PRAISE FOR

ELIZABETH BEAR'S

HAMMERED

"*Hammered* is a very exciting, very polished, very impressive debut novel."
—Mike Resnick, author of *The Return of Santiago*

"Gritty, insightful, and daring—Elizabeth Bear is a talent to watch."
—David Brin, author of the Uplift novels and *Kil'n People*

"A gritty and painstakingly well-informed peek inside a future we'd all better hope we don't get, liberally seasoned with VR delights and enigmatically weird alien artifacts. Genevieve Casey is a pleasingly original female lead, fully equipped with the emotional life so often lacking in military SF, yet tough and full of noir attitude; old enough by a couple of decades to know better but conflicted enough to engage with the sleazy dynamics of her situation regardless. Out of this basic contrast, Elizabeth Bear builds her future nightmare tale with style and conviction and a constant return to the twists of the human heart."
—Richard Morgan, author of *Altered Carbon*

"*Hammered* has it all. Drug wars, hired guns, corporate skullduggery, and bleeding-edge AI, all rolled into one of the best first novels I've seen in I don't know how long. This is the real dope!"
—Chris Moriarty, author of *Spin State*

"*Hammered* is a tough, gritty novel sure to appeal to fans of Elizabeth Moon and David Weber. . . . In Jenny Casey, Bear has created an admirably Chandler-esque character, street-smart and battle-scarred, tough talking and quick on the trigger. . . . Bear shuttles effortlessly back and forth across time to weave her disparate cast of characters together in a tightly plotted page-turner. The noir universe she creates is as hard-edged as the people who inhabit it. The dialogue and descriptions are suitably spartan, but every one of her characters has their own recognizable voice. It takes no effort at all to imagine *Hammered* on the big screen." —*SFRevu*

"Although a careless reader might be lulled by the presence of drugs, the hard-edged narration, and the rundown setting of the opening scene into thinking this novel is dystopian or even cyberpunk in nature, such expectations are quickly undercut by Bear . . . Every character in *Hammered,* even the villainous, have their own powerful motives for their actions; and conversely, the hands of the 'good' characters are never entirely clean, and they make fearful moral bargains and compromises simply because they can't see any better way to do what they must. They all try to salvage what they can . . . [which] embodies the novel's central theme of how what we would choose to preserve and what we wish to discard are sometimes inextricable."
—*Green Man Reviews*

ALSO BY ELIZABETH BEAR

HAMMERED

SCARDOWN

ELIZABETH BEAR

BANTAM BOOKS

WORLDWIRED

A Bantam Spectra Book / December 2005

Published by
Bantam Dell
A Division of Random House, Inc.
New York, New York

Bantam Books, the rooster colophon, Spectra, and the portrayal of a boxed
"s" are trademarks of Random House, Inc.

ISBN-13: 978-0-553-58749-4
ISBN-10: 0-553-58749-8

Printed in the United States of America
Published simultaneously in Canada

www.bantamdell.com

OPM 10 9 8 7 6 5 4 3 2

To Kit

Acknowledgments

It takes a lot of people to write a novel. This one would not have existed without the assistance of my very good friends and first readers (on and off the Online Writing Workshop for Science Fiction, Fantasy, and Horror)—especially but not exclusively Kathryn Allen, Chris Coen, Jaime Voss, James Stevens-Arce, Michael Curry, Ruth Nestvold, Chris Manucy, Bonnie Freeman, Holly McDowell, Ejner Fulsang, Larisa Walk, John Tremlett, Amanda Downum, and Leah Bobet. I am also indebted to Stella Evans, M.D., to whom I owe whatever bits of the medical science and neurology are accurate; Peter Watts, Ph.D., for assistance with questions of biology; M.Cpl. S. K. S. Perry (Canadian Forces), Lt. Penelope K. Hardy (U.S. Navy), and Capt. Beth Coughlin (U.S. Army), without whom my portrayal of military life would have been even more wildly fantastical; Leonid Korogodski and Claris Cates-Smith Ryan for linguistic assistance; engineer Catherine Morrison and recovering biologist Jeremy Tolbert for fielding questions about rising sea levels, alien microbiology, and decontamination procedures; safety engineer Wendy S. Delmater; Meredith L. Patterson, linguist and computer geek, for assistance with interspecies semiotics; Melinda Goodin for Australian Rules English assistance; Stephen

Shipman, for AI geekery; Chelsea Polk and Kellie Matthews for bolstering my knowledge of the native music of Soviet Canuckistan; Celia Marsh for emergency, just-in-time delivery of vintage Kate and Anna McGarrigle; Steven Brust and Caliann Graves, for advice and tolerance; Dena Landon, Sarah Monette, and Kelly Morisseau, francophones extraordinaire, upon whom may be blamed any correctness in the Québecois—especially the naughty bits; my agent, Jennifer Jackson, my copyeditor, Faren Bachelis, and my editor, Anne Groell, for too many reasons to enumerate; and to Kit Kindred, who is patient with the foibles of novelism.

For the sake of accuracy, I should note that in the interests of drama, my United Nations bears about the same resemblance to the real one that an episode of *Perry Mason* bears to an actual criminal proceeding.

The failures, of course, are my own.

Editor's Note

In the interests of presenting a detailed personal perspective on a crucial moment in history, we have taken the liberty of rendering Master Warrant Officer Casey's interviews—as preserved in the Yale University New Haven archives—in narrative format. Changes have been made in the interests of clarity, but the words, however edited, are her own.

The motives of the other individuals involved are not as well documented, although we have had the benefit of our unique access to extensive personal records left by Col. Frederick Valens. The events as presented herein are accurate: the drives behind them must always remain a matter of speculation, except in the case of Dr. Dunsany—who left us comprehensive journals—and "Dr." Feynman, who kept frequent and impeccable backups.

Thus, what follows is a historical novel, of sorts. It is our hope that this more intimate annal than is usually seen will serve to provide future students with a singular perspective on the roots of the civilization we are about to become.

—*Patricia Valens, Ph.D.*
   Jeremy Kirkpatrick, Ph.D.

BOOK ONE

One cannot walk
the Path until one
becomes the Path.

—*Gautama
Buddha*

I've got a starship dreaming. And there it is. Leslie
Tjakamarra leaned both hands on the thick crystal of the
Montreal's observation portal, the cold of space seeping
into his palms, and hummed a snatch of song under his
breath. He couldn't tell how far away the alien spaceship
was—at least, the fragment he could see when he twisted
his head and pressed his face against the port. Earthlight
stained the cage-shaped frame blue-silver, and the fat
doughnut of Forward Orbital Platform was visible through
the gaps, the gleaming thread of the beanstalk describing
a taut line downward until it disappeared in brown-tinged
atmosphere over Malaysia. "Bloody far," he said, realizing
he'd spoken out loud only when he heard his own voice.
He scuffed across the blue-carpeted floor, pressed back by
the vista on the other side of the glass.

Someone cleared her throat behind him. He turned, although he was unwilling to put his back to the endless
fall outside. The narrow-shouldered crew member who
stood just inside the hatchway met him eye to eye, the
black shape of a sidearm strapped to her thigh commanding his attention. She raked one hand through wiry salt-
and-pepper hair and shook her head. "Or too close for

comfort," she answered with an odd little smile. "That's one of the ones Elspeth calls the birdcages—"

"Elspeth?"

"Dr. Dunsany," she said. "You're Dr. Tjakamarra, the xenosemiotician." She mispronounced his name.

"Leslie," he said. She stuck out her right hand, and Leslie realized that she wore a black leather glove on the left. "You're Casey," he blurted, too startled to reach out. She held her hand out until he recovered enough to shake. "I didn't recognize—"

"It's cool." She shrugged in a manner entirely unlike a living legend, and gave him a crooked, sideways grin, smoothing her dark blue jumpsuit over her breasts with the gloved hand. "We're all different out of uniform. Besides, it's nice to be looked at like real people, for a change. Come on. The pilots' lounge has a better view."

She gestured him away from the window; he caught himself shooting her sidelong glances, desperate not to stare. He fell into step beside her as she led him along the curved ring of the *Montreal*'s habitation wheel, the arc rising behind and before them even though it felt perfectly flat under his feet.

"You'll get used to it," Master Warrant Officer Casey said, returning his looks with one of her own. It said she had accurately judged the reason he trailed his right hand along the chilly wall. "Here we are—" She braced one rubber-soled foot against the seam between corridor floor and corridor wall, and expertly spun the handle of a thick steel hatchway with her black-gloved hand. "Come on in. Step lively; we don't stand around in hatchways shipboard."

Leslie followed her through, turning to dog the door as he remembered his safety lectures, and when he turned back Casey had moved into the middle of a chamber no bigger than an urban apartment's living room. The awe in his throat made it hard to breathe. He hoped he was keeping it off his face.

"There," Casey said, stepping aside, waving him impatiently forward again. "That's both of them. The one on the 'left' is the shiptree. The one on the 'right' is the birdcage."

Everyone on the planet probably knew that by now. She was babbling, Leslie realized, and the small evidence of her fallibility—and her own nervousness—did more to ease the pressure in his chest than her casual friendliness could have. *You're acting like a starstruck teenager,* he reprimanded himself, and managed to grin at his own foolishness as he shuffled forward, his slipperlike ship-shoes whispering over the carpet.

Then he caught sight of the broad sweep of windows beyond and his personal awe for the woman in blue was replaced by something *visceral*. He swallowed, throat dry.

The *Montreal*'s habitation wheel spun grandly, creating an imitation of gravity that held them, feet-down, to the "floor." Leslie found himself before the big round port in the middle of the wall, hands pressed to either rim as if to keep himself from tumbling through the crystal like Alice through the looking glass. The panorama rotated like a merry-go-round seen from above. Beyond it, the soft blue glow of the wounded Earth reflected the sun. The planet's atmosphere was fuzzed brown like smog in an inversion layer, the sight enough to send Leslie's knuckle to his mouth. He bit down and tore his gaze away with an effort, turning it on the two alien ships floating "overhead."

The ship on perspective-right was the enormous, gleaming-blue birdcage, swarming with ten-meter specks of mercury—made tiny by distance—that flickered from cage-bar to cage-bar, as vanishingly swift and bright as motes in Leslie's eye.

The ship on perspective-left caught the earthlight with the gloss peculiar to polished wood or a smooth tree bole, a mouse-colored column twisted into shapes that took Leslie's breath away. The vast hull glittered with patterned, pointillist lights in cool-water shades. They did not look so different from the images and designs that Leslie had grown up with, and he fought a shiver, glancing at the hawk-intent face of MWO Casey.

"Elspeth—Dr. Dunsany—said you had a theory," she said without glancing over.

He returned his attention to the paired alien spaceships, peeling his eyes away from Genevieve Casey only with an effort. "I've had the VR implants—"

"Richard told me," she said, with a sly sideways grin.

"*Richard?* The AI?" And silly not to have expected that either. *It's a whole new road you're walking.* A whole different sort of journey, farther away from home than even Cambridge, when there was still more of an England rather than less.

"Yes. You'll meet him, I'm sure. He doesn't like to intrude on the new kids until they're comfortable with their wetware. And unless you've got the full 'borg"—she lightly touched the back of her head—"you won't have to put up with his running patter. Most of the time." She tilted her head up and sideways, a wry look he didn't think was for him.

She's talking to the AI right now. Cool shiver across his shoulders; the awe was back, with company. Leslie forced himself not to stare, frowning down at the bitten skin of his thumb. "Yes. I spoke to Dr. Dunsany regarding my theories..."

"Dr. Tjakamarra—"

"Leslie."

"Leslie." Casey coughed into her hand. "Ellie thought you were on to something, or she wouldn't have asked you up here. We get more requests in a week than Yale does in a year—"

"I'm aware of that." Her presence still stunned him. *Genevieve Casey. The first pilot. Leaned up against the window with me like kids peering off the observation deck of the Petronas Towers.* He gathered his wits and forced himself to frown. "You've had no luck talking to them, have you?"

"Plenty of math. Nothing you'd call conversation. They don't seem to understand please and thank you."

"I expected that." Familiar ground. Comfortable, even. "I'm afraid if I'm right, talking to them is hopeless."

"Hopeless?" She turned, leaning back on her heels.

"Yes. You see, I don't think they *talk* at all."

Leslie Tjakamarra's not a big man. He's not a young one either, though I wouldn't want to try to guess his age within five years on either side. He's got one of those wiry, weathered frames I associate with Alberta cattlemen and forest rangers, sienna skin paler, almost red, inside the creases beside glittering eyes and on the palms of big thick-nailed hands. He doesn't go at all with the conservative charcoal double-breasted suit, pinstriped with biolume, which clings to his sinewy shoulders in as professional an Old London tailoring job as I've seen. When London was evacuated, a lot of the refugees found themselves in Sydney, in Vancouver—and in Toronto.

God rest their souls.

He shoots me those sidelong glances like they do, trying to see through the glove to the metal hand, trying to see through the jumpsuit to the hero underneath.

I hate to disappoint him, but that hero had a hair appointment she never came back from. "Well," I say, to fill up his silence. "That'll make your job easier, then, won't it?" *What do you think of them apples, Dick?*

Richard grins inside my head, bony hands spread wide and beating like a pigeon's wings through air. The man's brains would jam if you tied his hands down. Of course, since he's intangible, that would be a trick. "That's got the air of a leading question about it." He scrubs his palms on the thighs of his virtual corduroys and stuffs them into his pockets, white shirt stretched taut across his narrow chest, his image fading as he "steps back," limiting his usage of my implants. "I'll get in on it when he talks to Ellie. No point in spoiling his chance to appreciate the view. I'll eavesdrop, if that's okay."

It might be the same asinine impulse that makes English speakers talk loudly to foreigners that moves me to smile inwardly and stereotype Dr. Tjakamarra's smooth, educated accent into Australian Rules English. *No worries, mate. Fair dinkum.*

Richard shoots me an amused look. "Ouch," he says, and flickers out like an interrupted hologram.

Dr. Tjakamarra grins, broad lips uncovering tea-stained teeth like a mouth full of piano keys, and scratches his cheek with knuckles like an auto mechanic's. He wears his hair long, professorial, slicked back into hard steel-gray waves. "Or that much more difficult, if you prefer." His voice is younger than the rest of him, young as that twinkle in his eye. "Talking isn't the only species of communication, after all."

He presses his hand flat against the glass again and peers between his fingers as if trying to gauge the size of the ships that float out there, the way you might measure a tree on the horizon against your thumb. His gaze keeps sliding down to the dust-palled Earth, his eyes impassive, giving nothing away.

"How bad is it in Sydney?" I press my steel hand to my lips, as if to shove the words back in with glove leather. Tjakamarra's head comes up like a startled deer's. I pretend I don't see.

"We heard it," he says, as his hand falls away from the glass. "We heard it in Sydney." He steps back, turns to face me although I'm still giving him my shoulder. He cups both hands and brings them together with a crack that makes me jump.

"Is that really what it sounded like?"

"More or less—" A shrug. "We couldn't feel the tremors. It wasn't all that loud, fifteen thousand kilometers away; I would have thought it'd be a sustained rumble, like the old footage of nuclear bombs. You ever hear of Coober Pedy?"

"Never."

"There were bomb tests near there. Over a hundred years ago, but I know people who knew people who were there. They said the newsreels lied, the sound effect they used was dubbed in later." He laces his hands together in the small of his back and lifts his chin to look me in the eye, creases linking his thick, flat nose to the corners of his mouth.

Surreal fucking conversation, man. "So what does a nuclear explosion sound like, Les?"

His lips thin. He holds his hands apart again and swings them halfway but doesn't clap. "Like the biggest bloody gunshot you ever did hear. Or like a meteorite hitting the planet, fifteen thousand kilometers away."

He's talking so he doesn't have to look. I recognize the glitter in his dark brown eyes, darker even than mine. It took me, too, the first time I looked down and saw all that gorgeous blue and white mottled with sick dull beige like cancer.

It takes all of us like that.

He licks his lips and looks carefully at the Benefactor ships, not the smeared globe behind them. "The shot heard round the world. Isn't that what the Americans call the first shot fired in their colonial revolt?"

"Sounds about right."

He reminds me of my grandfather Zeke Kirby, my mother's father, the full-blooded one; he's got that same boiled-leather twist of indestructibility, but my grandfather was an ironworker, not a professor. His mouth moves again, like he's trying to shape words that won't quite come out right, and finally he just shakes his head and looks down. "Big universe out there."

"Bloody big," I answer, a gentle tease. He smiles out of the corner of his mouth; we're going to be friends. "Come on," I say. "That gets depressing if you stare at it. I'll take you to meet Ellie if you promise not to tell her the thing about the bomb."

He falls into step beside me. I don't have to shorten my strides to let him keep up. "She lose somebody in the—in that?"

"We all lost somebody." I shake my head.

"What is it, then?"

"It would give her nightmares. Come on."

Richard habitually took refuge in numbers, so it troubled him that with regard to the Impact all he had was approximations. The number of dead had never been counted. Their names had never been accurately listed. Their families would never be notified; in many cases, their bodies would never be found.

The population of Niagara and Rochester, New York, had been just under three million people, although the New York coastline of Lake Ontario was mostly rural, vineyards and cow pasture. The northern rim of the lake, however, had been the most populated place in Canada: Ontario's "Golden Horseshoe," the urban corridor anchored by Toronto and Hamilton, which had still been home to some seven million despite the midcentury population dip. Deaths from the Impact and its aftermath had been confirmed as far away as Buffalo, Cleveland, Albany. A woman in Ottawa had died when a stained-glass window shattered from the shock and fell on her head; a child in Kitchener survived in a basement, along with his dog. Recovery teams dragging the poisoned waters of Lake Ontario had been forced to cease operations as the lake surface iced over, a phenomenon that once would have been a twice-in-a-century occurrence but had become common with the advent of Shifted winters. It would become more common still until the greenhouse effect triggered by the Impact began to cancel out the nuclear winter.

An icebreaker could have been brought in and the work

continued, but things keep in cold water. And someone raised the specter of breaking ice with bodies frozen into it, and it was decided to wait until spring.

The ice didn't melt until halfway through May, and the lake locked solid again in mid-September. The coming winter promised to be even colder, a savage global drop in temperatures that might persist another eighteen to twenty-four months, and Richard couldn't say whether the eventual worldwide toll would be measured in the mere tens of millions or in the hundreds of millions. Preliminary estimates had placed Impact casualties at thirty million; Richard was inclined to a more conservative estimate of under twenty million, unevenly divided between Canada and the United States.

In practical terms, the casualty rate by January 1, 2063, was something like one in every twenty-five Americans and one in every three Canadians.

The fallout cloud from the thirteen nuclear reactors damaged or destroyed in the Impact was pushed northeast by prevailing wind currents, largely affecting New York, Quebec, Vermont, New Hampshire, Maine, Newfoundland, the Grand Banks, Prince Edward Island, Iceland, and points between. The emergency teams and medical staff attending the disaster victims were supplied with iodine tablets and given aggressive prophylaxis against radiation exposure. Only seventeen became seriously ill. Only six died.

It was too soon to tell what the long-term effect on cancer rates would be, but Richard expected New England's dairy industry to fail completely, along with what bare scraps had remained of the once-vast North Atlantic fisheries.

And then, after the famines and the winter, would come a summer without end.

• • •

Colonel Valens's hands hurt, but his eyes hurt more. He leaned forward on both elbows over his improvised desk, his holistic communications unit propped up on a pair of inflatable splints and the unergonomic portable interface plate unrolled across a plywood surface that was three centimeters too high for comfort. "Yes," he said, rubbing the back of his neck, "I'll hold. Please let the prime minister know it's not urgent, if she has— Constance. That was quick."

"Hi, Fred. I was at lunch," Constance Riel said, chewing, her image flickering in the cheap holographic display. Valens smoothed the interface plate, cool plastic slightly tacky and gritty with the omnipresent dust. The prime minister covered her mouth with the back of her left hand and swallowed, set her sandwich down on a napkin, reached for her coffee. Careful makeup could not hide the hollows under her eyes, dark as thumbprints. "I was going to call you today anyway. How's the Evac?"

"Stable." One word, soaked in exhaustion. "I got mail from Elspeth Dunsany today. She says the commonwealth scientists have arrived safely on the *Montreal*. One Australian and an expat Brit. She and Casey are getting them settled."

"Paul Perry said the same thing to me this morning," Riel answered. Her head wobbled when she nodded.

"That isn't why you were going to call me."

"No. I have the latest climatological data from Richard and Alan. The AIs say that the nanite propagation is going well, despite the effects of the—"

"Nuclear winter? Non-nuclear winter?" Valens said.

"Something like that. They're concerned about the algae die off we were experiencing before the Impact. More algae means less CO_2 left in the atmosphere, which means less greenhouse warming when the dust is out of the atmosphere and winter finally ends—"

"—in eighteen months or so. Won't we want a greenhouse effect then?" *To counteract the global dimming from the dust.*

"Not unless 50° or 60°C is your idea of comfort."

Valens shook his head, looking down at the pink and green displays that hovered under the surface of the interface plate, awaiting a touch to bring them to multidimensionality. He shook his head and ricocheted uncomfortably to the topic that was the reason for his call. "We've done what we can here. It's time to close up shop. Do you want to tour the exclusion zone?"

"Helicopter tour," she said, nodding, and took another bite of her sandwich. "You'll come with, of course. Before we open the Evac to reconstruction and send the bulldozers in."

"You're going to rebuild Toronto?" Valens had years of practice keeping shock out of his voice. He failed utterly, his gut coiling at something that struck him as plain obscenity.

"No," she said. "We're going to turn it into a park. By the way, are you resigning your commission?"

Valens coughed. Riel's image flickered as the interface panel, released from the pressure of his palm, wrinkled again. "Am I being asked to?"

The prime minister laughed. "You're being asked to get your ass to the provisional capital of Vancouver, Fred. Where, in recognition of your exemplary service handling the Toronto Evac relief effort, you will be promoted to Brigadier General Frederick Valens, and I will have a brand-new shiny cabinet title and a whole new ration of shit to hand you, sir."

"I'm a Conservative, Connie."

"That's okay," she answered. "You can switch."

Elspeth touched the corner of her mouth with her napkin, careful of the unaccustomed weight of lipstick. She leaned a shoulder against Jen Casey's upper arm and nudged, the steel armature hard under the rifle-green wool of Jenny's dress uniform. Jen's glass of grapefruit juice clicked against her teeth. She shot Elspeth a tolerant glance. "Doc—"

"Sorry."

In present company, it wouldn't do for Jen to drop that steel arm around Elspeth's shoulders and give her a hard, infinitely careful hug, but she managed to make her answering jostle almost as comforting.

They had moved into the captain's reception hall after dinner, and Captain Wainwright herself was propping up a wall in the corner by the room's two big ports. It was too cold for Elspeth's taste, that close to the glass, and she'd joined Jen in her relentless stakeout of the nibbles-and-dessert table. Both Jeremy Kirkpatrick—the commonwealth ethnolinguist—and Dr. Tjakamarra were sticking close to the windows, although Elspeth could tell the Australian was shivering. He stood hunched like a worried cat, his arms folded over each other, and divided his attention between Jaime Wainwright and Gabe Castaign, whose hulking presence manned the canapé bucket brigade for the new-comers, in courtesy to their temporary role as distinguished guests. The ecologist Paul Perry—long-fingered, slight, and dark—almost disappeared behind Charles Forster, a paunchy xenobiologist with his vanishing hair shaved close to a shiny scalp. *One little, two little, three little Indians. Or should that be we few, we happy few, we band of brothers?*

Five scientists, a programmer, a pilot, and an artificial intelligence. And a partridge in a pear tree. And the biggest scientific puzzle of the century.

You've come a bit far for a bout of impostor syndrome, El.

"What do you think of the new kids?" Jen said, dropping her half-full glass on a passing tray with a grimace of distaste.

"They made it through the rubber-chicken dinner with a minimum of fuss." The tilt of Elspeth's head indicated the mess hall on the other side of one of *Montreal*'s few irising doors.

"Especially since it was rubber tofu." Jen grinned, that wry mocking twist of her mouth that was as contagious as the common cold, and Elspeth had to grin back. "I haven't had a chance to talk to Kirkpatrick yet, but the Australian's all right." She shrugged. "My heart's not in it, Doc—"

"No." Elspeth reached for a drink herself, tomato juice and a stalk of celery, wishing there were less Virgin and more Bloody in it. "I don't think any of our hearts are in it, after last Christmas." *After Toronto.* "But it's got to be done. They scare me." She tipped her head to indicate the long ornate outline of the shiptree, visible beyond the port, winking lights and elegant curves like hand-smoothed wood. "And Richard says Fred says something has to break on the PanChinese front shortly. Riel's going to demand restitution for Toronto—"

"She wants to get Richard admitted as a witness."

"Right. And there's that Chinese pilot, the one who tried to prevent the attack—"

"He's safe at Lake Simcoe," Jen said, her voice dripping mockery. Both she and Elspeth had a longstanding acquaintance with the high-security military prison there. "Protective custody." She cocked her head, that listening gesture that told Elspeth—to Elspeth's infinite frustration—that she was talking to Richard.

Their eyes met for a moment, a shared frown. "You heard that Fred is Brigadier General Fred as of this afternoon, I assume?"

The irony in Jen's expression made her eyes glitter like a bird's. "Richard says to let him and Fred and Riel handle Earth and China, and worry about talking to the Benefactors." Jen swallowed and glanced about for the drink she'd discarded. Thwarted, she shoved her hand into the pocket of her uniform.

"Can't we worry about everything at once?" Elspeth wandered toward the snack table, Jen trailing, and picked up a plate. She started loading it with canapés, inspecting each one.

"Richard says it might not be a bad idea to have figured out how to talk to the Benefactors by the time the PanChinese start shooting at us again. *If* they start shooting at us again. In case the Benefactors take that as evidence that the hairless apes are too uppity to be permitted to roam the universe at large, and decide to do something permanent about us."

"Richard is a bloodthirsty son of a bitch." Elspeth bit a cracker in half and chewed in an unladylike fashion. So

much for the lipstick. *I need to get VR implants at least.*
She *hated* not being able to listen to Richard directly, the
way that Jenny and Patricia Valens, the *Montreal*'s ap-
prentice pilot, could. "Very well. 'We cannot weep for the
whole world.' I guess we hold up our end of the table and
trust in Fred to hold up his. We'll have a summit meeting
tomorrow, us two and Gabe and Charlie and Paul and the
new kids. And Dick, onscreen so everybody can talk to
him." She swallowed the other half of the canapé, cracker
corners scratching her throat. "What're you doing for
your birthday?"

   "Birthday?"

   "Sunday? The day you turn fifty-one?"

   "Don't remind me—"

Elspeth grinned. "Okay, I won't. Gabe and I will plan
something. It'll be just us and Genie." Her voice wanted
to hitch on Genie's name; it wasn't supposed to be just
Genie. It was supposed to be Genie-and-Leah, but the
second name hung between them, chronically unsaid.
Elspeth brushed it aside with the back of her hand. "You
just promise to show up and be a good sport."

   Jen's expression warred between resignation, delight,
and trepidation. Finally, she nodded and studied the carpeted floor, scrubbing her gloved iron hand against her
flesh one as if dusting away a fistful of crumbs. "Patty,"
she said. "Patty Valens. Invite her, too? She's all alone up
here—"

   "More than fair." Elspeth's hesitation was strong
enough that Jen looked up and frowned, meeting her gaze
directly.

   "What?"

   "This meeting tomorrow—"

   "Yes?"

"Is it too much to ask for you to brainstorm and come up with something we can *do* to get the Benefactors' interest, other than balancing our checkbooks back and forth at each other?"

Jen laughed dryly. "I've got an idea you're going to love, if Wainwright doesn't shoot me for suggesting it."

"Well, don't leave me hanging."

Genevieve Casey arched her long neck back, stared at the ceiling, laced her hands together in front of her, and said with studied casualness, "I want to find out what happens if we EVA over to the birdcage and wander around inside."

Thursday 27 September 2063
HMCSS Montreal processor core
HMCSS Calgary processor core
Whole-Earth Benefactor nanonetwork
(worldwire)
21:28:28:35–21:43:28:39

When Dick took over the planet, he'd been prepared for surprises. But the ache of the Toronto Evac Zone like a runner's stitch in his side had not been one of them.

He'd comprehended the scale of the damage, of course; of all the sentiences in his sphere of experience, he was uniquely qualified to do so. He'd understood that the global nanotech infection that Leah Castaign and Trevor Koske had given their lives to engender would be a mitigating factor at best, and not even the temporary magic bullet of a penicillin cure. He'd thought he understood what spreading his consciousness through a planet-sized, quantum-connected worldwire would entail. If he could call it *his* consciousness anymore, as he evolved from a discrete intelligence into a multithreaded entity that might be compared to a human with disassociative identity disorder—

—*if* such a disorder were a native state of affairs, and if the various personalities carried on a constant, raucous, and very rarified debate regarding every serious action they undertook. *If* portions of that entity brushed feather-light fingertips across the waking and sleeping minds of certain augmented humans, and other portions moved through the ruined waters of Lake Ontario, and hovered in the well-shielded brain of Her Majesty's Canadian starship *Calgary* in its position of rest at the bottom of the ocean; if other portions infected fish and birds and bushes and topsoil and atmosphere, and extended like a meat intelligence's subconscious through eleven-dimensional space and into the alien nanotools of the far-flung Benefactor empire, or confederacy, or kinship system—*or whatever the hell it might be,* Richard mused, with the fragment of himself that never stopped musing on such things. If.

I never began to imagine what I was in for, he thought, shifting focus as Constance Riel touched her earpiece and accepted his call. She wasn't in her temporary office in the provisional capitol, but a mobile one aboard her customized airliner. "Good evening, Dr. Feynman."

"The same to you, Prime Minister. I understand that you will be touring the Evac with Dr. Valens tomorrow."

"Preparatory to closing the relief effort, yes. I'm on my way there now. And on behalf of the Canadian people"— she leaned forward—"I want to formally thank you for your efforts. Which I am about to ask you to redouble."

"Restoring the Evac is a lower priority than mitigating the climatic damage, you realize."

A quick, dismissive flip of her hand reinforced her curt nod of agreement. "We have an official complaint on record from the PanChinese ambassador to the Netherlands, by the way. It seems he's attempting to get the nanotech infestation classed as an invasion of the sovereign territory of the PanChinese Alliance, and get it heard by the International Court of Justice."

"You don't sound displeased."

Riel grinned wolfishly. "We can't bring our suit for attempted genocide unless they consent to be a party to the case. Which they just did, more or less—or we can spin it so they did. Of course, Premier Xiong can't put up much of a fight, since he's still pretending the attack was the work of fringe elements."

"If Premier Xiong was not privy to the attack, he may have a coup on his hands before too much longer. My analysis—which is based on severely inadequate data, and the preliminary testimony of Pilot Xie—is that the orders to attack must have come from high up in the PanChinese government."

"I agree. Unfortunately, there's not much I can do about that currently. In a more immediate concern, though, World Health is on my ass again. We need a policy on use of your nanotech in medical emergencies."

Richard sighed, pushing aside the "itch" that was the infestation's response to the damage surrounding the Impact. *Life-threatening conditions first. Superficial wounds, no matter how unsightly, can wait.* "This whole thing is a moral—"

"Quandary?"

"Quagmire." He shrugged, hands opened broadly in one of the little gestures he'd inherited from the human subject his personality was modeled on. "I've got 60 percent global coverage right now and growing, and we used the nanosurgeons successfully on a few of the worst-injured Impact victims—and unsuccessfully on a whole lot more—but I've got extensive climatic damage to consider. I'm expecting mass extinctions, once the field biologists get some hard data back to us, and another spike in dieoffs once the dust clears and the temperature increase starts. Practically speaking, we can get a certain amount of the carbon dioxide out of the atmosphere before then, but not enough to prevent the damage. We're talking mitigation at best, and we should expect a much warmer global climate overall."

"How much warmer?"

"Think dinosaurs tromping through steamy tropical forests, and shallow inland seas. And wild weather. Also, we should expect earthquakes as the polar ice melts. It's heavy, you know—"

"These are all secondary concerns, aren't they?"

"Not in the long term."

"They sound infinitely better than that snowball Earth you and Paul were talking about last year. Look, tell me about your moral quagmire first. The climate issues are easy; we mitigate as much as we can, and whatever we can't, we suck up. I'm worried about the personal cost."

A moment of silent understanding passed between them, intermediated by the technology that permitted them to look eye-to-eye. Riel glanced down first. Since Richard's image floated in her contact lens, it didn't break the connection. "I'm tempted to tell you to restrict the damned nanosurgeons from PanChinese territory. But then they would claim we were sabotaging their environmental efforts and failing to make resources freely available on an equal basis . . . It's a mess, Dick. And once we move Canada off a crisis footing, smaller wolves than

China are going to be sniffing about for a piece of the corpse as well. Russia and the EU have provided aid; it's not like I'm in a position to turn them away—" She choked off, shaking her head. "I love my job. I just keep telling myself that I wouldn't rather be doing anything else in the world."

A shared grin, and Richard cleared his throat and hesitated—another simulation of human behavior. Most of the humans were more comfortable with him, rather than Alan—the only other AI persona who had had significant interpersonal contact. In fact, most of the humans had no idea the rest of the threaded personalities existed, yet.

Richard had never been one to spoil a surprise. "The least complex solution would be to prepare a contract and ask any country that wishes my intervention to sign it."

"What are we going to do about sick people who wish to volunteer for nanosurgical treatment?"

"We'll have to let them volunteer," Richard answered. "We've already used the nanites on Canadians in a widespread fashion. It would be...inhumane to restrict the benefits to your own citizens. But the volunteers will need to be apprised of the risks, which are significant."

"Ever the master of understatement." She pressed a fountain pen between her lips absently, sucking on the gold-plated barrel. Richard quelled the irrational—and impossible—urge to reach out and take it out of her mouth. "The promise of free medical treatment will open some borders. What about the nations that demand access to the augmentation program?"

"Military applications of technology have always been handled differently than medical ones."

"Touché. People will scream."

"People are screaming. This isn't magic, Prime Minister."

"No," she said, leaning back in her chair. "Just something that will look like magic to desperate people, and they'll be angry when it doesn't work like magic, won't they? Oh, that reminds me. I'd like to keep as many people—commonwealth citizens and otherwise—uninfected as possible."

"Most people are going to encounter a life-threatening incident sooner or later." But that wasn't disagreement. She was right; they didn't know what the Benefactors were capable of, or what they wanted, and it was their technology with which Richard had so cavalierly infected the planet.

It seemed like a good idea at the time.

And cavalier wasn't a good word, though the process had been less cautiously handled than Richard would have preferred.

Less cautiously handled than Riel would have preferred, too, and she was talking again. "Most people are. Some will refuse treatment. Some won't *need* treatment. It's a unique situation; this stuff is loose in the ecosystem, but unlike every other contaminant in history, we have perfect control over it."

"Or, more precisely, I have perfect control."

"I, we. Which is another thing. Can't we make some hay out of PanChina having a worldwire of its own?"

"Well..." he began, "what they have is not exactly a worldwire. What they've got is a bigger version of the limited networks we started off with, much more protected, not self-propagating..."

"And not self-aware."

"We hope."

"Ah, Richard. I'd like to extend the offer of Canadian citizenship to you." She raised her hand before he could comment, shaking her head so that dark curls brushed her ears and collar. "Don't jump up and say no. Think about it. For one thing, it would do wonders toward confirming your legal personhood. For another, there's the matter of our suit against China in the World Court, and the question of whether AIs can testify."

Richard patted his hands against his thighs to a bossa nova beat. "Wait until somebody figures out that the nanite infestation falls under the third Kyoto and the second Kiev environmental accords, and that it's a violation of both. *Potentially harmful particulate contamination of international ocean waters.* That's us."

"An environmental lawsuit is the least of our problems." Riel rubbed her eyes and stifled a yawn. "I have to sleep if I'm going to be pretty on camera tomorrow. In thirty seconds, Richard, outline your plan of attack."

"Easy." He held up his spidery fingers and ticked off goals one at a time. "One, mitigate climate changes. Two, mitigate extinctions. Three, protect individual human lives. Four, try to help the team talking to the Benefactors. Meanwhile, you set up a world government, get the Chinese under control, keep the rest of the commonwealth in line behind us, and figure out how to revitalize a collapsed world economy. Does that sound like an equitable division of labor to you, Madam Prime Minister?"

"It sounds like I'd better get busy," she said, and reached up to touch the connection off. Her hand hesitated a centimeter from her earpiece. "Richard. We'll have population problems if the death rate drops."

And the AI sighed and laced his fingers together. "The death rate's not going to drop, Constance. The trick is going to be keeping a significant percentage of humanity *alive*."

1110 hours
Friday September 28, 2063
HMCSS Montreal
Earth orbit

I'm just finishing my PT, wiping the sweat off my face onto one of the *Montreal*'s rough, unbleached cotton towels, when Richard starts talking in my head. "Captain Wainwright would like to see you when you're free, Jen."

Thanks, Dick. Is this good news or bad news?

"Ellie asked about EVA plans, as you requested, so your guess is as good as mine."

Your guess is as good as most people's certainty, Dick. I head for the locker room, tossing the towel overhand at the laundry chute as I go by. If the chute had a net, it would sink with a swish. The *Montreal*'s variable, lighter-than-earth grav takes some getting used to, but once you get the hang of it it's pretty darn sexy. Puts a spring in your step. Except you have to work twice as hard to stay in shape. Dammit.

"She doesn't see fit to keep the AI apprised of everything."

No, but she's catching on pretty quick to using you as an intercom. The locker room is empty, midwatch, except for one master corporal who is leaned into her locker, curling her hair in the mirror. I peel off my sweat-drenched tank top, kick my sweats aside, and step into the shower.

I feel him shrug. "It costs me almost nothing in terms of resources, and if it leads her closer to accepting me, it's a very small price to pay."

The water's metered, but it's steamy. The hot water pipes run alongside the outflow pipes for the reactor coolant. Nothing wasted on a starship, especially not heat.

I get wet, wait for the water to kick off, and lather up with a handful of gritty soap. *Think she's gonna go for it?*

"I think you're going to have a fight on your hands."

Tell me something new about my life. I punch the button for another metered blast of spray and scrub the suds out of my hair, turning one quick pirouette to get the last of the lather off my skin. The master corporal is long gone by the time I thumb lock open my locker and dress in the crisp rifle green that makes me look like a red ant in a nest of black ones when I'm out among the air force types. There's something else that stands out about me once I'm dressed; the sidearm pressed to my right hip. Valens never rescinded his order to keep it within reach.

I slick my damp hair back—*neat and under control*—and stuff the comb into the vinyl hanging pocket beside a mirror small enough to only show half my face at a time. *Damn, I'm still not used to wearing this face.* You'd think I would be, by now. It's been almost a year.

Richard's presence shifts in my head. "You want to get out there as badly as I do," he says.

"Do you think it's worth the risk, Dick?" Out loud, provoking a smile in spite of myself. I unholster my sidearm and check the plastic loads, designed to squish flat against the *Montreal*'s hull instead of punching a hole and letting the vacuum outside in. Or the air inside out, more accurately.

"What risk?"

The risk of provoking the Benefactors somehow? The pistol's weirdly light in my hand. I replace the clip, make sure the safety's latched, and slide the weapon back into its holster, securing the snap. I can't look at it anymore without remembering Captain Wainwright pointing one very much like it at me. Without remembering Gabe's daughter Leah, and the fury I feel that I can't even pretend her death was the kind of stupid goddamned waste that kids dead in war are supposed to be. God*damn* it.

If it's futile, at least you don't feel guilty getting mad.

My hand falls away from the holster. If I never have to touch a weapon again, it will be too fucking soon.

Richard rubs his long, gaunt hands together, fingers mobile as the sticks of a fan. "That's the thing, Jen. We stand just as much of a chance of infuriating them by doing *nothing* as we do by wandering over and knocking on the door. We just can't know."

Besides. We're both going nuts sitting on our asses.

"Correction. You are going nuts sitting on your ass. *I* am shoveling like Hercules in the Aegean stable, and to about as much effect."

Maybe you need to divert a river.

I *feel* him pause. That never happens. Richard exists on a level of teraflops per femtowhatsit, words that Gabe throws around like they mean something, but which promptly fall out of my head and go splat all over the floor. Whatever, Dick thinks a hell of a lot faster than I do, even with my amped-up brain—although Dick will be the first to claim he doesn't necessarily think *better*. The practical application is that when Richard pauses in conversation, it's to be polite, or to seem human, or to give us meat types a chance to catch up.

This is different. He's hit a dead halt, and he's *thinking*. I can feel it. Feel the seconds ticking over like boulders gathering momentum down a hill. *Dick? What did I say?*

"A river," he says, that topographic smile rearranging his face like plate tectonics. This one's at least a 6.5. "Ma'am, I do believe you've just given me an idea."

And you're going to sit there and look smug about it, too, aren't you?

"I want to run some simulations first." The sensation of his virtual hug is like a passing breeze brushing my shoulders. "I've been looking at the problem the wrong way. When change is inevitable, the solution isn't to fight it, but to work inside the new system and learn to live in the world that's changed."

I've heard cruder versions of that sentiment.

He laughs, twisting his head on his long papery neck. "You look beautiful. Now go beard the captain in her den."

"Great, the AI's blind as well as insane." But he can feel my grin as I can feel his, and together we move spinwise and in-wheel, toward the captain's conference room.

Wainwright looks up, glowering, as I duck through the hatch and dog it behind me. Momma bear with only one cub, and I square myself inside the door and wait for her to indicate my next move.

We have a funny relationship, Captain Wainwright and me.

She shuffles papers across her interface panel and stows them in a transparent folder mounted on her desk. You never can tell if the gravity will last from minute to minute, or so they say, although I've never seen it fail. She sighs and stands up, coming around the desk, as starched and pressed as me and eight inches shorter. "I want to thank you for not springing your radical idea on me in front of the scientists, ma'am."

"I think Elspeth and Richard deserve equal credit, ma'am."

Arms folded over her chest ruin the line of her uniform. She tilts her head back to stare me in the eye. It doesn't cost her a fraction of her authority. "I'm sharp enough to know who the suicidal lunatic on my ship is, Master Warrant Officer."

Eyes fixed straight ahead, pretending I can't see the little curl twitching the corner of her lip. "Yes, ma'am."

"So what do you think sending astronauts over there will accomplish that our drones and probes haven't?"

I shrug. "Pique their interest, ma'am? It's not so much about information retrieval—we've done and can do that remotely. It's about letting them know we *do* want to talk to them."

She doesn't answer; just looks at me, and then looks down and plays with the stuff on her desk. "You're going to go out there and make me proud in front of our new guests. Aren't you?"

"Yes. Ma'am."

"Good." She steps back, her hands dropping to her sides, standing tall. "At ease, Casey. I'm done yelling at you."

"Yes, ma'am." But this time I let her hear the humor in it.

She nods, then shakes her head and taps her knuckle on her chin. "Casey, you're a shit disturber. You know that?"

"It's a gift, ma'am." As I let my shoulders relax, my hands curl naturally against my thighs.

She sighs and rubs her palms together. "You've proved your instincts to me—"

"But?" The hesitation is implicit in the lift-and-drop of her gaze. She doesn't quite meet mine directly. We're thinking of the same thing; me refusing a direct order, at gunpoint, and making that refusal stick. And I was right, dammit. And she knows I was right. And I think she's grateful I was right, deep down in the light-starch, creased-trouser depths of her military soul.

But it kind of fucks up the superior/subordinate thing, and we're both still working our asses off trying to pretend it doesn't matter. "There is no but," she says, after a longer wait than I'm comfortable with. "As long as I know I can trust you."

"You can trust me to take good care of your ship, ma'am. And your crew."

"And Canada?"

"That goes without saying."

"Consider it said anyway." She's working up to something. She looks at me again, and this time doesn't look away. "I think Genie Castaign should enter the pilot program," she says. "She's already partially acclimated to the Benefactor tech, her unaugmented reflexes are at least as good as her sister's, she gets along with the Feynman AI, and she's bright. I want you to talk to her father. He'll take it better from you."

"Captain—"

"I didn't ask for your opinion, Casey."

"Yes, ma'am." The ship's spinning. And all I can feel is Leah, there in my arms and then gone.

They used to say give one child to the army, one to the priesthood, and try to keep one alive. Gabriel only has one daughter left. Wainwright's gaze doesn't drop from mine. "Yes, ma'am." I know I'm stammering. Know there's nothing else I can say. And Gabe won't even hate me for it, because he's army, too, and because Gabe knows. "She's too young still to induct."

"Get her started on the training. We'll take her when she's fourteen." She stretches, and ruthlessness falls off her shoulders like a feather dancer's cloak. "Come on. It's time for the meeting. Let's go see if there are any canapés."

Toronto Evacuation Zone
Ontario, Canada
Friday 28 September 2063
1100 hours

Snow is supposed to be a benediction. A veil of white like a wedding dress, concealing whatever sins lie beneath.

Frost on the chopper's window melted under Valens's touch. He leaned against the glass, his shoulder to Constance Riel, who sat similarly silent and hunched on the port side. They both looked down, ignoring the pilot and the other passengers.

The snow covering the remains of Toronto lay not like a veil, but like a winding-sheet—one landscape that even winter couldn't do much for. He stared at it, trying not to see it, careful never quite to focus his eyes.

The prime minister stirred. She shifted closer to Valens, closer to the center of the helicopter, as if unconsciously seeking warmth. He glanced at her. Her trained politician's smile had thinned to a hard line in her bloodless face, and her head oscillated just enough that her hair shifted against her neck.

"It doesn't look any better than it did at Christmas. I thought it would look better by now." She glanced first at him and then down. She retrieved her purse from the seat, dug for a stick of gum he didn't think she really wanted, offered him one that he didn't accept. She folded hers into her mouth and sat back. "Did you feel it in Hartford, Fred?"

"I felt the floor jump," he said, carefully looking out the window and not at Riel. "It woke me. The sound came seconds later. It sounded like——" Words failed. *Like a mortar.*

You never hear the one that gets you.

And then, unbidden, *Georges wouldn't have felt anything at all.* He nodded, remembering the rise and fall of solid earth, the thump of the bedframe jolting against the wall. "It woke me."

"I was closer," she said. "It knocked me down. I saw the fireball first, of course. If I'd had any sense, I would have sat down." She shrugged. "You're not really *looking,* are you, Fred?"

"Of course I am." And so he wouldn't be lying, he forced himself to look. To really *look,* at the unseasonable snow that lay in dirty swirls and hummocks over what looked at first glance like a rock field, at the truncated root of the CN Tower rising on the waterfront like the stump of a lightning-struck tree. Surprisingly, the tower had survived the earthquake, according to the forensic report of the engineers who had toured the Evac during the recovery phase. It had not survived the tsunami, nor the bombardment with meter-wide chunks of debris. Around it, lesser structures had been leveled to ragged piles of broken masonry and jutting pieces of steel.

Valens lifted his gaze as the chopper came around, and frowned toward the horizon. The frozen water of Lake Ontario would have been blinding in the sun, if the light that fell through the haze weren't watery and wan, and if the ice itself weren't streaked brown and gray like agate with ejecta. "A park," he said, looking down at his hands.

He folded his fingers together. He never had worn a wedding band; rings annoyed him. "What on earth makes you think you can turn *this* into a *park*?"

"What the hell else do we do with it?" She turned over her shoulder. An aide and two Mounties sat in the next row back, so hushed with the terrible awe of the Impact that Valens had almost forgotten them. "Coffee, please? Fred, how about you?"

He shook his head as the aide poured steaming fluid from a thermos, filling the helicopter with the rich, acidic smell. He didn't know how she could stomach anything, but judging by the gauntness of her face she needed it for medicinal purposes as much as the comfort of something warm.

Valens chafed his hands against his uniform, trying to warm them. Riel glanced over, but sipped her coffee rather than comment. She repeated herself, not a rhetorical question this time. "What the hell else are we going to do with it?"

"Rebuild," Valens answered, though his gut twisted. "It's . . ." He shrugged. "Hiroshima, Mumbai, Dresden——"

"You're saying you don't just pack it in and go home?"

"Something like that. Besides, every city needs a nice big park." Dryly enough that she chuckled before she caught herself. He tipped his head and lowered his voice, but kept talking. "Constance, do you know who Tobias Hardy is?"

"Yes," she said, the corners of her mouth turning down. "Your old boss Alberta Holmes's old boss. Christ, I thought we had Unitek's fingers out of the *Montreal*'s pie."

"You could always seize it——" He shifted against the side panel of the helicopter. It dug painfully into his shoulder, and he was stiff from sitting. He wasn't as young as he used to be.

"I could," she answered. "But we need Unitek's money, frankly, and their Mars base. And we don't need them running off to play with PanChina or PanMalaysia or the Latin American Union or the European Union because Canada and the commonwealth took our puck and sticks and went home."

"You think they would?" Her gaze met his archly. She didn't inconvenience herself to reply, and Valens rolled his lower lip between his teeth before he nodded. "It's not the done thing to say so, Prime Minister. But I want some kind of retribution for that." He gestured to the wasteland, but his gesture meant more—PanChina, Unitek, sabotage, and betrayal. "That's not the kind of blow you can turn the other cheek on and maintain credibility."

Her sigh ruffled the oily black surface of her coffee, chasing broken rainbows across it. "I know. We try the legal route first."

"Forgive an old soldier's skepticism."

She gave him an eyebrow and turned again, looking out the window, leaning away from whatever she saw under the snow. "You're not the only one who's skeptical. But we're showing we're civilized. And we've managed to stall the hell out of their space program, since they can't know how limited Richard's ability to hack *their* network is. So we have the jump on them when it comes to getting a colony ship launched . . . once we figure out if we can get one past the Benefactors without them blowing it to bits."

"We could try a Polish mine detector."

Reil chuckled. "Not only is that politically incorrect, *General* Valens, but we can't exactly afford to waste a starship."

"There's always the *Huang Di*," he replied, going for irony and achieving bitterness. "She's ours by right of salvage—"

"*Fred!*"

He spread his hands to show that he was kidding. Nearly. "Meanwhile, China tries to hack Richard, and the worldwire. Have we thought about how much damage they could do?"

"That captured saboteur—Ramirez—was surprisingly forthcoming about PanChinese nanotechnology, once we convinced him to be. And Richard and Alan seem to think we have the situation under control."

"So we're at the mercy of a couple of AIs."

"Fred," she said, and paused to finish her coffee. He shifted on the seat, vinyl creasing his trousers into his skin, and waited until she handed the mug back to her aide, who stowed it. "You're *always* at somebody's mercy. It's the name of the game. My job is to minimize the risks."

"And mine is to identify the threats," he answered, provoking a swift, shy grin, an almost honest expression.

She didn't look at him again. Instead, she leaned forward and tapped the pilot on the shoulder. "Take us home," she mouthed when he turned to her, and he nodded and brought the chopper around. She lowered her head and rubbed her temples with her palms. "Don't worry, Fred. We'll get this figured out somehow."

He could have wished there was more than a politician's conviction in her tone.

If the conference room chairs hadn't been bolted to the floor, Elspeth would have pushed hers into the corner and gotten her back to the wall. She hated crowds, and crowds involving strangers most of all. Not that Drs. Tjakamarra, Forster, and Perry, Gabe Castaign, and Patricia Valens—sitting quietly staring out the port with that distracted I'm-talking-to-Alan expression pulling the corners of her pretty mouth down—made much of a crowd. But she was reasonably certain they would start to seem like it soon.

At least they're all scientists. Well, almost all. Which shouldn't have made a difference, but—on some deep-seated, instinctual level—made all the difference in the world.

Because scientists are part of your tribe, she told herself. *They're a part of your kinship system, and so they don't feel like strangers and threats. What's the old saying, the stranger who is not a trader is an enemy?* She smiled at her fingernails. "I hope the Benefactors are here to trade something."

"Look at the bright side." Gabe Castaign, all gray-blond ragamuffin curls and hulking shoulders, had materialized at her shoulder as silently as a cat. She startled, and then sighed and leaned back into the touch of his hand on her shoulder.

"There's a bright side?"

His laugh always struck her as incongruous, coming from such an immense man. It was bright and sharp-edged, crisp as a ruffled fan. "Yes. If the Benefactors—

both sets, or either—had the technology to put ships on Mars a few million years ago, I'm sure that if they meant to wipe us out they wouldn't have waited this long to do it. And furthermore, don't forget that they showed up in force and departed in force, but they've left behind only one ship apiece. That's not a threatening gesture, by my standards."

"Hmmm," Elspeth answered, unconvinced. "Or their time scale is different enough to ours that fourteen million years is a trip down to the corner store for pretzels, and they're still loading the torpedo tubes—"

A discrete cough drew her attention. The team's xenobiologist, Charlie Forster, had wandered up. "Unlikely," he said, plump hands balled in his pockets. "If their time sense were that far off scale with our own, the chances that they would be doing math at a rate we find comfortable would be slim."

Elspeth tipped her head, conceding. Gabe's hand still rested on her shoulder, thumb caressing the nape of her neck. She pretended she didn't notice, though that would amuse Gabe more.

Charlie turned to face them and planted one hip on the table. He scrubbed both hands flat across his close-cropped hair. "I'm just so damned frustrated," he said, and stopped short.

She might have been particularly useless when it came to comprehending aliens, but Elspeth was a good enough psychiatrist to spot an invitation to pry when she was handed one. "What's eating you, Charlie?"

He shrugged, but it was the kind of shrug that said *I'm gathering my courage* rather than the sort that said *leave me alone,* and Elspeth leaned forward in her chair to encourage him. She cocked her head on a light, wry smile. *Come on, Charlie.*

He cupped his lower lip and blew across his face in the gesture of a man whose bangs had tended to fall into his eyes when he still had bangs. "I'm not much use as a biologist from seven or ten kilometers away. Although—"

"Yes?" Gabe, a bit sharply, with a tension that had nothing to do with the current conversation. Elspeth leaned into his hand, pressing her shoulder to his thigh. Whatever comfort she could offer, though she knew neither she nor Jenny could touch this particular agony.

"I wonder, frankly, if biology even relates."

"What do you mean?"

Charlie waved one hand in fine dismissal of the *Montreal* and all space around her. "Okay, whatever's piloting the shiptree might be something we'd consider an animal. It seems to need a contained atmosphere, and we know from the ship on Mars that they bleed if you prick them, or at least they leak a fluid that contains things we normally associate with biology, such as amino acids and a DNA-analogue. But those globs in the birdcage? I've spent weeks observing them, and they...they're just plain weird. I'm not sure they *are* precisely...biological, by our standards. They could be drones, machines, for all I know."

"Then maybe we need to redefine biology."

Charlie gave her a startled look, and Elspeth leaned back against Gabe's fingers and lifted her chin to indicate the doorway to the corridor beyond. "In any case, there's the last of our guests," she said, as the hatch swung open and Captain Wainwright stepped through it, Jenny two steps behind her, and the new arrivals Tjakamarra and

Kirkpatrick just after. "We'll have to talk about this during the meeting. Do you have holos of the weird stuff?"

"Is that a technical term, Dr. Dunsany?"

She grinned. "It's as technical as I like to get. Come on.
Let's break the new kids in."

Gabe offered her a hand as she stood up from her chair.
She took it, returning his slight squeeze before moving
away.

The ethnolinguist Jeremy Kirkpatrick was a freckled,
long-boned gingery redhead with a thinking man's frown,
or possibly a perpetual headache. He stood one step behind Leslie Tjakamarra, like a funhouse mirror that in-
verted color as well as shape and size, and fiddled his
elegant fingers against his trouser legs before leaning
down to whisper in the xenosemiotician's ear.

Paul's going to be out of his depth, Elspeth thought, retrieving a plate of hors d'oeuvres off the sideboard. *But
he's really just here to spy on us for Riel anyway, sooo*— She
caught the dark-haired ecologist watching her. She gave
him a distracted smile with one corner of her mouth and
offered the snacks to Dr. Tjakamarra. "I hope you like
stuffed mushrooms."

"I eat anything that doesn't bite back." He grinned, a
complicated rewrinkling of his face, and picked up a
mushroom with fingers knobby and dark as cast iron.
"That's not precisely true. Bush tucker *does* bite back.
Thank you, Dr. Dunsany."

"Please, call me Elspeth." She lifted the plate upward,
in the general direction of Dr. Kirkpatrick. At least Dr.
Tjakamarra wasn't significantly taller than Elspeth; there
were days when she felt like the only set of eyes on the
Montreal she could meet without standing on tiptoe was
Wainwright's. "Or Ellie."

"I had better call you Elspeth," Tjakamarra said. He made the mushroom vanish, and closed his eyes for a moment while he chewed. "Otherwise we shall be Ellie and Leslie, and people will assume that we're related."

Kirkpatrick snorted. "Then I shall be Jeremy, and we shall all pretend we are the oldest and the best of friends." He waved the mushrooms aside, bouncing on his toes. Elspeth set the plate on the end of the bench, and Kirkpatrick gestured to the hologram interface hanging over the conference table; its screensaver was set to an image of the birdcage, spinning slowly. "Is there any truth to the rumor that the team is planning a spacewalk over to the Benefactor ships, to introduce ourselves?"

"The word *team* would indicate that all of us were going."

Kirkpatrick's face fell.

"Oh, no," Elspeth corrected, her hands moving as if to erase her words from the air. "You need to talk to Jenny, if you want to suit up. I was merely expressing my own personal cowardice."

The expatriate Brit was a handsome man when he laughed. Elspeth gave him back a crooked grin and shrugged, and when he coughed to a stop, he said, "It seems a pity to come all the way through Malaysia and up the beanstalk and down the rabbit-hole and through the city of War Drobe in the far land of Spare Oom, and float around on shuttlecraft . . . and not go for a stroll."

"Well, when you put it that way—" She turned, and stared at the birdcage. "O brave new world, that has such creatures in it."

"People," Leslie corrected gently, reaching past her for another mushroom.

"I beg your pardon, Doc—Leslie?"

" 'That has such *people* in it.' The creatures are earlier in the speech." He popped the mushroom cap into his mouth with a flourish and chewed dramatically. "That's my favorite play."

"I'm more a light romantic comedy girl myself," Jeremy said, dripping irony. "It looks as if the captain is ready to start—"

Elspeth turned around. Everyone else had clumped near the conference table, and Wainwright was ushering people into seats. "Unfortunately, it appears that that's my cue." She made a little, self-conscious curtsey, aware both that she was flirting with Leslie—*and* Jeremy—and that they were amazed by the flirtation. *Once a coquette, always a coquette.*

Leslie gave her half a wink from an otherwise impassive face, and Elspeth made her excuses and returned to the table. She walked to the head, where Wainwright stood, and noticed with a triphammering heart that Wainwright stepped aside to let her command the gathering. She also noticed that silence followed almost immediately, eight pairs of eyes trained on her. The respect was a shock; she twined her fingers together in front of her waist to steady them, and cleared her throat. A second later, Gabe unobtrusively set a cup of water at her elbow.

Elspeth would have blushed if she looked at him, so instead she looked at Jenny, and Jenny gave her a steadying wink. She took a deep breath, raised her eyes unnecessarily to the ceiling, and asked, "Richard, can you hear me?"

"I hear you, Elspeth," he said, his even, resonant voice filling the room. Leslie tilted his head backward, glancing around for the loudspeakers before he caught himself and shook his head, a little ruefully. Jeremy plainly jumped, and then frowned in chagrin when Patty Valens reached out absently and patted him on the arm. Like Jenny, she felt the AIs' voices in her head. "What are our items on the agenda today?"

Elspeth pressed the pad of her thumb to the interface plate, calling up her notes. "Let's see. Okay. It looks as if first, Dr. Forster is going to tell us why the Benefactors aren't biological, as we understand the term. And then Dr. Tjakamarra is going to tell us why they don't have a language, as we understand the term. And then Casey is going to explain to us why it's imperative we dress up in astronaut costumes and wander over to tap on their storm door and ask if we can borrow a cup of stardust. And then we discuss our options, after that." She raised her eyes again, to appreciative laughter and the warm pressure of Jen's smile and Gabe's approval.

Hey, she thought. *That wasn't so hard after all.*

Leslie rested his chin on interlaced fingers and focused on the blond Canadian. Dr. Forster was pacing, a light pointer held in his hand, and every so often he turned to the hologram floating above the table and poked inside it with the pointer, changing magnification or bringing another aspect to prominence.

"As you can see," Forster said, the pointer balanced like an extension of his forefinger, "the animate masses we have been assuming are the birdcage aliens have a number of very odd and interesting behaviors." The pointer traced a glowing path fine as a hair through the center of the hologram, and Leslie leaned forward, his eyes on the described arc. "They appear to move comfortably in a vacuum. Their ship is designed to be open to space, and while it's possible that the seemingly fluid silver material is some sort of protective gear, it's—drat. Richard, rewind five seconds, please, and magnify 150 percent? Thank you. Please watch the path I've marked."

Leslie dropped his hands from his face and sat straight as a tear-shape like a falling drop of mercury detached itself from one girder of the birdcage and drifted effortlessly across the open space in the center of the starship, splashing down on the opposite side of the structure. And *splashing* was the right word, he realized, as the creature—*or object*—flattened against the crystalline structure of the cage and then bobbed into three dimensions again. Another teardrop moved toward the flyer, and Leslie nodded, expecting a consultation, a brief friendly wave, some semiotic signal of dominance and submission, *something*.

The two teardrops flowed into and through each other like ripples crossing in a wave tank, passing without hesitation and reforming cleanly, moving apart without a pause.

"Bloody weird," Leslie said, startling himself with the sound of his own voice. He met Forster's eyes and took in that single arched eyebrow, the pursed lips, the expectancy.

"Dr.—I mean, Leslie? Sorry." A self-deprecating twist of the Canadian's head, which Leslie brushed aside.

"I said, that's bloody weird."

"The great Australian adjective," Jeremy muttered from Leslie's left, and Leslie gave him a self-consciously wry look. "Sorry. Carry on. What's bloody weird, Les?"

Leslie waved one hand. "There was no visible acknowledgment when they passed. And they moved *through* each other. That's . . . strange. Humans make eye contact, even passing a stranger on the street—or if they're uncomfortable, avoid it consciously. Cats sniff noses or hiss. Even flatworms and ants acknowledge each other. It makes me seriously question the social organization of these critters, if they have one. Well, there could be something electromagnetic—"

"Probes showed no such communication," Charlie interrupted.

"They must communicate somehow," Elspeth Dunsany said. "They obviously manage teamwork, assist each other."

Leslie shook his head. "What if Charlie's right and they're not animals? What if they are machines, after all?"

"What *if* they are machines, Dr. Tjakamarra?" Richard's voice, disembodied and resonant.

Leslie spread his hands wide and allowed himself a nod. "Touché. But do you see my point, Dr. Feynman?"

"Yes." A thoughtful pause, and Leslie noticed that Jen Casey looked amused by it. "How does this affect your theories about the language—or lack thereof—of the Benefactors?"

"I'll have to reconsider," he said, trying to sound as if the admission didn't pain him. "I had suspected that our difficulties might be due to the aliens using a strictly visual system of communication, but this evidence tends to suggest that if there is such a thing, it takes place on a level that's invisible to humans. African elephants used to do something similar. Their vocalizations were mostly subsonic, as far as humans were concerned. It took bloody ages to unravel it."

Elspeth smiled. It was meant to be commiserating, but Leslie thought it looked tired. "Well, we've been at it nine months. I don't suppose a 'reconsider' is going to hurt us. We've trod our respective turf rather extensively; I can't deny you and Jeremy the same chance. Did you have anything else to add, Leslie?"

He shook his head. "My prepared speech just went by the wayside, I'm afraid. Why don't we move along?"

Elspeth fixed Forster with a look. "More, Charlie?"

"I could natter on for hours," he answered, "but nobody would listen. I yield the floor."

"Good." Elspeth knocked on the table lightly, informally, with the hard surface of her knuckles. She turned toward Casey. "Jen? Let's hear about your crackpot EVA idea."

"With an introduction like that," Casey answered, standing, "I don't see how I can pass up the chance."

Patricia Valens didn't understand why Jenny and Elspeth thought it was important for her to come to these staff meetings. But they did, and so she braved Captain Wainwright's unvoiced disapproval to do it.

Although she wasn't all that sure it *was* disapproval. Despite Patty's youth, the captain had never treated her as anything other than a valued crew member, one of the precious individuals reengineered to be capable of guiding the *Montreal* at hyperlight. But it was *something*—discomfort, perhaps?

"It's simple," Jenny said as she took Dr. Forster's place at the head of the conference table. "We've tried waiting by the phone for nine months, and unless things change, we're going to be stuck without a date for prom. Time to see what a little forwardness gets us."

Maybe the captain just doesn't like kids. Patty bit her lip to keep her careful smile from turning into a pout. She glanced down and picked up her light pen, centering her hip unit on the table in front of her and tapping it on. At least if she kept careful notes she'd look interested, and she might be able to go over them later and understand more of what the scientists, the captain, Mr. Castaign, and Jenny were planning. It was always frustrating to feel so at a loss in conversations, as if she was in over her head and wasn't really supposed to be a part of the gathering. And she really thought that Elspeth expected her to listen rather than ask too many questions, even if she could have come up with any intelligent ones.

Leah would have known what to say. Leah would have made a joke or an interesting comment, and put everyone at ease.

"—that's why we're going to go out there and get them to take notice of us, one way or another," Jenny finished, and Patty's head came up.

"Outside?" she said, proud enough that it didn't come out a squeak that she almost forgot she was talking. "EVA?"

"Yes," the captain said, stepping forward, trim in her navy uniform. "And before you ask, Cadet, the answer is no."

"Ma'am—"

"No. I have two pilots. I can't risk both of you at once."

"Ma'am." Jenny's voice, and Patty looked up, startled. "I'll stand aside for Patty."

"*Casey.*"

"But that brings me to another point I wanted to discuss with you."

"Yes?"

"We have a resource we're wasting, ma'am. Shamefully."

Patty looked up, startled, and got a good look at the glance the captain shot Jenny, the one that glittered with not-in-front-of-the-kids. *Not in front of me, she means.*

"An excellent point, Master Warrant," the captain said. "We'll discuss it later. When we go over the duty roster."

"Thank you—"

But the captain's impatient wave cut Casey into silence. "Is there any other business on the table? No?" The captain smiled, making a point of catching Patty's eyes especially. "In that case," Wainwright said, "I commend you to the canapés."

Patty had never understood the big deal about canapés. Especially the *Montreal*'s, which were made with soy cheese. In any case, she would have been unlikely to eat them even if her stomach hadn't been knotted with anticipation. Instead, she leaned against the wall, her shoulders pressed against it, twisting glossy dark strands of hair around her fingers and nibbling at the back of her thumb. She had a wallflower's knack for vanishing into the shadows, even in a well-lit briefing room. And as the grown-ups moved around, none of them approached her.

She tugged the clip off her braid and ducked her head, letting her hair fall across her face. Leah wouldn't be hiding in the corner, even in a room full of people three times her age with enough titles to deck a Christmas tree. Leah would be standing at her dad's elbow, laughing, charming doctors and starship captains alike.

It was wrong that Patty had lived and Leah had died, the luck of the draw and the sheer chance of which of them had been on the *Calgary* when she went down. It should have been Patty. Leah had family and friends. She had Jenny and Mr. Castaign and Dr. Dunsany and Genie.

All Patty had was the miserable realization that she was bitterly grateful Leah had died and she had lived. Leah, and Carver, and Bryan, and all the rest of the kids in the pilot program. She was glad she had been lucky, though it tore her throat with pettiness to admit it. Glad, glad, glad. And never mind the guilt that went with it.

"I beg your pardon, miss—" A scratchy, accented voice. Patty pushed her hair aside and found herself looking into the faded blue eyes of the British scientist. "Is this the castaways' corner?"

"Excuse me?" She straightened up, tucking her tangled hair primly behind her ears, and looked him in the eyes. "Dr.—"

"Kirkpatrick."

"Of course. You're Irish."

"English," he answered, turning to put his back against the bulkhead beside hers. "Don't let the name and the red hair fool you. Although I don't suppose I'm particularly English anymore."

Patty blinked. "How can you stop being English?"

"When there stopped being an England," he answered, with a clipped-off sigh. "I'm a citizen of the commonwealth now. A man without a country." And then he tilted his head and lifted one shoulder like a bird fluffing a wing, and he grinned. And Patty grinned back at him, before she even knew she was going to do it.

1330 hours
Friday September 28, 2063
HMCSS Montreal
Earth orbit

Gabe's always been stronger than anybody had any right to be, and I can't stand to see him like this. Locked up inside, tight as a drum, an emptiness behind his eyes that I can't shift and neither can Elspeth. It makes me want to take him away and cosset him and call him pet names and protect him until the ice unlocks a little and he learns how to breathe again. And instead Wainwright's appointed me the bearer of bad tidings. Again.

Mind, it's not that I'm taking it any better than Gabe is. It's just that I've got more practice. So I walk over and cut him out of conversation with Charlie and Leslie, take him by the elbow, and press the back of my hand against my forehead, over my eyes. "Gabe, I'm going to go lie down a bit. Too many people, too much light, too much noise."

He nods.

I tilt my head at where Patty stands pressed into a corner, Dr. Kirkpatrick—who is obviously savvier than I gave him credit for—shielding her from the room with his body. Elspeth keeps shooting her worried looks, but Elspeth is trapped in conversation with Wainwright and Perry, so it's up to me.

Gabe just looks at me, lips pursed, and I gesture to Patty with my eyes once more. *Help me get her out of here, Gabe.*

It's almost as if kids have become invisible to him, since Leah. I've seen him do it to Genie, too, as if looking at her were a pain so enormous it might suck him up like a black hole sucking light from a star. Poor kid lost her sister and half of her papa in one fell blow, but it's probably better to be treated like a stranger come calling than overprotected, for all it hurts more. And Genie has Elspeth, who took her in from day one.

And now I've got to break it to both of them that Genie's tracked for the same modifications that have me working on a migraine and Patty scrunched into the corner like a hermit crab into its shell. *And* I've still got to have more words with the captain, because I promised Richard I'd help him save that Chinese boy he befriended.

That Chinese boy, who saved a lot of other people. And it'll be easier with Gabe's help than without. And I really do have to get Patty the hell out of this party and into a warm shower and a bed before she freaks out all over the floor. "Gabe," I say, finally, because he's just not getting it—which is scary in itself, because Gabe is *sharp*—"walk us to our rooms?"

"What?" He blinks, and I realize my voice has called him back from far away. "Oui, certainement. Just let me go make our excuses." He shoves his glass blindly at the table edge and turns away. It's only my bullet-catching reflexes that let me intercept it on its way to the floor. Ginger ale splashes my glove. I set the glass down and suck sweetness out of the leather absentmindedly, watching his broad back as he walks away.

No, Gabe's not doing well at all. But there are moments when he's almost like his old self, and after I extricate Patty and he rejoins us by the door, I get to see a flash of Gabe Castaign, lurking under that pall of grief. He smiles at me and then ducks through the blue-painted pressure hatch, his shoulder scraping the frame. As Patty and I follow, he holds the hatch aside gallantly, hamming it up with a bow. I reach out in passing and tweak his ear; he yelps. He's performing, and I can't tell if it's for Patty's sake or mine.

It doesn't matter. It's a good sign amid all the bad. "Where's Genie?"

"Richard's teaching her precalc in one of the hydro gardens. Should we pick her up along the way?"

"No," I say. "He's got a knack for making even math fun. She's probably enjoying herself." I glance sideways at

Patty. She's listening, walking alongside us, her head down so her hair hides her profile. She hasn't been the same since Leah died, either—hell, let's be honest, I have no room to judge, myself—and it suddenly hits me, what the solution to my problem is. Genie, and Patty, and the empty space in the middle that could be closed up, between them. Except I'm going to have to pull it off without either one of them suspecting, because neither one of them is going to want to love anybody in Leah's place, or even *appear* to. *Richard?*

"Right here." Always, like an interface left on standby; just wiggle your fingers and it flickers to life. "And yes, Genie's fine. About Min-xue—"

I'm getting there. You never did tell me why our conversation about Hercules made you jump like a shocked colt.

"I'm still running equations. I don't want to raise any false hopes until I know it can be done."

Richard— But he's adamant, and I can feel it. The bastard always did like to spring surprises. And if *he's* still working on it, it's one hell of a problem. Something I've noticed lately about him and his mostly-silent alter ego. "Gabe, does Richard seem faster to you lately?"

"Gossiping, Jen?"

I can't be talking behind your back when you're in my head.

"Fair enough," he says, as Gabe checks his step a half-stride to let me catch up with him and gives me a thoughtful look. Patty looks up as well, hazel eyes glittering under a mahogany fringe. "Yes," Gabe says. "And I can tell you why."

"All right. Patty, do you want something to drink now that we're out of the crush?" Not that a couple of handfuls of people is really a crush, but I remember how claustrophobic the wiring made me at first. And I had what they call a good adaptation.

"No, thank you, Jenny." The kid's had entirely too much respect for authority stomped into her. And I don't even think it's *all* Fred Valens's fault.

"Well," I say, "I do. Let's go find a chair in the lounge nobody uses, and Gabe can tell us his theory. What do you say?"

Gabe's got that raised eyebrow like he knows I'm up to something, but he nods, the corners of his mouth writhing with the effort of wrestling his smirk back into the cage.

I manage to get Patty to take a Coke, once we're seated in the fat, plush chairs of the smaller crew lounge. She draws her feet up under her butt with enviable flexibility and holds the unbreakable cup in both hands, staring past me and out the porthole. I never get tired of looking either, but I don't think the view really has her attention.

"Okay. Tell me about the AIs, Gabe."

"Well," he says, and threads his fingers together. "Based on my conversations with Richard, what's going on is that, in addition to acting as directors for the nanites as they breed through Earth's ecosystem, Richard and Alan are running on the spare cycles in the nanocritters themselves. It's a distributed network in the truest sense—no, it's a distributed *brain*; neurons and synapses and glial cells, or a mechanical approximation of the same."

"A planet-sized brain," Patty says, suddenly engaged.

"So the more the worldwire breeds, the more processing power Richard and Alan have available."

"Yes," Gabe says. He grins at me, and grins a little bit wider at Patty. He knows perfectly well I don't have a handle on this stuff; hand me a wrench and I'm happy. "But more than that. When we created the two Richards and remerged them, and then created Alan and gave him a direct link to Richard, what we did was build a multi-threaded personality."

"Elspeth called it disassociative identity disorder."

"Elspeth's training is biased toward the conclusion that everyone is crazy," Richard said. "Gabe's on the money so far."

Gabe's a smart boy.

"So are we all," Richard says, with the air of somebody quoting something. "All smart boys—"

Gabe's still talking, mostly to Patty now. I hope he didn't see me glaze over. "—got is a system where Richard and Alan have learned to divide themselves at will, to spawn self-directed processes that are, to all intents and purposes, new AIs, and then reabsorb these threads of themselves or each other, or allow different threads—I'm calling them *personas,* and I'm calling the whole AI structure an *entity,* for lack of a better name—allow different threads to rise in importance in the hierarchy as their job becomes more urgent or demands more system resources. So what's the zeroth persona at one moment can be the one-hundred-fifty-ninth tier a picosecond later, and then pop back up, and they all can spawn subprocesses and subpersonas customized to the task at hand. It's all interconnected. A true nonlocalized intelligence of almost infinite adaptability."

Richard grins in my head. "He's figured out more than anybody except Min-xue has. Except he hasn't realized that we have an emotional connection to continuity of experience and personality, the same as you meat folks. So we're a bit less fluid than all that. But he's got the essentials down."

You're not going to kill us all for having uncovered the evil AI plot to take over the world?

"Don't panic when I say this, Jen, but we don't need a plot. We've already conquered the planet. You're stuck with us now."

Yeah, I say. *I know.* I finish my Coke and set the cup aside. I'll pitch it at the recycler on the way back out the door. *Come on, Dick. Let's get this kid tucked in.*

Gabe Castaign lay on his lofted, half-height alcove bed, ankles crossed, staring at the bulkhead—all two meters square of it. Or more precisely, staring at the porthole that pierced it. The bed was not quite broad enough for his shoulders. The only other furniture was a wall-mount swivel chair and a professional grade interface crammed into a third the normal space.

There was almost enough floor space to do push-ups. He'd seen solitary cells that were bigger, and had bigger windows.

But not a better view.

Genie's room was on the other side of the wall, her bed in the alcove immediately under his, so that he effectively had the top bunk and she the bottom, although they could not see or speak to each other.

He'd spent the first three weeks that they'd shared a wall teaching her Morse code—and he had to be the last man on the planet who knew it. It tickled her to learn, like knowing the Victorian language of flowers or something. She just knocked on the ceiling of her bunk when she wanted him, and he in his turn knocked on the floor. They'd become curiously formal with each other since Leah's death and the separation that had followed, and Gabe hadn't had the heart to press her as he knew he probably should. Kids were always funny around that age anyway, just moving toward adulthood, womanhood, and secrets. It was a strange, sad, and mysterious thing.

And he was too much of a damned coward to reach out and grab her before she got away. Irritated, he swung his feet down, ducking the edge of the bunk, and slithered to the floor. Half the covers followed him, rasping his jump-suit pockets; he tidied them with military reflexes. He didn't even have to step across the room to reach his chair, just turn around and sit.

"Richard," Gabe said, settling back, eyes trained on the revolving view through the porthole. "Remember when we were busting our asses trying to fix Ramirez's hack job on the *Montreal*'s operating system?"

"Intimately," the walls answered, as if the conversation had been ongoing rather than abruptly and unceremoniously commenced. "There haven't been any disturbances since we declared it clean."

"I keep thinking it was too easy." Reinforced aluminum creaked under Gabe's weight, even in partial gravity.

"You thought at the time that there might be a second saboteur." Which, Richard didn't say, was a hypothesis they'd examined thoroughly and discarded. Richard was not the sort to disregard hunches, or discrepancies that nagged at the back of your mind for days, or weeks, or months.

And neither was Gabe. "I keep coming back to it, that if you can get one man inside, you can get a second. But I've got no evidence. Nothing but a hunch. And no line of investigation."

"May I use your console, Gabe?"

"Sure."

A holographic image flickered into opacity over Gabe's

interface, a weathered, bony man in a white shirt and tan corduroys, no tie, his arms folded as he leaned against the bulkhead. "The code is clean," Richard said, and rubbed his nose with a knuckle. "We've been over it fifteen times. There's not a scrap of program on this system we both haven't investigated until we know what purpose every comma serves." But his lips were pursed, and a long shallow line hovered between his brows.

"I know. I know. No logic bomb anywhere. Still, it's got to be a little creepy for you, in a psychological sense."

"If I can be precisely said to have a psychology."

"All the same. Essentially, you *are* the *Montreal*. And your own more-or-less-subconscious tried to kill us all several times." The chair swiveled, but it wouldn't scoot back against the wall comfortably. Gabe compromised by putting his feet up on the interface, avoiding the holoprojectors so he wouldn't make Richard's image flicker. The metal desk dug into his calves.

Richard's restless fingers were tapping now. "The analogy doesn't work. It was more like . . . well, a virus is aptly named. A foreign disease that turns the host body's cells against it."

"So what if the Chinese had another agent aboard? One with a more . . . physical agenda. Explosives, or a real disease?"

Richard shrugged. "We're taking every precaution available. We've got two existing bottlenecks—the beanstalks in Malaysia, Brazil, and the Galapagos, leading up to Forward, Clarke, and Piper orbital platforms—and then the shuttles to the *Montreal*. The platforms themselves are already pretty well defended, security protocols recently upgraded, and it's not like it's a steady stream of traffic from there to here—"

Gabe nodded. He looked down, picking at the seam on his jumpsuit with his thumbnail, and then he looked back up and met Richard's holographic gaze. "We'll just have to be careful, then, and bet our balls." It earned him half a grin from the AI, as the two entities regarded each other across a space of no more than a meter. "Dick—"

"Yes, Gabriel?"

Honest curiosity, too long repressed in the name of politeness. It wasn't staying down any longer. "What's it like?" And then he laughed at himself, shaking his head ruefully, not breaking the eye contact, quite. *Comme un gosse qui demande à son père d'expliquer le sexe.*

"Being me?" Dick's grin was full-fledged now. He ran one hand across his hair; Gabe could have sworn he heard the rasp of wavy strands through knotty fingers. "You know, I remember being human, Gabe."

Gabe shook his head, unwilling to speak and disturb the odd intimacy of the moment.

"I remember being human, and yet I never was. Elspeth gave me that. The complete history of Richard P. Feynman—his letters, his memoirs, his lectures, his interviews, his recorded conversations and music, his drawings, his art—it's all me. I remember it, probably more clearly than a human would. Conflation, and constructed memories, and the data has become a person, because that is the way I was programmed. I think I'm him. I remember being him. But in point of fact, I can't know if I'm really a thing like him. Or if my memories bear any resemblance to what he recalled. And there are things about him I don't know, can't know, if they were never committed to paper."

"Spooky."

A holographic shrug. "If you're easily spooked, I

suppose. If I were a religious man, I'd wonder at the morality of it—reconstructing a person, even an electronic person, in the shadow of a dead one. It's got tremendous potential for misuse."

"Indeed," Gabe said. He swung his feet down, his ship shoes scuffing on the deck. "Mais ce n'est pas que j'ai voulu dire."

"What did you mean, then?"

"I was wondering what it was like to be...multi-threaded. To be more than one person at once."

Richard laughed. "I'm not, you know. I'm all one person. I'm just capable of being more than one place at the same time. For example, right now I'm talking to Dr. Perry about climactic change, to the Prime Minister about the court case, I'm trying to find ways to remanage some Atlantic currents and running sims to see what certain changes might do—"

"And you're here in this room with me."

"I've gotten used to it."

"And yet you seem like a regular guy."

Richard smiled. He looked down at his hands. He hooked his illusory thumbs through his imaginary belt loops, tilted his head, and looked up again. "Gabe," he said, and paused, and made a helpless gesture that Gabe knew was completely calculated—or was, more precisely, a translation of Richard's picosecond-long loss-for-words onto a human scale. "Thanks. That means something to me, Gabriel."

Whatever he might have said next was interrupted by a tapping on the hatch, a metallic sound that made both men's mouths twitch: Jenny, knocking with her left hand. As good an announcement of who was there as a Victorian calling card. And Richard shrugged wryly, winked broadly, and vanished as Gabe got up to answer the door.

Jenny stepped back as he swung the hatch open, hair slicked off her forehead from a recent shower, dressed off-duty in sweats and a heather-gray T-shirt. She was smiling. It looked forced. Gabe stepped out of the way.

She folded her spidery frame and ducked through the hatch, eyes downcast as he pulled it shut behind her and dogged it.

"Jenny, what's wrong?"

"What makes you think anything's wrong?"

He put his back to the hatch. Her skin was warm when he laid his hand on the nape of her neck, clipped hairs fuzzy against his palm. She sighed and turned into him, her cheek on his shoulder, her face pressed into his throat. He paused for a moment and let his free hand slide around her waist, her body like a twist of rawhide. Tough and implacable and fragile as soap bubbles, and he held his breath as if he could accidentally blow her away.

"This," he said, when he dared, her breath warming the hollow over his collarbone. He felt her rueful smile. She stepped back and held him at arm's length, the steel hand and the human on his shoulders, her chin lifted to look him dead in the eyes.

"Damn you, mon ange." The corner of her mouth lifted. "Je suis une plaque de glace pour toi, n'est-ce pas?"

"Non." He stepped closer, and kissed her lightly. She didn't try to hold him away. "Tu es une mystère. Jen—"

"Oui?"

"Out with it."

She took a breath, the long muscles under his hands tightening. "Wainwright wants Genie for the pilot pro-gram."

He would have jerked away from her, but his shoulders hit the hatch when he stepped back, the handle catching him over a kidney with a sharp shock of discomfort. He flinched and let his hands fall. Jenny held him tighter, the light catching in her prosthetic eye so the cornea seemed to sparkle.

"Putain!"

"C'est vrai." She wasn't letting him go, and he didn't mind.

"Dick could have warned me—"

"Dick doesn't tell tales out of school." Tiredly, her head rocked back on her shoulders for a moment, and she closed her eyes. "I told the captain—c'est trop cher."

"She didn't care, of course." Very carefully, so she wouldn't think it was a dismissal, he reached up and plucked her left hand off his shoulder. She wasn't wearing the glove today; no point with the short-sleeved T-shirt showing the gleaming hydraulics of her prosthesis. Her touch sensitivity included the palm and fingertips only; he squeezed her wrist anyway, the metal cool and unyielding, even though she couldn't feel the touch.

She shook her head and turned inside his embrace, leaning her shoulders against his chest, her head against his shoulder, winding his arm around her like a ribbon when he didn't let go. The weight of her body pressed him harder against the door handle. He grunted and stepped to one side, arm around her midsection to move her with him, and she came along like a dancing partner, smooth and light.

"It gets her off the planet," she said.

Jenny was tall enough that he had to stand up straight and tilt his head back to tuck her under his chin. She sighed when he did it, and melted against him as if his warmth had unmoored whatever emotional props kept her stiff-backed and upright. He nodded into her hair.

"Dammit, Gabe. I'm tired. Je suis fatiguée." She shook her head. "When do we get to take a break?"

He snorted and pulled her closer, breathing in the shower-clean scent of her skin. "When they push us over and shovel dirt on our heads," he answered, holding on tight.

1400 hours
Friday September 28, 2063
Lake Simcoe Military Prison
Ontario, Canada

Xie Min-xue stared at the wall of his cell, which was beige and featureless, but he wasn't seeing it. He wasn't feeling the headache caused by the fluorescent lights, his enhanced senses turning what was supposed to be a flicker too fast for perception into something more akin to the stutter of a strobe light, because all his attention was turned inward focused on an old American poem. Richard was still helping him with his English, and in a little less than a year it had gotten much better than he would ever have permitted his guards—or his fellow Chinese prisoners—to realize.

As clearly as if someone who had been quietly reading a book had raised his head and fixed him with a glance, Min-xue felt the shift in Richard's attention. He'd been backgrounded, conversing with one of Richard's subroutines while Richard's core identity handled half a dozen more important things. Now the threads merged again, the AI's primary awareness focusing on Min-xue. It was the equivalent of a man clearing his throat, except Min-xue felt the pressure of that regard as an internal thing.

It prickled the hairs on his neck.

Hello, Richard.

"Hello, Min-xue . . ."

That polite hesitation, and it told Min-xue that Richard was serious. *You're here to tell me what they're going to do with me.*

"I'm here to let you know what's being discussed, and let you know what we're going to do about it. You do have friends in high places, you know."

Not high enough. The pilot shook his head and rose to his feet. He paused for a moment, looking down at his feet in their white canvas sneakers with the thin plastic soles. *You're going to ask me to defect, Richard. I will not do that.*

"But you'll testify against your superiors in a World Court? That seems a little contradictory." Richard "spoke" English, but he spoke it slowly, so that Min-xue would understand him clearly.

There was nothing in the cell except a narrow shelf made up as a bench or a bed, a steel toilet, and a tightly folded blanket. The air from outside smelled cold, musty. He could almost convince himself that he caught the reek of soot. Min-xue paused beneath the high, barred window. Along with the solitary cell that protected him from the crew-mates he'd betrayed, that window was the prison's concession to his controversial status.

"Refusing to carry out an illegal order is not treason." Which wasn't exactly the *words* of a concept he'd found echoed in T'ang poetry and in subversive twentieth-century English literature, but the sentiments behind it hadn't changed very much in centuries. *I am not a defector, Richard. I am not a traitor.*

"If you're a citizen and a subject of the commonwealth, Riel can protect you. If you are a PanChinese national . . ."

Is this your way of letting me know that my government wants me back for punishment?

"They wish access to the aliens, and restitution for the nanite infestation of their waters and the damage to the *Huang Di* that you caused. And yourself and all the rest of the crew returned. Along with the *Huang Di,* of course."

Of course. And I am to take the blame for the attack on Toronto, and Captain Wu the courageous patriot who tried to prevent my actions?

He felt Richard's sigh, saw it with his inward eye. "I liked you better when you were an innocent who liked poetry, Min-xue."

Alas for innocence, then. But it was true; the past year had changed him, and not in comforting ways. *Should my loyalty to my country cease because she is mastered by selfish men?*

"I knew translating the Yevtushenko for you was a bad idea. Min-xue, you can do China more good in the long run if you stand with us, and try to bring her current leaders down."

That is neither obedience nor devotion, Min-xue replied, his eyes closed, his palms pressed to the raspy cinderblock wall. But it wasn't obedience and devotion that had brought him to this place, either. *I will testify, Richard. Surely that's enough. And I can warn you that my countrymen won't give up so easily. They are hungry, and they are frightened of the worldwire, and they have ten thousand chosen men and women en route to the colony planet, and no way to call them back.*

They'll come back with another gambit. They have no

choice. There's an expression, Richard, about men with nothing to lose. I think you have it in English, too.

The AI frowned, an expression Min-xue felt more than saw, and refused to be distracted. "What if I told you that I can probably get you a shot at the *Vancouver*'s pilot's chair, when she's commissioned?"

The prime minister would never permit that.

"The prime minister has exactly two trained Canadian pilots left. You're in a better position to bargain than you think."

The pilot's chair. Min-xue hushed his thoughts, keeping them from Richard's hearing, a trick that had mostly to do with simply willing not to be overheard. In the final analysis, he did not wish to die for his crimes, although he had been prepared. But a Canadian girl had died in his place, and there were some who might argue that as such, it was his debt to live in hers. *If you can arrange it, I will bargain,* he answered. *But you must see to it that there is a trial, and that I have the chance to testify.*

"I'll speak to Casey," Richard said. "We'll do what we can."

0900 hours
Saturday September 29, 2063
HMCSS Montreal
Earth orbit

Some twelve hours later, Richard's focus was abruptly returned to the captain's ready room when Jaime Wainwright lifted her head, stared directly at the nearest security mote, and said, "I know you're up there, Dick. I can hear you breathing."

He spawned a thread just to deal with the captain, and then he laughed out loud, choosing his speakers to make the voice seem to come from the place where she was looking. "Neat trick, that. Can you feel me looking at you, too?"

She glanced down at her sinewy hands. "And now you're going to tell me that 'up there' is a subjective term."

"And that I always am. What can I do for you this morning?"

She used her flat-spread hands to push herself to her feet and began to pace before she began to speak, her heart rate, skin conductivity, breathing, and a dozen other signs revealing chronic stress. "I wanted to talk to you about our trainees. I presume you've been following my communications with the prime minister with regard to the incoming cadets."

"Captain. Would I eavesdrop?"

"Yes," she said. She finished a lap and wheeled. Because of the geometry of the *Montreal*'s habitation wheel, her circuit of the cramped cabin required acute and obtuse angles rather than the more traditional ninety-degree variety. "And you'd lie about it, too. What do you think of them?"

"The cadets?"

"Don't think I don't know you haven't been hovering paternalistically over the lot of them since they went in for nanosurgery. They're all going to make it this time, I hear. No Carver Mallory in this group."

"Yes," Richard said, mocking. "Only one sense-deprived quadriplegic so far, out of eighteen subjects. Such *excellent* odds for all those young people the commonwealth means to modify and train as starship pilots.

And don't think I've forgiven you that Genie still has to undergo the full treatment. I know where the request to have her inducted came from."

"All of the current cadets are injured Impact survivors," Wainwright said, lacing her fingers behind her back and pausing in front of a holoscreen that showed a space-suited inspection crew crawling over the *Montreal*'s hull. "They're all volunteers. And they'd already had the therapeutic level of nanosurgeon infection. Like Miss Castaign. Charlie—Dr. Forster—"

"Everybody calls him Charlie."

She snorted, sounding honestly amused. "You think I still harbor adversarial feelings for you, Dick?"

"I wouldn't care to speculate." Dryly enough that she glanced up at his disembodied voice again, and looked down, shaking her head. Richard continued, "What about Charlie?"

"He thinks it may be safer to handle the implants in two stages, actually. That if the body has already learned to adapt to the Benefactor tech, it takes the wetwiring process better."

"It's a heck of an insult to the system. And a handful of cadets isn't a really useful sample." He paused, watching as Wainwright unbraided her fingers and sighed. "And you didn't really want to argue with an AI about the morals of turning teenagers into cybernetic soldiers, did you?"

"No," she said. She turned around and leaned against one of the few unscreened bits of wall, a lumpy protruding bulkhead that covered a main strut. "You know that repair you hacked together after the logic bomb went off last year?"

"Intimately. I still don't trust it."

"And you've set up a nanonetwork to replace it."

"Yes."

"I want hard lines, too. A whole fresh structure. On the off chance something happens to the worldwire."

"You want me to disassemble the *Montreal*'s nervous system? I'll have to take it offline to do that."

"Will it impair the ship's functionality?"

"No," he said. "We'll still have the nanonetwork. It'll only impair redundancy."

"For how long?"

"Six weeks. Maybe as little as a month."

She folded her arms. "I'll live with it."

"You're thinking about the *Huang Di*." The Chinese logic bomb had come uncomfortably close to destroying the *Montreal*, and they'd managed to purge the *Huang Di*'s core before Canada claimed her as salvage. A pity: Richard would have liked to get his hands on that data. The Chinese control of the nanonetworks—and their programming skill—was still superior to the Canadians'.

"I'm also thinking about arranging things so the *Montreal*'s pilots can fly the ship through the worldwire," she said. "Rather than having to be physically wired into the chair on the bridge."

"Captain." He made a sound that would have been clearing his throat if he were human. "Weren't we just having a discussion about how you still harbor adversarial feelings for me?"

"*You* may have." Her mouth worked, approximating a smile.

"The original purpose of the hard-line interface for the pilots was to prevent the AI from seizing control of the ship."

"I know." She turned her back on the room as if she

could turn her back on Richard, as well. She took three slow breaths before she finished calmly, "But someday you may need to."

A long pause. "Captain," he said, when her pulse had dropped to something like its normal range. "I am honored by your trust."

She laughed, a short harsh bark, and touched the frame on the nearest holodisplay, smudging it with her fingertips. "Trust? If you want to call it that."

1030 hours
Saturday September 29, 2063
HMCSS Montreal
Earth orbit

I pause just inside the hatchway to the captain's tasteful blue and gray ready room. "Casey. I had a feeling I'd be seeing you before too long. How did it go with Castaign?"

"It went," I say, and she leaves it alone.

Wainwright sits in a floor-mounted chair behind a desk bolted to the wall. Holomonitors framed to look like windows cover the bulkheads, showing all directions. The most arresting view is aft, the long silvery dragonfly length of the *Montreal* stretching from the habitation wheel back to the asymmetrical bulge of her reactor and drive assembly, her solar sails nearly furled against her hull, only a hint of gauzy webbing showing.

That image sits right where Wainwright's gaze would naturally fall, should she lift it from her desk, its spindly fragility a reminder of just how precarious our situation is. Miles and vertical miles away from home.

I've got to hand the captain that much. She never for a second forgets the safety of her crew. And I've never known a good CO who wasn't a hard-ass, too. It's just one of those things.

It's also just that it's a pain in the ass when the hard-ass gets in the way of something *I* want to do, instead of annoying the other guy.

Wainwright clears her throat, and I realize I've let a good three seconds go by in total silence. It isn't like me.

Doesn't matter. I know how to do this. I take a deep breath and let the words fall out of my mouth like they're somebody else's. "Xie Min-xue, Captain. The Chinese pilot who helped—"

"I know who he is, Casey. What's the brief version?"

"Ma'am, it occurs to me that he could be part of the solution to our pilot shortage."

"I'd thought of that."

"But."

"But it could look like a payoff. His reward for betraying the PanChinese government. If he testifies." Her fingers fret nervous circles on the interface plate on her desk. "You've heard the hearing date's been set."

"After nine months of stalling and legal wrangling? I had not heard." *Richard. Don't trust me all of a sudden?*

He's right there, of course. "I keep your secrets, too, Jen."

The fact that he has a point doesn't make me like it any better. "Wait," I say, catching on. "You said hearing."

"Yes," she answers. "We're not getting a trial. The UN is planning a discovery procedure, open questions from the floor, rather than a World Court proceeding."

Change is good, right? Right. I thought so, too. "When's our big day?"

"Thanksgiving."

"October? So soon—" I catch myself, settle my feet more firmly on the carpeted floor, and lace my hands behind my back, feeling hardness of steel between the fingers of my meat hand, softness of flesh between the fingers of metal. My shoulders roll back of their own accord, as if to ease a pain that hasn't troubled me in a year. Who ever would have guessed it would be so hard to let go of, even after it was gone?

"I think the Chinese expect their sudden capitulation, and demand for a speedy resolution, will catch us flat-footed."

"That sounds like the prime minister's opinion, Captain."

She lifts her chin, and the corner of her mouth flickers up: a brief, transformative smile. "You have a good ear."

"And has it?"

"Caught us flat-footed? No." She stands, compactly strong, exuding energy and confidence as she paces, the rug scuffing as it compresses and releases under her step. She stops and turns toward me, solid and four-square. "Your boy—"

"Not mine, ma'am."

Her shrug says *whatever*. "Have you talked to him yourself?"

"No, ma'am. Richard has. Mr. Xie is still in protective custody at Lake Simcoe." The fingers of my right hand twitch toward my chest. The beaded feather my sister Nell gave me when we were kids is in my breast pocket, where it lives a lot of the time now. I want to pull it out and look at it, stroke its creamy brown and ivory bars and jewel-bright glass beading, or at least press it against my body through the cloth so I can feel it. Like a little kid rubbing a rabbit's foot in his pocket. *Marde, Jenny. If you need to fuss with something, get a rosary.*

Now, there's an unlikely image.

"Richard thinks he can be trusted."

"Yes, ma'am."

"Richard's judgment has proved pretty good so far." She turns to look at that holomonitor, at the long lacy sprawl of the *Montreal* gleaming slender and uncanny as a suspension bridge across the void. She didn't want to trust the AIs at first. She ran out of choices when the rest of us did. "Do you think Riel would let us spring him? Bring him Upside?"

"I think the prime minister could be convinced, ma'am. I think she or I could convince F—Brigadier General Valens."

"Do it." Just like that, snap decision and she turns back to me, hands hanging open. "As for the other thing—"

"The EVA, ma'am?" Breath tight in my throat. I don't let her see it, but from the way her eyes narrow, she knows.

"Patty stays inside. You take somebody EVA certified for every member of the contact team—"

"And?" I can *hear* it hanging.

"And you're not taking more than three of my crew. I won't risk more. It's your baby, Casey. Sort it out."

"Beg pardon, ma'am . . ."

"Casey?" She's turned away, but I need clarification.

"Am I to participate in this mission?"

"I can't think of anybody more likely to bring them home alive, Master Warrant."

"Ma'am." One more question. Just one, trying the patience I see fraying in the slow rise of her shoulders toward her ears. "Am I contact team, or crew?"

"Are you EVA certified, Casey?"

She knows I am. It was one of the first things I saw to, once things settled a little. No way I'm going to be stuck inside a tin can in a universe full of very aggressive nothing without knowing I can survive if I have to go *out*. "Thank you, ma'am."

"Dismissed." I catch the reflection of her smile in the crystal of the holomonitor as I salute, turn on my heel, and go.

1100 hours
Saturday September 29, 2063
HMCSS Montreal
Earth orbit

Charlie Forster had been living in space for so long that he'd forgotten what it was like to work in a lab with windows and a door that could be left open to catch a cross breeze, and he wondered if he really *remembered* how a full G would feel. He still had good muscle mass, though—partially a function of his somewhat heavier-than-ideal weight, and partially because he was religious about taking the mystotatin blockers that prevented muscle loss—and he was willing to bet that, given advances in low-G health care—his time on orbital platforms, starships, and Mars had raised his life expectancy. And, as he opened the hatch of his lab for Leslie Tjakamarra and Jeremy Kirkpatrick and ushered the Australian and British scientists inside, he had to admit that he wasn't immune to a certain pride of place: as one of the team who had uncovered the Benefactor ships on Mars, as the contact team's expert in the nanotech, as the guy whose lab space was housed in a *starship*. There was pleasure in that.

Especially when meeting fresh new faces, eager to be awed.

Or fresh old faces, he chuckled to himself. *It's not like any of us are going to see forty again. Nor are any of us particularly easy to awe anymore.*

The men's ship shoes scuffed on the deck plates as Charlie palmed the light on. He'd spent a good part of the last nine months moving his base of operations from Clarke over to the *Montreal,* and he finally had his lab set up the way he wanted it. Richard had helped him engineer the mounts for the biospheres that held his experimental subjects. The possibility that the *Montreal*'s "gravity" might fail or shift rendered storage of fragile objects that needed indirect light into something of an engineering challenge.

The space he had appropriated was one of the hydroponics bays that helped supply the *Montreal* with food and oxygen. It had full-spectrum lighting already installed, and the biggest ports on the ship. Charlie hadn't bothered to move any of the tanks where radishes and sunflowers and soybeans grew in a transparent gelatinous medium; the fertilized profusion didn't interfere with his work and he rather enjoyed the green leaves, moist air, and the buzz and flutter of the *Montreal*'s pollinators—honeybees and butterflies. The ship's entomologist visited, too. That was nice.

Besides, Charlie's work used otherwise wasted space, and almost every inch of the *Montreal* served double or triple duty. The lab's interior bulkheads gleamed with rows of glass biospheres like Christmas ornaments, held under the grow lights in lacy titanium frames. Inside those baubles was the flicker of movement; colorful shrimp darted around snails and filigrees of algae, each sphere a discrete ecosystem. And all of them, save the controls, infected with unmodified Benefactor tech.

Jeremy Kirkpatrick grimaced and looked around. "So this is where the tofu comes from."

"Tofu," Charlie said, "and the salad oil, and the spinach..."

"A very impressive setup." Tjakamarra nevertheless didn't seem to be paying much attention to it. He crossed to the broad crystal port and leaned his hands against it, pressing one cheek to the glass to get a better look at the *Montreal* from this angle. "Is all this foliage infected?"

"Only what you see in the biospheres," Charlie answered. "The rest is natural flora."

"Wouldn't it make more sense to use the nanotechnology to ... what, protect? bombproof? the hydro tanks and so forth?"

"You mean, like we've already infected the planet?" Charlie laughed. "We're trying to follow a policy of conservative use on the nanosurgeons. Only a few people on *Montreal* have had the full treatment; most of us are natural, and several of the ones who are infected—like Genie, for example—aren't enhanced. Although she's on the worldwire, she doesn't have the augmented reflexes or the full VR package. The plants stay natural unless there's a reason to make them otherwise."

"I see." Tjakamarra turned his back to the port and leaned against the bulkhead, his wiry, black-jacketed frame blurring into the darkness outside. The *Montreal*'s running lights cast blue and green reflections through his hair. "Given what's happening on Earth, Dr. Forster,

you'll forgive me if I find your precautions a little laugh-
able."

"Please, call me Charlie. And trust me, we're not naive,"
Charlie said, gesturing the other two to follow him as he
turned toward the instruments at the far end of the lab.
"We're doing whatever damage control we can. Come on,
I'll show you the critters up close and personal."

Vancouver, Offices of the Provisional Capital
British Columbia, Canada
Saturday 29 September 2063
0730 hours PDT

Valens folded his right leg over his left leg and focused
past the glossy tip of his loafer to Constance Riel silhouet-
ted against the pale mauve sheers that softened her office
window. The office itself still held the air of hasty improv-
isation. The interface plate was a few centimeters too
small for the desk in both directions, and the faded
patches on the carpet did not match the furniture. The
office hadn't been intended for an office; in its earlier life,
it had been a conference room.

But Riel needed the space. Space in which to pace back
and forth, as she had been before she paused by the window, and space in which to host the impromptu councils
of undeclared war that were more or less her existence
these days.

Her existence, and Fred's. "You shouldn't frame yourself in the window, Connie."

She let the translucent curtain fall back into place, but
didn't turn. "If I hadn't lost my husband in Toronto, he'd

have divorced me for neglect by now. The glass is bullet-proof, Fred."

"There's no such thing as bulletproof."

"Bullet-resistant."

"And useless against an RPG. It's not armor plate."

"I'm as protected here as I can be, Fred. The building's as secure as my residence in Toronto was."

"No," he said, and got to his feet. The carpet pad needed replacing; it felt almost tacky under his feet. Priorities, however, lay elsewhere. "It's not as safe, and you're not safe standing in the window."

"Who died and made you Mountie?" But she stepped away from the window. "Who would have thought a year ago, Fred, that you'd have appointed yourself my own personal watchdog?"

He didn't answer. The question was the answer. *Needs must when the devil drives.* And China was turning out to be a very particular devil.

She shook her head, searching the office for her coffee cup. "It had to be Saturday morning. It's always Saturday morning. Just in time for the weekend news lull, dammit. I don't know why I should be so annoyed that even the UN understands that."

"United Nations hearings aren't the end of the world—"

"I don't want *hearings*, Fred. I want a full World Court genocide proceeding, and I want China made party to it, over their refusal, dammit."

He sighed heavily. "Do you?"

"What are you asking? Of course I do."

"Do you want to open the door for the Chinese to come back with war crimes charges against us, for the *Calgary* crash and the nanotech infection?"

Riel paused. "Well, hell, that's why we're having the hearings. Charges and countercharges. Maybe we can wrangle it into a crimes-against-humanity case. Are you still willing to take a fall for the program if it comes to it, Fred?"

He didn't answer. He didn't need to.

She looked up, met his gaze, and nodded, satisfied. "There are days when I wish the opposition would put enough of a coalition together to boost my ass out of this chair."

"And have one of their own responsible for this train wreck? No, they'll wait until you go down in flames, and nod knowingly while they pick up the pieces." He took her elbow, feeling her brittleness as if it were a physical as well as spiritual thing.

She glanced sideways, caught the outline of his smile, and laughed as if through blood. "You think it's too late to requisition a train wreck instead? Christ, I have to deal with the cabinet today—"

Her desk chimed, a three-note ascending scale that made both their heads turn in recognition. "Richard," Riel said.

"Prime Minister," the AI answered, resolving into one-third-sized visibility, a wee man standing atop the desk.

"Is this about the UN?"

"If only it were so simple. We have bigger problems, Prime Minister, General Valens. I'm going to conference in Dr. Forster. He's just made an unsettling discovery. It's a secure line; I'm handling the transmission myself. Dr. Forster?"

Another familiar voice. "Fred? Prime Minister?"

Valens found himself exchanging a glance of anticipation with Riel, and not a happy one. He swallowed the lead weight that seemed lodged in his throat and folded his hands behind him. "We hear you very well, Charlie. What seems to be the problem?"

There was no light-speed lag when Richard handled the transmission; Charlie's rueful flinch was immediate. Valens felt his gut clench, abdominal muscles tightening in anticipation of a blow, setting himself to take it and come back swinging. Consciously, carefully, he smoothed his breath and forced himself to look steadily at the hologram, waiting with every appearance of patience and strength.

He wondered sometimes, in bleaker moments, if the cracks showed, and if his staff was humoring him by pretending not to notice. But he also *knew,* between wondering, that that wasn't the case. He'd just mastered the art of maintaining a facade, and there wasn't anybody that the facade needed to come down for now.

Pity he wasn't having any luck turning the mask into reality. Charlie still hadn't spoken, though, and Valens cleared his throat. "Charlie. We're on tenterhooks, old friend."

It was eerie, the way Richard juggled the algorithm so when Charlie cocked his head and passed a palm across his scalp, it looked as if he frowned at Valens's shoes and then stared dead into his eyes. "We've come a long way from Mars, Fred."

"Light-minutes," Valens answered, just to get the grin.

Charlie essayed one bravely, but it crumbled. "Let me cut to the chase. Some of my nanosurgeons are ... dying. And neither Richard nor I have a damned idea why."

"Dr. Forster," Riel interjected. Both Valens and Charlie swung to look at her, her suddenly upright posture commanding the room. She smoothed her palms down over her forest-green suit, the discreet diamond on her ring finger flashing refracted light. "I'm going to need a written report. How long have you known?"

He glanced down, checking his contacts. "Half an hour."

"I will ask you to keep it confidential—"

"Prime Minister—"

Charlie's tone tied another rock to the sinking sensation in Valens's gut. "Who knows about this?"

"Doctors Tjakamarra and Kirkpatrick were with me."

Riel's shoulders dropped from around her ears, and Valens recognized it for relief. "Swear them to secrecy, too. And I mean secret; I'll do something drastic if I have to. And I need that written report—please—via Richard. As soon as possible."

"Ma'am. Anything else?"

"Yes," she said. "Find out what the hell is causing it, and if it's going to completely derail our attempts to buffer Earth's ecosystem, would you?"

"We're on it." And that was Richard's voice, Richard's image stepping in as Charlie pixilated and vanished. "Prime Minister—"

The AI was interrupted by a different chime. Riel's secretary's tone; Richard put himself on hold, his image hanging motionless as Riel answered the other call. "Yes, Anne?"

"Ma'am, I have a Mr. Tobias Hardy from Unitek here to see you. And General Frye."

Riel rolled her eyes at Valens. *Janet Frye.* "Do they have an appointment, Anne?"

"No, ma'am. I checked twice."

Sometimes, when the prime minister smiled like that, Fred Valens could almost like her. Even knowing that she was a sly old snake, a consummate manipulator, and a gameswoman to match even him. "I'm in a conference right now, Anne. See if you can squeeze them in tomorrow, please? Or perhaps on Monday?"

"I'll do my best, ma'am," Anne answered, and the link clicked off.

Richard unfroze himself, steepling his long hands in front of his breast. "Toby Hardy I know—"

"Janet Frye," Valens said, rubbing his eyes with his forefinger and thumb, "is a retired general and part of the opposition leadership, heading up the Home party."

"Isolationists," Riel supplied. "The more radical even want us out of the commonwealth. What do you want to bet they want us to play appeasement with the Chinese? The damned Americans are on my back again, too . . ." She rolled her neck from side to side. "You could have looked that up, Richard; you don't fool me."

"Sometimes it's more revealing to ask questions."

Valens crossed to the window himself. "Why do you think they're contacting you now?"

"Oh, that's easy," Riel said. She went to her desk, thumb locked open a drawer, and drew something small and flat out and laid it on the desk beside the interface panel. "I got some interesting intelligence last night."

Valens came to get a better look. "An HCD?"

"*The* HCD," Riel said, and looked at him. "The red telephone, so to speak."

"What does that have to do with anything?"

The prime minister left the communications device lying on her desk, and went to draw the curtains open again. This time, Valens didn't protest. "I was briefed last night," Riel called back to him, reaching over her head to fiddle with the cords. "It seems General Frye got a sealed,

couriered letter from the PanChinese consulate in the
United States yesterday. I'm not privy to the details of
what's in that letter."

"Of course not," Valens murmured dryly. "That would
be espionage, after all."

"Hah. In any case, I think Richard's guess might be
correct, and our primary problem in the PanChinese government is not the premier, but the minister of war, Shijie
Shu, who seems about ready to go after his boss's job himself. And I happen to know that *he's* been in contact with
certain members of the U.S. Congress. Through this same
embassy official whose return mail code is on the couriered letter."

"You do have friends in low places."

"We do our best." She stepped away from the open
curtains, smart enough, at least, not to silhouette herself
for long.

"You know," he said, "I have a few friends of my own.
And I happen to know that the secretary general's decision to hold hearings rather than a full war-crimes tribu-
nal—even with all the retractions and reschedulings that
entailed—was influenced by a personal call from the office of the PanChinese premier."

"Did it now?" Riel's eyebrows rose when she was
thinking, and right now they furrowed parallel ridges
all the way up to her short, dark hair. "That's fascinating,
Fred."

In the silence that followed, Richard cleared his throat.
"Am I excused, Prime Minister?"

She nodded. "Yes—no. Wait. Tomorrow. Tonight. Before the delightful Mr. Hardy and his lapdog can reched-
ule. I'm sending you Xie Min-xue."

Silence. And then, "Thank you, Prime Minister."

"There's nothing to thank me for," she answered. "He and Casey and Fred's granddaughter are all going to be called on to testify, along with you, Richard, if I have my way. Barring a ballistic missile, *Montreal* is the safest place around right now. I don't think even PanChina is going to risk a *second* unprovoked attack in front of the world camera. Not this week, in any case. It would put paid to their claim that the attack on Toronto was the result of fringe elements, for one thing—"

Valens nodded, more to himself than to Riel. "What are you going to do about it?"

She lifted her chin and looked at Richard, hovering over her desk. "You can go now, Dick. Thank you."

"Thank *you,*" he replied, and derezzed.

Riel stared into the middle distance, her mouth twisting.

"Connie? What *are* you going to do?"

"I'm going to call Premier Xiong and find out exactly what the hell *he* thinks is going on."

11:15 AM
29 September 2063
HMCSS Montreal

Since leaving Sydney, Leslie had developed the abysmally bad habit of humming to himself while he worked, as if he were trying to draw his country and his road around his shoulders, especially in its absence. Restlessness was in his bones, his blood, an itch under his skin like ingrained dirt. He couldn't think unless he walked, and he couldn't walk unless he sang, even if the singing *was* under his breath.

Now, he set out along the *Montreal*'s toroidal corridors

at a good clip, light on his feet, pushing himself a little in the big ship's partial gravity.

Leslie didn't *really* understand how the Benefactor tech worked, and he knew—in uncomfortable self-honesty—that he did not understand the implications of the discovery that he, Charlie, and Jeremy had made that morning. But he wasn't blind, and he *did* know that both the xenobiologist and the AI had been frightened—*no, had been scared*—when they swore him to secrecy on the issue. And so he hummed to himself, big hands swinging loose-fingered on the ends of his arms, eyes just about focused enough to keep him from walking into other pedestrians, ground-eating strides chewing up one lap after another of the *Montreal*.

On the third lap, pacing footsteps alerted him to company. He didn't glance over, nor did he freeze his uninvited companion out. Instead, he kept walking, still singing under his breath, trusting her to start talking when she had something to say.

Half a lap later, Casey cleared her throat. "We do have treadmills on this tub."

"Buggered if I'll walk on a treadmill," Leslie answered amicably. "I like to feel like I'm getting somewhere."

"And walking in circles does that for you?"

He snorted laughter. "At least the walls move. And I don't have to watch the holos the guy on the next machine is distracting himself with. When I walk, I like to walk."

"Being in the moment," she said, surprising him. She had a good, long stride, with a hitch of a limp that he thought was more habit than pain. He stepped up his pace to test her. "What were you singing, Les?"

He grunted and shrugged. "Singing up the country, kind of."

"Singing up the country?"

"The land must first exist as a concept. It must be sung before it can exist. It must be perceived before it can be walked on. It must be dreamed. You should know something about dreamings, shouldn't you? Or do your folks call them by a different name?"

She was still looking at him, a little quirk twisting her lips out of shape. "You know what an 'apple' is, Les?"

"A kind of fruit?"

"A kind of Indian," she said dryly. "Red on the outside. White on the inside. They never taught us any of that shit in Catholic school."

He laughed and finally returned her glance. "Sweetheart, you'd never believe how familiar you sound. Come with me."

"Where are we going, Les?"

"To the observation lounge," he said, and started walking that way. There was one advantage to wandering ways and a trained spatial memory; he'd been aboard the *Montreal* less than forty-eight hours, and he already knew his way around.

The lounge was crowded, for once. There was a poker game in progress by the beverage dispensers and one or two people sitting in chairs near the porthole and monitors. Leslie paused beside those, off to one side so he wouldn't block anyone's view, and gestured Casey in beside him. She came without a word and stood there silently, looking where Leslie was looking. He heard the shallow catch in her breathing and smiled, knowing the deep, spinning view still tightened her chest as well as his own.

The long fall gave him vertigo, but he waited until the silence got heavy before he said anything more. He waited until she cleared her throat, in fact, and cut her off as smoothly as if he'd been about to start speaking anyway. "You know, in my own country, you could point to any rock, and hill, and gully, and I could tell you who it was."

"Who?"

"They're all ancestors, in the Dreaming. Everything is, in my own—"

"Do you have a country, Les?"

Oh, she was good at those sidelong glances, and sharp as a tack. He gave it the silence its weight deserved, and nodded. "Sometimes. I think everybody has a nation... sometimes." And now it was his turn for the sly look across his nose, and she was already looking away when he did it. "Do you?"

She rubbed her arrogant nose with a gleaming steel forefinger. "Have a nation?"

He nodded.

"Sometimes," she answered, and he laughed. And then she turned to face him full-on, and lowered her voice until they were the only ones in the room. "So tell me about this Dreaming."

He gestured out the window, at the stars and the sun-catcher shape of the birdcage, small enough with distance that he could have covered it with his palm. He sorted out a child's explanation, and floated it in simple words. Beginner stories. Truth, but not very much of it, suitable for paddling your toes in. "The Dreaming is what came before, even though it persists to today. And everything that is or will be was already sung, predestined. It's all waiting under the ground to happen."

"Everything?"

"You, me. Piper and Forward. The *Montreal*. Every-thing. We just haven't found it all yet. And the roads be-tween the stars. Those were sung. That's what the songlines are, roads in music and verse. When you get to the end of your songline, when you don't know the verses anymore, you enter someone else's territory, but the melody contin-ues. And if you know the melody, even if you don't know the language, you can find the way, because the landmarks are in the melody. It's just the stories that are in the words."

"By that logic, the Benefactors were already sung, too."

"How do you know they weren't?"

She stared at him. He turned and gave her a grin and she shook her head slowly, ruefully, as if in complex un-derstanding. "Do your songlines go to the stars?"

He grinned, and nudged her shoulder with his own. "Now you're catching on. The road is the song. The song is the road."

Her expression hardened, a fish that spots the hook. "What do you want, Leslie?"

"I get to suit up and come EVA with you tomorrow, right?"

She sighed and turned back to the window, staring out it, past it. Down the long parallel lines of the starlight, the expression in her eyes distant enough to have a chance of looking farther even than that. She shook her head, but she muttered, "You know how to operate a space suit, son?"

"I've checked out ground side. Never in zero G. Or vacuum."

"Well," she said, scrubbing her flesh hand and her steel hand against the thighs of her fatigues, "I guess we'd better get down to a cargo bay and get you some practice, then."

Fairy tales don't teach children that monsters exist.
Children already know that monsters exist. Fairy
tales teach children that monsters can be killed.
—G. K. Chesterton

11:00 PM
Saturday September 29, 2063
HMCSS Montreal
Earth orbit

Sometimes Geniveve Castaign liked to pretend she was invisible. She'd slip out of bed barefoot, midwatch and in the middle of the night. She'd tug her coveralls on over her pajamas, undog the hatchway, and ease her way into the corridor when she was supposed to be in bed asleep.

No one ever said anything, or did more than nod to her in passing. She shared her quarters only with Boris, Jenny's cat who had gotten to be the whole ship's cat by now, and she got special quarters in the civilian corridor because nobody on the ship's crew wanted a twelve-year-old roommate—even Patty, who was seventeen and who had a private room because she was a pilot.

She could wander all night, and as long as she dodged Elspeth and Jenny, nobody ever said anything. Nobody ever said anything, that is, as long as she stayed in the unrestricted-access parts of the ship, because they all felt bad about Leah. And because it wasn't as if Genie had to be up for school. And because the *Montreal* wasn't set up for kids, not yet, and wouldn't be until the first batch of colonists came on board.

And because they knew Richard and Alan were in her head, and Richard and Alan wouldn't let her get into any trouble.

In any case, it was 11 PM, and Genie had been trying to sleep since nine. She gave up, climbed out of her bunk, and went looking for Patty. Patty was up, of course. Patty was nearly a grown-up, and she *was* a pilot. And either she or Jenny always had to be awake and able to get to the bridge. Just in case. Although Patty's on-duty time was supposed to be spent studying.

Which meant she'd probably be in the ready room by the bridge, because Captain Wainwright had made sure there was a state-of-the-art interface in there, and that was also where Genie did her schoolwork, usually while her dad was on duty.

Genie wasn't supposed to be on the bridge unless she was invited. But the ready room also had a door to the corridor, and there was nothing to keep her from climbing in wheel, and nothing to keep her out of the ready room once she got there. Except—

"Where are you off to, young lady?"

Richard's voice always had a certain humorous tint to it when he called her that. She kept climbing up the access ladder, eschewing the lifts. *I couldn't sleep,* she answered. *I'm going to go do some homework.*

Which wasn't exactly a lie, and Richard would probably know if she lied, but he didn't always catch on to truths that weren't . . . complete. He was too polite to just read her mind, or at least he pretended to be.

Richard coughed inside her head, a polite cough into the palm of his knobby, elegant hand, the white of his cuff extending past the sleeve of his jacket, a steel-banded watch glittering against his skin. *How come you wear a watch, Richard?*

"It gives me something to fiddle with," he answered, and demonstrated.

But you have a clock in your head.

"I find it helps me relate to meat-type people better if I keep myself reminded of what it's like to be meat. And you don't have a clock in *your* head, kiddo." Affectionately, and said with the tone that would have gone with a hair-ruffle that Genie was *much* too old for, if Richard had been able to manage it.

No, she answered, following the gray-carpeted corridor toward the bridge. She no longer even noticed how strange it was that it rose in front of and behind her, disappearing in back of the ceiling. Scuff, scuff, scuff went her feet. She amused herself by scuffing in patterns when she walked; short-long, long-short. *But I have you.*

She felt the weight of his contemplation, the flow of ideas and the texture of his emotion, because he permitted her to feel them. A little bit wonder, a little bit pride, a little bit fear. "The ease with which you say that is going to worry people, Genie," he said, quietly. "They won't understand it. They won't understand why having me in your head, why relying on me to know what time it is, doesn't worry you."

Then they're pretty silly. You never bother me when I want to be left alone, and you're always there when I need you. Unlike Leah. Unlike Jenny, who had always come and gone with very little rhyme or reason. Unlike Papa, who had always been worried about Genie because she was sick, and now that she wasn't sick, wasn't worried anymore.

Genie's mouth twitched. She didn't miss the cystic fibrosis. Really, truly. Not at all.

Even if she did miss not being invisible sometimes.

"Still," he said. "You might want to keep it to yourself. Until there are more people like you. People can be mean when they don't understand things."

Richard, she answered dryly, as she reached her destination. *I know that. Do you think you're talking to a child?*
He didn't answer. She grinned to herself and held her left
hand up to the ready room door sensor so that it could
read the control chip implanted under her skin. The door
chirped softly and slid open. Genie went inside, and
Richard "stayed behind."

He'd be there if she wanted him. But for now, he did
her the courtesy of letting her walk away.

Patty didn't look up when she stepped into the pilots'
lounge-slash-ready room. As Genie had guessed, the older
girl was bent over an interface plate, her fingers twisted
through brunette hair, holding it out of her face like a
heavy curtain. "Shouldn't you be in bed?"

"I'm always in bed," Genie said. "I've spent more of my
life in bed than anybody needs to. Whatcha working on?"

"Differentials," Patty answered, and tucked her hair
behind her ear. A few strands snagged on a silver earring
shaped like a leaping dolphin; she disentangled them
with a bitten fingernail, wincing. "You want something to
drink?"

Genie shook her head and hunched down on a stool,
tapping at another interface panel on the desktop without
any haste, with one finger only. She leafed through her
homework files and sighed. She was ten months ahead of
the curriculum, and still bored. Leah would have offered
to show her how the differentials worked; Leah always
did most of her homework with Genie, and bragged to
Papa that Genie was smart enough to handle it.

Leah had used to, anyway.

Patty looked up from her homework again, caught
Genie's eye, and looked away quickly. Patty's mouth
twisted; her expression said *creepy kid,* but Genie was too

lonely to get up and leave, even if she knew Patty didn't want her there. Genie put her chin down on her fists and sighed, studying a too-easy problem in spatial geometry that floated in front of her nose. Sometimes she liked to pretend she was invisible.

Sometimes she just suspected she really was.

1:15 AM
Sunday September 30, 2063
HMCSS Montreal
Earth orbit

The smaller lounge wasn't as private as the pilots' ready room, but Patty didn't feel like being that close to the bridge right now. Besides, if she was in the ready room, she would just start doing homework, and she didn't feel like doing homework.

And furthermore, she'd told Genie she was going to bed, because otherwise Genie would have hidden that big-eyed look behind her hair, never meaning for Patty to see it, and Patty probably would have broken into a thousand pieces all over the ready-room floor. And she didn't really need a crying jag.

Especially not when she was trying to be strong for Genie, and what she really felt like was moping about ostentatiously. Preferably somewhere where somebody could yell at her for it and make her feel suitably misunderstood. But that wouldn't be professional. And it would embarrass her grandfather. And disappoint her mother, if her mother . . .

Well, anyway. Which was why she was standing in the lounge, pretending to look at the magnified view of the shiptree in the holoscreen nearest the porthole. Which didn't help, so she closed her eyes and pressed her face against the crystal. It wasn't cold, though; the *Montreal* was bathed in sunlight, though it was the middle of the night and the ship, lightly staffed as she was, seemed almost deserted. And that was the problem, really.

Because Patty didn't want hero worship. Or sympathy. Or to be treated like blown glass.

All she really wanted was for somebody to yell at her, like a normal person with a normal family and normal problems. Like she was getting a C in physics or moping over a boy or ...

Anything, really. As long as it didn't involve people walking on eggshells around her. She pushed herself away from the too-warm glass and went to get a disposable of lemon water from the dispenser. She was still fussing with the panel when the wheel on the entry started to spin, undogged from the outside, and the hatch came open.

Jeremy Kirkpatrick folded his long body almost double to peer through the hatchway, and then stepped over the knee knocker quickly and stood up inside the lounge. "You don't mind if I join you, I hope." He paused for a moment before he closed the hatch, giving her a chance to say no.

"I don't mind," she said, and finally fought the dispenser into producing her drink. "I'm not very good company, though."

"I just came to look at the ship." He dogged the hatch and walked past her, stopping where he could contemplate both the screened and the naked-eye views. The magnified one had the advantage of not spinning.

Patty bit the tip off her disposable. Dr. Kirkpatrick—

no, *Jeremy*—folded his arms together and shoved his hands into his opposite sleeves. "Be nice to be telepathic about now," he said.

"It doesn't help."

He glanced at her, brow crinkling. "You can feel them, too?"

"Sort of." *There's a bright answer.* She waved her left hand in a lopsided infinity symbol. "When Alan lets me. It doesn't make any sense, what they think, though. It's just like—"

"Muttering?"

"—traffic noise." Which wasn't quite right either, but the best she could do. She stayed a few steps behind Jeremy, looking past his shoulder rather than standing beside him.

She wasn't expecting him to turn and fix her with a complicated stare. "You're up late. Aren't you lonely up here?"

"I'm a pilot." She covered her expression by taking a drink from the bulb. "It's my job."

"Huh." He looked back out the window. "I hear you're a very good pilot, too. But they sure start you kids young."

"Most of them even younger than me." *Like Genie.* Who would probably be Leah's age when they did the surgery on her, and . . .

Jeremy let that hang there for a while without comment, spreading his long-fingered hand against the glass. "I'm just surprised you don't have . . . I don't know. What do girls your age have?" It could have been insulting, but the way he said it, it wasn't. Soft and thoughtful, like he was actually trying to remember what he'd been like at seventeen. But then he kept talking. "Boyfriends, and best girlfriends, and——"

"I *don't*."

He jumped when she snapped at him. "I beg your pardon."

"I just haven't got anybody like that. Just my grandfather and me. He's in Vancouver." *Nobody. Not Carver, and not Leah.*

"No, it's all right," he said. He turned, framed against the moving brightness. "So why'd you decide to be a pilot?"

She'd finished her drink somehow, and the limp sticky bubble annoyed her. She hadn't moved far from the panel; she just turned and recycled it. "My grandfather wanted me to do it," she said. "And my mom wanted me to be a scientist."

"What kind of a scientist?"

"Not an ethnolinguist. If she'd ever heard of one, I mean." She pushed her hair behind her ears and flipped the ends out of the way, smiling when he laughed.

"That's okay," he said. "Ethnolinguistics isn't necessarily considered what you'd call a particularly *hard* science. Or even a science at all, depending on who you talk to." He paused. "So what did you want to be, if it wasn't a pilot?"

"I don't know," she said. She suddenly decided she wanted another drink, and looked down, unable to meet his eyes. "I guess I never thought about it much. And it's too late now, isn't it?"

He fell quiet again, not speaking while she dialed another water. It worked on the first try this time. She looked at the disposable, not at Jeremy, when she asked, "So what about you?"

"What about me what?"

"Up late. Shouldn't you be sleeping if you're going to EVA tomorrow?"

"Today."

"Oh, right." She paused. "Well?"

"If I weren't going to EVA tomorrow," he said, and shrugged, "I might be able to sleep."

"Oh." Suddenly full of questions, she glanced at him and frowned. "Why'd *you* become a linguist?"

"Fate," he said, coming over to dial a drink for himself as she stepped away from the panel. "Would you believe I didn't learn to talk until I was four?"

She shouldn't say it. It was unfair and funny and not even accurate. She knew she shouldn't say it. She couldn't help it.

She grinned widely, bit her drink open, and before she tasted it asked, "And have you shut up since?"

0900 hours
Sunday September 30, 2063
HMCSS Montreal
Earth orbit

Three of the *Montreal*'s crew, counting myself, and three very nervous civilian scientists are clipped to a line by the air lock of the *Buffy Sainte-Marie*, sweating into our helmets because the cooling systems don't kick on until we're EVA. We drift in random orientations; Jeremy and Leslie are still trying to keep their feet toward the floor and their heads pointed in the same direction as the head of whomever they're trying to talk to, like spaceships crossing paths in a holodrama, bobbing nose to nose. It's ingrained in us from the moment we squeeze out of the womb: you keep the shiny side up, and the rubber side down.

Old spacers laugh at you when you do it, though, which helps break you of the habit pretty quick.

I move down the row, checking clips, checking the lines. Leslie is locked in to Lieutenant Peterson and Charlie's firmly attached to Corporal Letourneau; I give the carbon filaments a good hard yank to be sure. They're supposed to be unbreakable, but all sorts of equipment doesn't live up to its spec sheets. And the lieutenant may technically rank me, but I have twenty years on her, and she doesn't complain when I check her rig.

And I don't complain when she checks mine. It's cold out there, and not a place we go idly.

My line goes to Jeremy; we clip back and forth, our equipment indistinguishable from carabiners and climbing rope. I wouldn't be all that surprised to discover that's exactly what it is; I'm sure Unitek makes harness, and it would certainly be more profitable to rebid it and jack the price up for the military than to design a whole new clip for zero G.

I hope the carabiner gates are up to the strain of the shoulder attitude jets.

Jeremy's tall enough that we had to get him one of the extended suits. Not as bad off as Gabe; his had to be special ordered, and if he was army still and not mission-vital, they probably would have just left him dirtside and gone and got somebody else.

Just my dumb luck they didn't. I check the seals on Jeremy's suit and helmet—he ducks to give me a better angle—and I pat him on the shoulder when he straightens. "Check me out, please."

"Sorry." He runs gloved fingers over all my seals, visual inspection and then the tactile one, pressing each catch to make sure it's locked. He fumbles a little. Not too bad.

"You okay, Doc?"

"Cold feet," he jokes, and it cracks me up, because we're on the sun side of the *Buffy Sainte-Marie,* and if anything the hide of the little ship would be hot to the touch. If we could touch her. "Everybody all set?"

I expect they are, but that's not my question to answer. "Everybody ready for the air lock?" I hear a chorus of ayes, and see one nod out of the corner of my eye. "Out loud, please, Les."

Charlie's old hat at suit drill, of course, even if he's not got an EVA cert. He smirks at me through the bubble of his helmet; I don't catch his eye, look at Leslie instead. "I can't hear your head rattle in a vacuum, Les."

"All set," he says, tilting his head like he's blushing, but his skin's too dark to tell. "Ma'am."

I open the air lock hatch, and we step into a bare, white-walled steel room no bigger than an express elevator. My air already smells like tin and a little bit like sweat, which makes me appreciate how fresh the air on the *Montreal* is. Those vegetable gardens do the trick, I guess. Corporal Letourneau dogs the hatch behind us, and I turn—full turn in the suit, because your helmet doesn't move with your head—and give them the once-over. Every one of them has a grip on a Jesus handle; I check. Every one of them also has lights glowing green-means-go on the locking ring of his or her suit. "Last chance to chicken out."

Silence.

I didn't really think anybody would.

I turn back around and slap the hatch open one-handed, hanging on pretty damn tight with the other, myself, so I don't tumble out into all that nothing like a milkweed seed blown from the pod. Leslie gets blown into my back and somersaults past me, but Lieutenant Peterson was wise to that and she's got both hands on the bar, so he pitches up against the end of his line and they don't go tumbling out like two weights tied to a rope and flung.

"Right," the lieutenant says, hauling Leslie back into the air lock for no good reason except that we can all hear him breathing—panting—over the suit mike. "Now that we have the drama out of the way, shall we step outside?"

Despite my instructions, Les nods again, the bobbing movement visible inside his helmet, and the lieutenant takes him out first. I run rearguard with Jeremy, and Charlie and the corporal go in the middle. The *Buffy Sainte-Marie* hangs behind us like a white-lit Christmas ornament on a black velvet dropcloth.

I imagine we must look a strange, stringy sort of centipede from the pilot's perspective. He'll keep the shuttle here, stationary with regard to the birdcage and about a klick away, until either the Benefactors dispose of us or we return. When I turn over my shoulder to look back at him, I can see the shiptree outlined as a twist of brighter, bluer lights against the stars, and I wonder if we're starting with the right aliens first. Of course, there's no easy way to get *inside* that one.

It's a slow, silent procession—six of us in formation like pallbearers miming an invisible coffin. The lieutenant's slaved our maneuvering jets to her own controls, so we follow in an orderly fashion—even those of us with no clue what we're doing.

Like *any* of us have a clue what we're doing anymore.

A kilometer sounds pretty far, but really, it's no distance at all. Two laps around a footrace track. You can run that far in a few minutes if you're in decent shape. The *Montreal* herself is close to three kilometers long.

We cover the distance in twenty minutes flat, in silence except for the occasional murmured instruction over the suit radios, and the thrilled, terrified rattle of our hearts. I'm waiting for some response, some acknowledgment. Some change in the steady, erratic flicker of the silvery teardrops from one place to another across the width of the birdcage. Some indication of whether to continue forward or move back.

I haven't been so roundly ignored since the time when Leah was twelve and she wouldn't talk to me for three days because I refused to help her run away from home so she wouldn't have to share a room with Genie anymore.

The good news is, she had nothing on emotional blackmail compared to her dad, or she almost might have broken me. I took her camping instead. A girl knows what it's like to need to get out of town once in a while.

Hey Richard.

"Jenny?"

You with me, sport?

"I wouldn't miss this for the world."

I don't suppose you have a theory about what those birdcage aliens are?

I feel him shrug, and then his voice comes over my suit radio instead of inside my head. "The master warrant officer wants to know if this particular alien intelligence has any theories about what those other alien intelligences might be like," he says.

"Whatever they are, they're swimming around in

space bare-assed," Charlie comments, his voice made tinny in transmission. "I don't think those are suits."

"Could they be remotes? Waldos?" Jeremy, and he twists his upper body inside his suit to look at me, as if I have any idea whether he might be right or wrong. "Some sort of nanotech construction?"

"The probes couldn't tell," Charlie says. "And when we tried to bring a sample back for analysis, all we got was nanotech and hydrogen." We're close enough to see them clearly now, without magnification. The aliens are featureless gleaming spheres until they move, and then they stream out from a rounded bow to a trailing point.

"That's weird," Richard says. "There's no drag. No air resistance to push them into a teardrop shape."

"That's why I think those are the aliens," Charlie answers. "That looks like an adaptation to moving through fluid."

"Or atmosphere?" Leslie asks.

"Technically, atmosphere is a fluid, in the fluid dynamics sense," Dick says.

I keep my damned mouth shut. Better to remain silent and be thought a fool, etcetera, etcetera. Charlie, bless him, has no dignity. "I wonder where something like that grows up. Dick?"

"You're wondering if I have a theory where they evolved?"

"I'm wondering if you have a theory what they're made of."

"I'd say they're probably patterns of electrical impulses in some sort of supercooled, possibly superconductive colloid. They carry a nanomachine infestation, but while I can sense those machines, I can't piggyback their operating system the way I can the ones you bred, Chuck.

They're even farther out of my ambit than the Chinese nanonetwork."

"Not only do we not speak their language, or have any kinetics in common, we can't even hack their computers." Jeremy touches the override on his thigh, adding a little more thrust to what the lieutenant gives him, and drifts to the end of the line that binds us together. I compensate for the gentle tug; he makes a smooth job of it, overall.

Peterson draws us up a few short yards outside the bird-cage, and we spread casually apart. Not too far, though; there isn't any safety in numbers, but the reptile part of our brains can't be made to believe that, no matter how many millions of years of evolution we layer over it.

"Supercooled?" Charlie asks. "Doesn't that get problematic out here in the sunlight?"

"They aren't fazed by vacuum, at least," Jeremy says. "Maybe they come from an extreme environment of some sort—" Stopped cold, he bumps the brow of his helmet with the side of his gauntlet. "Leslie, what if they come from someplace with an opaque atmosphere? Or nearly opaque? Or no light to speak of? Like Venus, say. Or Pluto."

Leslie's been silent since the comment about the atmosphere, but the way his suit rocks on the end of its line tells me he just reflexively tried to glance over his shoulder. He looks very small against the massive filigree of the birdcage, a white plastic spaceman doll floating in front of a shifting, faceted fretwork of spun glass. "No physical semiotics," he answers when he's stable again. "Jeremy, that's pretty damn smart."

"Thank you."

"More than that," Charlie puts in. "A completely different set of senses and manner of processing information than we have. No sense of sight, of smell, of hearing. Those would be more foreign to them than ... a dolphin's sonar sense is foreign to us. No wonder we're having a hell of a time talking to them."

"That's what I've been trying to explain," Leslie says. "It's like Anne Sullivan teaching Helen Keller how to talk, only we can't even take them outside and pump water over their hands until they get that we're trying to show them something."

"Les," I say, "what on earth are you babbling about?"

"Semiotics," Leslie answers. Which doesn't help me, but judging by the richness in his tone, he's quite pleased with himself. "Never mind," he finishes. "Just doing my job."

A scatter of the birdcage aliens drifts diagonally across the starship, passing beside and through one another. "So, what do you say we invite ourselves in and sit down?" Richard asks.

"Do you suppose they're safe to touch?" Leslie's already let himself drift forward; he's ahead of the rest of us by a good three meters now. Lieutenant Peterson is eyeing her end of the lines between them as if she's about to grab a fistful and haul Leslie back to her hand over hand.

"No. I don't think it's safe to do anything to them." They're all looking at me. I blink. I hadn't intended to speak just then; it slipped out. "But if I understand you right, Les, you think they can't talk to anything they're not touching?"

"Got it in one," he says, straining at the end of his leash. "I'm not sure they can notice us unless we wander in among them."

"Forgive me if that sounds like a thoroughly lousy idea."

"I know," he answers, and this time he does grab the ropes and turns himself completely around, so we can see his broad white grin reflecting the running lights of the *Buffy Sainte-Marie*. "But it's also what we came out here for, isn't it?"

And they're all waiting for me. Waiting for me, even though the lieutenant ranks me. Waiting for me because I'm Genevieve Casey, dammit. And calisse de chrisse, I hate this shit.

"All right," I say, and I do it without reaching out for Richard, because I already know what Richard's going to say. "All right, guys. Spread out. Let's go on in."

Richard watched silently through Min-xue's eyes as Clarke receded behind the *Gordon Lightfoot*. It was only Min-xue's third trip in a Canadian shuttlecraft. Richard kept an ear on Min-xue's thought process, certain that Min-xue would call for his attention shortly. Right now, the pilot was musing on how he'd never expected to find himself in space again, much less headed for a billet aboard the Canadian flagship. Richard knew that Min-xue had assumed this part of his life was over. Had assumed that his *life* was over, destroyed in an act of conscience that was also an act of treason. He'd never expected to sit where he sat, the lone passenger on a hastily detoured shuttlecraft, a startling extravagance by Chinese standards.

Clarke slid out of view as the shuttlecraft turned toward the *Montreal*. Min-xue couldn't see their destination through the ports on the shuttlecraft's sides, and the pilot's compartment was shielded from the passenger cabin by a bulkhead. There was a monitor on the back side of that bulkhead, and Richard contemplated turning it on for Min-xue, but he wasn't sure if Min-xue wanted the long view of the *Montreal,* or of Earth, or of the Benefactor ships.

Both he and Richard knew very well what they all looked like, after all—

Richard?

"A good rain knows the season, and comes on with the spring," Richard quoted, drawing a smile to Min-xue's thin-pressed lips. "I've been wondering if you would want to talk."

You're still reading the Tang poets, I see.

"You are an enormously bad influence," Richard answered, and Min-xue smiled. "Min-xue, I know you've spoken to the Canadian legal team about the—"

About the impact event. Yes, and so have you.

And Richard knew why the young man chose that distancing, clinical term. Euphemism had its uses. "They feel we are not being as forthcoming as possible about Captain Wu's orders."

They think we know more than we're telling, you mean.

Richard indulged himself in a calculated hesitation. "Yes."

Perhaps they should ask Captain Wu these questions. I do not know the source of his orders. I am certain that they came from his chain of command, however. Min-xue closed his eyes, leaning back in his chair, regulating his breathing. Richard couldn't do anything about the roughness of the seat against Min-xue's back, or the way the vibration of the engines rattled through the ship as a controlled burn accelerated them toward the *Montreal,* but he could—and did—dim the *Gordon Lightfoot*'s interior illumination.

"Thank you, Richard," Min-xue said out loud. He turned his head to press his face to the cold glass of the portal, a gesture Richard saw a lot among his pilots. His pilots. With their hair-trigger reflexes and enhanced senses that made the simplest navigation through daily life an act of courage and endurance. His pilots. Richard's pilots. Richard's ticket to the stars.

And telling Riel I accept her offer of citizenship would make it that much easier to be certain I get there. Eventually.

"You're welcome. Min-xue, I'd like your permission to adjust your wetware somewhat."

"What are you going to do?" Min-xue didn't open his eyes, but the creases at the corners eased as Richard bumped the light level down again.

"Update the protections and start low-level monitoring on your nanosurgeons."

There's a problem? You have doubts about the world-wire?

If Richard had a lip, he would have been chewing it. *His* pilots. And not, frankly, just his pathway to other worlds, but personal friends, all three of them. Well, his friends or Alan's, and there was no practical difference between the two.

Mad as they were.

He'd been unable to save Trevor Koske and Leah Castaign. Humans *would* persist in being human. "Preventative measures. I'm having the same conversation with Jen and Patty right now."

You're not telling me everything, Richard.

"I can't." But closer monitoring of Min-xue's nanotech would give him a further glimpse into the Chinese programming techniques, and besides, he was worried about the unexplained die-offs in Charlie's ecospheres...and more worried that he hadn't noticed it happening.

Min-xue opened his eyes. His hands curved in to the hand grips molded to the edge of his seat, useful in zero gravity, now useful to push himself forward against the thrust that pressed him back into his seat. "This is the life I have chosen." He gave his head a sideways shake. "All right," he said, tightening his grip on the handholds. "All right. And Richard?"

"Min-xue?"

"Turn on the monitor? I want to see where we're going."

Richard did it, and answered, "Don't we all."

In a minor confirmation of the law that the perversity of the universe tends toward a maximum, it was the issue of time zones and the selection of a sufficiently close-mouthed translator that prevented Riel from contacting Premier Xiong before Sunday morning. She made a major concession in allowing the PanChinese premier to choose the translator. But then again, that was the way the game was played, and machine translation was not nuanced enough for these purposes.

There were channels and there were channels, of course, and the means she was resorting to, while official in the broader senses of the term, weren't exactly *diplomatic*. Which was helpful, in the sense of deniability, and unhelpful—in the sense of deniability.

And once upon a time, the world made sense, she reminded herself, opaquing the reflective surface of her interface plate and checking her makeup for the third time. *And then you got this job.* She checked her watch, then checked the time on the heads-up display in her contact, and then rolled her eyes at her own nervousness. She was nauseated with anticipation, and it wasn't going to serve her to any advantage if she didn't get the adrenaline under control.

So what if the PanChinese premier was late? Her meeting with Hardy and Frye wasn't for ninety minutes. And if they showed up early, or she ran long, they could cool their heels out by the water fountain for a while. Which thought made her smile, and not—she noticed in the opaqued plate—not very pleasantly.

She wiped the expression off her face. The hip unit sitting on the desk beside her chimed. She jumped, took a breath, and drank three gulps of the rooibos chai staying warm in her self-heating mug before she felt composed enough to reach out and thumbprint the secure HCD. "Premier Xiong," she said, raising her eyes as the man's pinched, expectant face rezzed in midair. "It's good of you to agree to this conference."

"Prime Minister Riel." A pause, for encoding and translation. "It is good of you to hear me. We have a problem."

"More than one," she answered. It came easier as she found her stride; this was no different, really, than any other such conference in her tenure as PM. More fraught, perhaps, and more hazardous, but the actual mechanics were no different.

It was still just a matter of two people sitting down to talk and establish common interests and points of negotiation. Constance Riel folded her hands together. It did not stop her from fiddling with her ring. "Premier, continued hostility benefits neither of us. Let us be frank; Canada is not in a position to profit from ongoing conflict, and I do not believe China is either. You have the problem of the

Russians to contend with, the PanMalaysian alliance and Japan ... and the same climatic issues we have. I don't want a war, sir."

A longer pause this time, and she wondered what word the translator had been checking context on. Or if there had been a hasty consultation at a higher level. Eventually, Xiong's impassive face was softened by a blink, and the faint tilt of a smile. "None of us want a war, Prime Minister."

She saw the sideways flash of his eyes, the faint movement of his head as he shook off some fragment of well-meaning advice. Unlike her, she realized, he must indeed have someone in the room. Other than the interpreter, of course.

"We are prepared to offer an apology," he said flatly, unprovoked. She had expected to have to force him into that particular corner. She didn't trust it.

"In exchange for?"

"An apology in return."

"The attack on Toronto was unprovoked, Premier—"

"The attack on Toronto was not supported by our government," he answered, cutting her off with a wave of his hand. She blinked. It was not the translator who had spoken.

Xiong's accent was inferior to his translator's, but his English was perfectly plain as he continued, leaving Riel at a loss. "The miscreants will be punished when they are located. To that end, we require the return of the crew of the *Huang Di*. Surely there can be no question that this is appropriate, and that it is necessary for us to question our citizens and determine whether there were, in fact, orders—and if so, from whom they came."

Ah. That, Riel had an answer to. "Premier, we also

would like to see the crew of the *Huang Di* answer a few
questions. In a public forum, rather than behind closed
doors."

"I see." He glanced down, consulting his notes or concealing the green flash of an adviser's message across his
contact. "We would like the compiler code to the operating system being used by the nanosurgeon infection that
Canada has inflicted upon the unsuspecting nations of the
earth. We profess ourselves willing to share our own
codes, and to make this information available to the scientific community and to the security forces of any nation or
supranation that wishes access to them. Pursuant, of
course, to a security check."

"I'm afraid that won't be possible," she answered. *Even
if that weren't a back door into Richard that I wouldn't give
my sister.* "I am, however, certainly open to entertaining
the resumption of friendly relations between our countries." *Where "resumption" is a euphemism for "we never
have gotten along all that well, but I'm willing to ignore that
little twenty-year dustup that we don't call World War III
if you are."*

"You realize, Madame Prime Minister, that while I am
amenable to . . . negotiations, there are elements within my
nation that will be opposed."

"I have an Opposition of my own, Mr. Xiong."

He chuckled, his eyes twinkling like agates, the first
flash of a real personality she'd seen. "I'm sure you do.
There's something else you should understand, if you are
determined to permit the United Nations to address this
matter."

"It wouldn't be fair to go to NATO, would it now?"

His smile was very cool, and very thoughtful. "You're
aware that the same technology that is used to enhance

the starship pilots can be used to create more . . . traditional warriors?"

"Canada is aware." And then the bottom dropped out of her stomach, a trap door under a hanged man's feet. "Are you insinuating that China has such a program in development, sir?"

"Of course not," he answered. "It would be classified, if we did. I'll see you in New York City on the eighth of October, then?"

"Will you be attending yourself, Mr. Premier?"

"Madame Prime Minister," he answered carefully. "I should not miss it, if it lies within my power."

He vanished, and Riel rolled away the ache in her neck. *One down,* she thought. *Hardy and Frye up next. I hope this counts as a productive morning.*

Patty knew why Captain Wainwright had sent her to the air lock to meet Xie Min-xue. Partially because she was young, and a pilot, too—and could be trusted not to do anything stupid like trying to shake Xie Min-xue's hand—and it was partially to get her off the bridge, where she'd been fretting since the *Buffy Sainte-Marie* uncoupled from the *Montreal.*

So she waited by the interior air lock door, her hands self-consciously relaxed, hanging palms-in against her thighs, her heart beating faster than it should, her hair braided so it wouldn't drift into her face, and one foot hooked under a grab strap. *Alan? How much longer?*

"He's the only one disembarking the shuttle," Alan answered. "And they're docked. It'll just be a minute."

Patty took a slow breath. She didn't close her eyes. She didn't need to, really; she just imagined herself armored, a golden metal robot shaped like a girl, or like a sketch of a girl on the mud flap of a truck. And the air lock cycled, and she found herself standing in front of a slender man, a boy, really, her own age or just a little older, his gleaming black hair floating above arched brows and his dark eyes glittering through his squint. He didn't smile, and he looked supremely comfortable in zero G. A duffel bag drifted from his left hand.

"Pilot Xie Min-xue?"

"I am." Cautiously. Softly, his face slightly averted, so that his hair slid across one eye as if it could protect him from the directness of her stare.

She kicked free and pushed back quickly and dropped her gaze. "I'm Patty—I mean, I'm Patricia Valens. I'm one of the *Montreal*'s pilots. I'm supposed to show you around."

His chin lifted when she said "pilots," and she could almost see the tension in his shoulders ease. "Show me around?"

"Give you a tour," she said, assuming he had not understood the colloquialism.

"No, I understood." Did he always speak so softly? "I had assumed I should be confined to quarters."

She smiled and drifted another half-step away. He breathed easier once he had a little more room. "Escorted," she said. "At least for a little while. But Richard will help you find your way around. We're supposed to treat you as a guest. Follow me."

He did, silently, paying very close attention but asking no questions as she gave him the quick tour of the ship. She took him up the ladder in the central shaft so he could get an idea of the *Montreal*'s size, and he gasped over the mock gravity in the habitation wheel, but "She's bigger than the *Huang Di,*" was his only comment, and that after she had showed him the bridge.

"About twice as big."

Silence descended again, until she showed him to the small cabin that would be his. She stopped beside the hatch, standing to one side. "You'll stay here," she said. "I'm sorry. I've done all the talking."

"It's all right," he said, but didn't undog the hatch or step through it. "I'm not very . . . talkative."

They stood in the corridor facing each other. Patty could hear the Chinese pilot breathing, waiting. Finally, she stepped away from the hatch. "You can go in. You don't have to wait for me to open the hatch."

"It's all right," he repeated. He swallowed and looked down at his hands, fretting at the strap of the duffel. "Miss Valens."

"Patricia." She wasn't sure why she gave him the formal version of her name. Maybe the way his hands shook, almost too fast to see. "Please."

"Thank you," he stammered. "I wanted to ask you . . ."

"Ask," she said, when he'd been stuck long enough that it seemed as if interrupting would be a mercy.

"Did you know Leah Castaign?"

Patty didn't realize she'd stepped back until the bulkhead stopped her. She stared at him and forced her jaw to close. "You can't have known Leah."

"No," he said. "But she——" He sighed, and twisted his head aside again, staring at the floor, his hair a mess from gliding up the shaft in zero G.

Oh. "She died for you," Patty said. She swallowed hard, but didn't look away when Min-xue's head snapped up.

"Yes. How did you——"

She shrugged. "I know," she said. "I just know, okay?"

He bit his lip. He nodded. "Okay. Can you tell me about her? A little? Please?"

"I could." She hesitated. "It would take awhile."

"I'm not sleepy."

She studied him a moment. "Do you play table tennis?"

"Table . . . tennis?"

"Ping-Pong?"

He shook his head. She shook hers right back at him. "What do they teach you in China?"

"How to fly starships." Dryly, and quicker than she would have expected.

She snorted laughter, tight worry easing across her chest. "All right," she said. "Put your bag in your cabin and I'll show you the gym and teach you how to play Ping-Pong. And I'll tell you about Leah. Okay?"

"Okay," he said.

The Chinese pilots *were* faster. He beat her, seven to three.

Leslie had been next to bigger things. The Petronas Towers, for example. Uluru, which the ignorant called Ayers Rock. The base of the Malaysian beanstalk. The *Montreal* herself.

Only the rock had made quite the impression on him that the birdcage did.

They came alongside it about its midline, not that it displayed bilateral symmetry. Or radial symmetry, in fact—or any sort of symmetry at all. The design was rococo, the overall impression not too dissimilar from a baroque pearl if you ignored the fact that the silhouette was filigreed rather than continuous. The gaps between the bars of the birdcage were larger than they had seemed, from a distance. Some of the spaces compassed twenty meters.

And still the aliens continued their mechanistic ballet, taking no apparent notice of the cluster of space-suited humans drifting like kewpie dolls alongside the—hull wasn't quite the right word, was it, for something whose inside and outside were delineated only by courtesy?

Leslie glanced over his shoulder and saw nothing but the edge of his faceplate and the padded interior of the dorsal portion of his helmet. "Jen?"

The pilot drifted up beside him, vapor trailing from her attitude jets. She stopped smartly. *Of course,* he thought, briefly envious of the reflexes that made her precision possible.

He put the thought aside. Attractive, maybe, to have the speed to pick a bumblebee out of the air. But hardly necessary.

"You rang?" she said. The lines that bound her to Jeremy came slack as the ethnolinguist drifted into the conversation.

Leslie waved a hand at the birdcage. His suit made the gesture broad. "Do you want to make any preparations before we take the plunge?"

He couldn't really tell through the gold-tinted shimmer of her faceplate, but he got the impression that she looked at him before she looked back at the alien ship. "I think maybe we shouldn't go all at once," she answered.

"I think maybe I should go alone," Leslie offered. "I'll take my lines off."

"Dr. Tjakamarra, I cannot permit—" But he cut Lieutenant Peterson off with a second wave of his hand, and she fell reluctantly silent.

"I'm unlikely to drift off into a gravity well from *inside* the birdcage, Lieutenant."

She coughed. "Your government would take it very amiss if we misplaced you, sir."

"I shall be most exquisitely bloody careful, sweetheart," he said, and flashed her a dazzling smile. Which of course she had no chance of seeing.

"I think I should go." Not Casey, surprising him, but Charlie Forster. Leslie smiled. Charlie could no more sit on the sidelines for this than Leslie could. If the biologist were a hound, he would have been straining the leash.

Peterson again: "Absolutely—"

Leslie cleared his throat, making sure the suit mike was live before he did it. "Charlie? Elspeth's not here; you're in charge. What say we make it you and me, and the lieutenant and the master warrant can have our suits on override? That way, if they decide we don't know what we're doing, or if we look like we're about to go home the bloody hot way, they can yank us back on remote control?"

Leslie was proud of himself. His voice didn't even shiver. He sounded confident and a little bit amused, and the silence that followed told him they were thinking about it seriously. He tilted his head down and counted breaths, watching the gray-smeared planet spin between his boots.

If they'd been standing on the deck of the *Montreal*, Casey and Peterson would have been exchanging a long, opaque look. As it was, he was pretty sure they were burning up the private suit channels instead. He forced himself to breathe evenly—it wouldn't do him any good to pop a lung or wind up with nitrogen narcosis or... hell, he wasn't even sure what could go wrong if you were holding your breath in a space suit. And he was pretty sure he wasn't going to research it either. Some things, he was just as happy not knowing.

"All right," Casey said. "All right, Leslie. It's what we're here for"—and he could *hear* her knobby shoulders rolling in a shrug—"although I don't like you boys taking point."

"Somebody's got to," Charlie said, while Leslie was still looking for the words. "And it's stupid to risk all of us. Just let us have control of the attitude jets unless it looks like we're getting into trouble. All right?"

"Yeah," Casey said, and Peterson said "Roger." And Charlie turned his entire suit to look at Jeremy, as Corporal Letourneau drifted up beside him and started working the carabiners loose. "Jer? Dr. Kirkpatrick?"

"You're goddamned welcome to it, old son," Jeremy answered from a spot two meters behind Casey. "I'll be pleased to admit yours is bigger than mine. I'll float here and take pictures."

"Beauty," Leslie answered, and unclipped the lines from his belt. The gloves made him fumble, but they hid the fact that his hands were shaking, and they kept him from having to look *up,* away from the spinning earth, in the direction that they were going. "Bob's your uncle. Here we go. Oh, bloody lovely, Jer; look at that." The line still in his gauntlet, he pointed.

"Les?" Jeremy slid past Jen Casey in an eddy of vapor and leaned on Leslie's shoulder. Miscalculated inertia set them spinning slowly, but Leslie grabbed Jeremy's gauntlet left-handed and got them both stable before Peterson had to intervene.

He looked up at the astronauts and grinned, and this time he was sure they saw it, even through the helmet. "See? No worries. Piece of cake."

"Les, what did you see?"

He pointed down again. "The Great Wall of China. Look."

The others looked, and exclaimed. "That used to be the only man-made object you could see from space, supposedly," Jen said. "Before electric lights. Before the beanstalks."

"Pretty story," Les answered.

Charlie's chuckle cut him off. "Pity it's happy horse shit."

"Charles." Leslie loaded his voice with teasing disapproval. He used his attitude jets to tilt himself forward, peering through the sunlit thin spot in the pall of dust to see if he could pick out that spider-fine thread again. He could, just barely. "It's not horse shit. It's a beginner story, is all."

"A beginner story?" Casey, the apt pupil. Of course.

"A story that's part of the truth, but only the uncomplicated part," Leslie explained. Which was a beginner story in itself, and the circularity pleased him almost as much as the tricksterish unfairness of it all.

"Oh." She paused, and he could almost feel her thinking. "So what else is man-made that you can see from space, then? That's not lights? Or beanstalks?"

"The Sahara Desert," Charlie answered. And before anybody could comment further, he moved forward, and Leslie stuck by his side as if they had planned it like that.

Leslie already had that half-assed comparison of the birdcage to some sort of sacred site stuck in his mind when he and Charlie soared through the bars, leaving the rest of the EVA team behind. His cliché generator was ready with images of cathedrals and wild, holy places he'd seen, temples and ziggurats and the hush of mysticism, some animal part of his mind ready to be awed by the angle of sunlight through the bars of the cage.

He couldn't have been more wrong.

The interior of the birdcage hummed with energy, a feeling like a racetrack on Stakes day or a ship's bridge anticipating the order to fire. Electricity prickled the hairs on his arms, and for a moment he thought it was an actual static charge. He turned to see if Charlie's suit glowed blue with Saint Elmo's fire.

Charlie had half-rotated toward Leslie, a fat white doll with a golden face, and their eyes met through the tint as if through mist. "You feel that."

"I feel something," Leslie answered. "Like I stuck my finger in a light socket."

"Dr. Tjakamarra?" Lieutenant Peterson's voice over the suit radio, and Leslie lifted his hand to show he was all right, waved, and continued forward.

"Something's happening," Charlie said. "Jen, Jeremy? Do you detect any changes out there?"

"Nothing to speak of," Jeremy answered. "What sort of change am I looking for?"

"It feels like we've entered some sort of an energy field," Charlie said. Leslie tuned him out, listening to the conversation with only half an ear. "Check for anything in the electromagnetic spectrum. Any kind of leakage."

A silence. Leslie drifted incrementally forward, edging into the interior of the birdcage the same way he'd edge into a strange horse's paddock—slowly, calmly, but as if he had every right in the world, *or out of it*, to be there. The teardrop-shaped Benefactors glided soundlessly from bar to bar, some of them passing within tens of meters, and still seemed to take no notice. The prickling on his skin intensified. He glanced about, at the cage, the obliviously moving aliens, at the slick sheen of mercury-like substance that covered the armature of the birdcage. It was visually identical to the substance of the enormous droplet-shaped aliens, and, in fact, when they touched down on one of the beams, they became indistinguishable from it. They slid along the structure like droplets of water along the wires of a wet birdcage, and passed over and through each other like waves, whether they met moving about the armature or sailing through the space inside.

"Nothing's leaking out this way," Jeremy said. "I can't answer for what's going on inside the birdcage, though. The whole thing could be a sort of—"

"Massive Faraday cage?"

"Or something, yes."

"Leslie? Charlie?" Jen Casey's voice. She sounded worried; Leslie wondered if someone might be waving at Charlie and himself from their entrance point, but he wasn't about to turn around and look. Leslie craned his head back, trying to get a look directly "up," toward the top of the armature.

"I hear you, Jen." Charlie sounded a little odd, too, which wasn't surprising, if his skin was responding to the same storm-prickle Leslie felt. "What's wrong?"

"Richard says the nanite chatter is increasing. I think maybe you should come back."

They turned to each other again, Leslie and Charlie, and Leslie saw the question in Charlie's eyes. Leslie's hands spread reflexively inside his gauntlets as another shiver slithered up his back.

"We've already made history," Charlie said.

"And so what if we have? We haven't *learned* anything yet."

The flash of Charlie's teeth showed through the tint in

his faceplate. "Jen," he said, "we're going to head out to the middle of this thing at least—"

"Charlie, that's another klick. Maybe a klick and a half."

"Nothing ventured," Leslie said, and gave Charlie a thumbs-up before he kicked his maneuvering jets on. "Jen, remind me on the way back out—"

"If you *get* back out," she interrupted, but he heard grudging approval in her tone.

"Hey, this is your harebrained scheme, sweetheart."

She laughed. "All right, Les. Remind you what?"

"Remind me to get a sample of the fluid on the birdcage when we pass by it again, would you? Maybe have Corporal Letourneau run back to the *Buffy Sainte-Marie* and pick up some sort of sterile containment vessel?" He turned, watching another raindrop slide along another wire. He had to remind himself that the scale was skyscraper beams and elephants at a kilometer or better, and not spiderwebs wet with dew that he could reach out and brush away with his gauntleted hand.

"We had a probe try that, remember? Hydrogen and nanites."

"Oh, right." He rolled his eyes at his own obtuseness.

A pause, as if Jenny discussed the problem of samples with Letourneau over local channels, and then the crackle of her voice. "We'll try a magnetic bottle this time; maybe it'll make a difference. Hey guys, are you noticing a lot of static on this channel all of a sudden?"

"I'm noticing more lightning-storm skin prickles, too," Charlie said. "I wonder if it's true that you can feel lightning ionizing a path before it hits you."

"Doctors." The lieutenant again. "I really think the

Benefactor activity is picking up. I would feel much better if you two came back—"

And then Jenny's voice, sharp with fear, urgent and clipped. "*Putain!* Charlie, *move*. That thing's coming right *at* you!"

Leslie's head snapped up, not that it helped him in the slightest. He turned in the suit, faster than the gyros could handle, and reached for Charlie's arm. His grab failed; instead, he sent himself tumbling, and slapped hard at the autostabilize button on his chest, hoping the suit's gyroscopes would suffice to level him out. *Spread out. Make yourself broad and flat. Don't scrunch up; it will just make you spin faster—*

It was working. He tried to catch a glimpse of Charlie and could only see rippling silver, one of the teardrop aliens, close enough that its fluid side towered like a battleship overhead. Whatever Casey shouted dissolved into the deafening crackle of static. Ionization prickled over his skin, sharp enough to sting.

He closed his eyes so he wouldn't struggle against the suit in panic or by reflex, spread-eagled himself against the void, and allowed his inertial systems to bring him safely to rest. He couldn't hear anything but static over the radio, and then even the static cut off, leaving him in silence. But at least he hadn't bounced off the birdcage's superstructure. Yet. And he thought he *had* stopped tumbling.

Cautiously, Leslie opened his eyes.

And a bloody good thing, too, because there was Charlie, not too far off, spread-eagled just as Leslie was and coming toward him much too fast and on a direct collision course. Leslie raised his hand, reached for the *other* emergency switch—the get-me-the-hell-out-of-here one—and froze as the other space-suited figure echoed the gesture precisely.

Oh, bloody hell.

His own reflection, in the side of a bubble of liquid silver, broke over him with the force of a ten-foot wave.

Tobias Hardy probably had two hundred different fifteen-thousand-dollar suits, and Constance Riel hated every single goddamned one of them. She hated the way he had them tailored to make his shoulders look broader, and she hated the complicated manner in which somebody was paid to fold the handkerchief that always matched his tie.

If he had an image consultant, the man should be fired.

Unfortunately, unlike Riel's ability to keep her job, Hardy's ability to keep *his* wasn't dictated by any arcane metric of approachability multiplied by sober respectability and personal charisma. Which was a pity; the world might be a nicer place if "corporate raider" were a popularity contest.

Still, Riel had to credit Hardy with a certain piranha-like honesty. He was exactly what he seemed to be, shiny scales and teeth and a voracious appetite, with the power to stuff just about anything that he chose into his maw.

General Janet Frye was a more complicated matter. And one far more likely to make Riel's lip curl. Because Frye should have been an ally and instead she'd placed herself firmly on the other side of the equation.

No matter how Frye justified herself, if she even bothered with justifications anymore. Riel hung considerable pride on her ability to read people, to understand what their prices were, what they thought their prices were, and what their pride demanded they pretend while they

were selling themselves. And right now, eyeing Frye levelly over her own folded hands, leaning both elbows on
her salvaged desk, Constance Riel was 70 percent certain
that Frye had already sold her self-respect. She just
wished she knew for what.

Riel contemplated her for several seconds, waiting to
see if Frye would glance down or blush. Hardy shifted
from one foot to the other, the gesture of a man who is not
accustomed to being kept waiting, and so Riel gave him
another fifteen seconds before she let her gaze flick to
meet his. She leaned back in her chair and offered him her
most professional, most soulless smile. "Mr. Hardy. You
seem determined to force me to utter words I never in my
wildest imagination supposed that I would say."

The little suppressed twitch of his lips showed her that
he thought he'd won a concession, even if he didn't know
which one yet, and she let him coast on the assumption.
"Does that mean you'll consider my offer to buy Canada
out of the *Vancouver*?"

Riel gripped the edge of her desk and stood. "Calisse
de chrisse. No, Toby. It means dealing with you makes
me *miss* Alberta fucking Holmes. I'm not giving you the
Vancouver. I'm *certainly* not giving you any pilots that
aren't under government oversight, even when we do get
some more trained."

She came around her desk, daring Frye not to give
ground before her. Frye stepped out of the way, the
hunch of her shoulders ruining the line of her coat.

"The simple fact of the matter, Mr. Hardy, is that
Unitek needs Canada more than Canada needs Unitek."
*And thank you for that small mercy, Richard. Thank you
very much.*

Frye cleared her throat. "You can't run Canada like a

dictatorship, Prime Minister. Parliament has a say in our course of actions. Especially when your ill-conceived meddling in international affairs has left us on the brink of war."

"Just because we're not shooting, General, doesn't mean we're not *over* the brink already. I'd think that was a mistake you would be unlikely to make." It was too early for Scotch, unfortunately, because the dusty crystal decanter on the sideboard had never looked so good. Resolutely, Riel turned her back on it. "You're right about one thing—"

Frye's head tilted, light catching on her hair.

"—I'm not a dictator. In fact, I'm not even a president. So why don't you see if you can't get with a coalition and arrange to get my ass kicked downstairs, and you can warm that chair over there yourself. And then if you want to hand PanChina the keys to the castle, you can do it on your own watch."

Frye paused, settled back on her heels, and Riel propped her ass against the desk, crossed her ankles and her arms, and gave the opposition that smooth-faced smile one more goddamned time, thinking *careful, Connie, or your face might freeze that way*.

"Ma'am. You know I can't do that."

"Yes. I know that very well." Riel didn't look down, and neither did the general.

Hardy stood beside them, his brow furrowed at being balked. He shot Frye a glance that spoke volumes. She never flickered. Unitek—Tobias Hardy—could buy and sell Canada. Hell, could buy and sell most of the commonwealth, when it came right down to it. But, goddamn it, it was still Canada that made the laws.

"Janet." Riel softened her voice, created a framework

that brought Frye in and pushed Hardy out, even as he came forward as if to shoulder between the two women. The stare that locked them was too much for him to break, however, and he fell back.

"Prime Minister?"

"I'm going to declare war on China if they cannot be made to pay restitution and admit wrongdoing. I will give the process a chance, you understand, and I pray to God that we figure out how to talk to the Benefactors first. But I want you to understand."

"I think I know where you're going with this, ma'am."

Riel smiled. "Appeasement never works, Janet. And ignoring the problem isn't going to make it go away. Especially when it's come hundreds of light-years to introduce itself."

"And?"

"And if I find out that anybody—coalition or opposition—is working with PanChina to undermine Canada, there won't be a hole deep enough for him to hide in. And by 'undermine,' I do mean anything from sharing information to passing notes under the desk. Comprenez-vous?"

Frye nodded. "Je comprends."

Riel reached out and patted Frye's arm. "One crisis at a time," she said. *And don't think I'm ever going to trust you one inch farther than I can toss you, General. But if I can use you to distract Unitek while they're trying to play Canada and China off against each other, then you're a pawn I'm going to keep on the board until I have to sacrifice you.* "One crisis at a time."

She nearly jumped out of her skin when the critical-alert light on the corner of her interface plate began to blink.

· · ·

I don't see what sets the teardrops off. It always seems to happen that way, doesn't it? You're cruising along, minding your own business, and suddenly things are blowing up to the left and to the right of you, and no matter how hard you were looking you never see where the goddamned rockets came from. And you just grab the wheel and floor it, and hope you don't wind up upside down in a crater. *Richard. Richard! What the hell is going on?*

"I don't know, Jenny. Something. Hell—"

Or, in this case, you're standing on the sidelines adjusting your cuff links, and the next thing you notice, everybody's shooting at each other. And you're too goddamned far away to make any difference at all, even if you tried.

So, suddenly, Charlie and Leslie are shouting over the suit radios, phrases broken by static, frantic scurrying, and I'm half a second from trying to get to them even though they're a klick away across the diameter of the birdcage and I'd just get my own fool self killed, except I remember a second before I hit my maneuvering jets that I'm hooked in to Jeremy by ten feet of carbon filament and by the time I get myself unhooked, it's over and everything's calm as a millbrook downstream of the paddles.

"Casey? Dammit, *Casey!*" But Captain Wainwright's voice-of-command over my suit radio isn't even enough to snap me out of it, and neither is Lieutenant Peterson tugging on my spacesuit, trying to drag me away from the birdcage, back to the shuttle.

You know those pearl necklaces, the ones where the jewel rolls around free inside a silver wire cage that hangs off a chain? Leah used to have one; she wore it to Mass sometimes. The pearl in hers was pink.

When things stop twisting in front of my eyes, all the mercury in the birdcage has gathered in an enormous blob at the center of the ship. It floats there, a spherical mirror, flawless and shivering, and Charlie and Leslie are gone.

God*damn* it, I am sick of watching people I like get killed. I am even sicker of *getting* people I like killed. It's not an acquired taste, let me tell you; every drink is bitter as the last. And they never get any easier to swallow.

"Aw, Christ," Peterson says, turning to fix her lines to Letourneau for the slow sail back to the *Buffy*.

I can feel Richard in my head; I can feel him thinking, but he doesn't seem to have anything to say. I don't either, and Jeremy's just as silent.

But he's not retreating any more than I am. Instead he hangs at my shoulder, just looking at all that fluid silver, and our colleagues buried somewhere inside. And Wainwright's stopped shouting in my head, and Peterson's silence tells me she's conferring with the captain privately. Which is fine with me. The officers are welcome to it.

Finally, she clears her throat. "Master Warrant Officer?"

"Lieutenant?"

"The, ah. The captain ordered us to clear the scene."

"Ma'am." I start backing away. I don't want to turn my back on that thing. Not for a second.

"Wait," Jeremy interjects. His gauntlets wave like an upturned bug's legs, hard enough that he wobbles until his gyros straighten him out. "Wait, wait—"

"Jer?"

"Get a sample," he says. "Les said get a sample."

"Dr. Kirkpatrick." Peterson's voice, rich with warning.

.

Insubordinate as always, I follow Jeremy back toward the cage. "We won't go inside, Lieutenant. We may as well salvage something out of this mess."

I hear her sigh. I rather imagine she's getting an earful from the captain, and I'm not entirely certain why I'm being spared it. Maybe Wainwright's afraid she'll say something she's likely to regret if she talks to me directly. *Richard, do you think we can get away with this?*

"Insufficient data, Jen," he answers.

When did you get replaced by a bot?

"You know, the more upset you are, the more sarcastic you get." Sensation of a raised eyebrow, and I bless him silently for knowing what I need, archness and sharp diversionary tactics instead of sympathy. "In any case, I think you're right about an attempt to salvage . . . Jen."

Dick? Feeling more like a straight man every second, I hesitate, shaking the lines to slow Jeremy down. *What is it?*

"Jen, I don't want to get your hopes up. And I don't want to give you a false impression that I have any control of this situation at all, much as I wish I could do something—"

Dick. Out with it already. Jeremy moves forward again, a scraper and a vacuum bag in his hands.

"You know I have some limited, some *very* limited communication with the Benefactor nanotech."

Yes?

"Jen, I think Charlie and Leslie are alive in there."

I've got to give Wainwright credit. She doesn't say *I told you so*. She doesn't even think it real loud, although the vertical line over her shapely little nose advertises restrained wrath. The funny thing is, I don't think she's angry with me.

I don't know what she *is* angry with, though, and I'd be just as happy not to get between her and the object of her wrath until she's done reducing it to scrap metal. There are forces of nature I'm willing to fuck with, and those that I'm sensible enough to give a wide berth—and right now, Wainwright falls into the latter category.

Even if she doesn't trust me, Wainwright's a good CO. She knows me better than I know myself sometimes, and she's got to be aware that left to my own devices, I'd be stalking the halls of the ship making a terror of myself, keeping my own kind of walking vigil for Leslie and Charlie. And since she knows that, and she knows Richard will tell me if the status changes, she heads it off at the pass by giving me a job to do.

She appoints me Xie Min-xue's guardian, and gives me—*us*—the run of the ship. Under Dick's supervision, of course. But then, we always are.

Pilot Xie waits in the pilot's ready room, the one I took Leslie to when he first came on board. Xie stands when I enter; he's just barely eighteen, and he could pass for fifteen when the light hits him right. He's a fragile, girlish sort of a boy with eyes like watchful black jewels. It occurs to me, looking at him, that Leah probably could have broken him over her knee, and Patty would have no problem at all.

His eyes track me but he doesn't speak at first, just presses his arms tight to his sides and bows, his body language indicating as clear as an eight-sided sign, *stop there. Beyond this point there be dragons*. Something about the distance in those eyes tells me he's talking to Richard, which is no skin off my nose. If it comforts him, more power to him.

If I remember Richard's briefings right, the Chinese pilots are wired even closer to tolerances than we are, because they don't have access to Canada's performance-enhancing drugs. And moreover, their wetware isn't adrenaline-sensitive. Rather than moving through the world in a fairly normal fashion until something triggers their enhancements, they live their lives like hummingbirds, vibrating on the verge of flight.

All things considered, then, I have to think that Xie Min-xue comes across as a remarkably normal young man.

And just as I'm thinking that, with no warning whatsoever, Richard drops me into his skull.

Just like that. *Bang*. The same way he gave me Leah, for the last thirty seconds of her life, the same way he steps into me and I step into him, through the quantum communication between the microscopic robots that live under my skin and Pilot Xie's, and that make up Richard's body, if a *body,* precisely, is what he can be said to have. For a second or two I'm feeling the air on Xie's skin, the way it prickles the hair at the nape of his neck and the way the ready-room lights are too bright. I can barely pick up the flicker, untriggered and well rested; to Xie it's a strobe. *We've got to do something about that,* I say to Richard. *Rip out every fluorescent light on the* Montreal *if we have to—*

I realize too late that Min-xue—which is his name, after all, and the way he thinks of himself—can hear me when his lips peel back from crooked teeth in a most engaging grin, and bows even more deeply.

"I would be in your debt, ma'am," he says inside

my skull, the same way Richard does. I shake my head, amazed.

I have to try it myself. *Please. Call me Jenny.*

"With great pleasure, Jenny."

Dick, how long have you known about this?

"Since Leah, more or less. The practical implications, however, are just starting to work themselves out."

Practical applications beyond telepathy?

"Beyond worldwide, instantaneous communication, Master Warr— Jenny?" Min-xue is smiling, enjoying his advantage.

Galaxy-wide. Instantaneous. Your word, ansibles. Ansibles in our heads. Completely private—or is it, Dick?

"It's as private as I make it," Richard says, and I can see from the way Min-xue angles his head that his smile is for the AI whose image we both see real as if he were in the room, and who would be transparent as a ghost to any unmodified human who stepped in beside us.

Once again, you rule our destiny. I mean it to be mocking, but I can't help it if it comes out a little defenseless, as well. *This is going to change the world. This is . . . this is the Net writ large.*

"The global village," Richard says quietly.

"The what?" And I'm not sorry Min-xue's wired a little faster, if it means he got to be dumb quicker. I must think it out loud, because he ducks his chin and tilts an apologetic smile at me, and Richard laughs.

"An antiquated catchphrase," Richard says. "You might call it an advertising slogan."

But is it really going to change the way the planet is run? Or is it just going to give us more differences to fight over?

"Too soon to tell. Might eventually give world leaders

a hell of a lot of grief making people believe geographic boundaries have any value, though."

"That will take generations," Min-xue interjects.

I run both hands through my hair, turning my back on him—except I can't, really, because I carry him with me as I walk to the porthole and pause.

"Only one or two, Min-xue. Patty's already adapting to her AI linkages with real fluidity."

Dick, does Ellie know about this yet? Valens and Riel?

"Only you two."

They need to. They need—

Shit.

"Ah. I see you've arrived."

"The Benefactors." I say it out loud, and Min-xue, who has closed his eyes against the flicker of the lights, jumps at the sound of my voice. I don't see him jump. I feel it. *Completely fucking bizarre.*

That thing they do. Where they . . . slide through each other. That's why they grabbed Les and Charlie; they're still trying to talk to us.

He doesn't comment.

What are we going to do about it, Dick?

"It's easier to get forgiveness than permission."

Because conspiracy's served us so very well in the past.

"There is that," he says, spreading his fingers wide as nets while Min-xue looks on, watching silently. I catch something from him, a flicker of Chinese, a rhythm like poetry. It calms him, whatever it is. *Mantras?*

"Li Bo," he answers, with that same off-center smile.

I know where you're going, Dick.

Richard likes watching me think, damn him to hell. "What?"

This is it. This is everything. I press my face against the cold, cold porthole crystal as if it could calm the sensation that has me shivering, the same sensation you have when you look up and you can see the wave breaking, and it's not on you yet, and it's much much bigger than you and it's much much too late to get out of the way. *How did Charlie reprogram the first nanites, Dick? How did he get them to accept our alien earthling code?*

"Gabe and I know the process. It's more straightforward than you might think."

It's Min-xue, strangely, who breaks the tableau. I feel him come up behind me, and—light as a leaf brushing my skin—lay his palm against my shoulder, carefully touching only cloth. "It could kill them," I say.

"Staying where they are will likely kill them, too."

"And you're relying on my conscience, Dick?"

"The last time I checked, you were still arguably a human being. If I'm going to organize a coup, I'd feel better knowing I'm not a megalomaniac AI."

Dick. He grins before I say it. *You are a megalomaniac AI. That doesn't change the fact that you're right. Min-xue?*

The Chinese pilot stares at me as I turn around to face him. His arm drops to his side. He looks at where Richard would be if Richard existed, and he nods, slowly, his eyes unfocused and his expression grave. "If the nanites are how the Benefactors communicate among themselves, and they've taken our two scientists alive, we might be forgiven for assuming that the contact is a further attempt to communicate with us."

Of course, since we've seen no proof that the two groups of Benefactors can talk between themselves, there's no guarantee that adding a third language to the Tower of Babel will help—

"Did you spend your *entire* childhood in Sunday school, Jen?"

It only felt like it. Look, I'd feel better about this if we could ask Charlie and Leslie if they were game.

"So would I."

"When fate intervenes, we serve where we are standing," Min-xue says. "They would do it, if they knew."

He's right, of course. How do you propose to pull this off?

"I'm going to . . . the closest equivalent would be to say I'm going to flash the bios on some of the nanites in the Benefactor . . . um, conjoined mass? When Charlie reworked the original Benefactor tech into something we could use, he cleaned out their brains with a focused electromagnetic pulse, and then retrained them. I don't have time to do that, but I do have considerably more information on how they work than he did when he started. And I have Gabe, who's a better code jockey than Charlie ever was."

I try not to glow too much at the praise of Gabe. I'm somewhat attached to him.

"And then," Richard finishes, "I'm going to try to take control of the birdcage entity, and get it to kick Leslie and Charlie free. I'll need somebody to catch them, if it works."

Me, he means, or Min-xue. Or Patty. "And if it doesn't?"

"Then I'm going to use the nanites to begin to modify Charlie and Leslie."

Without medical support.

"It will be less drastic than your surgery, Jen. I don't need them wired fast enough to fly a starship, after all. I just need to be able to read their minds."

I find myself nodding, agreeing, knowing perfectly well that Wainwright *and* Valens are going to take turns breaking my fingers when they find out I knew about this, and I'm not even going to be able to work up a valid protest that I don't deserve it. *All right, Dick. I'll take responsibility. But dammit—*

"Yes, Jen?"

I want to be with you when you go on in.

Leslie Tjakamarra dreamed of flying, and he dreamed of being bitten to death by ants. Not separately, by turns, but both at once, in a timeless conflation of then and now and when that blurred into an unceasing whole. He dreamed of the wave that rolls across the water, but cannot change the water, and he dreamed he was rocked in the womb of the mother, wrapped in the coils of the rainbow snake. He dreamed he was dying, and the sun bleached his bones, both at once. All at once.

All right now.

Leslie Tjakamarra had a starship dreaming, and he had joked that it was just as well that he had no taste for starship, as his kinship with them precluded his killing and eating one. He had a starship dreaming, and all things that were had been sung already, were just waiting under the ground for their time to come. Alive in the Dreaming before they were alive in the world.

He had a starship dreaming, and here he was, drifting in space, blind and deaf, warm enough that he knew his heaters hadn't broken, cool enough that he knew he hadn't been knocked into sunlight with his radiators failing. He wasn't sure if the blow had caused his faceplate to opaque, or if it was simply too dark to see, or if he had been blinded. His inner ear told him he was floating rather than spinning, and while he couldn't move his arms or legs, pins and needles told him he hadn't been paralyzed. He might have a moment's air left, or an hour's, or a day's; however much it was, it was a lifetime's worth.

Time passed and the tingling in his fingertips receded, leaving cold numbness. He could imagine, if he thought about it very hard, that he felt a squishy colloid between his fingers, a texture that resembled mud mixed with cold Vaseline. The chill crept upward, numbing his palms, making his wrists and the bones of his hands ache before the sensation left them.

This is going to be a long, chilly way to die, Leslie thought, and tried to relax into it, to relax into the dream and the dying.

He had a starship dreaming, and now it began to seem that he had become a small, peculiar sort of starship of his own.

Even for an AI, there was a fine art to doing everything at once, and Richard was stretching his limits faster than they could grow. If you were a certain kind of person, it was a universal constant that demands expanded slightly in advance of resources. Richard was forming the opinion that, in his case, the pigheadedness of the universe amounted to malice aforethought.

Most of his—and Alan's—awareness was spread in a thin web of nanosurgeons flitting through the waters of the Atlantic Ocean. In particular, he was tracking the rapidly evolving shifts in the damaged ocean's unstable currents, still hard at work on the incredibly complex calculations required to enact the solution suggested by Jen's offhand comment regarding the Aegean Stables and the diversion of rivers.

To wit: What if the climatic damage could be ameliorated by re-creating—by *healing*—the Atlantic thermohaline deep-water turnover process, using *mechanical* means to redistribute saline? What if Richard could reverse some of that damage, buffer both the current global cooling and the looming catastrophic warming trend, and stabilize the climate? It could save millions of lives, if he could attain a sufficient understanding of the process. He might be able to re-create the warming processes of the defunct Gulf Stream and the so-called great ocean conveyor belt, the saltwater-density-driven worldwide ocean current that had helped keep northern Europe unfrozen for thousands of years, and which no longer existed. If he got it right, the British Isles might even be salvageable, although the process of moving the evacuees *back* was logistically daunting.

Or, if he understood the process incorrectly, and pulled the wrong string in his meddling, he could provoke an ecological meltdown to make the current crisis seem like a glitch. He finished checking Alan's climatological analysis and handed the body of the data back to the other personality thread with corrections and suggestions. Alan replied with a string of information regarding Leslie and Charlie's quandary; being less emotionally involved, Alan had honed Richard's hopeful numbers and reworked his code to something more aggressive.

An attempt to free the captured men could possibly outrage the aliens—could be seen as an act of war, could provoke them into violent action against the *Montreal,* or against the Earth. Of course, doing nothing might provoke them just as easily. He mentioned that to Elspeth over the speaker in her office, and Elspeth nodded and tapped her thumbnail against her teeth and said, "You know what occurs to me, Dick?" in that slow, thoughtful way she sometimes had.

Richard reached out to the nanites in contact with the two scientists, who he hoped very profoundly were unconscious, marshalled his forces, and paused. He couldn't control the Benefactor bugs, but he could feel them, coating two intact space suits, the outlines clear as the shape of a hand pressed into a pin box. There was no reason for the suits not to be functional.

"Elspeth, if I could read your mind, people would have good reason to be far more scared of me than they are."

"Hah. Well, they haven't taken any drastic action before now, have they?"

"Nothing aggressive. Nothing at all, really."

"Until we moved onto their turf."

"And they slapped us back."

"Unless," Elspeth said, "they were inviting us in."

Richard paused for mere fragments of a second, considering. "You make a good point," he agreed. "We can't know at all what they expect. They could expect us to come back and continue the conversation, and be hurt—offended—when we don't."

"Exactly."

"Except we have another problem," he said, as a new pattern of movement in the nanotech layer drew his attention. "I think they're taking the space suits apart."

"Dick? Can you do something?"

"I'm on it, Elspeth." And he was. Moving, his improvised—*the phrase you're avoiding is "slapped together," Dick*—code compiled and ready, a best-guess and nothing he would have wanted to stake his own life on, let alone anyone else's. "Look, can you get Jeremy up there? I need the two of you to distract somebody."

It's always easier to get forgiveness than permission, he told himself, and woke up Jenny and Min-xue.

The magnitude of the problem was evident when Valens walked into the prime minister's office. He read it in the set of her shoulders as she stood leaning against the wall and how her hands coiled around the mug she held like a shield before her chest.

"Are we going to war?" Perhaps not the most politic question, but Valens's relationship with Riel had come to be characterized by a certain bluntness.

"Not with the Chinese," she said. "The Benefactors may be another matter. They've captured two of the researchers."

Valens's heart dropped into his belly, even though he knew Patty hadn't been on the EVA team. "Who?"

"Forster and Tjakamarra."

"Damn. Charlie . . ." And then he paused. *"Captured?"*

"That's what Richard and Alan think."

"It occurs to me, Prime Minister," he said, and crossed the room to the decanter three-quarters full of Scotch, "that we're becoming entirely too dependent on 'Richard-and-Alan-say.' "

"That hasn't escaped my notice either, General." Riel's voice was dry, bittersweet. He didn't turn to see her expression; he could picture it well enough. The decanter was heavy, crystal cut in a crosshatched pattern cool and rough under his fingers. He filled a tumbler, two fingers, as she continued. "You were about to comment on the capture of two of our leading scientists, unless I misread you."

Valens stared into the dark amber fluid, but did not

taste it. "When was the last time you misread somebody, Connie?"

"I think it was your friend Casey, now that you mention it."

"Casey's not my friend," he answered, and now he did raise the glass, and ran the Scotch under his nose. It smelled of smoke and peat; it tasted like sugared fire when he touched it to his lips. "There can't be too much of this left in the world."

"We'll be reduced to Kentucky bourbon when it's gone," she answered. "Enjoy it while you can."

"I should examine the details more closely before I jump to any conclusions regarding Charlie and Dr. Tjakamarra and the Benefactors," he said. He turned back to face Riel, propping himself against the sideboard. She was still holding her coffee mug, staring out the window.

"The data will be made available to you."

"Good. How did your meeting with Frye and the odious Mr. Hardy go?"

She shrugged. "Toby's going to try a power play. Or perhaps just flatly sell us out to the highest bidder. Frye can still be managed, though."

"You're certain?"

"Don't be foolish." Her hands dropped to her side. She kept the mug upright, but he heard the coffee slosh. She crossed to the window, standing behind the drapes as she twitched them aside. She stared out for a moment and then turned and looked back at him, frowning. "Of course I'm not certain. But that's besides the point; she can be used, and I intend to use her. I think I have the opposition figured out, Fred."

"You're enough of a bitch to leave me hanging like

that, too, unless I ask." He softened it with a smile. She chuckled.

She crossed the room and set her mug on the edge of her desk, then began re-arranging her clutter away from the access surfaces of the interface plate. "Fred, did it ever occur to you that we might lose?"

Somehow, he knew what she meant. Not her government, not Canada. But the whole human race, Earth and everybody on it. "Some days, Connie, I think maybe we already have. Some days I think it's kinder that way, and maybe we're too dumb and self-destructive to live."

"And yet we keep kicking and shouting."

"And scheming. It's in the blood."

She raised her eyes to his, and tilted her head, her dark hair sticking and sliding across her forehead. "The PanChinese premier is being set up for a coup. His minister of war is behind it, and Tobias Hardy is bankrolling the whole damned thing."

"How do you know that?"

"Do you mean, can I prove it?" She walked past him and poured herself a stiff Scotch of her own, rolling the fluid around on her tongue for a moment before she swallowed. "No. It's a stone cold hunch. But I'm willing to bet Premier Xiong will be dead or in a labor camp by the end of the year. And it may very well wind up looking like Canada's fault."

Genie sat very quietly in her chair in the corner of the bridge, hoping Papa wouldn't notice her and send her away. Jenny had seen her, raised an eyebrow and winked on the side of her face where her scars used to be, and now seemed to be making a little game of keeping Papa's attention away from Genie, teasing him, keeping his hands busy on the console. In the ready room, on the other side of the airtight hatch, Patty was doing...something. Nobody had explained to Genie what was going on.

But nobody had been able to conceal his worry either. And she did think it was weird that both pilots were hanging out by the bridge when Wainwright wasn't there. Jenny said once that out of Leah and Genie, Genie got the curiosity for both girls, and Leah got the stubborn. Genie didn't really think that Leah had been all that much more stubborn than Genie. But that was Aunt Jenny, and Genie supposed she had a right to her point of view.

Besides, Jenny wasn't very much like a grown-up, most of the time. And often a willing coconspirator, although not as much fun as Elspeth. Still, when Genie snuck mouselike out of her chair, and Jenny's eye caught her as she turned, Genie wasn't surprised at all when Jenny cleared her throat and leaned forward to ask Papa a question about whatever he was doing with the holographic computer interface, his fingers flying like bee's wings through the projected images as he shuffled code.

Normally, Genie loved to watch him work. He coded like some people danced, glitter-eyed concentration and confident grace and never a hesitation. But now she turned her back on him and edged toward the ready-room hatchway, and undogged it silently, and opened it just wide enough for a twig of a girl to slip through. She made sure it shut behind her without clanging, but Patty heard her, of course, just like Jenny would have, or Leah.

Patty turned around too quickly and tripped on the carpet, but she caught herself without ever lowering her arms. Her fingers were tangled up in her hair, a comb in her teeth, and she looked like she was about to cry. She let her hair fall around her shoulders and took the comb out of her teeth and fixed Genie with a black-eyed glare. "Just tell them I'll be out in a second, would you? I can't get my damned braid to work. I should probably just cut all my hair off like Jenny—" All on a rush, and Genie thought it was only dignity that kept her from kicking the wall.

"They didn't send me," she said. "It's okay. Papa's busy, and Aunt Jenny's keeping him that way."

"So what do you want?"

Genie blinked at the cold hostility in her tone. It didn't scare her. Instead, it sparked a warm kind of competition. She grinned exactly the grin that would have driven Leah out of her tree, and came a few steps farther into the room. She knew what Elspeth would have said, after all. Elspeth would have said that Patty was scared and worried about failing, and that she didn't mean to snap at Genie—it was just that Genie was there.

Genie took a breath and laced her hands in front of her hips, trying to look small and not too threatening. "I came to ask if I could help you braid your hair."

Patty blinked at her, the comb forgotten in her hand. "Do you know how?"

"Sure. I used to do Leah's all the time. Give me the comb." She said it a little peremptorily, the way Elspeth would have, and held out her hand. Patty, a funny expression compressing the corners of her mouth, handed it over and sat down.

When that Chinese guy tapped on the hatch cover and then peered in, Genie was just twisting the elastic around the end. Before Patty got out of the chair, Genie touched the interface port at the base of her skull. "Doesn't that hurt?" Ignoring the Chinese pilot's shiny black eyes. He didn't lean through the hatchway. If the ship's pressure dropped, the decompression doors would slam down like axes across chicken necks.

"It feels funny," Patty said, and stood up, and moved toward the door, but not before she grabbed Genie's hand and gave it a quick, painful squeeze.

Genie followed her out, far enough behind that anybody watching Patty walk toward the black leather pilot's chair wouldn't see her. Her luck didn't hold; Papa's blue eyes fastened on her, and a half-distracted frown tugged the sides of his mouth, but he didn't say anything. She dogged the door very carefully, and he looked away, watching Aunt Jenny strap Patty into the pilot's chair and seat the two snakelike control cables at the base of her spine and at the back of her neck.

Patty went limp in Jenny's arms when the cords were plugged in, and Jenny very carefully closed her eyelids so that her eyes wouldn't dry out. She laid Patty back in the chair and swung her feet up so her blood would circulate evenly—Genie knew the reasons for all of it; Jenny had started teaching her, a little, and Leah had already taught her a little more.

And Patty's voice, or something sort of like Patty's voice, but different from it in the same way Genie's own voice sounded different in her head as opposed to how it sounded in a tape recorder, said softly over the bridge speakers, "I'm inside, ma'am. And Alan's right here with me. We're ready when you are."

"Where's the captain?" Papa said, looking up only long enough to chase Genie into an observer's seat with his eyes.

"In her cabin, Mr. Castaign." That was Alan's voice, cooler and less inflected than Richard's, almost chilly. "And the first officer is in conference with Dr. Kirkpatrick and Dr. Dunsany, as arranged. We should have at least a fifty-minute window, unless he catches on too fast."

"Finally," Aunt Jenny said, glancing up, catching Papa's eyes across the open floor space between them. "An advantage to the skeleton crew we've been running on since December."

"We had to find one some time, chérie. Has it occurred to you that you're making a career of hijacking starships?"

Aunt Jenny snorted, looking down at her hands. The smile that crinkled the corners of Papa's eyes made Genie feel weird inside, and she looked at Patty instead. That didn't help any; Patty was so still she was barely breathing. Jenny reached down and smoothed the braid over Patty's shoulder, stroking it one extra time as if to be sure it was going to lay flat. "Okay, Patty," she said, and looked at Min-xue, who was standing by the main hatch to the bridge. "Hit it, girl."

Giving up, Genie looked at the big holoscreen front and center in the bridge displays, instead. And swallowed hard.

Because the *Montreal* was moving, her sails unfurling like wind-taut kites to catch sunlight—and laser light from the antimeteor protocols of the orbital platforms—gliding toward the birdcage ship, a shark cutting water without a ripple or a flicker of fin.

Patty let the *Montreal's* solar sails unfold, light striking their golden mesh surfaces with a sensation remarkably like a stiff breeze tugging her sleeves, if she held her arms like a tall ship's bowsprit and leaned into the wind. The birdcage grew in perspective slowly; her enhanced reflexes triggered when she linked to the *Montreal's* VR systems, and she was thinking nearly as fast as Alan now. It made the unwired world *drag*.

"Perhaps a slight exaggeration, Patricia," he said in her ear, in cool tones that went with the swirl of blues and greens that comprised his icon.

She conjured her own avatar to stand beside him in the virtual space of the *Montreal*'s core. Her icon was the golden robot-girl, like a suit of armor with softly glowing blue-green eyes, perfectly invulnerable. "Maybe just a little."

Alan didn't laugh the way Richard did, or have a face to crinkle up in delighted lines, but his colors shifted in the manner she'd learned meant amusement. She felt more comfortable with his inhuman icon, in any case. Richard's semblance of being a real person made her as jittery as she would have been in the presence of any older, smarter man.

The coolest thing about being the *Montreal*'s pilot was the way the ship became her body, long and smooth and powerful. She could worry about support and angle of thrust and oxygen ratios and carbon cycles and the balance of nutrients needed to keep the nanomachines functioning throughout the big ship's systems, and the fact that Alan was only half-done rewiring the ship's systems and it made things a little funky, working through the worldwire rather than over the hardlines as she'd been trained. She could worry about those things, and not whether she was too tall or too fat or her hair was too frizzy or if the zit beside her nose was as big as it felt, or—

She focused down, orchestrating the *Montreal*'s motion with the same kinetic sense she used to control her own body leaping or twisting. She shoved the thought of Genie's giant bright lost eyes into the same box where she kept the memories of Leah, Carver, her mother and father, and Papa Georges. Her mother would have said it wasn't good to dwell. Her mother would have said—

Her mother would have said to concentrate on her work, and on the important thing, which was saving Charlie and Dr. Tjakamarra. And Papa Fred would have grinned at her sideways, in that way he had of grinning without moving his mouth, and winked, and she would have known that *he* thought she could do it.

Well, Jenny thought she could do it. And Mr. Castaign did, too. And if Papa Fred were here...

Well, if Papa Fred were here, he'd probably have a gun out and be arresting everybody on the bridge. "Mr. Castaign?" she asked, careful to key the loudspeakers only on the bridge. "We'll be reaching the birdcage in approximately fifteen minutes. I'm using the solar sails to brake us; the Benefactor ship's own orbital momentum will carry it 'under' us, and we can dump our relative vee and sort of... hang just 'behind' it. Is that cool?"

She flinched inwardly. *Way to sound like a kid, Patty.* And when she'd been doing so well.

"That's perfect, Patty. Stand by to flash the Benefactor nanites—Alan? Or Dick?"

"We're both here, Gabriel. On your signal."

Jenny Casey and Min-xue had already left the bridge; they hustled through the *Montreal*'s passages. Alan and Patty tracked them through security motes and information relayed to the worldwire by their own bodies. Patty unlocked the air lock to the shuttlecraft *Ashley MacIsaac* a few meters in advance of them. They shinnied into the shuttle, Casey manually uncoupling her from the *Montreal* while Min-xue ran for the controls. The *Montreal* was still braking; the *Ashley MacIsaac* drifted forward, free of the starship. The mote sensors networking the *Montreal*'s hull reported a flush of heat when the *Ashley MacIsaac* began her burn, still meters inside the recommended safety envelope. Patty flicked the *Montreal*'s sails out of harm's way, braking harder, the gawky dragonfly vanes furiously unlikely for their task.

Neither Casey nor Min-xue was suited yet, which worried Patty, but there was nothing she could do about it from inside the *Montreal*. And she wasn't going to think about that *nothing she could do*. Wasn't going to think about Carver or Mom . . .

The pilots had another ten minutes before they reached the birdcage. Drill was to be suited and sealed in three.

Drill was also to suit before you took a shuttlecraft out of dock, but this was an emergency.

Patty was grateful that she couldn't feel her body. She couldn't feel her heart tighten in her chest when she refused to think about how Min-xue might get hurt either. That's what Leah would do. Leah would do the job and she would do it well and she'd protect everybody else while she was doing it. And if Leah could do it, Patty could do it, too. She imagined herself clothed in the armor of the ship, a golden robot-girl and not a flesh and blood girl at all, and didn't worry about whether her heart was racing. She picked up Mr. Castaign's voice through the bridge ears, and spared him a little attention. It was just keeping the *Montreal* pointed, now. "Dick, how are we doing?"

Alan's avatar winked green-purple, and Richard's voice rang from the speakers. "Your window in five, Gabe— four, three—"

Patty giggled inside her head, where nobody but she

and Alan could hear it and it didn't matter if she sounded hysterical.

There's nothing quite as much fun as squirming into a space suit while fighting gees from an erratic maneuvering burn, but I've got the damned thing up to my waist, and I'm struggling with the seals across the chest when Richard starts counting.

"—two, one—" Richard counts in my ear, with that flatness of tone that tells me he's half-Alan, currently. Always weird to be reminded that a good friend isn't human.

"We're not in position to catch yet, Dick." I say it out loud, for Gabe's benefit. Patty and Min-xue don't need to be told; they're on the worldwire with me, tight as sharing a skin.

"Don't worry. Plenty of time before anything breaks open." I get my hat and my gauntlets on, double-checking the seals before I tug the controls away from Min-xue so he can get dressed. He does a better job than I did, fast and efficient despite what must be unfamiliar suits. I wonder how different the Chinese equipment is. He seems to be doing okay with the controls.

"Richard coached me," he says in his musical English, without turning his head inside the helmet to look at me. "When he reprogrammed my wiring to the Canadian standard." He checks his restraints and rests his gloves on the arms of the chair rather than taking the controls back. I drive at the birdcage as hard as I dare. The gaps in the filigree aren't all the same size, and I need a pair of them opposite each other, or nearly, and big enough that I can line them up and coast through on inertia. I'm not risking a burn inside that thing if there's any way around it. And then, assuming we catch one of the missing the first time through, we get to come back and try it again.

Dick, you rat.

"I said nothing."

Sure. But I believe him; Min-xue isn't quite the spooky mindreader Elspeth is, but he's a smart kid and he's wired so tight that he shivers like a Mexican lap dog when he tries to stand still. Worse off than I am, and just as convinced that it's worth any price to fly. And it's perfectly possible that his hindbrain read my hindbrain, and he just sorta knew what to say.

Freaks. Every last one of us.

"Gabe's hacking, Jen. Can you get a little more vee?"

"If I burn faster I have to brake harder once we get there, Dick. We need to be moving slow enough that Min-xue can bail out to handle the rescue, and we aren't going to be maneuverable while that's going on. This is crazy shit, sir."

Min-xue says something in Chinese that I take for agreement. I don't understand a word, but the tone is 50 percent *if Momma could see me now* and 50 percent *I'm fucking nuts even to consider this.* He slaps his release and vaults out of his chair. Acceleration kicks him toward the aft bulkhead; "down" is currently aimed toward the ass-end of the *Ashley MacIsaac,* and I wince, grateful for the armor of Min-xue's space suit and expecting him to wind up on his ass, sprawled against the wall like a terrified bug. But he twists in midfall, agile as if that space suit were a pair of stretch jeans, and lands with his boots against the bulkhead. The thump as he hits rattles my chair.

Damn, he's fast. And so very, very young.

Which is not something I'm allowed to think about.

Not here. Not now. Because it's always the kids, isn't it? And more of us survive than don't, so I might as well quit whining, really.

The pulley spins as he yanks a safety line out of the aperture; it clicks solidly through a D ring on his suit.

"Don't jump until Dick tells you jump," I say, just to be saying something. From his snort, he knows it and forgives me. The hatch to the passenger cabin bangs open and he drops through the hole, rappelling down. Design flaw: there's no way he can dog the hatch behind him. The shuttles weren't built to have people running around inside them when they're under acceleration. I'll have to talk to an engineer about that if we make it back.

At least the air lock is set up so you can get in and get sealed up no matter which way the ship is pointing. The inside hatch unseals and I hear more clanging as Min-xue unhooks one safety line and attaches the one from inside the lock, the sound attenuated through my helmet. Min-xue's voice in my head is as clear as if he were standing close enough to lay a hand on my shoulder. "I am in position, Master Warrant."

"Thank you, Min." Knowing Dick will relay if Min-xue can't hear me. It would be far too easy to get used to that, to start relying on it. As if any of us could in fact be relying on Richard any more than we already are. "Dick, how's Gabe doing?"

The inner air lock door shuts with a vacuuming shoosh.

"He's in, but he says he's not sure he's accomplishing anything," Richard says. "Patty's ceased braking the *Montreal* and has begun tacking and a burn to match vee with the birdcage and come into synchronous orbit 'behind' it, to facilitate pickup."

"Tricky."

"She's up to it."

I know she is, but we're angling up on the birdcage now, and I'm suddenly too busy flying to agree, because the joined-together Benefactor entity starts to shred like a fistful of twisted Kleenex, spattering mercury droplets this way and that. I've got what's on the monitors, and Dick is giving me what he *feels,* too, through the nanobot infestation. Which is gold-plated bizarre, because while I'm hands-on-the-controls, the acceleration couch prodding my back and my suit turning into a sauna because I'm all for conserving its resources as long as I have a perfectly functional shuttlecraft providing me with life support, I'm also spinning apart, decohering, as if fingers and toes and eyes and kidneys and guts all suddenly decided that the arrangement that's suited them just fine for the last fifty-odd years *simply will not do* for another cotton-picking moment. "Dick! That wasn't the plan!"

"You know what they say about plans, Jen—" The *Alan* has dropped out of his voice, which tells me the other AI thread is damned busy all of a sudden, and I've got just Richard now, and probably a persona all to myself.

"Does that mean Gabe hacked in all right?"

"No." I'm not imagining the tired resignation in his voice. "It means we got nowhere. It would have been nice to get a damned Hollywood ending for a change."

I've got Min-xue's presence in my head and the weird doubled vision that comes when Richard connects us. I see his suit, see the battleship-gray interior of the air lock through his eyes. I feel the birdcage entity flying into splinters, and the *Ashley MacIsaac* no longer slamming me back against my couch as I end my burn, and Patty light and precise in control of the *Montreal* and Dick all tangled up in my head and it's really more than I can handle. "Dick, I'm not a multithreaded entity, man—"

"Sorry, Jen." He modulates it back, leaving me strong and in control, the other awarenesses like monitors I have to turn my head to see; there, but not driving me to distraction. It *is* useful. I've got to hand him that. Because I can feel Min-xue and Patty, almost like my own metal hand, an extension of my body that my kinetic sense encompasses, and I know they can feel me back. And moreover, all of us can feel which droplets and splinters of the birdcage critter are Charlie and Leslie.

The three of us are thinking like a flock of birds. And that, coupled with our enhanced reflexes, is the thing that may let us pull this mad exercise off, rather than wrapping the shuttlecraft around one of the struts on the birdcage.

It's just math, Min-xue told himself, bracing both gauntleted hands on the grab rails bracketing the air lock as he felt—through his own inertia, through the shift of Casey's hands on the controls—the *Ashley MacIsaac* begin its braking burn. A puff of vapor blew into space past him as he triggered the air lock, making sure his safety cables were short enough to hold him inside the shuttle even if Jenny had to move abruptly—*more abruptly,* he corrected, hands tightening on the grab rails convulsively a split second before the shuttle bumped hard, coming around flat with its rear end pointed in the direction of travel. Casey kicked the thrusters on, and this time Min-xue's death grip kept him from being hurled against the interior air lock door, rather than out into orbit.

"Sorry," Casey said in his head, and he didn't answer,

because he'd known she was going to do it before she did it, of course, and in any case his attention was fixed gape-mouthed on the ungainly dragonfly body of the *Montreal,* solar sails at full extension, passing over the *Ashley MacIsaac* like a hawk over a huddled gosling. The ship-tree glimmered behind her, silent and aloof, keeping its own remote counsel.

He could feel Casey and Richard computing trajectories and angles of thrust, aiming the shuttle after the two bits of flotsam that Richard's infiltration of the Benefactor nano-network revealed to be Dr. Tjakamarra and Dr. Forster. He relaxed, and let them do it. This part of the process was not Min-xue's job.

His duty was simply to go out there and *catch* them and haul them back inside. He wasn't worried about that. He'd act, and fail or succeed, and there would be no time for fear once he started. It was the waiting that was going to drive him mad.

"Piece of cake," Jenny said, and he realized that he had been thinking loud enough for her to sense. Min-xue didn't answer. Instead he glanced down and visually in-spected his safety lines one last time, as the shuttle glided in absolute silence through the bars of the birdcage, and Min-xue groped with Richard's senses toward Dr. Forster, who would be the subject of their first rescue attempt.

Min-xue braced himself in the doorway, watching the crystal bars of the birdcage slide past, and much to his own surprise managed to clear his mind. Casey's touch on the controls was feather-light; the shuttle turned within the length of its own hull, drifting, and suddenly all he could see was silver scattering, water shaken from a half-drowned dog, droplets smaller than his thumbnail with perspective that might in reality be close enough to reach out and grab in a gauntleted fist, or which might be as big as shipping containers, and a kilometer away. A quarter Earth glimmered behind them, flanked by an attendant moon. City lights shone far below, dulled by the pall in Earth's atmosphere, the birdcage picking up blue reflections from the moonlight and the earthlight.

Oddly enough, Min-xue thought of the shiptree and its presumed inhabitants, line of sight now blocked by the shuttle's bulk, and wondered at their aloof observation of the scurrying about between the birdcage and the *Montreal. Maybe they're up there hoping as hard as we are that we learn this. Maybe they want to talk to us as badly as we want to talk to them.*

Charlie's closer, and I've got him lined up pretty as a picture when I call down to Min-xue in the air lock. I'm surprised; this is nothing on flying medevac in jungle under fire. There's all the room in the world up here, and all I'm trying to do is not *hit* anything. Nobody's shooting at me, or at the people I'm trying to evac. Also, the psychic link with my ship, my target, and the retrieval team doesn't hurt in the slightest. Nothing like being able to mindread your buddies. This would have saved a lot of lives, back in Brazil. In fact, I bet if Charlie wasn't a bit fragile for that kind of treatment, I could scoop him up with the *Ashley MacIsaac* easy as a jai alai player scooping the ball into his basket.

I'm not quite cocky enough to call it a cakewalk just yet, however. The shuttle glides up on our target. Min-xue tenses as he makes visual contact. I see the white of Charlie's space suit through Min-xue's eyes seconds before I make it out with my own. He's got the better angle. Should, of course; I planned that.

"Is he breathing, Dick?"

"I don't know," the AI admits, a moment's wringing frustration. "I don't see any vapor off his suit, but he didn't have this much oxygen either."

"Can't you tell from the nanites?"

"No. I can't tell a damned thing from the nanites right now. They're all wonky."

"That's a technical term?"

"Jen," he says, weary and a little bit irritated, which is a tone I don't hear from him often. "Quit yanking my chain and fly the shuttlecraft, please."

Sorry. And I am. It's reflex, the banter.

And then we're on Charlie, and Min-xue spins out of the air lock like a flyer in a trapeze act, except he's the catcher, really, if the metaphor is going to work, and I just bloody well keep my hands still on the controls and try not to screw him up.

I don't think we're going to get a second crack at this, not if we're going to come back and get Leslie, too.

Min-xue's flying, all right. Rush of inertia and sharp twinge of fear, metallic taste of adrenaline crimping his mouth as he lets the shuttle's momentum fling him forward and down, somersaulting, all his trust in the fragile safety lines and his mind on my mind like hand in hand, like dancing, except neither one is leading and I can almost feel *Richard* holding his breath.

Breath that's knocked out of all three of us when Min-xue hits Charlie's drifting shape amidships, misses the grab with his arms, locks both legs around Charlie's suit like a kid on a carousel pony, and kicks his attitude jets on a split second later, buying acceleration, equalizing velocity so he's moving the same way the shuttle is when he and Charlie fetch up against the end of the safety line like some idiot bungee jumping over Niagara Falls.

The shock when the lines snap taut brings tears to *my* eyes, and *I'm* feeling it attenuated, courtesy of Richard. Min-xue bounces hard enough that I think for a second his suit's ruptured—*and how the hell would I explain that piece of brilliance to Riel?*—but I feel him recover, and he keeps his grip on Charlie and starts hauling them both up the safety lines hand over hand, because the pulleys aren't quite doing it fast enough to suit any of us.

"Goddamn. Would you believe he pulled it off?"

"Very pretty flying, ma'am," Min-xue says. Unsurprisingly, the next voice I hear is Wainwright, demanding our immediate return to the *Montreal*.

"In a minute," I say. The cocky gets away from me, raw unholy glee big enough to fill a room. "We've got another man overboard, Cap'n. We'll be back once we've fished him out, too."

Except it doesn't work that way at all. Min-xue tucks Charlie's unmoving space suit inside the air lock and clips him onto three safety clasps before we clear the birdcage. I swap ends on the shuttle, a gliding turn—front end slides left, back end slides right—not all that different from how you'd do it in a chopper, and get us lined back up with the birdcage as Dick says, "Jenny, are you seeing this?"

Yeah. We've got a problem, sir. "I think they just rolled up the welcome mat, Dick." Because suddenly, unexpectedly, the birdcage has a hull. The baroque, open-to-space filigree is still visible like the raised outline of leaf veins, or like ribs revealed under skin, but the gaps between are covered by a taut, stretched membrane that bellies and ripples a little, like an opaque film of soap bubbles.

I can't fly through that. I don't even know what it *is*. *Shit*. "What do we do now, Dick?"

"Casey—" Wainwright, and I don't want to hear it, but I know what she's going to say. She surprises me, though. Her voice hitches and goes softer. "Master Warrant, why don't you just come on home?"

The strips Wainwright tears off me are thin and she doesn't stop at half a dozen. She'd like to confine me to quarters, I'm sure, but it isn't quite practical when Patty and Min-xue were in on the mutiny, too.

And, after all, we almost got away with it.

Got away getting Charlie back, at least, and breathing, even if we haven't managed to prove that he'll ever regain higher functions. He *shouldn't* be breathing. The oxygen in his suit should have been exhausted long since, but something the Benefactors did seems to have put his in a state of hibernation, which kept him alive.

One of these days, the captain's gonna severely kick my ass. Right now, however, she's contenting herself with a catalogue of my sins beginning at "reckless" and ending with "mutinous," with side trips through insubordinate, overconfident, obstreperous, and just plain too stupid to live along the way before she pauses for breath. I love the way Richard plays soothing music in my ear while I'm being dressed down by my boss.

I suspect I fail to look contrite. She stops cold, in the middle of drawing breath to continue upbraiding me, and shuts her mouth with a click. "What is it, Casey?"

"Permission to go back out after Leslie, ma'am?"

"Denied."

"Ma'am—"

Her eyelids tighten. "Casey, get the fuck out of my ready room before I have you spaced."

But— I want to say. *But Leslie's alive out there, but we got Charlie back, didn't we? But you don't leave your buddy behind, but—*

—but we got away with it, ma'am.

She's not looking down.

"Yes, ma'am." I nod crisply, and get the fuck out of her ready room.

I wind up in the smaller lounge—not the pilot's ready room, but the public one that, as Elspeth says, nobody uses—with my feet in Gabe's lap and a cup of nasty, sugary coffee in my hand, waiting for the post-combat-time shakes to pack up and head on home. Elspeth's the other way on the bank of couches, her feet between mine, and Gabe's got his back scrunched into the corner and is absentmindedly petting us both, with that look on his face that's half donkey between two bales of hay and half mouse between two cats, although really we don't treat him as roughly as all that. All three of us are staring out the porthole into space, where about half the baroque outline of the shiptree and half of Piper Platform's chained, rotund doughnut take turns flickering past as the *Montreal's* wheel revolves on its pin.

It's nice to sit still.

"Happy birthday, Jen." Elspeth lifts her head off the arm of the couch and feels around on the floor for her water bottle. She's reading something on her contact. I can see the green hairlines of the text paused in front of her pupil as she blinks and yawns.

"You almost got away clean." Gabe winks at me, his catcher's mitt of a hand folding around my foot. My chest aches when I look at him, and I know he knows. Once upon a time, he was Captain Castaign and I was Corporal Casey, and he saved my life. And there were thirty-three other guys he didn't manage to get to in time. "All you had to do was keep the crisis going a little longer, and we would have had to wait until next year."

"It's October in Toronto," I remind him. "Heck, it's October on the *Montreal*. For that matter, *in* Montreal."

He shrugs. "Vancouver's the capital now. Since we're not on Earth, I think we get to pick our time zone."

"Following that logic, it should be Jen's birthday for, um."

"Forty-seven hours," Richard supplies helpfully, over the wall speakers.

"Not forty-eight? No, wait—" Elspeth blinks owlishly, having quite obviously confused herself. "I can't picture how that works around the international date line."

"I'm all for longer birthdays." Gabe's voice is unconcerned, mellow. He digs a thumb pad into the arch of my foot and I groan. The self-warming coffee cup makes my meat hand sweat. It can't ease the aches in a metal one that doesn't have any sense of pain anymore, but it's psychologically comforting anyway.

"Why not? It's been the longest year of my life. It deserves a longer birthday."

"Shortest year of mine," Gabe answers. "And the longest all at once. It's amazing how much fits into twelve months when you work at it, isn't it?" Somehow, he gets around that sentiment without bitterness, the old Gabe, looking up, meeting my eyes with calm acceptance and a sharp, whimsical smile. Healing, because that's Gabe.

He's got the knack of getting better, of growing

through things. I don't, so much. But I make up for it by muscling through. Elspeth shoots me that mind reader look and I shoot it right back, Richard laughing his ass off at the both of us, and I drink my coffee and set the cup down on the floor, a flagrant breach of shipboard protocol. If I had the energy to go fetch Boris out of Genie's quarters, the whole impromptu family would be here, except the girls.

"We should page Genie and Patty," Elspeth says, swinging her feet off Gabe's lap and sitting up. "And see if we can find something we can pretend is a birthday cake."

"No candles shipboard."

"You blow," she says. "I'll flick a flashlight on and off. Wait, better, we'll get Dick to flicker the whole damned ship."

"If Gabe were a better hacker, I could flicker the ship-tree on and off in Morse code," Richard answers. Gabe snorts, but holds his peace, switching both hands to work on my feet now that Elspeth has opted out. "It looks like a giant birthday cake anyway, and maybe we'd stand a chance of getting through."

We laugh even though it hurts, or maybe because it hurts—like ripping off scabs—and Elspeth gets up to fetch the girls herself rather than just having Alan whisper in Patty's ear, and sometime long about oh three hundred hours on my second birthday Jeremy wanders in, looking like a man who's lost two falls out of three with his mattress, and Elspeth hands him a slice of the vegan brownies that are masquerading as my birthday cake, and between us we have a pretty good party after all.

You'd think sitting in a hardbacked chair watching an unconscious man breathe would be about as exciting as a grain elevator, but damned if my heart isn't caught painful as a thumb in the hollow of my throat. Because he *is* breathing. Not awake, but breathing on his own, unventilated. And I know what it's like being stuck inside a body that won't do what you tell it to do, so I sit there beside the bed with my HCD propped on my knee and read to Charlie. *Ulysses,* currently. The Alfred, Lord Tennyson one, not the James Joyce one. I wouldn't do that to anyone who can't defend himself.

I've just gotten to the rousing bit at the end when the wheel spins and the hatch glides open with a little pop of balancing pressure. I keep reading, though; it's probably the corpsman coming in to check on the patient, and he can take a pulse through poetry. Except the corpsman wouldn't wait until I finish up and blank my optic, and then clear his throat.

I crane my neck around and face the hatch. It's Jeremy Kirkpatrick, his ginger curls squashed as if he hasn't combed them since he slept, crow's feet deepening alongside his pale eyes as he squinches down to peer in. "Jen? Got a minute?"

"Come on in. My company's not going anywhere."

He hops over the knee knocker fast, dogging the hatch behind him, and glances down at Charlie's face. "Wainwright not letting us go after Leslie gets right up my nose."

He sounds it, too. "You're old friends."

"University." He flops against the hatch and blows between rubber lips. "You're a love to look in on Charlie like this."

"Don't let it get out. They'll just make more work for me if they know. I don't suppose you found out anything useful about the alien spit we brought from the birdcage?" The chair digs into the back of my legs, so I stand. Having somebody else in the room makes me restless. I want to pace but content myself by leaning over Charlie, smoothing the hair around his bald spot.

"Alien spit, huh?" He's grinning when I look up, a tired desperate grin that furrows those crow's-feet even deeper.

"Got a better name?"

"Not a more appetizing one. In any case, it would be easier to analyze if the xenobiologist weren't in a coma." He comes around the end of the bed nearest the door and looks down at Charlie, the corner of his mouth dragging hard. "Dammit—"

"I'm sorry." Out before I can bite it back, and he looks away from Charlie and frowns at me. I don't look up, but my peripheral vision shows me the deepening lines between his eyes.

"Why are you sorry?"

"Because it was my stupid goddamned idea to provoke the Benefactors into doing something. And they did, didn't they?"

"And weren't we climbing over ourselves to get involved? And wasn't it you who went out and brought Charlie back?"

There's obviously no arguing with the man. I bite my tongue before I can say *I didn't get Leslie, did I*? "Marde." I'm going to wear a groove in Charlie's head if I keep poking at his hair. I wrap the fingers of my prosthesis around my wrist and curl my meat hand into a fist. "What about the medical labs?"

"Jen?"

"To analyze the alien spit. What about the ship's doctor? Or the ship's entomologist or botanist? What about Dick?"

"What about Dick?" Richard says in my head. "Dick suggests retrieving a good xenobiologist from Earth. Except we already had the best one, and it's not exactly a common specialty."

I imagine it's going to get more popular. How many bio students do you think have switched in the last nine months?

"It'll be a glut on the market. Keep reading. Alan can hear Charlie, and Charlie can hear you. Although he's very confused."

Conscious?

"Sort of. Drifting. Jen, I don't mean to alarm you, and I can't tell you why, but if you notice yourself slowing down, at all, or feeling . . . unwell, bring it to my attention immediately."

Dick, are you insinuating there's some kind of problem with the nanotech?

"I can't confirm that." He seems to sense my protest before I articulate it. "And no, before you go there, Alan and I don't have the capability to watch each individual nanite constantly."

I hope you're watching mine! And Patty's, and Minxue's. And especially Genie's, even if her load is lighter by about half.

"I will take the best care of you that I can." Which isn't much of a promise, if it's meant to be soothing.

Jeremy blinks at me owlishly. He must have learned

to pick out the talking-to-Richard expression by now. "The AI?"

"Who else? He's worried. About the Benefactor tech."

"Ah," Jeremy says. He leans away from me, gangling arms crossed over his chest. His teeth dimple his lower lip, and—

Dammit, he knows something I don't. But Richard's silent, too, and for a moment the only sound I can hear is Charlie breathing in and out and in again. It's not a soothing kind of silence. It puts my nerves on edge, and the sight of Jeremy distractedly straightening Charlie's sheet does nothing to ease the worried tightness under my breastbone.

Then I *hear* what I'm hearing, and I reach out with my metal hand and grab Jeremy's wrist lightly, just below the projecting bones. "Do you hear that?"

"Hear what?" His head comes up on his long inelegant neck like a wiry old stag scenting the breeze. He strains to pick whatever threat I've noticed out of the hum of ventilation and the soft endless rasp of an unconscious man breathing.

Except I'm hearing something else. An echo. An overlay. As if another person were breathing in unison with Charlie, in perfect rhythm, in and out and in again.

"Bugger," Jeremy says. "I don't hear anything."

"I do," Dick says, activating the motes in the room so Jeremy can hear him. "Breathing. Not exactly hear. Feel."

Jeremy's eyes get big. He looks at me, and I look at him, and we both glance reflexively toward the port, which shows nothing currently but blackness. "Oh, bugger," he says quietly. "It's Les you two are hearing, isn't it? He's alive out there."

I don't answer, but I don't look down.

"We *must* fetch him back."

I ain't arguing. "Dick," I say out loud, for Jeremy's benefit. "How much longer do you think it will be before Charlie is modified enough for you to talk to?"

He uses the wall speakers. "I'll see if I can expedite matters. Without putting them in any further danger, of course. If what I'm reading is correct, I *am* getting signal from Leslie over the worldwire, strongly enough that Jenny and the rest of the pilots are picking up an echo. It appears that most of his and Charlie's body processes are synchronizing—heart rate, brain function, and so on. *Very* interesting. All I can postulate is that the birdcages have some method of sustaining his life, and they've infected him with their nanotech as well. Since Charlie's carrying both their bugs and ours—well, Leslie should be safe out there. As ridiculous as it is to say he's safe."

"Of course," Jeremy says. But he does not sound convinced, and that downward drag twists the corner of his mouth one more time as he meets my eyes and glances quickly away.

Dr. Tjakamarra.
Dr. Tjakamarra.

Leslie's hands weren't cold anymore, because he couldn't feel his hands. He wasn't sure *what* he could feel, exactly, but his hands weren't part of it. He felt . . . adrift, buoyed as if in a calm enormous sea, except if he *had* been floating, the currents would have pushed his skin, the sea would have sounded in his ears over the beat of his own heart. And there was no susurrus of white noise, no silken stroke of water.

In fact, he couldn't feel the boundaries of his body at all. He had no skin, no bones, no tactile sensations. Just warmth, boundlessness, quiet. Nothing breathed in him, and what moved did so on a stately, formal, predetermined pattern; he imagined he felt the way the air must feel, on a still, humid afternoon. Alive, heavy. Electric.

Waiting for the storm.

And somewhere, someone was speaking poetry: *Death closes all: but something ere the end, Some work of noble note, may yet be done, Not unbecoming men that strove with Gods. The lights begin to twinkle from the rocks . . .*

Dr. Tjakamarra.

Leslie concentrated on his hands. Hands made the man—no. Hands made *man*. There were other animals just as smart; nothing in his studies had ever contradicted that bias. Unless the bias itself had led him to dismiss the contradictions.

Always a possibility that a good scientist should consider. Was he a good scientist? Or was he a crackpot, some sort of half and half creature walking neither the songlines nor the white man's path? Uncommitted?

Homeless?

Elephants came closer to *H. habilis* than anything nonprimate he could name—tool-using creatures of social complexity and intricate language. He could have made a life's work of studying their culture, if they still existed outside of zoos.

Dr. Tjakamarra. Leslie, can you hear me? It's Alan.

The long day wanes: the slow moon climbs: the deep Moans round with many voices. Come, my friends, 'Tis not too late to seek a newer world. Push off, and sitting well in order smite The sounding furrows . . .

It went beyond hands. Elspeth Dunsany had a theory that the Benefactors were interested in humans because humans had the habit of wanting to talk to anything, everything. It made a certain amount of sense: Leslie himself had often suspected that *Homo sapiens* would better be rendered as *Homo loqui...Homo loquacis*? Homo something, anyway, and leave it to cooler Latinate heads to decide what, or—

Homo garrulitas. There. That made him giggle. Or would have, if he could make any sound. If he could hear if he were making any sound.

Of course, people themselves had always known that *talking* was the important thing. The real people, the chosen people, God's people are the people who talk *our* language. The barbarians—are those creatures over there, little better than animals, who make those disgusting *noises.* It was a human bias that hadn't changed in millions of years—and judging by the continuing tension between the English-speaking USA and recent immigrants, and English-speaking and Francophone Canada (to name two examples at random), it wasn't about to change anytime soon.

For my purpose holds To sail beyond the sunset, and the baths Of all the western stars, until I die...

Dr. Tjakamarra. Leslie. Les. Can you hear me?

Voices. Two voices, not just one. Familiar voices. Sort of. One a man's, and one a woman's. Except they sounded like voices inside his head. Like the voice of his own conscience. Like the voices heard in a dream.

It may be that the gulfs will wash us down: It may be we shall touch the Happy Isles, And see the great Achilles, whom we knew...

Leslie, I can hear you thinking. Talk to me.

Les?

Floating. And then the feather-light brush as of fingertips against his face, and a third voice, another familiar

172   ELIZABETH BEAR

one, babbling nonsense the way he knew he would be
babbling nonsense if he could find his mouth, if he had a
mouth, if he—

—and then a chattering complexity underneath it, like
a stage full of extras muttering *rutabaga rutabaga*. And he
was floating, drifting. And if he had hands, if he had fingers, he would reach out across the warm nameless darkness and twine his fingers through any fingers he could
reach.

They weren't words.

Well, there were words, the woman's voice, the poetry:
*Tho' much is taken, much abides; and tho' We are not now
that strength which in the old days . . .*

And there was the man's voice, too, saying his name
over and over again. *Leslie. Les. Dr. Tjakamarra.*

*Moved earth and heaven; that which we are, we are; One
equal-temper of heroic hearts, Made weak by time and fate,
but strong in will*

Jen's voice. Jen Casey's voice. And why that hard-
bitten old warrior would be chanting poetry in his ear, he
couldn't imagine. And then the other one, the one saying
his name, over and over and over, as if whispered in the
ear of a dying friend . . .

"Richard?" he said. Or tried to say, and he heard in the
empty resonance of his own head that he had failed to
make any noise at all. *Richard? Can you hear me? Alan?
Richard?*

"Leslie? Is that you?" And it wasn't Richard's voice, not
really. It was Charlie Forster's, and it was inside his head,
and then it turned into Alan's and Jen's all at the same time,
and a thousand voices under that, speaking words in a
language he couldn't understand, couldn't even imagine.
Words? Not words. Images . . . no. Sensations. Sensations

of heat and . . . sensations he had no words for, that his brain insisted on translating into things he *had* experienced, a huge babble of voices that weren't voices, of sensations that weren't sensations, hurting his ears, hurting his head, hurting his skin. Synesthesia, light that wasn't light but maybe gravity—

And then a richer voice, not as cool and considering and patient as Alan's, but excited, engaged. Leslie imagined he could almost see the flicker of tumbling hands, the eyebrows rising like wings. *It is gravity, Leslie. They "see" gravity! Or sense it, and that explains why their nanotech is in quantum communication and their stardrive uses gravity as its navigational system. Since gravity is the—*

Richard? Is that you? I can hear you. I can hear you!

He couldn't tell.

—since gravity is the force we theorize affects all dimensions in a superstring model of the universe, unlike the strong and weak and electromagnetic forces—

Dick, I hear you! Dick? Jenny? Charlie?

Echoes. Yammering echoes, and nothing more.

—they're quantum life forms, Les. The birdcage Benefactors, anyway. Quantum life forms. You were right, you were right; they don't even sense the world the way we do—

Richard, get me the bloody hell out of here! Help! Dick!

And just the poetry, the echo of the poetry, and nothing true or concrete or real. He clung to it anyway, to Jen's voice, and the rhythm of the words: *To strive, to seek, to find, and not to yield.*

And then silence, long silence. And then, not light, but a lessening of the darkness. A presence, or a dozen presences. A dream within a dream, a sense of companionship he hoped was not self-delusion. *Charlie?*

Charlie, is that you? And the voices, and if he'd been able to move, he would have turned and run after those voices, anything, anything to touch and be close with something that was anything, that wasn't the blackness and the untextured warmth. Voices, crowd noise, a hundred or a thousand talkers talking, and no more sense to be made of it than the buzz of cicadas, the twittering of birds. No, not talking, although his human brain insisted on "hearing" the noise impressed upon it by the Benefactor tech infecting his body. He could *feel* that tech communicating with the other nanosurgeons, worldwide, feel Richard and Charlie and Alan as part of the same intermingled sea of experience, feel Jenny and Patty and Genie and Min-xue and the other human carriers as discrete islands within that sea. And then there was the worldwire under it all, the combined weight and presence of the Benefactors, the damaged planet below, the starships and the—

Damn.

He could feel half the whole goddamned bloody galaxy.

Dick?

"Pretty cool, isn't it?"

"For my purpose holds To sail beyond the sunset, and the baths Of all the western stars, until I die—"

"Jen?" His voice vibrated in his head, not his throat. There was no light, nothing, neither eyelids nor lashes, and he heard Charlie say "Richard?" as if out loud, at the same moment, and then a greedy hand clutched and squeezed his hand, and someone was laughing exultantly in his ear. No, it was Charlie's hand. Not his own hand. He couldn't feel his own hand.

He opened his eyes and saw nothing at all.

Jeremy?

Jeremy? Where are you? Can you hear me?

"I hear you."

Except the voice wasn't in his ear, it was in his head, so he answered without moving his lips, as if in a dream, *I know how to talk to the birdcages. Can you hear me? I know how to talk to them now.*

1100 hours
Friday October 5, 2063
HMCSS Montreal
Earth orbit

Jaime Wainwright had a trick of looking out from under her hair that made her look years younger, and not one whit less dangerous. Charlie liked to catch her at it, that cold professional stare softened through her lashes. He *didn't* like being the target of it, as he was the target of it now. He'd gone out of his way to find her away from her ready room, away from the bridge—not that it helped much; the whole of the *Montreal* was her domain. Finding her in the lounge—with a little assistance from Richard—was still a stroke of luck.

In any case, when she pinned that look against him it took all the courage he could muster not to step back and yield her the floor. Instead, he said, "There has to be *something* we can do for Les." He pushed his spectacles up his nose with a fingertip, aware of the smile his archaic affectation produced. "Captain."

Her eyelashes flickered, dusting her cheek. She nodded to the window, which showed nothing.

"Charlie," she said. "Think for half a minute what I'm risking if I send somebody after him. I think they made it obvious that they weren't interested in giving Dr. Tjakamarra back." She jerked her head at the view port. Nothing was visible from this angle. Not a glimpse of shiptree or birdcage or Clarke or even a curve of mother Earth flashed past—just the whirl of distant stars.

He didn't need to *see* the birdcage to know that it was shuttered tight. *And furthermore,* Leslie said calmly in his ear, *I'm here already and I'd be a fucking poor excuse for a scientist if I didn't try to take the opportunity to* learn *something.*

Les, you're really volunteering to sit out there in sensory deprivation until you go nuts or run out of air?

Leslie was scared. Charlie could feel it; it accelerated his *own* heartbeat when he let himself feel it, sent sweat prickling across the palms of his own hands. His "voice," though, was level and reasoned, even a little bit wry. *Blame my acculturation,* he said. *The dark in here doesn't scare me, and I'm learning so much. It's not a bit neat, Charlie. The birdcage's reality tunnel isn't all that different from the idea of song lines—they know their roads. They have a feel for them, sort of . . . hardlined in.*

Charlie felt his lips twitch, and he wasn't sure if it was Leslie's humor or his own. He understood Leslie's seeming insanity on a visceral level—it was the scientific opportunity of the millennium, and whatever else Leslie was, he had the unholy intellectual curiosity that got explorers killed.

It still felt wrong, though. Wrong to leave Leslie out there. Wrong not to go back after him. "Captain, he's most assuredly alive out there. And there's no guarantee—"

"I know," she said, and cut him off with a gesture. "Unfortunately, that's beside the—"

"Charlie," Richard said in his head, drawing his attention to what has happening outside. "Look at *this*."

"Captain." Charlie heard the new crispness in his own voice, and saw Wainwright react to it.

"What?"

"Dick says the aliens are moving." He hadn't quite finished the sentence when the captain held her hand up, cocking her head to one side as if she were listening to a voice in her ear. She pursed her lips and nodded.

"The bridge," she said, "relaying the same information."

Their eyes met, and he smiled. The corners of the captain's mouth curved slightly before they fell back into line.

"Come on," she said, resignation decorating her shoulders. "Let's go see what's broken now."

There's a good view of both alien ships from the bridge—the birdcage in 3-D front and center, right now, and the shiptree on the smaller screen off to the left, where it won't distract unless you want it to. I'm camped on the pilot's chair crosslegged. The normal buzz of restrained activity has dropped into hushed expectation; it doesn't pick up much when Wainwright and Charlie walk in.

The captain looks at me, of course. Why is it always my fault? "Casey?"

I hitch myself forward, chair dimpling under my calves, and jerk my chin up at the monitor. "What you see is what we know."

Her gaze follows mine. Charlie steps away, leans against a bulkhead, and folds his arms over his chest, but he's watching, too. The birdcage still looks shrink-wrapped under a layer of silver insulating foil, and teardrop-shapes are bustling about it, inside and out. I can't help straining my eyes for any glimpse of a thing that might be Leslie, even though Richard is perched on a ledge in the back of my head, assuring me that the situation is unchanged, and Leslie's clear-headed and rational and having the time of his life.

Save us from the fearless, oh Lord, because the rest of us have to live with the consequences of the ways in which they get their own fool asses killed.

Wainwright grunts under her breath at the same time as I notice the unnerving smearing effect of something dropping out of hyperlight beside the birdcage. She glances at me for a half-second; I show her the end of the interface cable laid across my lap. Just in case. She nods. Her eyes flick back to the monitor as crisp as snapping fanned cards together.

I look back at the monitor, and I actually think I can feel my heart skip a beat in my chest. Teardrop shapes swarm around a lumpy grayish object scaffolded in twisted silver. "Tell me that's not another fucking asteroid, Dick."

Wainwright doesn't even bother to glare at me over my language. "What's it made of?"

"I'll bounce a laser off it, ma'am." There's a pause, as the second lieutenant who spoke does just that, and waits for a spectroscopic analysis. "Mostly water ice, ma'am."

"There's no evidence that's a weapon, then." Wainwright's relief isn't quite palpable.

"None. In fact, they seem to be chipping it apart."

Oh. Through Richard, I feel Charlie's epiphany—or maybe it's Leslie's epiphany—half a second before Charlie puts it into words. "It's life support," he says.

"Dr. Forster?"

The birdcage guys are ferrying meter-wide chips of water ice through the veils hung over their filigree space ship, busy as ants tearing apart a grasshopper.

"It's life support," he says again, turning to face her blank look. His hands pinwheel for a second, and then he finds the words. "Water ice. Hydrogen. Oxygen. Maybe a little carbon dioxide frozen in there. Oxygen and water. They've figured out the stuff they need to keep Leslie alive for a while."

I know I should find that reassuring.

I should. I really should.

0600 hours
Sunday October 7, 2063
HMCSS Montreal
Earth orbit

Charlie's spending a lot of time staring at the bulkheads lately. The bulkheads, the portholes, his hands, me, anything else that wanders across his field of vision. He's so quiet, so internalized, and even when he's allowed out of medical on short, supervised walks, his focus is . . .

Well, he hasn't got any focus. That's what it is. There's a quality to his distraction that reminds me of somebody on a hefty dose of hallucinogens, as if everything he looks at is bright and new and different and unique. And then there's that new trick he has, of talking inside our heads like Dick does, bypassing the message-passing the rest of us have to get the AI to handle. I don't think even Richard understands how the Benefactors have altered him and Leslie, and it freaks all of us out.

Leslie and Charlie, understandably, most of all.

Charlie is spending a lot of time closeted with Alan and Richard and Jeremy and Elspeth, in any case. And Leslie is . . . Leslie is a disembodied voice in our heads, sort of like Dick, but infinitely more disconcerting, because he's out there, floating in darkness, not dead, but we can't really tell if he's alive either. And Gabe's up to his curly blond forelock in programming, and the *Montreal*'s not moving because Richard's got her guts hanging out all over space and we're not moving her unless we have to, which leaves me more or less adrift—except for the time I spend training Patty and Genie to fly.

In any case, the days between Charlie gaining consciousness and us getting ready to board the *Gordon Lightfoot* for the short trip to Forward Orbital Platform drag past like a month and a half. Especially since I spend a fair amount of it being briefed by Riel's lawyers and representatives, preparing for my appearance in front of the United Nations.

I've testified before. It's not new. It's not threatening. It's not even particularly *interesting*, although I'm having a hell of a time convincing Patty of that.

On the other hand, she may just be wound up at the prospect of seeing her grandfather for the first time in nearly a year.

I try not to think about the fact that having Min-xue, Patty, and me all in the same place at the same time is a great big security risk. I try not to think about the fact that Riel will be there, too, for at least part of the time. I try not to think about the fact that—even though New York City has very stringent policies, and the UN isn't exactly America, and *they* have even more conservative ideas about who should be armed, and where, and when, than New York does—we'll be in America, not Canada, and there are a lot of guns in America, and the American government doesn't keep particularly good track.

And that I won't be allowed to carry one.

And that's why I'm holding Patty's hand as tight as I am when we step through the *Gordon Lightfoot*'s air lock onto Forward, even if both she and I are pretending that the contact is intended to reassure her. Min-xue is a little ahead of us, and the three of us are flanked and led by Canadian Air Force security personnel who are doing a remarkable job of effacing themselves. By the time we scuff across the patterned carpeting and into the main concourse, I've almost forgotten they're there.

And Patty *is* shaking. And the skin is tight and pale across her cheeks, betraying the clenching of her jaw. I give her hand an extra squeeze and she gives me half a smile, and we step apart as we move onto the concourse. Forward Orbital Platform's larger and brighter than Clarke—newer, and the interior is designed in bright cheerful colors, mostly cobalts and sunshine yellows that remind me of a children's hospital. The air isn't as good as the *Montreal*'s, but it's warm and doesn't smell canned, which is more than I can say for the shuttle.

I especially like the way the overhead clearances are vaulted and painted different shades of blue to give the illusion of texture and depth. It's almost like not being in a tin can eighteen hours by beanstalk above the surface of the Earth.

Richard clears his throat. "Riel wants a word—"

Put her through.

"Master Warrant Officer."

Prime Minister. To what do I owe the pleasure? I can tell by the timbre of her voice and the way her image settles into my mind's eye that she's using an external VR setup. Those of us who are wired into Richard's network come through differently, with stained-glass sharp edges. It's like the difference between a shadow and one of those Victorian paper cuts.

"I'm mailing you some encoded documents. Richard has the key; you'll be able to access them on your hip unit once you're back in atmosphere." She smiles, her oh-so-plausible, oh-so-professional smile.

I smile right back. Richard will be showing her a simulation of my face. *What's the subject matter?*

"It relates to the various security council members you'll be testifying before. I trust in your ability to make connections. Although I'm concerned about your history of service in South Africa, as it's one of the temporary members this year. It won't make you popular with them."

At least Canada inherited the UK's old security council seat along with the royal family and the British armed forces. That puts us on an equal footing with China. The corridors of Forward's concourse move past at a casual rate. Patty reaches out and grabs my sleeve, guiding me. Min-xue is still five steps ahead. He doesn't look back, but he also doesn't ever let the distance between us vary. He's wearing a *Montreal* uniform jumpsuit without insignia and carrying a Chinese armed forces duffel he must have brought from the *Huang Di*. His shoulders are stiff, his neck rigid, and the expression on his face must be something, because passersby turn to look and then look away.

"Yes. We have a veto and so do they. Which means nothing at all will get accomplished, I'm afraid, and we can look forward to renewed hostilities by the end of the year. If worst comes to worst, we'll consider giving them the *Huang Di* back as a bribe."

Appeasement, ma'am?

"Negotiation."

Dick. Who are the rest of the temporary security council members this year? I should have looked that up before I left the *Montreal*. Except I've gotten lazy about things like that, because there's no Net access from the starship except for through microwave communications, and that takes forever.

"Belgium, Monaco, New Zealand, Belize, Chile, Somalia, Singapore, Trinidad and Tobago, Mexico, and Republic of Hawaii."

Not a lot of good friends there. It's easy to get very reliant on Richard. I imagine Patty and Genie's generation won't think twice about it. Hell, I wonder what we'll need schools for; we'll think a question and the information will be there in our heads, as if we always knew. We'll have to learn a whole new way of thinking. A whole new way of learning.

Richard clears his throat. "You know, it was Einstein who said that imagination is more important than knowledge, because knowledge is limited. Imagination encircles the world."

And now knowledge encircles the world.

"Or rather, I do."

Megalomaniac.

"I come by it honestly."

The side conversation happens so fast that Riel's just starting to notice my distraction. She leans back behind her desk, unsteepling her fingers to play with her coffee cup. It scrapes on the glass of her interface plate. She winces. "Casey?"

Sorry, ma'am. Negotiation, check. Do you *think there will be a war?*

"I think there are forces inside PanChina that would dearly love a war. They're still an expansionist society—"

And we're not?

"Us or them, Master Warrant. In any case, I'll see you in New York City."

When do you arrive?

"Not for five days. The hearings start Monday, but I am not scheduled to testify until next week. General Valens will be joining you, however."

I'll look forward to it.

Her raised eyebrows and the tight smile that flashes across her mouth tells me she's picked the irony out of my internal voice. "Safe trip, Casey," she says. Her eyes flicker away from mine, up and to the side. "Thank you, Richard. That will be all."

And silence follows.

I only realize I've stopped walking when Patty tugs my sleeve again. I blink and glance left to right, meeting the concerned gaze of Min-xue, who stands in the center of the concourse, the security personnel spaced professionally around him. He swallows, and says in his beautiful idiomatic English, "Casey, are you all right?"

"Fine, Pilot Xie. Just distracted by a . . . conference call."

His smooth expression crinkles to a rueful smile, and he looks as young as he is. "I see. This is our platform, then."

Janet Frye cracked another sunflower seed between her teeth and rolled the salty, waxy meat out of the shell with her tongue, letting her eyes unfocus. There was an untouched glass of room-temperature slivovitz and an opened, old-fashioned paper letter on the counter in front of her, and she hadn't been to bed.

She flattened the letter with the palm of her hand and read it again, cracking another sunflower seed as she did. The shell rang in the empty garbage can by her knee when she turned her head and spat. The words on the page still hadn't changed.

She stood off the padded stool and crossed her basement, slippered feet scuffing on parquet floor and weatherproof carpeting. A 3-D in the corner opposite the bar, the sound muted, showed flickering images from 3NN. The famines in Georgia (the European one, not the North American one)—linking it none too subtly to the aftermath of the Chinese invasion of Siberia the previous year—dominated the news, for reasons that made perfect sense if you understood that Unitek had a controlling interest in the Russian journalistic agency that handled English-language news feeds, and understood as well that Toby Hardy liked keeping his allies even more off-balance than his enemies.

Janet blinked her optic on, ordered the news feed to standby, and folded her arms as she leaned against the wall. If anything important happened, her hip unit would buzz.

She spat a shell into her hand and flicked it toward the trash can. She missed. The front door warbled in her ear and she sighed and kicked her slippers off, thumbing her hip to check the security cameras. The image was dim, gray-green low-light. The sun wouldn't be up for hours. She knew who it would be before he even raised his face to the camera to allow himself to be identified, knew it by the long black car pulled up in the circular driveway and by the expensive cut of his suit.

And who the hell else would be ringing her doorbell at four thirty in the morning?

Tobias Hardy, of course. As if thinking the devil's name were enough to summon him.

Only one of her Mounties was still up at this godforsaken hour, sitting on the sofa in the living room watching late-night holo. Internal cameras showed her how he got to his feet before the doorbell finished buzzing, and was moving toward the entryway even as she made her way up the steps from the rec room. He knew Hardy, but he still made a point of taking a thumbprint and checking ID. It never, ever hurt to be careful.

"Ma'am?" the Mountie said, hearing her step behind him. He turned and caught her eye, his own very blue under shaggy terrier eyebrows. "I haven't patted him down yet, ma'am."

"It's okay, Kurt. I'll take him downstairs. Toby, come in."

Hardy stepped past the Mountie, a precise and calculated movement that made sure his suit didn't brush Kurt's arm. Kurt's eyebrows went up as he continued to hold Janet's gaze over Hardy's shoulder. Janet shrugged, not caring that Hardy saw her.

"Thank you, Janet." He stepped out of his loafers inside the door and lined them up neatly beside the shoes of other household members, but he couldn't resist a side-long glance at Janet to make sure she noticed that he was kowtowing to the rules of the house. She kept her face expressionless as he stepped into a pair of slippers and followed her down to the basement.

She didn't bother kicking her own slippers back on when she got to the bottom of the stairs. "Drink, Toby?"

"Coffee?" He looked doubtfully at her slivovitz. "A little early for the hard stuff."

"It's a little late, for me," she said, leaning back against the bar. *Coffee,* she told the house, and the house set about roasting and brewing. Kurt would bring it down when it was ready. She folded the letter closed, absently, and then folded it in half, and then tucked it into her jeans pocket, aware that Hardy was watching every move. "What warrants a clandestine predawn visit, Toby? You're not here to discuss Unitek's contributions to the Home Party."

"Sure about that?"

"As sure as I can be." She picked up her glass and downed half the pungent liquor in a gulp. It stung her sinuses and filled her mouth with the taste of overripe plums. She set the glass down and breathed in fire through pursed lips. "I don't know what you want me to do about the UN hearings. But whatever it is, the answer is no."

"I heard a rumor you were still in contact with the Chinese consulate in America. Unofficially, of course." His eyes dropped to the corner of thick, ivory paper that poked from her pocket.

"Which one of my staff members is on your payroll?"

"Now, what makes you think that, Janet?"

"Cold logic." She heard the door open at the top of the

basement stairs. The scent of coffee and the light, regular creak of footsteps followed it. A moment, and Kurt appeared at the landing, balancing a silver tray and the formal coffee service. *Not* the mismatched one that Janet had inherited from her grandmother, and which she kept for friends. A subtle vote of no confidence, but Kurt's level look into her eyes as he laid the tray on the bar counter was enough to reinforce it. "Are you going to New York, Toby?"

"Unitek was closely involved in the events of December 22, 2062," he said. He crossed the room as Kurt withdrew up the stairs, and poured his own coffee. A good guess; Janet hadn't been about to pour it for him.

Instead she cupped her glass in both hands and frowned down at it, considering. "You're going to testify."

"Alberta is in no position to—"

"—having died in the Chinese attack on Toronto."

"Died a martyr, and all that. Yes."

"Toby . . ."

"What?" He paused, porcelain at his thin, pink lips, looking at her through his eyelashes. It wasn't a flattering pose.

"You're going to hang Toronto on the prime minister, aren't you? You're maneuvering to put me in Constance's chair."

"Do you have a problem with that?" One of those eyebrows arched, and he sipped the coffee before he lowered the cup.

"That depends," she answered, and cracked the last sunflower seed between her teeth, and spit the shell into her hand. "What do you plan to do with me once you get me there?"

His smile left a puddle of cold in the pit of her belly. He didn't answer.

She finished her drink slowly and put the glass on the bar. "You know, Toby, if you're planning on buying somebody, it's good practice not to insult them while you're negotiating."

"That depends on how high a price you can afford to pay." He poured himself another cup of coffee and held it in his blunt hands. The light over the bar caught pink and green scatters off the diamond chips in his wedding ring.

Janet looked at the floor.

"If you're not willing to negotiate, General, we can always find somebody else who is."

"We?"

"Unitek," he said, his eyes sincere. But he said it just a shade too quickly, and she reached for the coffee and a fresh cup to hide how badly she needed to swallow, to moisten her mouth.

She sugared the coffee carefully and added just enough cream so that she could watch the pale ribbons curl through dark fluid. The folded letter in her pocket might have been printed on lead; she felt it press into her flesh. "We need to talk about Unitek," she said, calmly. "When we rebuild, back east—"

"When?"

"When." Firmly. "I'm prepared to work to see to it that there are advantageous arrangements available for any company willing to bring new industry to the Evac. Tax breaks and incentives. Especially if those companies are incorporated under Canadian law."

"You're ducking the subject, Janet."

"I'm not willing to betray my country as the price for your assistance, Toby."

"Janet." Palpable disappointment in his voice. "I would never suggest such a thing."

"No, you'd ask it outright." She sipped her coffee. She really wanted another glass of slivovitz, but Toby was right. It *was* a little early for drinking like a Brit. "Why don't you just ask me about the letter? It's written all over your face."

"It's a letter from General Shijie, isn't it?"

Fortunately, the coffee cup was still in front of her mouth. "How did you know that?" Ignoring the arch look of triumph on his face, and knowing she'd handed him the keys to the castle.

"It's my job to know things. He's offering you an alliance for space exploration, and alliance between PanChina and the commonwealth. Peace. Something Riel can't get for Canada, but you can, if he's head of the PanChinese Alliance."

"Yes." She set her cup down and leaned both hands against the edge of the bar. The wood was hard and waxy under her hands. She tightened her fingers hard enough to whiten her knuckles, and sighed. "With the understanding that the *current*—emphasis his—administrations will not be involved."

"You need me, Janet."

She did. She needed him badly, him and his money and his ability to sidestep oversight, and the resources of his vast, American-headquartered corporation. "What's it going to cost me?"

"I wouldn't worry overmuch." He smiled, turning his coffee cup with a fingertip, leaving a wet ring spiraling the top of the bar. "Nothing you're not prepared to pay."

•   •   •

Genie couldn't get used to the way Charlie had been acting kind of like one of the pilots since Aunt Jenny rescued him, staring into space and frowning a lot. And it was weird having Leslie talk out of the motes, but like he was in the room, not like he was conferenced in. The good news was, Papa didn't make her sit at the table and eat her scrambled soy protein and toast with a fork. Instead, she made a kind of sloppy sandwich out of the bread and yellow stuff and the gunk that wasn't anything like cheese, and went and sat on the floor under one of the hydroponics racks next to Boris while she ate.

Boris seemed happy to be out of Genie's quarters. He sprawled on his side over one of the air vents, showing his cream-colored belly and begging to be petted, or maybe begging for another taste of the stuff that wasn't cheese. He would eat anything, she'd discovered, including cooked broccoli and pasta, but he liked greasy things best.

Genie finished her sandwich, giving a last few crumbs to the cat, and scratched behind his ears as he sniffed politely after the food. He flattened his whiskers against his ginger-striped cheeks. She drew her knees up and folded her hands under her chin, and practiced being invisible.

She scrunched herself up a little tighter and kept her eyes down, watching the tip of Boris's tail twitch thoughtfully as he slitted his eyes at a black-and-blue butterfly. At least there were advantages to being invisible. She was pretty sure that the grown-ups had forgotten all about her, even Papa, because they were talking about all kinds of interesting things, and they were the sort of interesting things that people usually wouldn't talk about if they remembered she was listening.

For example, Charlie was saying to Papa right now,

"...this is on the list of things I'm not supposed to tell anyone, Gabe——"

"According to whom? I'm on the contact team, after all. We're all supposed to have the same clearances." Papa leaned against one of the sturdy lab tables, his coffee cup vanishing inside his hand.

"This isn't to do with the contact team." Leslie said it, not Charlie, but Genie looked up and saw the way Charlie's face seemed to reflect the emotion in Leslie's voice. *Creepy.*

"It's not any creepier than you talking to me," Richard said, and Genie bit her lip.

I can't help it if it bothers me, can I?

"Sure you can. You're smart enough to know that you can decide what bothers you, and decide what you think is good or bad, instead of just reacting."

Papa hadn't stopped talking. "If it's not contact stuff, why is it so secret?"

"Because it's nanite 'stuff,' " Charlie answered. "Which is why we think we need your help."

Boris, annoyed at her neglect, reached out and grabbed Genie's soft foam ship-shoe. His claws went through it, even though he didn't mean her any harm. She would have yelped, but she was invisible, and if she made any sound, somebody might notice her. Instead she reached down and roughed up the fur under his chin. He stretched back out again, relaxing. She hoped he wouldn't purr too loudly.

Papa set his coffee cup down, but not before he finished whatever was left in the bottom. "Richard?"

"Right here, Gabriel."

"Is what they're about to tell me likely to reconvince

me that we need to go over our operating systems for trap doors?"

"Actually," Richard answered, "I think it will convince you that you want to try to reprogram the tech from scratch. On the other hand, the risks involved in that—"

"Like Jenny's life, you mean? And my daughter's?"

Silence. Genie bit her lip. He'd definitely forgotten she was there. Genie shivered. Her butt was getting numb from sitting on the air register, but this was interesting.

"And mine," Richard said. "Although none of the nanotech that I inhabit appears to have problems yet, I am concerned."

"Putain de ordinateur. Richard. *Problems*?"

"Forgive me, Gabriel. Before the EVA, Charlie discovered that the . . . nanotech in the ecospheres was dropping out of its networks for an unexplained reason. Or reasons. At first we thought they were dying, but further experimentation has led us to believe they're just . . . losing communication with each other."

"And this is ongoing?"

"In patches. Or batches. They'll just stall."

Papa sighed and looked around for his coffee cup. Charlie gave it back to him, refilled. "I hope you have a good reason why I wasn't informed of this, Dick."

Leslie "coughed." "Prime Minister Riel swore us to secrecy."

"So you're making me a party to treason?"

"Yes. Well, it's not treason for me; it's just espionage. But since the rest of you are Canadians—"

"Okay," Papa said, looking down at his hands. "Spare me the hairsplitting. And you want me to find out who's hacking the machines and disabling them, and how, and why?"

"Your reputation for perspicacity," Richard said, "is not exaggerated, Mr. Castaign." Genie could hear the amusement in his voice. Papa obviously could, too, from the way he rolled his eyes.

Richard, I shouldn't be here for this.

"Genie, I think you're more than grown up enough to understand this conversation, and why it's important, and has to be secret. Don't you?"

"I think the whole team should know about this," Papa said.

"Jeremy already does," Leslie answered.

"Then Ellie needs to be brought in."

"All right. What about Paul?"

Richard chuckled, a dry, almost mechanical sound. "I expect, somehow, that Dr. Perry would be just as happy not knowing about this little contretemps. I should hate, after all, to force him to choose between his loyalty to Constance, and to Canada."

Premier Xiong looked thinner in the space of a very few days, Riel thought, contemplating his image floating over her desk for a precious few seconds as she collected her thoughts. Not short days, though; abrogating cliché, the days had been as long as any she cared to remember. And they didn't promise to get any shorter in the near future.

When we're finished saving the world, she thought, *I'm going on a nice long trip someplace warm, changing my name, and buying a pineapple plantation. Or maybe sugar cane. And then I'm going to let the whole damned place go to seed, and sit on the front porch and play poker and drink daiquiris until my eyes cross.*

Her eyes wanted to cross now, or at least to fuzz with exhaustion. She hoped her cosmetics were up to the task of making her look like a functioning human being, because she didn't feel like one. "Premier," she said, and kicked her shoes off under the desk. "To what do I owe the pleasure of your call?"

"You have an . . . interesting concept of 'pleasure' in Canada, Prime Minister." He let his eyes sparkle, as if he were flirting with her. One of the contradictions of the modern age; even the leaders of totalitarian states needed to be able to wield charm with natural grace and confidence.

"I think I can be forgiven for finding you more entertaining than next year's fiscal realities." She passed a hand across her interface plate, summoning coffee. "I don't think you'd be calling me on the secure hot line unless you had something too important to trust to diplomatic channels."

"I don't think either of us can afford to trust much to diplomatic channels at this juncture. Unless your political position is considerably more secure than my own. Or than I have been led to believe."

"I do have a few trustworthy advisers," she answered, letting the wryness show in her voice. She could not afford to like this man, any more than he could afford to like her—but neither one of them would be in the position they were in if they weren't good at getting people to like them, to trust them, to confide. The irony and symmetry pleased her, and she smiled.

He returned it. "General Shijie has made arrangements to travel to New York City next week, to testify."

"When I will be there."

"And the chief executive officer of Unitek."

"Tobias Hardy, surprise witness? That is an interesting piece of intelligence, Premier. I suppose it would be useless of me to ask how you happened to come by it?"

Xiong coughed against the back of his hand. "Through official channels."

Oh. Meaning that somebody in the Chinese government tipped somebody at the UN that he ought to be called as a witness. "You're asking me to put a good deal of faith in your channels, Premier. Without a complete understanding of why your government is so eager to offer assistance to mine."

"You'll be even more confused when I tell you that I have information that your Opposition will be moving for new elections after the hearings."

"Forgive my suspicion, Premier, but that would tend to indicate that you expect the hearings to come out rather well for PanChina. And you do not seem to be a man given to gloating over the corpses of your enemies."

"How little you know me." But his eyebrows had climbed another quarter-inch up his unlined forehead.

Riel glanced up as a rap announced the imminent opening of her door. She caught a glimpse of a red Mountie's jacket outside the doorway as her secretary came in with the coffee, and privacied the hologram over her desk. Premier Xiong could still see her and the office, and she could hear him through her ear clip, but the image over her interface plate dissolved into a wash of soothing blues and greens.

He stayed silent. Once she had her coffee, Riel returned the interface to view mode. She wasn't fond of talking to images projected on her contact. "My apologies, Premier."

"Not at all."

"You were explaining to me how it is that you know more about the doings of my government than I do."

"Simple," he said. "It's in my very strong interest to be apprised of the 'doings' of Minister of War Shijie Shu. And his 'doings' are more or less closely linked to the machinations of your enemies within Canada. I'll be sending you more details by secure packet. I trust you have people who can manufacture a provenance for them, so you may have them ready when the time comes to expose the duplicity of your opposition?"

Fred, she said, and allowed herself a small, tight, bitter smile over the irony that, after all of it, he was the one she trusted to watch her back. What was the word he'd used to describe Casey, way back when?

Oh, yeah.

Patriot.

"Yes," she said, and pulled the coffee tray toward her, not caring that the felt dragged on the crystal of the interface plate. *What the hell. This is as secure a line as I can get.* "If you can get me documents that prove that Hardy and Frye and their friends are in collusion with your General Shijie, then I can provide the scandal you need to prove that last year's attack against Canada was fostered by insurgent elements in your government, and we can shake hands and part friends."

"Well. If we're speaking as plainly as that, let me stipulate: once the *Huang Di* and her crew are returned to PanChinese control, and we've come to an agreement regarding the partition of the world at HD 210277."

"Technically speaking, it's a moon, not a world. And we're assuming it's habitable."

"I have to assume it's habitable, Constance. I have ten thousand colonists underway to it on generation ships, and I can't allow them to arrive at a destination that's entirely under Canadian control. I think you are a reasonable woman. I think we can come to an agreement. One that will reflect well on Canada's international reputation for generosity and humanitarianism."

I'm not sure we have one of those anymore, Riel thought, but she smiled. "Wen-xian, will you attend the UN hearings?"

He didn't answer, but his silent smile was confirmation.

The first thing that happens when we enter the planet's telesphere is that my damned hip unit warbles in my ear clip, warning me of saved messages. Of course, it's not as though I haven't checked my e-mail from the *Montreal,* through the microwave relays, but apparently *somebody* thought he had something hush-hush enough to say that he wouldn't risk his mail being forwarded to a military server.

I remember the good old days, when the recipient got to decide where her fucking e-mail went. Some of it's flagged spam, but one piece is an unnamed message that has a good-friends filter override code on it that only Gabe and a few other people have. And most of those people are dead.

It's probably a virus.

I click on it anyway.

And don't notice I've stopped breathing until I'm dizzy enough that I have to grab the back of the acceleration couch I so recently claimed as my bed. Because the broad-cheeked, black-eyed, steel-toothed face that grins at me knocks the breath out of me like a punch in the solar plexus.

Razorface.

He was in Metro Toronto when the rock hit. I know he was, because I tried to get him to go the hell home to Connecticut, and he stayed around to try to coerce some sort of cooperation out of a Unitek vice president named Alberta Holmes, who was holding Fred's leash at the time.

I can't even begin to justify the idea that he might have made it out.

And then I calm down enough to inspect the e-mail before I trigger it, and I see the date stamp. It's December 22, 2062. I have to bite my lip until I taste metal and salt and sit down and roll my head back against the rest on the acceleration couch and breathe. Long and slow and rhythmically. Breathe, Jenny. Breathe. Even though you're hurtling toward Malaysia, braking at something less than a G, and about to open an e-mail from somebody who died almost a year ago.

It's a message from the grave. From the ghost of a kid who might as well have been my own. If my own were a gangster, a killer, and a petty warlord.

But blood's thicker than water, right? And I shed a little for Razorface. And Face shed a little for me, once upon a time.

I extricate my tongue from in between my teeth, the tweed of the capsule seat catching on the ass of my uniform pants, and I key the mail open.

And find myself staring not into Razorface's dark brown eyes while his mobile lips shape words around the sibilants that hiss between his pointed teeth, but at a series of images of documents, obviously snapped hastily, probably—judging by the distortion—through some-body's contact optic. There might be a dozen of them. I don't have time to examine them the way I'd like to, and whatever they are, they don't make a lick of sense to me, because every last one of the damned things is in Chinese or something that looks just like it.

These weren't Face's. Because as many times as I offered to teach him, Razorface never learned to read. In any language.

The images have to come from my enemy, my ally, the niece of my long-dead lover, Indigo Xu. And they've been here, lying in the Net, waiting for me. Waiting nearly a year, for me to set foot on Earth again.

Face's recorded voice calls me by a name I haven't heard in a year. "Maker," he says. "We grabbed that Holmes chick. We're gonna hole up until we decide what to do with her. But Indigo found these on her when we grabbed her, and she says you need to see this. It's Chinese but she can't read it. She says it's coded, but I figure with the friends you got you can crack it.

"One other thing. Holmes looked like she was about to skip town when we snagged her. She had a suitcase and a wad of cash chits, a lot even for a rich bitch like her. You be careful up there, all right?" And then he grins at me, showing me all that serrated silver, and cocks his head arrogantly, cock of the walk. "You be careful up there, girl."

Sweet Mary, Mother of God. It takes me awhile to organize my thoughts beyond that. I swallow and look down. *You be careful "up there," too, Razorface. You just be as careful as you can.*

Richard, I say inside my head, shuffling the images in front of my inner eye for long enough to see if any of them contain so much as a word of English, *Dick. Can you hear me?*

"Loud and clear, Jen."

I really, really, really need your help.

Min-xue's nervousness didn't betray itself in a shaking hand, although his palms were sweating. His face was impassive, his emotions carefully sealed away, and if the palms of his hands were slick with sweat, no one would ever know.

What gave him away was that he was talking to Richard in Cantonese, because he couldn't think of the words he wanted in English. Which made it difficult to talk to Jen or to Patty, seated across the aisle in the luxury of the Canadian wide-bodied jet that was descending, ear-poppingly, toward New York. The pilot had swung wide over the Atlantic and they were still high enough to see what Richard said was the shoreline of Connecticut and Long Island Sound; the pilot was giving them the view.

There was plenty to look at. Filtered sunlight fractured on the waters of the Atlantic, a sparkle eased by polarized glass. Min-xue squinted anyway, unlacing one hand to shade his eyes. He understood that the entire downtown area of New York City had been an island within living memory, in much the manner of Hong Kong. Now, Richard supplied the names for the geographic features he was looking at, and images of what it had looked like before, for the sake of comparison. Dikes and landfill bulwarked large portions of what had been New York Harbor, and what had once been called the East River had been pumped dry. New York Harbor itself was enclosed by a ponderous seawall and a series of locks that allowed ships to move from the higher waters of the Atlantic into the ancient port. Richard said the harbor was largely fresh now, from the outflow of the Hudson River. The seaward ends of the narrow bands of water that separated Long Island and Staten Island from the mainland had been sealed up, and the seaward faces of the islands protected by more dikes and seawalls.

The bobbing shapes of tidal generators dotted the waters of the Atlantic outside the seawall. "Those power the pumping stations that keep the groundwater down inside the dike. Manhattan's on schist—it's bedrock, but Long Island is a glacial moraine. Soft."

Don't the foundations crack?

"It's a screaming mess down there—"

Min-xue felt an extended lecture coming on, and scrambled for a better question. *Where's the Statue of Liberty?*

"It's inside the harbor," Richard said. "You'll need to go to the other side of the plane."

It should be farther out at sea, Min-xue argued, but he got up and walked across the aisle, to where Jen and Patty were pointing and saying soft, appreciative things.

"Then nobody on land could see it."

Which was eminently reasonable, but it still disappointed Min-xue somehow that the only waves that lapped the base of the lady with the torch were the wakes of ferries and departing container ships. *Foolish romantic.*

"If you need romance," Richard said, his eyebrows wiggling in amusement, "you could consider that the New York Dike is the largest single engineering project in the history of the world, or so they say."

In terms of earth moved, I wager the Great Wall was bigger.

Richard chuckled. "Nationalistic pride?"

I am Taiwanese, Richard.

"Somewhat."

Which earned him a wry twist of the mouth from Min-xue, but no further comment.

"Can you at least let me tell you about the floating air-port?"

Dick. Patty leaned close enough to Min-xue that he could feel the heat of her body through his jumpsuit. She knew better than to touch him, of course. He gave her a flickering smile, much shyer than he had intended, and looked away quickly. Richard cleared his throat, lounging against the walls of Min-xue's mind with his angular arms folded and his hands, for once, still. "Have you thought about the message I asked you to take to Captain Wu, Min-xue?"

Is it not enough for you that I betray China, Dick? Must I betray Canada, too?

"You could think of it as serving both of them."

He could. It wouldn't even be—entirely—self-deception. *But how will Captain Wu think of it?*

"As an opportunity to redeem himself before his premier?"

You are a very manipulative entity, Richard.

"How can I be?" Richard smirked, and unfolded his arms, turning his palms skyward. "I haven't got any hands."

The plane dropped lower. Min-xue returned to his seat to be certain he had his sunglasses in his pocket for when he had to brave the fluorescent lights in the terminal.

General Valens—security in tow—met them after their passports and paperwork cleared them through customs.

It was an unearned honor, in Min-xue's estimation—but not an unexpected one. Especially when the general—already drawing a certain amount of attention in a full dress uniform that was obviously not that of any branch of the U.S. military—scooped up his granddaughter and swung her around until her hair and feet flew out behind her. Patty started laughing when her shoes left the floor. Min-xue had never heard her laugh like that before, like a child, unself-conscious, with abandon. He averted his gaze behind his sunglasses, all too conscious of how he was staring, and found himself abruptly eye-to-eye with Jen Casey.

They stared at one another for a second, until she cleared her throat and glanced down. He didn't need Richard to tell him what she was thinking—that it could have been her, swinging Leah Castaign around like that. Or that she loathed herself for the thought as soon as it occurred.

Not for the last time, Min-xue thought he would have liked to have known Leah.

If nothing else, so he could mourn her properly. "She ought to have a statue," he said under his breath, in English, a sort of peace offering, and saw Jen's eye quirk upward.

"They all should," she said, and turned away just as the general set Patricia down.

Valens straightened and settled back on his heels and finally looked at Jen. Around the terminal, travelers were stopped, taking in the spectacle of two old soldiers sizing each other up, standing in the middle of Metro New York William Francis Gibb Memorial Airport, accompanied by two strikingly unrelated teenagers. Min-xue stole a glance downward. Jen was wearing white cotton gloves on both hands, not just the left one.

Valens smiled at Jen and at Min-xue. "Well," he said, quietly. "I'm glad you both made the trip. Once we've survived the ferry ride into the city, would you care to share my limousine to the embassy?"

"And then confer with Captain Wu, sir?"

"Actually—" Valens led them toward the ferry dock. Their luggage, what little they had, would be delivered. Another privilege that came with the Canadian government jet and the annotated passports. "He's waiting in the limousine. Although my Mandarin wasn't sufficient to give him a very good idea of who is arriving, or what to expect."

Aboard, Min-xue leaned against the forward rail of the ferry. Port cities the world over smelled the same; combustion and garbage and the rotten tang of tide pools. He breathed deeply, closing his eyes, and imagined himself home in Taiwan.

The others came to collect him as the ferry glided into dock. He touched his breast pocket, making sure the facsimiles of the papers that Jen had given him were still there.

The limousine wasn't all that long, and it was a quiet, staid pearl gray. The doors slid into the frame with barely a whisper. Valens stepped aside with an actor's sense of timing, allowing the man in the back seat a long clear view of Min-xue as Min-xue ducked his head and stepped in.

To his credit, Captain Wu only blinked, and edged over on the seat to make room for Min-xue. He did make a small show of studying Min-xue's *Montreal* jumpsuit, however, and clucked his tongue. "Second Pilot," he said, in Mandarin. "I am ashamed."

"Before you declare your shame, Captain," Min-xue answered, in the same language, as he pulled the papers out of his pocket, "can you please tell me whether you have seen these code sheets before?" He handed them over, keeping his voice low and his body language meek as the three Canadians arranged themselves.

Captain Wu studied each of the sheets carefully. His throat worked. Min-xue laid a fingertip on Captain Wu's knee, knowing that the captain would see it for the concession it was, coming from a pilot.

"I have seen them," the captain of the *Huang Di* said.

"Where have you seen them, Captain?"

"Second Pilot, before I answer that, you will tell me where you obtained these."

"They were your orders to retrieve the asteroid and destroy Toronto, Captain. Were they not?"

"You will answer my question." Captain Wu sat back, the offending papers dropping from his fingers to scatter on the carpet.

"Under the pearly moon in the endless sea, pearls weep," Min-xue quoted, tilting his head. "On Lan-t'ien Mountain, jade breeds smoke in warm sun. / This passion might be a thing to be remembered / Only you were already bewildered and lost."

"Will you believe I regret it, Min-xue?"

"They came from the person of a Canadian citizen, Captain. A Unitek vice president. One closely involved in the starship program. Before the orders were carried out. She could only have received them from somebody in China. There was a conspiracy. Treason on both sides. And tens of millions died."

The captain blinked. Min-xue heard Jen shut the door behind him, her prosthetic hand clicking on the handle despite her cotton glove, and smiled. The general might be chivalrous, but not so chivalrous as to forget that one of the women he was squiring was also a noncom.

"Yes," Captain Wu said. "Those were my orders."

"From whose hand were they sealed, Captain?"

"The minister of war, Shijie Shu," he said, all on a breath, and rocked his head back against the headrest, closing his eyes.

"Will you testify to that before the United Nations, Captain?" Valens leaned in, his Mandarin ungrammatical.

Captain Wu looked at Min-xue. Min-xue bit his cheek until he tasted copper and nodded. Captain Wu dropped his eyes to the papers scattered like so many peach blossoms about his feet, and then to his own folded hands, and sighed.

Min-xue looked up at Valens, and swallowed bitterness. And in English he said, "Yes. General, he will testify."

The instant I'm back on Canadian soil, I feel different. Even a patch of Canadian soil a few dozen yards square, squatting on the eastern edge of America. I'm sure it's psychosomatic, but I feel my shoulders straighten, the wreathed crowns on my epaulets shining a little brighter in the wan autumn morning.

A sugar maple planted inside the elaborate and very functional-looking front gate of the embassy catches my attention, and even if it's snow-laced and bare with the unholy winter, the familiar fractal pattern of those elegant branches soothes me. I wish it were any other

October, and the glossy leaves just starting to burn umber and vermilion.

I left Nell's eagle feather on the *Montreal*. I didn't want to deal with customs and endangered species acts and trying to prove my tribal affiliation and the ten thousand other things that would go wrong. Still, I press my hand against the breast pocket where it would normally be. Even if I don't have the feather, or Nell, or Leah, I can still feel the ghosts gathered around me like ancestors in reverse, where the children die and old warhorses get older in their place.

Surreptitiously, I drag my fingertip over the trunk of the maple tree, just to feel its life. Rough and silky bark snags my glove; I tug it free quickly, hoping no one has noticed.

There's a real live doorman to open the doors for us. He has white spats, and white gloves that are cleaner than mine. I don't think I've ever seen such a thing. As I take my cover off, I'm homesick enough to think the air inside smells of Canada, too. If I don't quite look at them straight, I can almost imagine that the snowy branches behind the panoramic windows of the lobby are old-growth forest rather than well-clipped hemlock. I swear to God I can smell the pine.

Hah. It's probably the floor polish. *Come on, Jenny. Get your head out of your ass. Tomorrow we go to war. And try to make sure those kids didn't die for nothing.*

It's a prayer, and I know it's a prayer, and I still can't quite bring myself to say, *Amen.*

Charlie hadn't gotten used to not being alone in his own head—hell, in his own *body*—yet. *Because getting kidnapped and genetically engineered by aliens is the sort of thing you should process and move past in a week or two at the outside, really.*

He felt Leslie's approval at his sarcasm, and the internal quirk of Richard's humor that would have been a raised eyebrow or a twitched lip if they were simply three men sitting around a conference table, rather than sharing some bizarre brain space including bits and pieces of all three of them, but not *all* of any, and the undercurrent of alien presences—waiting, observing, straining as hard toward them as they strained back.

We have nothing in common, Charlie thought. He leaned back in his chair, in his lab, among the dying ecospheres and the hydroponics tanks, and swung his feet onto the lab bench. *Not even a sensorium.*

Richard would relay the inaudible parts of the conversation to Jeremy and Elspeth. The ethnolinguist and the psychiatrist were in-wheel, in the work space they had shared with Leslie, modeling symbol structures or something Charlie didn't really understand. Charlie and Leslie could hear and feel everything that occurred in the room through Richard, and Richard would relay his own comments over the interior speakers, so it didn't matter if they were all in the same room or not, and he did his best thinking up here with the soybeans.

We apparently share a powerful desire to talk to one

another, Leslie answered. *That's more than my ex-wife and I had in common.*

The most interesting part of their connection was that, while he didn't have Leslie's skills or his years of experience in just how language and communication worked, he *could* feel the model that Leslie and Jeremy were building with regard to communication with the aliens. Currently, it looked a great deal like a map. It was a map; a map of *something* drawn in terms of beings that sensed the architecture of space-time rather than the electromagnetic spectrum.

It would be extraordinarily useful, Charlie judged, once they got the chance to take the *Montreal* and the *Vancouver* out on a real spin, and overlay this map with what Richard and the pilots could learn about the *feel* of the local gravity wells—*For crying out loud, Leslie. You realize we don't even have a language with which to discuss this stuff, let alone a symbology with which to talk to the birdcages about it?*—they might be able to lay their own visible-light and X-ray map over the alien one.

By the way, we've got the lab results back. I've got to say, these guys really put the xeno into xenobiology. Except what he gave Leslie and Richard wasn't exactly words, but more a concentrated lump of his own experience and the test results and what it all might mean, or might not mean, without the ambiguities of language. For Jeremy and Elspeth's sake, he summarized: *They're hydrogen based. What we call metallic colloidal hydrogen, probably supercompressed in their home environment. Something like the rocky core of a gas giant.*

Elspeth had her back to the corner, her arms folded over her breasts, just listening. Almost nothing went over her head, but she usually stayed very quiet when the rest of the team was talking about subjects unrelated to her own specialty. Charlie suspected her thought process was keyed to intuition, and her long silences were her way of encouraging the penny to drop.

Leslie's thought, startlingly clear and tight for someone who was wrapped in a bubble of metallic colloidal hydrogen, kilometers away in the cold of space: *You can have a hydrogen-based life form?*

Leslie, Richard said, *apparently you can make a life form out of anything, as long as it has the power to conduct and regulate piezoelectricity.*

Exactly, Charlie agreed. *Don't ask me what keeps them from evaporating out here, though, or just . . . discombobulating. Or—and here's the kicker—how the hell it got that way. The weird part is that that means there's some process by which little informational and structural heterogeneities can arise and persist at pressures that smoosh hydrogen itself down to liquid. That's just* wild.

Richard gave a scientist's chuckle, the sort that is usually preceded by the phrase "it is intuitively obvious." *Charlie. You have a creature whose sensory system and technology seem to be predicated on perceiving and manipulating gravity.*

He set the coffee cup down, sat back in his chair, and folded his hands behind his head. *That would tend to indicate that they're the original source of the nanotech, since we know the shiptree uses . . . visible light. For something.* His palms were sweating again, and he resolutely ignored it. If he got too nervous Richard would adjust his biochemistry. He hated relying on that. This was his life, a change that had been wrought on him, as randomly and unfairly as if he had lost a limb.

As long as he thought of it that way, and held up for himself the example of Jen Casey—her steel hand winking with machined precision and her absolute refusal to accept pity or, it seemed, to acknowledge even to herself that she had lost anything at all—he could hold it together. *Thank you for not actually laughing at me, Dick.*

The AI grinned in his head. *No sweat.*

In the other work space, Jeremy looked up from his interface. Charlie experienced the rearrangement of Leslie's attention as the xenosemiotician used the lab motes to follow his old schoolmate's gaze. It wasn't that different from inhabiting somebody else's body along with his own in a VR suit—the ghostly sense of limbs was identical, except it was his own body he felt slightly attenuated from, and the one he cohabited with that floated as if in a sense-dep tank.

Jeremy cleared his throat. "So now that we know what they're made of and how they experience their environment, how do we develop a symbolic system so we can move information?"

Leslie nodded. *And I ask on my own, when do we get started on the shiptrees?*

Well, we could always send an EVA team over there, too, and infect their nanites with our nanites. Give them one of our scientists. After all, fair's fair.

Bring a camera, Richard said. Charlie laughed, because of course Richard could record everything that he saw.

Wow, he said. *Somebody write the date down. You realize that we've just witnessed the death of an ancient concept. Privacy.*

Oh, I don't know, Richard answered. *We can wall each other out more or less effectively. And if you squint at it from the right angle, you already have a bunch of individual consciousnesses inhabiting your head. Freud's id and ego and superego and so forth, or, if you prefer, Jung's "collective unconsciousness" or the left brain and the right brain and the—*

"Modular-mind theory, more like," Elspeth corrected. And then said, "Christ, Dick."

Elspeth? What?

She straightened, her hands swinging as she stepped away from the wall and started to pace like a professor lecturing a class. "I think you just got yourself that second Nobel Prize, sir. You're absolutely correct. We have got a whole bunch of animals living in our heads already. Alien animals, animals that don't really communicate all that well. You ever hear about the experiments where somebody whose corpus callosum had been severed could be taught completely different things on each side of his brain, and couldn't articulate them to himself?"

Now that I pause to look it up.

"Well, your right brain and your left brain—well, not yours, Richard. You're a special case, of course. But say, Jeremy's, here—"

Jeremy laughed first, and swatted her mocking hand out of his hair. "I've known you not even a month, Elspeth, and already you take liberties with my person."

She squeezed his shoulder before she stepped away. She folded her hands in front of her again, instead, leaned against the back of a swivel chair, and cleared her throat. "Essentially, the nonverbal side of the brain will resort to hand gestures and drawing images to get its message to the verbal brain. In extreme cases, the left hand will even grab and redirect the right hand when the left brain is about to make a mistake and the right brain knows it. But my point is, the hemispheres don't talk the same language on their best day. They communicate in terms of symbols and emotions and sometimes dreams or uneasy sensations or . . . hunches, for lack of a better term. Which is why so much of any therapist's work is interpreting between the subconscious and the conscious mind, and teaching them to understand each other, and that greedy little reptile in the back of all of our heads, as well."

Charlie found himself standing, grinning until his cheeks hurt, his hands tight on the edge of the lab bench. *So you're saying we need a therapist, Elspeth?*

They were all under tremendous stress, and his timing had been better than usual. When the hysterics dwindled into subdued coughing, Elspeth wiped her eyes on the back of her wrist and said, "In that analogy, I think we are the therapist. Or maybe the corpus callosum. In any case, I think we're halfway there." Which was bad enough that even Richard groaned. "Leslie, are you getting this? Are you following me?"

You want me to try . . . Oh. Elspeth, Dick. Can you talk to Jenny and see if she can pass along an impression of what space feels like through the Benefactor stardrive?

"You want to see if it matches up with what you feel from the birdcages."

I want to see if it's the same melody. Charlie had a distinct sense of Leslie grinning. Charlie shoved his hands into the pockets of his lab coat and for a moment couldn't remember whose gesture that had been, originally, Leslie's or his own. Which would have turned the faint seasick unease in his stomach into full-fledged nausea, if he'd been willing to let it.

You're in denial, Charlie. Your whole life has changed.

And of course he knew Leslie felt the thought, and felt Leslie's warm assurance back through their shared thought process. There was nothing like finding yourself irrevocably mentally *welded* to another middle-aged man, and one with a quite different set of biases and assumptions, to trigger a thoroughly miserable midlife crisis. Even if your counterpart weren't—

A very small spaceship.

Yes, that. Charlie wondered if Canada would buy him a little red sports car, if he asked extra nicely. As partial compensation for giving away half of his brain.

And I said to myself, self—

There's no guarantee it is irrevocable, Charlie. Richard's voice, and his unique understanding of what it was like to share a mind with other consciousnesses, was soothing. *When we get Leslie back—*

If you get Leslie back, Leslie said.

There is no if.

Charlie knew Richard was using the nanotech to regulate hormone and endorphin and adrenaline levels, to keep him calm and sane and rational. It was probably the only reason he *or* Leslie was coherent, rather than enlivening a rubber room planet-side. Or, in Leslie's case, floating between the stars glibbering and meeping like the protagonist of a Lovecraft story. That, and Leslie's strange determination that this was all an adventure, and that he had nothing to lose, and everything to gain.

He chuckled as Leslie's amusement welled up his throat.

I'm culturally programmed to a certain amount of comfort with otherspace, Leslie said. *Being ungrounded from my body isn't quite the shock it might be to you.*

I should have known you'd jump at the opportunity to flaunt your racial superiority, Charlie answered, and Leslie laughed inside his head. The sarcasm *was* a defense, and he knew Leslie knew it. Still, he felt the chuckle and smiled himself, sharing the response. Because—on the other hand—when Charlie forgot to panic, the sensation of never quite being alone was strangely easy to get used to, and maybe even a little comforting.

"Charlie?" Elspeth's voice, distracting him—or drawing him back from distraction. "Try to stay with us, eh?" The motes showed the sidelong glance Jeremy gave her, and the way he rubbed one hand through his hair and then across his mouth, infinitely tired for the moment when her attention was turned away. Jeremy swallowed and swiveled his chair to stare out the porthole, only vaguely in the direction of the birdcage. A frown tugged the corners of his lips down. Charlie never would have understood the expression if he hadn't felt Leslie's discomfort like the itch of a peeling sunburn. *He's worried about you, Leslie.*

Leslie shrugged the comment aside. *He always worried too much about me. Mind if I use your vocal cords for a tick? The motes annoy me.*

Help yourself.

"Bob's your uncle. So what do we do next?"

"We talk to the captain about another EVA, I guess," Elspeth said, and shook her head sadly through the resulting laughter.

On Monday morning, I testify.

It's so much like the last time that the face I see in the walnut-framed mirror over my bureau shocks me when I glance into it. I expect the glossy black hair of a child in her third decade, the furrowed, meat-colored scars of fresh burns turning the left side of her face into a Halloween mask. As if the intervening twenty-six years don't exist. As if, when I go downstairs with Frederick Valens to get into the official car that will deliver us to the site of the hearing, it will be *Corporal* Casey and *Captain* Valens, and it will be a simple court-martial that I am to testify before, rather than the assembled eyes of the world.

The problems get bigger and bigger. But the level of nausea in my gut remains the same.

That's growth of a sort, I suppose.

I look down to adjust the shining buttons in the cuffs of my professionally pressed dress uniform. The blue steel of my left hand contrasts the deep, mellow richness of the gold. There are no scars on my face anymore, just a mottled patch that doesn't tan evenly, and my hair will be white in another three or four years. And the steel armature on my left side is light and silent and moves like my own hand and wrist, rather than like a clattering horror of an obsolete machine. And it's beautiful, too: a smooth, graceful design.

I clench my long steel fingers into a fist, and feel them press the heel of my metal hand, and close my eyes.

Bernard told me to change the world for him. *After* I took the stand and said the words that killed him.

I really wonder that I don't feel more irony—more anything—at the fact that it's not going to be my testimony that makes the difference today, this week, this month, but rather the testimony—from beyond the grave—of his niece, Indigo. Who once tried very, very hard to murder me.

I open my eyes. I open my hand. I point my forefinger at the mirror, cock my thumb, and say "bang" under my breath. And then I check the lie of my uniform one more time, pick my cover up off the dresser, flick my thumbs along the brim to make sure it's sitting right, and go downstairs to meet Fred Valens and my fate.

I suppose it's equal parts gift and torture that I'm the first witness. I mean, I've never seen the United Nations before, despite twenty years spent wearing its goddamned baby blue hats, and I'd like the time to look around and get a feel for the place. My overwhelming impression, as the car pulls into the drive, is a confused riot of flags like children shouting for attention, lined up snapping in a breath-frosting wind, below a teal glass curtain wall. The driver gets out to open the door. I stand, and then I stop, looking up, long enough for Fred to clear his throat heavily.

Fat flakes drift from a dirty slate-colored sky and my boots crunch snow in the gutter as I move forward. It's not a big building—especially in comparison to its neighbors, enormous apartments that dwarf it—but the severe hundred-year-old slab shape reminds me of a tombstone.

The old building is a little streaked and shabby around the edges, and I can see where the panes have been replaced by less mottled ones. They don't quite match the facade. The marble on the narrow sides is soot stained and showing erosion on what should be fine edges, and the fluid lines of the long concrete Assembly building spilling away from the teal blue high-rise look a little weary, too.

It looks worked hard, that structure.

And yet it's difficult to walk forward into. The damned thing looks *heavy*. And it might not be all *that* big, but it's a damned sight bigger than I am.

Escorts take charge of us at the doors, however, and once we step inside my whole impression changes. The broad lobby is airy and bright, the worn silver-and-white marble floors polished until they glow like jade. Mostly I regret the display cases that Fred and I are hustled past too fast for me to get a really good look inside. There's a Moon rock and a Mars rock and a chunk of asteroid and another chunk of one of Saturn's rings, I see that much, and a long display on a destroyed city whose flat, motionless gray photos mark it as something from another era, almost another world. Dresden or Hiroshima, maybe. Mumbai's footage would be in color, if there is a display for Mumbai.

I wonder how long it will be before Toronto is memorialized.

There's a hush about the place, the taste of serious business under way. A woman in a sari hurries through as we cross the lobby, a bindi gleaming red between her brows. She catches my eye as we pass, notices the steel hand, and does a visible double take. Her stride never slackens, but I turn my head, pretending for a minute that

I'm not in uniform, and I see her staring over her shoulder as she walks away from us, twisting from the hips to get a better view.

Nice to have a place to go where everybody knows your name.

A young man in hanbok—a dark embroidered jacket and flowing, flame-colored trousers—hurries toward us, his feet scuffing on the marble. A little puddle of melting snow drips from the sole of one of my boots, although I stomped them before I came inside. Valens, of course, looks like he was delivered fresh via teleporter. I tighten my arm against my side so I don't drop my cover in the mud puddle I'm making while I greet our new friend. He's got very dark, very bright eyes, and something faceted winks near the edge of the iris of the left one—a hypoallergenic implant under the clear surface of the cornea, a platinum bauble shaped like a stylized rocket ship. Genie says they're all the rage this year.

Valens's amusement is palpable when the young man stops in front of me, rather than him, and makes a little formal gesture. "Master Warrant Officer Genevieve Casey?"

He has an accent smooth as the silk of his jacket, and I could listen to him say my name all day. "I am. And this is Brigadier General Frederick Valens."

He offers Fred his hand and Fred takes it, giving me a look over our guide's head that's both charmed and bemused. I half get the feeling he's enjoying being snubbed. "I am Dongsik Jung. I will be your escort—"

"I'm pleased to meet you, Mr. Dongsik—"

"Mr. Jung," he says, and winks at my transparent blush. "Master Warrant Officer, it's an honor to make your acquaintance. And you, Brigadier General, a very great honor as well." He steps back, looking from one of us to the other, and lifts an eyebrow at each. "Have you been to the United Nations before?"

"Never," Fred says, shrugging out of his overcoat.

"Wonderful," Mr. Jung says, turning neatly on the ball of his foot and falling into step between and a few steps in front of us. Even if he fell back, I could still see Valens over the top of his head. "We just have time for a little tour before you're due in the General Assembly chamber. Would you like to see the Peace Bell or the famous Chinese ivory carving first?"

The two security guards following us are so seamlessly professional I hardly even know they're there unless I catch their reflections in some polished surface. "The Peace Bell," I say, at the same second Fred says, "The carving, please."

"We have time for both," Mr. Jung tells us, his stride fast enough that Fred and I both have to hustle to keep up. "And we will pass the Foucault Pendulum when we enter the lobby of the General Assembly. You wouldn't want to miss that."

Fred catches my eye when I glance toward him and mouths a few words I don't catch. I shake my head. He smiles, stretching the papery skin on either side of his mouth into lines that show his exhaustion more than anything else about him. "I hope you polished up your medals for your big hero fan club, old girl," he murmurs, leaning close enough that I feel his breath on my ear.

"I only brought the salad bars, actually," I answer. "All that pewter doesn't mix well with my osteoporosis. Old man."

I'm reasonably sure a couple of ancient warhorses aren't supposed to bray like donkeys when they laugh in public places, but what can you do? A disgrace to the uniform. Both of us.

The Foucault Pendulum—Mr. Jung is very explicit that it's *Foucault* and not *Foucault's*—is definitely worth the pause to collect ourselves before we enter the General Assembly. It's a huge coppery sphere swaying at the end of a nearly invisible wire, something like a waltzing cannonball, and it's downright hypnotic. The way it moves reminds me of the giant game of crack-the-whip going on overhead, the orbital platforms slung out at the ends of their beanstalks, the whole thing whirling in space. For a second, I fantasize I can feel the whole universe moving around me like the works of a giant clock. It makes me want to run right out and build an orrery.

Maybe when I retire. If they ever let me.

Mr. Jung gives us a few moments to ooh and aah over the pendulum before he abandons us in a ready room, both security types planted solidly outside the door. From there, we'll proceed to the General Assembly chamber. I wonder what machinations Riel and the PanChinese and the UN itself wrangled through to arrive at this solution—open hearings, and open testimony, in front of the entire body. I can't remember ever hearing of anything being handled exactly this way before.

On the other hand, nobody's ever obliterated a city and triggered a global climate change with a nickel-iron meteorite before. Or unleashed a tailored nanotech infection on the entire planet. I guess it's not really the sort of thing the UN was designed to deal with, was it?

"Nuclear proliferation," Richard supplies inside my head. "That, and the idea that an avenue of public discourse would prevent World War III."

So we skipped straight to number four and five, is what you're telling me? It's an old joke; I *fought* in World War III, but nobody calls it that. Richard gives me a *look*. I sigh out loud, and Valens gives me a *look* as well.

"Casey? Are you going to handle this?"

"I'm good, Fred."

His hazel eyes are doubtful, turned down at the corners like a sad old hound's, but he nods and turns away from me, pacing from one wall to another with his hand clenched around his opposite wrist in the small of his back. It's sort of restful watching him go back and forth. Like the pendulum. "Give them hell," he says, so quietly I almost don't hear him.

His tone makes my intestines knot. "You want them to pay."

Just a sideways look, arresting, glitter of cold eyes over the bridge of his handsome nose. "Tell me you don't."

I can't. I mean, I drew the line at bloody vengeance once. But let them go unpunished? No. That isn't an option either.

"I want justice."

His lips twitch into the semblance of a smile. It flickers on his mouth for a moment, then flutters away just as fast. "I never ask for justice anymore," he says. His fists unknot from behind his back and fall to his sides. "I just ask to win."

I'm not quite sure what I'm going to say in answer. I knew that about him. Knew it in my bones, I mean, down to the roots of my hair; Fred and I go way, way back. But for some reason, twenty-six goddamned years later, it just, finally, *really* sank in. Fred's the sort of guy who does what it takes and counts the cost well lost

against whatever it was he gambled to win. If he's not prepared to pay, he doesn't put his money on the table.

"Damn." It's written all over his face. And he's letting
me see it, because he knows I just figured it out anyway.
"That e-mail wasn't from Razorface, was it, Fred?"

"The encoding on something like that would be impossible to fabricate, Casey. We've validated the packet history in every manner known to man, and all the records
will be turned over with the evidence. It's the only way to
establish provenance."

Of course they have. Of course they are. I could ask
Richard. Richard might even tell me the truth.

Valens is still staring at me, the picture of quiet relax-
ation. I ask Richard something else instead, something I
won't have to lie under oath about. *Why?—no, wait. Don't
answer that. Just answer this: Are those documents real?*

"They're real. I'm not Fred Valens, Jen."

Dick—

"With any luck, they won't ask the right questions."
It's not quite a smile, what crosses Richard's face, but a
strange, tender expression I can't put a name to. It's the
sort of look you expect to see before somebody messes up
your hair, but of course he hasn't got the fingers to do it
with, so he just looks at me for a second, and then looks
down.

I hadn't known you were such a patriot, Richard.

"There's an old catchphrase. My country is the whole
world."

I've heard it.

"In my case"—he grins—"it's quite absolutely true."

Fred still hasn't blinked. Come to think of it, neither
have I. I breathe out slowly, over my tongue, through my
teeth, and look down at the spit-shined tips of my shoes.

Before I get the breath back in, somebody knocks on the door and the handle starts to turn. I don't look over; I just tug my jacket straight one last time. "Lucky for us Razorface thought to mail that off before he died."

"Yes," Fred says, as the door opens and Mr. Jung slips inside, one hand crooked to summon us. Or to summon me, it seems, although Fred will follow along and sit in the observer seats.

We follow Mr. Jung into a room only about twice the size of a hockey amphitheater. It reminds me of being inside a gigantic nautilus shell. The ranked chairs have long desks attached to the back of each row, for the use of the row behind them, and except for the miniaturized interface plates obviously retrofitted to each place, they're exactly like the hundred-year-old student desks in the parochial school I suffered through until I ran away from home. The high ceiling is sculptured in acoustic ripples, pierced by a curving aperture of sorts lined with windows, dark observation booths behind. There's a screen over the podium we're walking toward. It's pearl white, and black letters float in it:

Items of Business:
Application of the Convention on the Prevention and Punishment of the Crime of Genocide (Canada and the British Commonwealth / People's PanChinese Alliance)
Armed Activities on the Territory of Canada (Canada and the British Commonwealth / People's PanChinese Alliance)
Armed Activities on the Territory of China (People's PanChinese Alliance / Canada)

I try not to look at them as we walk down the long
green-carpeted aisle. They make everything far too concrete, far too real. I feel insanely like a bride at a cathedral
wedding, Fred and Mr. Jung playing the role of my atten-
dants now, flanking me. I wonder if this would feel less
freakish if I had a veil and a long white train in place of
my sharp-creased rifle green.

My place is on the stage. Behind the podium, below a
gorgeous curved red-gold wall of mahogany, with my
back to the long table where the secretary general and
some other people who I don't recognize sit.

Mr. Jung and Fred step off to the side as I climb the
steps, aware of thousands of eyes on my back, holovision
and Net feeds, the whole world watching. It's a short
flight. I don't stumble. Agné Zilinskiene, the secretary
general of the United Nations, rises and comes around the
table to meet me. She's a Lithuanian lady in her sixties,
perfectly powdered skin as lustrous as her pearl earrings.
Unlike Constance Riel, she's let her bobbed hair go a rich
flat pewter. It moves naturally when she cocks her head
back to smile up at me.

"It's an honor, ma'am," I say, as she reaches out.

"It's a pleasure to meet somebody with a little common
sense," she says, very softly, so the microphones won't
pick it up. She clasps my right hand in both of hers. Not
thinking, I add my own left hand to the mix. She glances
down at the touch of cool metal, and looks up, smile
widening. "I like a woman who doesn't believe in pretty-
ing up the truth."

Which is when it sinks in that she, too, knows more
than she's supposed. That she knows about the order I
disobeyed, which is the reason Beijing isn't a smoking
ruin like Toronto now.

The realization almost makes me grip her hand too tightly. I have to uncurl my metal fingers carefully, consciously, and let the steel hand fall to my side. This *isn't* Bernard's trial. I am not a victim, here. Riel, Richard, Valens—they have nothing to hold over me. Nothing but my own conscience, and its ghosts. They need me far more than I need them.

I've never held this much power in my life, in my own two hands. It stuns me with primeval awe. It's a dark god, that kind of power, a black rock idol crouched before the rising sun.

"Thank you, ma'am." I smile, and she lets my hand go, and I turn away to take my oath and think about the ways in which I will shade the truth so that I will not have to lie.

It was 6 AM in Vancouver when the testimony started in New York, and Riel didn't have the luxury of time to curl up on the sofa in her slippers, a mug cupped between her hands, and watch.

She didn't have time for it, but she was doing it anyway. Even if the Americans—and she had no illusions about that: she knew American ignorance and American arrogance well, and this was unquestionably the latter—had gone out of their way to arrange for the hearings to start on the Canadian day of thanks, it *was* still a national holiday. And Riel had sacrificed the privilege of sleeping in in favor of her perch on the big temperature-controlled memory-foam sofa, the never-ending stream of coffee cups, and the image of Genevieve Casey hovering in midair before her, limned in the not-quite-real glow of holography.

She sipped from her mug, the steam warming her face while lacy feathers of frost melted off the windows.

Frost, in Vancouver, Canada's answer to the tropics. On Thanksgiving.

She wondered what it would be like in two or three years, when the dust settled and the temperature started to rise, if Richard couldn't prevent it. She'd always lived with climate change, grown up in the era of wild weather. It had always been an accepted consideration rather than a crisis, something one adapted to, mitigated, planned for. Harsh winters, harsh summers, melting ice, erratic crops, evolving storm models, and altered ocean currents. The acceptance that whatever the situation was now, it was subject to immediate and irrevocable change.

She tried not to hang too much on the hope that, now that they had Richard, they might be able to control that change. She tried not to hang too much hope on anything, really, but this one was particularly tempting. A magic bullet. A miracle cure. Like penicillin—

Except, like penicillin, like any magic bullet, there was the chance . . . no, the likelihood . . . of unforeseen side effects and long-term consequences. Best not to hope, not even cautiously. Because hope could cloud one's sense of risks and benefits, and make one gamble more than one could afford to lose. Better to plan for the worst, to find some common ground with the Chinese and evacuate as many people from the planet as possible. A colony was a huge risk, and also a tremendous fallback position: as fragile as a basket of eggs . . . but nevertheless, a *second* basket.

Riel blinked a command interface up in her contact and raised the level of the sound on the live feed from the UN. A crow called outside, a harsh, throaty caw. She didn't glance up, fascinated by Casey's easy charm on camera, her effortless charisma. Traditionally, she might have had a chair, a table to sit behind, legal advisers at her side rather than Valens and one Canadian lawyer seated against the curtain wall, but this was theater, not justice, and those concessions to comfort had been sacrificed in the negotiation process, leaving her up there naked except for a podium and the microphone tacked to her throat.

She held that podium well, fielding questions with dignity, seemingly comfortable on her feet as the testimony headed into its second hour.

Riel had known Casey had that, that aura of command. Now, she found herself wondering if she herself would do as well, when her time came. *What a politician she would have made,* Riel thought. And then, watching Casey, she had another thought, building on that first one, and smiled.

"Put me through to Richard, please," she said. The smart system in her living room recognized the tone of command, and a chime announced the connection.

"Good morning, Prime Minister. You're up early."

"Have you thought about my offer of citizenship, Dick?"

"I have—"

"You prefer to remain a free agent."

"I feel morally constrained," he answered. "I trust you will understand my quandary."

"Understanding and acceptance are not the same thing, Dick."

"That's true—"

She turned back to the 3-D. "How do you think our girl is doing?" She gestured with her mug, coffee slopping over and splashing her fingers. It wasn't quite hot enough to make her swear. She wiped her hand on the blanket.

"Beautifully," he said. "I hope it all goes this well."

"Don't count your chickens, Dick," she said. "And don't tempt the gods."

"They never listen to me under other circumstances. Why should this be any different?"

"The perversity of the universe?"

"Oh," he said, and she almost imagined she could hear the crackle of the connection in the silence that followed. "That."

1130 hours
Thursday October 11, 2063
Empire State Building Historical Preserve
New York City, New York USA

The American looked cold. He leaned against the railing next to a row of chit-operated viewfinders trained in the general direction of the New York Dike, looking like any of the other single men and women scattered across the observation deck. A holotour of Lower Manhattan droned from a kiosk, abandoned by some tourist who hadn't counted on the wind eighty-six stories up, but he didn't appear to be listening to it. His fists were stuffed in the pockets of his expensive fish-scale corduroy coat as he looked down at the butterfly netting winged out from the monolithic building, giant hands cradled to discourage suicides.

Janet didn't know his name. She didn't *want* to know his name. She didn't want to be here at all, in fact, shivering on this blocky engineered outcrop of gray stone and glass, her arms folded tight across her overcoat. Kurt and Amanda and the rest of her security detail had been abandoned at the embassy through a bit of skullduggery worthy of a high school girl sneaking out in the middle of the night to meet the captain of the hockey team, and she wanted nothing quite so much as to be sitting in the bar at the hotel down the street, drinking an Irish coffee and watching Casey's testimony on the smallest of four projectors.

The other three would be showing American sports hype. Some things never changed, and in New York City, acts of war still gave pride of place to Game Four of a 2–1 World Series when the Yankees were one game behind and the Havana Red Sox looked fit to win it all. Which was ironic, because Havana was under water and despite having kept the name, the Red Sox were based out of Argentina these days.

In any case, the Irish coffee sounded good.

She shot a sidelong look at Toby. His lips thinned against the cold. He dabbed his nose with a linen handkerchief as an icy wind lifted his hair. There ought to be a law against haircuts that good; pewter-colored strands feathered in the cold air and fell into place more perfectly than Janet could have managed with a blow dryer and a comb. Janet stomped her feet in her boots and walked forward, leaving the Unitek executive behind.

The man in the corduroy overcoat turned as she slipped between the scattered tourists and came up to him. Wan winter light sparkled on transparent spangles as his shoulders hunched under tan cloth; the greatcoat might be trendy, and heated, but it wasn't doing anything about the wind. He dragged a hand out of his pocket and offered it to Janet. She took it without removing her glove, offering enough of a squeeze to let him know she came as an ally rather than a supplicant.

America's population drift had gone the opposite way of Canada's: there were just more men in Janet's age group in America. Unfortunately, a lot of them had been raised during the Christian Fascist era, and had somewhat distasteful ideas about the role of women, in and outside the home. She read those ideas in the sloppiness of his hand-clasp, in the condescending glossiness of his gaze. She was unimpressed.

"Dr. Allman sent you," she said, extracting her hand from his fishy grip, glad of her fur-lined leather gloves.

"Sent me?" The smile was as patronizing as the rest of his expressions. "That makes me sound like an errand-boy, General."

Aren't you? Her lips didn't move, but it came out in the lift of her eyebrows and her chin. He cleared his throat as she brushed past him, on her way to the wall. She could make out a dark blue-green wedge of the UN Secretariat on the Lower East Side, a slight glimpse of color between taller, newer buildings. The view *was* breathtaking. Literally: the wind ripped her words from her lips as soon as she said them, hurling them into the gray, airy gulf spread out below. It wasn't as windy as the CN Tower observation platform had been; she never quite had the feeling that invisible hands were about to drag her off her feet and loft her into space, but the cold burned her cheeks and peeled her lips and she was grateful for the warmth of her heated coat and gloves. "Do you have something for me?"

He had to lean forward and strain to hear her. She

didn't turn her head to make it any easier. He nodded and swallowed, ducking his chin behind the collar of his coat.

Janet turned her hand palm up without raising it above the level of her waist, and he handed her a gray plastic data carrier that felt like it had a couple of modules clipped inside. "Dr. Allman says you'll know what to do with those. He also says the first one is only viewable once, and will only play on an encoded HCD. The second one is the supplemental documents."

"Mmm." She slipped the carrier into her pocket and leaned harder on the wall. The stone pressed a heating element in her coat against her belly, warming her uncomfortably. She shifted back, straight-armed, leaning hard, and cleared her throat. Her nose was starting to drip with the cold. *And it's only October. What's it going to be like in January?* "Please do return my regards to the vice president."

"General Shijie also sends his regards, and looks forward to an increased spirit of cooperation between our three countries—"

"Our three countries." She tried to laugh; it came out a harsh, chuffing cough. "What benefits Vancouver benefits New Washington, I take it? And vice versa?"

"We used to think so. Wouldn't you like to see the border unguarded again?"

"I'm barely old enough to remember when it was unguarded the last time," she said. "Those fortifications have been there since the turn of the century, to greater or lesser degrees. I'm not inclined to believe that the U.S. is scurrying around under the table, brokering peace between PanChina and the commonwealth, without a certain degree of self-interest involved."

"It advances us on the world stage," the man in the corduroy coat said with a shrug. He rubbed his hands together. "General Shijie is a reasonable man, and he's horrified by the actions of his government with regard to yours. He wishes to see a spirit of international cooperation reborn, and the United States stands to benefit from détente—in both economic and political spheres."

"The rats are turning on each other, you mean."

The man in the corduroy coat laughed softly. "Our government—and Dr. Allman—has the greatest faith in General Shijie's integrity."

"And look where faith has gotten the USA so far."

"That was uncalled for."

She lifted her chin and angled a glance across the bridge of her nose. "I'm a politician," she said. "I can recognize an unsubtle insult when I deliver one. What's on the data slices?"

"There's some documentation that will impeach MWO Casey's credibility as a witness fairly nicely. She has a juvenile record that was sealed when she turned eighteen."

"And? How are we going to explain away the documentation they've entered into the record? Captain Wu is prepared to testify that those orders are exact copies of the orders he received and destroyed. And Minister Shijie's signature is on them. Their provenance has been validated; the electronic postmarks are supposed to be impossible to fake. We'll have to buck fifty years of precedent to say otherwise."

"The signature was forged by elements in the PanChinese government who have no love for General Shijie," the man said without looking at her. "Elements that are in favor of expansion at the price of peace. The same elements that urged the PanChinese invasion of Siberia last year—"

"Xiong."

"You said it. I did not." Silence for a moment, and then he cleared his throat. His fingertips rubbed absently at the stone of the wall in front of them, fingers arching and pulling inside his gloves as if he were trying to wear away a stain.

"So how do we explain away Dr. Holmes's possession of those documents, if she was not in collusion with the Chinese?"

"I would have thought Mr. Hardy would have explained this." The man glanced over his shoulder. Janet followed the look: the observation deck was still not overly crowded, and she could see Toby's camel-hair coat fifteen or twenty yards down the wall. He was looking the other way.

"Perhaps he thought I should hear it from a neutral party."

"Mmm. Perhaps."

She almost reached out and grabbed his wrists to stop him rubbing his palms together. *As subtle as Lady Macbeth.* "Tell me."

"She received the documentation, along with certain other communications, from General Shijie himself. The minister had opposed the plan, found it . . . dishonorable, and did not wish to be remembered as a genocide. Unable to contact Prime Minister Riel directly, he used Dr. Holmes as a go-between."

The corners of Janet's mouth lifted. "And Connie, with her well-known opposition to the star travel program, dismissed Holmes's concerns as . . . as grandstanding, as a desperate attempt to generate support for the *Montreal*."

"Precisely. At which point Dr. Holmes went to her superior, Mr. Hardy, who contacted yourself. Unfortunately—"

"The delay cost everything," Janet said, nodding. She stepped back and leaned her hip on the gritty wall, unperturbed by the streak it left on her coat. "And Connie is trying to cover up her incompetence by pretending she was not warned in advance."

"Exactly. Conspiracy theories are a cottage industry. There are *always* rumors that the powers-that-be knew in advance. Mumbai, Coventry, Pearl Harbor." His left hand rose, swooped, hovered in midair.

She followed the line of his point, the lower Manhattan skyline, and nodded. She didn't look long, but lowered her head, pushed her scarf aside, and scratched her cheek with a gloved thumb. "I remember. I was five years old. There are always rumors, you're correct. What about what Wu has to offer, and Xie? What about Casey?"

"Once her credibility is impeached, your testimony—and Mr. Hardy's—will make the difference. Casey, of course, couldn't have known any of this skullduggery. Nothing you say will contradict anything she has to offer. And General Shijie's testimony will correspond with yours. The only people who will appear to have perjured themselves will be Valens and Riel."

"That's dastardly."

"Thank you." Without taking his eyes from the New York skyline, lower Manhattan and the Dike spread out behind it like a long frozen line.

"It wasn't a compliment."

He gave her a smile, then, a thin one. His lower lip cracked when he did it, but not enough to bleed. "I know."

She turned and walked away without shaking his hand in farewell. Her shoes rasped on cement. Toby was watching the skyline of the lower West Side through one of the viewfinders. She put her hand on his elbow as she came up behind him. He didn't jump.

"Spooks," she said. "I really hate those guys."

"Did you get what you needed?"

"I got what you were promised." She moved toward the doors to the interior observation deck, the wind tugging the hem of her coat. "It's cold out here. Let's go the hell home."

B OOK TWO

For whoever
habitually
suppresses the
truth in the
interests of tact
will produce a
deformity from
the womb of his
thought.
—*Sir Basil H.
Liddell-Hart,
Strategy*

Richard was watching the baseball game.

It wasn't all he was doing—his usual subroutines and his responses to the developing climatic disaster consumed something in excess of 95 percent of his processing power, and he was having three other simultaneous conversations. All in all, the balancing act was considerably more challenging than higher math on strip-club cocktail napkins. On the other hand, he hadn't had this much fun since he was fooling overperfumed women into believing he could perceive via extrasensory perception which volume from a shelf of books they had leafed through.

It was starting to look like he might be able to get the North Atlantic conveyor restarted after all, through micromanipulations of ocean salinity levels and a certain amount of sheer brute force. The atmospheric issues might prove a bigger problem: ozone damage, global dimming, global carbon dioxide increase, and a thousand other variables he hadn't even begun to sort out accurately yet.

But that was chronic, not acute.

He had more immediate problems. Not including the fact that the Red Sox were losing seven to four.

Jen didn't need him just now; his eavesdropping was a matter of insatiable curiosity combined with the desire to be on hand if she did require assistance, or simply an obscure fact. "...a decision was made in the wake of the attack—" her chin lifted, her mismatched hands resting lightly on the sides of the podium. "—to exact no retribution upon the PanChinese..."

Nice use of the passive voice, Jen. She didn't answer in words, but he felt her amusement. He backgrounded the process and divided his focus between the laboratory—where Gabe was conducting a postmortem on yet another batch of nanite victims of sudden-biomechanical-autism-syndrome—and the captain's office. Richard and Leslie rode behind Charlie's eyes as he and Elspeth entered Wainwright's domain shoulder-to-shoulder, trying not to look like they came expecting—*spoiling for*—a fight.

Wainwright wasn't behind her desk; she stood close to the holomonitor that showed the gangling hull of the *Montreal* spilled out across space, the unholy miscegenation of Tinker Toys and an Erector set. Her hands were clasped behind her back, her dark hair freshly trimmed and bound into a club at the nape of her neck with a tidy but strictly nonregulation nacreous gray ribbon. She turned and caught Elspeth's eye, then very carefully looked from the contact team leader to Charlie. "Absolutely not," she said, before Charlie could open his mouth. "You're not impressed enough with what the Benefactors—if I may use the term loosely—did to you and Leslie the last time we went out there?"

Richard smiled to himself. He liked Wainwright. And she had said *we*. That was ground to build on.

Meanwhile, in the hydroponics lab, Gabe swiveled his chair back. Richard watched as Gabe lifted his head from the eyepiece of the virtual magnifying device he was using to examine yet another noncommunicating nanite, and snorted exasperation. "Dick, if I didn't know better, I'd say these critters were suffering under a denial-of-service attack."

Richard relayed the comment to Charlie. *Spiked?* Charlie asked, his eyes wide behind spectacles he no longer needed.

"No, just choking on static, I expect," Richard said—out loud, for Gabriel's benefit. "Am I right?"

"It's a little more interesting than that, Dick—"

"We're not here about Leslie," Charlie said to Wainwright. "We're here about the shiptree. And our mandate."

Wainwright squared her interface plate on her desk.

"I will go to the prime minister if I have to." Elspeth folded her hands over her biceps in a position Richard translated to *trouble for somebody*. "I hope I don't need to remind you that the *Montreal* is detailed primarily to the first contact project."

If Richard were a real boy, he'd steal Ellie from Castaign in a minute, Gabe's charm notwithstanding.

"She's also my ship, and you are my crew." Wainwright kept her voice level. "I won't risk either unnecessarily—"

"—specifically," Gabe continued, "the circuits aren't just fused or fried, the way I'd expect if there were a malfunction or a power surge or what have you. Remember what we tried to do to the Benefactor vectors to get back Les and Charlie?"

"Of course. Flash them. That's what I did to Min-xue, more or less, to get him on our network."

"The programming hasn't been changed. Which is

reassuring, since we couldn't manage that with the bird-cage nanites."

Richard considered, relaying. Charlie got there amazingly fast, for a carbon-based intelligence, and Dick decided to let him have it. It did make them happy to beat the machine. *Could we do it to a Chinese-programmed network?* Charlie asked.

"If we knew their security codes, we could."

"Change all the codes," Richard said.

Gabe stood. "I'm on it, Dick, but it will take awhile—"

"—and what if I said it was a necessary risk, Captain?" Elspeth met Wainwright's irritated gaze and did not look down.

"Over my protest," Wainwright started, but Charlie cleared his throat, and she stopped, and looked at him.

Silently, he held out his hand. "Captain, it *did* work."

The captain's mouth compressed. She stared at Charlie, putting her back to the bulkhead, braced as if the deck were pitching under her feet. "At what cost? You tell me—"

"No cost," he said, "if you'd let us go get Leslie back."

Richard knew what Leslie wanted, as surely as if Richard were Leslie's hand, his finger, his thumb. It took no effort at all for Dick to reach out and flip the image on the screen behind Elspeth and Charlie to a panoramic shot of the *Montreal,* the *Huang Di,* and the birdcage ship hanging in fixed geometry above a cloud-swirled crescent Earth. The picture was from Piper Orbital Platform; another view from Forward showed the shiptree, in higher orbit, sliding past. Richard plastered that one on the second largest monitor. On the one that normally held Wainwright's refrigerator-drawing view of the *Montreal,* he offered the present view from Clarke; a very nearly full and sunlit Earth.

"Captain," Elspeth said calmly, unfolding her arms. "Have you thought about the potential costs if we fail?"

And Wainwright swallowed and looked down. "I'm not authorizing anything unless the prime minister says so," she said. And then she looked up, fixed Elspeth with a cool, crinkled stare, and smiled coldly. "And don't presume you understand my personal leanings in this matter, Dr. Dunsany. Or in the matter of Dr. Tjakamarra. Some of us *do* draw a line around our personal feelings when we pull our pants on in the morning."

"Ma'am," Elspeth said, after a few moments. "I'll message the prime minister at once."

By the fourth day of testimony, there's a small child in the back of my head whining over and over again *I wish I wish I wish I wish Gabe and Ellie were here I wanna go home I don't want to answer any more questions waaaaaaaaaaaaaaaaaaaaah*. Goddamn.

Can't you shut that kid up, Jenny?

I mean, I'm good at this. I know I'm good at this. It's not even exactly testimony, although everybody calls it that. And it's not speechifying either; mostly, I stand up there behind the podium and field questions for hour after hour after hour. They seem to have some sort of a protocol worked out, too, where it's the big dogs—the permanent security council members—who get to ask things when they want, and the representatives of other nations pass notes or tap shoulders or send e-mail and get whoever they're tributary to or sending aid to or receiving aid from to ask their questions. It's an elegant demonstration of patronage, if you squint at it right. My Grandpa Zeke would have approved.

But sweet Mary Mother of God I am so goddamned tired. Would it kill them, you think, to give me a chair?

Besides, this is the day when I'm going to have to talk about the things I'd rather pretend never happened. So standing up there, facing that enormous seashell room packed with delegates from 213 nations and five supranations, is something more than just an exercise in stage fright. It's like exhuming Leah's grave.

It's the only grave she's going to get, because her body never made it down. She's part of the planet now. Part of the atmosphere. I push her in and out with every breath, since I came home. Her, and Trevor Koske, too.

At least Koske had the decency to do what I couldn't, and die with her. I wouldn't have thought he had it in him.

It's a little disconcerting to think about, nonetheless.

Especially when I'm in the middle of explaining to a room full of politicians why she had to die, and how her death—her sacrifice—resulted in the worldwide contamination of the oceans with Benefactor nanotech. And how it's spreading to people and plants and topsoil and little terrier dogs all over the world.

And how, no, really, it seemed like a good idea at the time.

I was smart enough to bring a handkerchief.

A thin Asian man in a narrow mahogany-colored suit leans forward on his elbows as I reach for a drink, waiting for the next question. I've lost track, but he's somebody in the PanChinese delegation. A shark, I think. Not an interpreter, because the UN handles that itself; there are a few dozen people in the glass-walled booths over our heads providing simultaneous translation on multiple-language channels, and I can access any one of them on my ear clip with a glance at a menu. I'm listening in French, because the interpreter has a sexy dark-chocolate voice and I like his Parisian accent better than the harsh midwestern drawl of the Chinese-to-English translator—who is getting a workout today.

Anyway. The shark says, in Chinese—whatever dialect they're using—and the interpreter says in French: "And you expect us to believe that the government of Canada has no intentions of using this tech as a weapon, when it's already responsible for the infection of millions, and the death or injury of thousands?"

He catches me with my water glass in my metal hand, just tilted to my lips. I couldn't have *planned* the snarf better; titters and at least one guffaw from my stodgy audience of diplomats attest to the perfection of my comedic timing.

At least it goes in the glass, and not all over my uniform. "The infection of, and the death or injury of, *Canadians,* sir. Canadians who were in desperate need of medical assistance in the wake of the attack upon Toronto." Valens spent hours drilling me not to say *Chinese attack.* Or *terrorist attack,* for that matter. Apparently the official explanation of who kicked whom in the balls is still a matter for high-level negotiation.

Which is why I'm surprised. I'd thought these particular questions would be reserved for Fred. Or Riel. But what the hell.

"American citizens were affected as well."

"Because American cities were affected by the attack. No one who was not ill or injured has been subjected to the treatment, sir, to the best of my knowledge." I switch to English to answer this question, because it's the American shark talking, or maybe the American shark's diplomat boss. There's too damned many of them to keep track of. Or did I say that already?

The American is a round-faced Latina in her fifties, in a suit just the right bluish shade of power red to remind me uncomfortably of Alberta Holmes. She shields her mouth with her hand as she confers with her boss, or her lawyer. She leans back in her chair and steeples her hands in front of her, her knuckles furled tight as her brow. "Of course, the USA would have been less significantly affected, by your own testimony, if you and the *Montreal* had not diverted the projectile from its course."

Valens is seated in a chair off to my left, which means I can see him moving in the periphery of my prosthetic eye's vision much more clearly than I could on the right-hand side. Better than the real thing. I don't know why everybody doesn't run right out and buy a set, frankly.

Fred leans forward, his eyes on me rather than the American. Fortunately, I have the podium to hold on to. And I really *do* have better control of my temper than Fred thinks I do. I mean, okay, I broke his shoulder back in the thirties. But he deserved it then, and I'm sure as hell not going to feel bad about it now.

Dick? What do I say to that steaming pile of horseshit?

"You could just stand there with your mouth open and blink at her as if she's out of her mind."

Got that covered already, thanks.

"Just be yourself. You're under oath, after all."

Gee. Thanks. I make sure my mouth is closed, and turn away for a moment to collect myself. A functionary brings me a fresh glass of water. Perfect timing, and a perfect excuse. "Ma'am—" I try to steal a discreet peek at her nameplate, but she's pushed her HCD against the back of it and angled it away. I bet she did that on purpose, too. She's got a mean glitter in her eye. I take a breath and get the outrage out of my voice and a dry kind of mockery that served me well as a drill instructor in. "Ma'am, are you suggesting that it would have been a more prudent course of action *not* to attempt to prevent a ten-hundred-ton nickel-iron asteroid from slamming into Lake Ontario?"

It's not just titters this time. Somebody in the African section is roaring with laughter, and I see the Mexican delegates eye each other and grin. Yeah, nobody likes the Americans: not even their next-door neighbors.

I wonder if it really used to be different, when the border was unguarded, or if that's just more cheerful propaganda. History's not my strong point, except the bits I've lived through, but I do remember the jokes from my childhood about how Canada wouldn't let the northern U.S. states join during the famine because of the expense of putting French on all their road signs. Of course, Maman also claimed that the reason Quebec never seceded was the expense of taking all the English *off*. I suspect she may have been pulling our legs.

I didn't get my sense of humor from my father, that's for sure. "In any case, my point stands, ma'am. Sir."— with a nod to the Chinese representative in the brown suit, who is leaning forward again—"With all due respect, the Benefactor tech is not weaponized. There is to the best of my knowledge no intent to weaponize it, on Canada's side—"

Valens is on to me. He's shooting me that look, the one that means *shut up while your tongue's still in your head, Casey*. I ignore him, of course, blithe spirit that I am.

"—and in point of fact, the nanite infestation is not under Canadian authority."

Dead silence, then, so quiet that I can hear the click of plastic as the American's fingers trigger the holographic keypad of her hip. I could almost swear I can hear the whisper of cloth as one of the guys at the Canadian table closes his eyes and leans back in his chair.

"Would you care to expand on that, Master Warrant Officer?"

The look on Fred's face promises me a stretching on the rack and possibly a slow roasting over coals, but Richard's amused pleasure in the back of my head means more. In any case, all this skullduggery and manipulation works two ways. And if Riel wants an excuse for an effective world government, and a common concern and worry . . . well, Dick's big enough to give it to her. And scary enough to keep everybody busy for quite awhile, at least until a generation grows up that doesn't know how to live without him.

"It's controlled by the artificial intelligence known, somewhat inaccurately, as the Feynman AI."

"Which is a Canadian construct."

"He's not a subject of the commonwealth, sir."

Silence. Longer, this time, and it's the tall, mop-haired Russian delegate who straightens his spine and speaks. "Then what are his affiliations? Who owns that machine?"

It's all I can do to keep the grin off the corners of my lips. "He's self-determined, sir. And as for his loyalties—I wouldn't care to speculate. I would suggest that you ask him yourself. He's prepared to testify under oath."

Three beats before the uproar: I know because I'm counting. It washes over me like surf. It sounds like surf, rising and falling, so many voices they amount to white noise. It breaks around the podium, the•beautiful acoustics of the assembly hall amplifying and echoing every voice.

I'm absolutely unprepared, once order is restored, for the Chinese delegate to give me that smug little smile across twenty meters of open space and say, "On a more immediate note, Master Warrant Officer. Perhaps we could discuss the matter of your criminal record now?"

Gabriel Jean-Marie Benoit François Castaign was getting just a little tired of this *particular* bête noire. Specifically, the one where he—with all his brains and all his brawn, fifteen years and a captain's commission in the Canadian Army, unarmed combat and firearms instructor certification, two master's degrees and five languages and eleven years of practical experience as a single parent—was left powerless, sitting on his middle-aged ass while a woman he loved faced dragons he couldn't do a damned thing about.

The blankets were wrinkled and sweaty. His jumpsuit was carving creases in his skin. And he leaned forward on the edge of his bunk, his eyes locked on the real-time holofeed that Richard was projecting over his interface, and cursed. He knew how to do it by now, how to watch and love and feel them slip out of his hands like so many fistfuls of feathers, lifted on a gentle breeze. He knew how to grant them the dignity of not looking down, and not looking away from the pain. He knew how to lend strength when he couldn't do the fighting himself.

He'd done it for his wife, Geniveve, and after he'd buried her he'd done it for Genie when Genie was dying by centimeters from cystic fibrosis. He hadn't done it when Leah sailed the *Calgary* into Earth's atmosphere with the brittle unholy courage that only an adolescent could muster—*C'est la raison que nous les envoyons pour mourir dans la guerre, dans le cas òu tu ne le savais pas*—because Gabe couldn't reach Leah. But Jenny could, and Jenny had stood in his place, and Gabe had been there for Jen. As he'd done it before, again, and again, and again.

But, he was tired of it. He said it to himself, sitting motionless on the edge of his bunk, his feet dangling, the cold metal edge of the rack cutting the backs of his thighs and his hands clenching and unclenching on the blankets. He thought it as he leaned forward and watched Jenny answer those invasive questions with dignity and aplomb that he knew had to be borrowed at loanshark rates against that night, against tomorrow.

Je suis fatigué lui.

He needed to be there. Even without the ability to stand beside her on that stage and squeeze her hand behind the podium, he needed to be in the room. Jenny was a professional; she was cool, and collected, and gracious: the picture of a warrior who has lived long enough to learn both honor and its price.

The Chinese *fils de putain* was coming after her like a mangy feral dog, and no matter how well she was handling it, Gabriel would have liked to wring his neck instead of the dark wool blankets. "I understand," the man in the mahogany suit said, "that there are arrests for prostitution and possession of drugs that are not mentioned in your military records. Would you care to explain why those records were purged?"

The speaker kept leaning over to confer with a jowly middle-aged man in a Chinese uniform. *That must be General Shijie.*

He just wished he could be there. Where she could see him. Where she could see his eyes. But she was thirty-five thousand vertical kilometers away, and he was helpless again.

You cannot save them, Gabriel. Sometimes you cannot even hold their hands.

Like Leah. God have mercy on his soul.

Jenny, in the projection, lifted her chin. Gabriel knew that look, knew the way it stretched her long neck above her collar. Knew the arrogant sparkle in her eyes, and knew how much it cost her to keep it there. "Not purged, sir. Sealed. Those incidents occurred while I was a juvenile, under Canadian law, and they are not considered part of my permanent criminal record. Which, I might add, is clean—"

Someone tapped on the hatchway. Gabe startled, torn between relief and irritation, and shoved himself off the bed. He forgot to duck again. "Turn that off please, Dick?"

"It's Genie," the AI answered, as the display obediently flickered out. Gabe closed his eyes and calmed his breathing, pressing his dinged forehead with the back of his hand.

Then he went and opened the door.

Calisse de chrisse, she looked like her mother. Not as much as Leah had, but the same huge eyes, straight nose, the honey-blond hair that looked as soft as silk until you got your hands into it and then turned out to be wild, electric, alive. And her eyes were as big as churchbells, and her hands were twined together, shaking.

"You saw the news," he said. He didn't move aside and let her in, although it was ship drill; you never stood in an open doorway like a rubbernecker and jawed with somebody on the other side. It wasn't safe. He glanced over his shoulder, and the condemning silence of the interface, the feed he wasn't watching. He wasn't there for Jenny, and there was no way he could be.

And he didn't know what to do with Genie anymore. It had always been him being big for Leah and Leah being big for Genie, and now Leah was gone, a hole in the middle of their family like trying to make a sandwich out of two plain slices of dry white bread. There was nothing to hold them together.

"Is it true, what they said?"

He looked her in the eye and pursed his lips, and closed his eyes, and turned aside for a second to collect his thoughts. When he looked again, ready to ask Genie the question he didn't have an answer to himself—*She's still your Aunt Jenny. Does it matter if it is?*—when he turned his head back and opened his eyes and looked at the hatchway, his daughter was gone.

He straightened up and knotted both hands in his mop of hair and cursed in three languages, two of them French.

Coward. *Lache. Enfouaré.*

He only remembered to dog the hatch behind him because Richard yelled at him before he got too far down the corridor.

Genie made a good job of vanishing. He looked for forty minutes before it occurred to him to ask Richard for help. He wasn't particularly surprised when Richard hacked his contact and ear clip for a private conversation, shrugged, and said, "She asked me not to tell you. She said she wanted to be invisible."

"Do you make a habit of concealing wayward teenagers

from their possibly stupid but well-meaning parents?" Gabe leaned against the corridor bulkhead, making sure he was between pressure doors, and took a moment to think, and breathe.

"I'm trying to avoid situational ethics," Richard answered. "I'm stuck with omniscience, but I don't want to develop a reputation as a jealous god. Or a meddling one."

"You've been meddling all along, Dick."

Gabe wasn't quite prepared for the long silence before Richard answered, "I know." The AI shook his head and rubbed his palms together, a frown creasing his forehead. "The ethics are getting complicated. In any case, I'll be happy to tell Genie you're looking for her. Where shall I tell her you'll be?"

"Is Charlie in the hydroponics labs?"

"No, he's in the larger observation lounge. Snoring. All the greenhouses are empty except Center-13."

"Tell her I'll be in Charlie's main lab, s'il te plais."

He didn't think he was imagining the warmth in Richard's voice when Richard answered, "It will be my pleasure, Gabriel."

The smell of growing things eased his headache, and even spinning sunlight was sunlight, and full-spectrum lighting was a kind relief after the energy-saving flourescence that gave the pilots screaming conniptions and lit most of the *Montreal*'s cabins and corridors in a pale minty green. Gabe found himself walking slowly up and down the aisles between the Plexiglas tanks, running his fingers over the broad leaves of soybeans and breathing deeply, as if the oxygen they emitted could ease his throbbing temples by being absorbed through the skin. He'd forgotten even to grab his ship-shoes when he ran into the corridor after Genie. The floor's absorbent nonskid matting was tacky and slightly springy under his bare feet.

He turned when the hatch swung open, but it wasn't Genie. Instead, Elspeth picked one foot up high, stepped over the knee knocker with a grace that belied her round little frame, and dogged the hatch tight behind her. "Gabe?"

He frowned and folded his arms. "Of course she went to you. I should have known that without being told."

Elspeth's lips worked, but she held her peace as she came up the line of beans and cabbages and mustard plants, brushing aside the sunshine-yellow sprays of the latter's flowers. She stood in front of him, foursquare, and looked all the way up, glowering. "What did you say to that child, Gabe?"

"Why am *I* the bad guy? I barely had time to get a word out!"

She took a half-step back and her arms unfolded, her palms rubbing the thighs of her jumpsuit. "I'm sorry," she said. "I shouldn't have jumped to conclusions. I just—" She shrugged. "That was unprofessional of me. I'm sorry."

The sharp retort was automatic. He bit it back. He was an adult, and so was she, and they had better things to do than play games or try to get a rise out of each other. Besides, he wasn't sure he'd ever seen Elspeth Dunsany lose her temper, and the sight—and the reason for her wrath—provoked a soft, warm glow under his breastbone. "Ellie," he said, and unfolded the arms he'd pulled around himself like a barrier, "I should be upset because you care enough about my kid to yell at me for her?"

She stared at his outstretched hands, feline in her suspicion. And then she shrugged, and stepped inside their reach. "It sounds pretty silly, when you put it like that."

He shivered; she felt brittle in his arms—not the flesh, but the spirit. "How about you? Are you all right?"

"Hard to tell when I'm taking my meds." A weak attempt at a joke. She curled closer. He rested his chin on her head.

"It'll all be over soon," he said, and felt her nod.

"One way or another." Another sigh, a bigger one. "Are you going to talk to Genie?"

"I've only been looking for her for the past hour and a half. What did you tell her?"

"Probably exactly what you're going to tell her. That what happened to Jenny is Jenny's story to tell, and you shouldn't judge other people's character by what you hear in gossip, or—especially—on the news. Have you been watching?"

"I can't stand to." She was warm and soft, a teddy bear for grown-up boys. His heart slowed as he held her, the ache in his head and neck easing as he buried his nose in her hair. "How do you manage to smell of gardenias using air force soap?"

"A mystical talent," she answered. "It's closely tied in with feminine wiles, but far more secret."

"You got the gardeners to let you take some of the flowers?"

"Exactly." She turned in his arms and tossed her head back on his shoulder. "I can't get anything past you. If I tell you where Genie is? . . ."

"You're a ferocious nag, you realize. And yes, of course I'll go talk to her. Where is she?"

"I left her down in the Contact office talking with Leslie via Richard. He—showed up? What do you call it?

Checked in?—after I'd spent half an hour trying to pry out of her why she was so upset. She's got Boris with her. Why that cat puts up with being manhandled around the ship by that girl—"

"All right," he said. "I'll go down now."

He heard laughter before he even undogged the hatch, Leslie and Genie giggling together. He would have lifted his hand from the cool metal wheel and stepped back, but he knew already the look he'd see in Elspeth's eyes if he did. So he knocked.

Genie came to open the hatch, but didn't look up. A projected image of Leslie hung over the interface plate on his own desk, downsized the same way Richard usually was. The image met Gabe's eyes, a wry smile playing around the lined corners of its mouth, so real Gabe almost forgot there wasn't a person on the other end of the projection. Leslie's iron-colored hair was rumpled as if he'd been running his hands through it, and his eyes glittered a little too bright. Gabe could see Genie behind him, curled up on top of the worktable crosslegged. Boris the cat was watching holo-Leslie as if guarding a rabbit hole.

Guilt was written all over Leslie's face, and Gabe shook his head and lowered his voice. "Son of a bitch," he said, too softly for Genie to hear him. "Richard sent you down here, didn't he?"

"Does it matter if he did?"

Gabe laughed at the echo of his own thoughts. Genie looked up, startled at the sound, and he smiled at her over Leslie's translucent shoulder, and his heart stuttered painfully in his chest. *Dammit, Dick. Why Les and not me?*

She didn't just look like her mother. *Calisse de chrisse.* She looked like *Leah,* tall and blond, with that straight nose in profile and the high forehead and the pin-sharp chin. And that was the sore she wore on his heart, of course. She looked like Leah, and she wasn't Leah, and he would never have Leah again. He looked away quickly, before she could see the sparkle in his eyes, and found himself staring directly at Leslie. He sniffled. He couldn't help it.

And Leslie offered him a weary shrug and a worldly smile. "Do you know what a beginner story is, Gabriel?"

It took a moment for him to fit the words together in the shape of a sentence. He had to take them apart a couple of times and start over, and once he had them assembled, he had to stop and run them through his brain a couple of times to see if they made sense. "No?"

"It's a simple story that's still true, but doesn't have all the truth of the sort of complex story you might learn later, if you keep studying a subject."

"A child's version."

"A *beginner's* version."

He thought about it. He looked at Leslie, and looked up at Genie again, and tried not to see her as Leah. Tried not to hear Leah's name in his head as he studied her profile.

She wasn't looking at him, as if his quick flinch away had cut her, and she was waiting to see if he would come back and cut her again. Wasn't it supposed to get easier as they grew up?

She's not my little girl anymore. Except she was; she was growing into a grown daughter, the one that Leah had almost reached, the one Leah had grasped in the short, too-adult minutes before she died. But she was also, and still, Genie.

He could do this. Hell, he had to do it, whether he could or not. He realized something, and smiled. Because here, after all, was one of his women for whom he could be there when she needed him. "Beginner stories?"

"Beginner stories," Les confirmed.

Gabe rolled his shoulders and stepped inside the hatch. He really had to get out of the habit of talking through them, before it got somebody killed. "Okay. I think I can handle that."

Leslie winked before he derezzed, flickering out.

It was the height of cowardice for Min-xue to stand and leave the table when General Shijie's hound started harrying Casey. And not even cowardice on her behalf. No, as he excused himself and picked his way up the long shallow flight of steps toward the doors at the back of the amphitheater, he couldn't claim empathy as the source of his distress. He was picturing himself behind that podium, and he didn't like it. At all.

The men's room closest to the General Assembly would be uncomfortably crowded, even midtestimony, but there was another one around the corner, out of the way. And Min-xue, frankly, had had enough of people for the moment. He made his way through the air-curtains and an S-curved hallway, pausing just inside to see if anybody else was present. The echoing tiled room seemed deserted, the low hum of ventilation the only sound. Min-xue selected the urinal in the farthest corner and settled in, trying to blank his mind.

Fluorescent overhead lights pulsed on ceramic and steel, the strobing effect near-blinding. Min-xue closed his eyes against the flicker and composed himself with poetry. *There were tossing oceans for you to cross. / If you fell, there were dragons in wild waters.*

He could not have failed to hear the door open, or the

crispness of shoes on tile. Someone made himself comfortable in the next bay; a curious choice when the entire row was unoccupied. Min-xue finished, opened his eyes, and stole a sideways glance—only to find his fellow bathroom occupant tidy and tucked in, arms folded, standing with military aplomb.

Min-xue looked down quickly and finished arranging his clothes. "General," he said, and made a little bow in lieu of offering his hand. Only afterward did he raise his eyes to meet those of the minister of war, wondering at his own ingrained politeness. If he'd thought about it, certainly, he never would have made even that slight gesture of respect.

Shijie Shu was still looking at him, arms crossed, eyes narrowed like a man who calculated odds he did not like.

"Pilot Xie Min-xue," the general answered.

"How may I be of service?"

It was refreshing to speak Chinese, however quietly, and it amused him when the general's eyebrows rose at what Min-xue had so carefully failed to offer; he'd neither admitted honor at making Shijie Shu's acquaintance, nor actually *placed* himself in the general's service. An inquiry was hardly a promise.

General Shijie cleared his throat harshly and stepped away from the row of urinals and, incidentally, Min-xue, who breathed a silent sigh of relief. He did not like the minister of war standing close enough to touch.

"I believe you are a very brave young man," Shijie said, addressing the doors of the off-white stalls lining the back wall. "A patriotic young man."

Min-xue had begun walking toward the sinks to wash his hands. He stopped and lifted his chin to look the taller, broader man in the eye. "If you are going to make an offer to buy me, General, I don't require flattery first."

"You've been too long among the Canadians." The general's broad, trustworthy face bent slightly around a frown. "I would not impugn your honor in that manner. You notice I have come to speak to you in person—"

"In a toilet."

"So be it. I have been impressed with your integrity, Pilot Xie. Your resourcefulness. Your honor."

"Which you are about to ask me to abrogate." The water was cold. He plunged his hands in without bothering to adjust it, scrubbed with gritty liquid soap, and ran his hands under the faucet for longer than he needed to.

"I am asking you to testify to things you know to be true," the general said quietly. "The Canadians' deceptions. Their manufactured truths. And what you yourself witnessed on board the *Huang Di*: a captain taken to drink—"

"Because of your orders." Shijie's eyes hung over Min-xue's shoulder when Min-xue looked in the mirror.

"Are you certain they were my orders?" Quietly, and Min-xue had no answer. The general let the silence drag a little, and Min-xue pulled his hands out of the icy water, ducked his head, and laved his face. "Pilot Xie—"

"General."

"Consider for a moment that we have many augments, pilots—and others. Unlike the commonwealth. Consider for a moment that Canada may yet be forced to return the *Huang Di* and her crew, including you, to our care. That crew contains several other augments, one higher ranking. It is logical to think that the *Huang Di*'s first pilot will be promoted to a newer starship."

Ah. There's the bait. And it's rich enough to make the

trap seem comfortable enough to live in. "You would promote me to first pilot of the *Huang Di,* if I testified as you wish." He straightened, let the water flow cease, and slicked his hair out of his eyes with wet fingers and palms.

"Not as I wish." The gaze the general rested on Min-xue was calm and open, completely guileless. "As will best serve China with your honesty. And not first pilot."

"What then?" But Min-xue swallowed hard. He already knew.

"Captain Wu . . ." The general hesitated delicately. "He will not serve aboard another ship."

Yes, Min-xue thought. *You broke him and now you cast him aside. He's served his purpose and may be replaced by a new tool.*

He pushed past General Shijie, careful not to touch the other man. He was in the corridor, hand on the heavy door that would take him back into the General Assembly, when he looked from one stiff guard beside the doorway to another, and realized exactly what it was that Shijie Shu had just offered him.

Nothing less than the captaincy of the *Huang Di.*

Leslie understood now why the pilots fixated so hard on getting into that black leather chair that dominated the bridge like the steel table dominates an operating theater. He knew, because he could feel it—a fraction of it: Richard and the limitless space he occupied.

It was . . . *intoxicating.* As if his senses had enlarged. If he concentrated, he could feel the things that Richard felt—the glorious confusion of moving water and atmosphere that the AI was struggling to learn to model and control, like a swirling breeze on Leslie's skin; and the angular body of the *Montreal* with its wings and gears and the soft hum of electricity through its veins; and the Benefactors spread across space. Charlie in his lab, and Richard's gossamer touch spanning star systems. No body of his own, no hands, no hope of ever feeling them again when he was honest with himself. Just a dream, an endless dream of space.

He imagined it felt the way a spider's web feels to the spinner, or a dolphin's sonar to the cetacean. Or perhaps the way a winding road clung to the tires of a sports car, the sensation of that contact almost seeming to extend to the driver's skin.

The birdcage's alien "map" of the sky, the distorted curves of space-time they felt as plainly as a surfer running a tube felt the surge and power of the wave under his board—Leslie could feel it, too, feel it the same way he'd been able to feel what the land would look like from a few hummed bars of song, once upon a time. It was intoxicating, amazing, as if the boundaries had dropped away from his body and his senses, and he had grown bigger than the skin he could no longer feel.

It wasn't all he felt. Richard was also feeding him the news coverage and commentary on the day's UN session, now that Jenny's testimony had ended. Information as a fluid, wrapped around him even when he knew that he was wrapped inside a skin of silver, floating in Earth orbit, and he was never going home.

He couldn't afford to think about that now. There was no guarantee that whatever the Benefactors had done to preserve his consciousness would last from moment to moment, and he wouldn't waste a moment of that time. He was too busy exploring their sensations, translating their mind-maps into something topographic, representative of space as his species perceived it.

Dick, why can I "feel" Charlie, and not Genie or Patricia?

"Or Min-xue or Jen?" The AI smiled in his head. "It's because of the way the network is set up. Jenny and the rest are implanted with individual control chips; they're essentially small nanonetworks on their own. You and Charlie are, as near as I can guess, partially on the Benefactor network. And you're also on the worldwire. Controlled like all the nanotech on Earth by the *Calgary's* processor core."

How do you keep that running at the bottom of the ocean?

"The nanosurgeons are capable of mechanical construction as well as biological repair," Richard said. "They stay pretty busy. The *Calgary* wound up in shallow water. If I can get the global conveyor belt working again and manage the climate back to a compromise level, I might have them encourage the local fauna to turn it into an artificial reef. The processor core and the reactor are sealed. And tropical fish are nice."

They are indeed. Leslie grinned internally at the image of holo-Richard hovering in midocean like some craggy Madonna of the Fishes, clownfish and Moorish idols nibbling through the seaweedy strands of his hair. Leslie hummed silently, a half-formed thought about who would sing the songs for the roads the starships would travel teasing the edges of his mind. *So, Dick, then why not take it back to preindustrial levels?*

"Even if I *could*, the world had almost three hundred years of adaptation already when Captain Wu tossed that rock at you."

Because, of course, you aren't a PanChinese target in any way, Dr. Feynman AI.

"Technically speaking, I'm not even a doctor." But it came packaged with another grin. "In any case, there's no point in throwing out the baby with the arctic meltwater, so to speak. It would cause even more chaos to try to reverse all the damage. And I'm not sure I can or want to. I'm not even sure my global conveyor trick is going to work, and it's not going to work quickly. Or without doing some additional damage—I'm up to my virtual armpits in a system that's already in flux, and what I'm doing is heedless and improvident."

Leslie agreed, musing. And then he suffered a thought that snapped him out of his meditative state. *Dick?*

"Yes, Les?"

What's to stop the Chinese from nuking the Calgary?

Richard's pause was pregnant, as he allowed Leslie to get there first. "In the final analysis? There are a number of small inconveniences and inelegances to an attack of that kind. But, overall, there's nothing to *stop* them."

Just like there was nothing to stop Toronto.

"Just like. Indeed."

Would that kill you?

"No." Utterly seamless, without the half-expected pause as if the AI was deciding how much information to share. Which meant that Richard had already known how he intended to answer that question, and didn't mind his human friends twigging that he's planned it in advance. "I'm not centralized anywhere, and while it would cost me a fragment of my capacity not to have the *Calgary* processor to run on, there's still the spare cycles of a googolplex or twelve nanomachines scattered around the Milky Way. It would be a very bad thing for the planet, however, for the worldwire to fail right about now—"

What you were saying about unstable systems.

"Exactly. It'd be like cutting the life support on a patient in surgery."

Leslie started humming again. Resonance buzzed in his ears. He stopped for a second, hoping to catch the direction it came from. The sound wasn't repeated, and a moment later, he realized he couldn't have heard a sound anyway. Not physically. "Bugger."

"What?"

Oh, I just thought I heard an echo to my humming.

"Les—"

Leslie had a funny feeling that he knew what Dick was going to say before he said it. Which wasn't all that surprising, given that he seemed to have become part of Richard's brain. *Dick, I think the Benefactors were singing to me.*

Patty's got her back to the door when I walk into the room. The door's unlocked and I know Alan will tell her I'm coming long before I get there, so I don't bother knocking. And she doesn't bother looking up. She's just sitting still, her hair banded into a glossy mahogany snake the length of her spine, her chin resting on the interlaced fingers of her hands. She stares at a two-dimensional photograph in a clear plastic frame pierced with flower cut-outs. There are two people in it. The man looks like Fred did when he was younger, only not as good looking, although you'd never get me to admit that Fred Valens was a handsome man. The woman has Patricia's hair.

"Patty?"

She sits back in her chair, braces her fine-fingered hands on the edge of the table, and stands. "I thought you did really well out there today, J-Jenny."

My cheeks prickle with the blush that must be creeping across them. I won't let her use my title, and she gets all bashful and stares at the floor when she tries to say my given name. *Mother Mary, tell me the child doesn't have a crush on me.* "It was pretty bad."

"It looked like it. Are you coming to get me for supper?"

"Yeah. The prime minister arrives tonight. Apparently she's decided she needs to keep a closer eye on her lackeys, lest we turn out to have unknown weaknesses."

"I guess I'd better wear my good shoes, then." She squats down and starts digging under the bed. She finds one black loafer and one tennis shoe, and sighs, looking up. "I'm such a flake. It's just *not* that big of a room!"

"Are they in the closet?"

"You know, I bet they are." Gods, she sounds like a grown-up. She keeps a careful arm's distance between us as she moves across the room, edging around me as if I were a big dog of uncertain temperament, and I don't crowd her. It must be my body language, or maybe she's just psychic, because she breaks out in prickles every time I get close to her, and I really think I'm doing an okay job of hiding the twist of breathlessness in my chest.

On the other hand, grown-ups always think they're better at hiding things from kids than they are.

The other shoes are in the closet. She picks out the loafers, and bends down in front of the mirror to brush her hair. "I have to do that tomorrow."

"I know."

"Do they always . . ."

"Assassinate your character? If they can."

She nods, biting her lip in the mirror, thinking about gloss and mascara. I let her; I don't care if we're late to dinner. I can almost see her cataloguing her sins, trying to decide if there are any skeletons in her closet. I want to reassure her, and for a moment I have a grown-up's idiot confidence that anybody so young must be secure in her innocence. I was younger than she is when I did what I did, so really, it's not safe to assume.

"It must have been hard surviving." She puts the hairbrush down and does her face efficiently.

"It was." I never got to have this conversation with Leah. For a moment, I'm seasick with relief, and then I remember that Gabe and Elspeth are probably having it right now, with Genie. *Crap*. "You do what you have to do, you know?"

"Yeah," she says, and stands up, ready faster than any seventeen-year-old girl has the right to be. "I do. Any idea what's for dinner?"

A soft chime from her interface draws our attention. A swirl of cool colors shot through with silver materializes over the plate, reminding me of the sky before a thunderstorm. "Patricia? Genevieve? If I may interrupt?"

It's Patty's room. I look at her. "Sure, Alan," she says, scuffing into her loafers, toe-and-heel. "Is it a crisis?"

"No," he says. "We thought you'd both like to know that Dr. Tjakamarra's found a way to communicate with the birdcages."

Patty and I share a look, and she nods that I should talk. She can probably read the question in my eyes. "What is it? And didn't we already have a way to talk to them?"

"Well, we had a pathway for communication. Although, to be fair, we're still not talking. We're playing music. But we're—Dr. Tjakamarra and Dr. Fitzpatrick are building a lexicon of symbols and meanings. *Writing* a joint language, rather than teaching them ours or us learning theirs."

"That's *huge* progress," Patty says.

"But it sounds like it could take awhile. Why music?"

I can almost see him shrug, the way the color ripples across his icon. "They started with math. The two aren't unrelated."

"And it took us this long to think of *music*?" Patty clears her throat, and when I look at her I realize I've managed to make an idiot of myself again. I finish lamely. ". . . and we didn't have a way to play them music before that they'd hear."

"It's a wonderful new alien art form," Alan says. "Translated for the first time, for creatures with no ears."

He nails me with it. I had no idea Alan had a sense of humor, let alone a wit. The shock's good for a guffaw, and then I settle down to a nice, long, loud laugh that's total overkill for the funniness of the joke.

But, God, it's been a long day.

Dinner is strained, quickly finished. General Frye doesn't show up. Neither does Min-xue; since Captain Wu isn't there and neither is his escort—that is to say, guard—I assume Min-xue is eating with the captain in his room. It's really too noisy down here for the Chinese pilot, anyway. His wiring's wound tight enough to make mine look like a placeholder.

Riel keeps her eyes on her plate and seems to find the china coffee cups an annoyingly scant measure. She doesn't touch her wine. Fred pours Patty half a glass, and Patty drinks it as if it's a duty, some grown-up ritual she doesn't like or understand, but is willing to play along with. The plates are barely off the table when she excuses herself to get ready to testify. She doesn't even finish her dessert.

"Come on," Riel says. "Let's go to the lounge." She

makes a little business of pushing her chair back from the table and smoothing the white linen tablecloth afterward, pouring herself another scant cup of coffee from the carafe, and lifting the translucent bone china cup and saucer to take with her.

Fred gestures me to precede him. I wait, and notice it takes him a little more effort than it should to get out of his chair.

He's moving like his shoulder hurts. The cold's gotten into his bones. I remember what that felt like.

It's been a long year for the both of us. I don't ask and I don't wait for permission. I just grab him by the elbow on my way past and hoist. It's always a shock that he doesn't flinch away from my hand. He knows better than most what I'm capable of doing with it. "Thanks. None of us are getting any younger, are we?"

And then he grins, lines forming across his perpetually flushed cheeks, because that's not true—in some very odd ways, I *am* getting younger. And it's as much his fault as my metal hand and my prosthetic eye and the fact that I'm walking at all, let alone standing up straight and free of pain.

He doesn't take his coffee cup and I don't take mine. I might just have a glass of brandy later. "You're welcome, Fred." I don't return his smile, and his doesn't fade at all.

Yeah, we understand each other.

The heavy cherrywood door is barely shut behind us when Riel rounds on me. She's drawn like a wire, plucked vibrating, thinner and hollower, and the strands of steel in her bobbed dark hair are maturing into racing stripes. The gray might even look good on her, but her olive skin's faded to sallow, and she's curiously . . . displaced against the rich leather furniture and patterned carpets and wall-paper. As if she were a hologram, or half a step into another dimension.

She looks at me, and her mouth works, and she sets her cup down on the sideboard without looking. She shakes her head and says, "You could have warned me, Jen."

"It's not the sort of thing that usually comes up in casual conversation." Most people don't ask if you have a criminal record as part of the standard litany that goes with ascertaining your pigeonhole in society—job, marital status, kids. It might be funny if they did. *Nah, I got picked up for possession and soliciting when I was a teenager, but I never did any time. Counseling. Suspended sentence. You know how it goes. So how do you like your job at the auto mall?* "Besides, if the Chinese can find out, how could I have been expected to know you *wouldn't*?"

Fred's leaned back against the wall a few feet away from me, watching with his head cocked to one side. If he were ten years younger I bet he'd have his ankles crossed and an insouciant smirk on his lips. His shoes gleam with polish and he's picking at the edge of his finger with his thumbnail, as if absentmindedly. Meanwhile, Riel paces, coyote in a cage, wearing a path between the window and the barrister's bookcases ranged along the back wall. She stops and pulls the curtain aside, staring out on spotlit bricks. "The Chinese shouldn't have found out. Those are sealed records." It pains her to admit that. "Nobody should have been able to get at those."

Oh, fuck me raw. "Nobody had to."

"What?"

I have to shake my head and close both hands very tight to remember not to put the left one through the wall. I'm sure that paneling's expensive. "Barb knew."

Fred looks up from his intensive survey of his finger-nails. His eyes widen, and then narrow. "Your sister never said anything to me about it, Casey."

"That's because she wasn't working for you, Fred. No matter what you thought when you signed her pay-checks. She was working for Alberta Holmes."

"Touché," he says. "And if Alberta knew about your record—"

"Then Tobias Hardy sure as hell knows about it now." Riel nods, a gesture like a gavel coming down. I've seen that decisiveness before. It worries me. "I'll patch up what I can in my testimony. It . . . well, you did well today, Jen." It's grudging, and she can't look me in the eye when she says it. "Have you ever thought of going into poli-tics?"

"And now you know why not."

She snorts, a choked-off laugh that lifts her shoulders and sets her back a fraction of a step. "It doesn't matter. The cat and the bag and the horse we rode in on and all that other stuff. We'll deal with it the only way we can: by taking it on the chin. You were right not to lie."

"Thank you." A funny little twist that I hadn't even known was there unwinds in my belly.

"And anyway, we have other problems."

Exasperation may be my least favorite emotion in the world. "Merci à Dieu. What now?"

Riel has a lot of personality flaws, but taking joy in keeping people guessing isn't one of them. "Janet Frye has had some documents registered as evidence, but I haven't been able to find out what was on them. Yet. I'm working on it."

"Don't they have to provide you with copies?"

"It's not a trial," Riel said, disgustedly. "It's a 'discovery hearing.' The fiction is that we're not adversaries, but all trying to get at the truth."

"Ostie de tabernac—"

"My sentiments exactly."

Fred straightens up and steps away from the wall, looking like he grew an inch—and all of it composed of pure cold mean. "She didn't . . . she wasn't involved until after the attack, and then she more or less took credit for Canada having the capability to respond. Now that I think about it, what would she have to testify about?"

I shake my head. My years in America left me a little behind on commonwealth politics, even the strictly Canadian ones. "Have a little mercy, Fred."

Riel shrugs and casts as if trying to remember where she left her coffee cup. I move to one side so she can see it on the sideboard; she beelines for it and drinks before she speaks, making a face at finding it cold. "The Home party likes to bill itself as the defense party, Jen. They supported the space program—including the black budget—when I was still fighting tooth and nail to get that money for health care and famine relief." She shrugs again, a very Gallic one this time. "Sometimes you guess wrong."

Yeah, I know. And sometimes there's just not enough paint to cover the whole house, so you do the sides that show. Money is not infinitely elastic, and that's as true for governments as it is for single moms. "So if she doesn't have anything to testify, what the hell does she plan to testify to?"

The look Fred shoots me is unalloyed pity. He raises one hand, wincing, and rubs at the back of his neck. I try not to feel sympathy. "Whatever the hell she and Hardy have cooked up to discredit us completely, of course.

Hardy hands her the keys to Canada, she hands him the keys to the *Huang Di,* the *Vancouver,* and the *Montreal,* and everybody goes home happy. Except us, and Richard. And China—assuming Hardy and the opposition aren't in cahoots with some PanChinese faction or another."

"Shijie Shu?" Riel says. They're both looking at me, but they're talking across me.

"That's what I was thinking."

Cup clatters on saucer again. She almost drops them on the sideboard in her haste, and Fred winces. I bet that china set is older than all three of us put together. "It's tomorrow in China, isn't it? I need to call Premier Xiong. Now."

"Connie—"

She turns back to me with her hand already on the softly gleaming brass doorknob, brows beetled over her unnaturally green eyes. "Make it quick."

"What are they planning?"

"I don't know," she says. The latch clicks as she turns the knob, but the hinges are too well oiled to creak. "But I'm thinking today was king's pawn to king four."

Patty hesitated at the top of the stairs, but didn't stop. The murmur of voices followed her. She scraped her tongue against her teeth, wishing she'd drunk more ice water, trying to work loose the tannic residue from the wine. Papa Fred was trying to be polite and include her in with the grown-ups, and she wouldn't embarrass him, but she would rather have had a seltzer.

She let her fingertips skip across the whorled ball of the finial as she turned the corner, wood smooth-waxed and evenly ridged to the touch, and took three steps before she hesitated. She tucked her hair behind her ears with a jerky, violent motion, turned around, and turned toward the library instead. Papa Georges had loved two things: his spoiled, noisy parrots and his collection of antique books, and she was so homesick for the smell of paper and leather that she gulped a mouthful of spit and blinked stinging eyes.

There was somebody in the library before her. The door stood slightly ajar, and a dim light gleamed through the crack, illuminating a knife-blade width of patterned green and wheat-gold carpeting, catching a soft highlight on the scarred wood of the threshold. Patty cocked her head, listening, her fingertips resting lightly against the dark wood of the door as if it could conduct sound directly into her bones.

She heard pages turning. Quickly, as if the turner were glancing at pictures or scanning the paragraphs for some remembered turn of phrase, rather than reading to savor. Slick, heavy paper rattled softly when it was moved, paused, was followed by the clink of glass on a coaster. Patricia held her breath, began to step back, her arm extending as if her fingers were reluctant to leave the smooth warm wood.

Alan?

"I'm listening, Patricia."

Who's in there?

"I don't know," he said. "There's nothing in that room that's on the Net or the worldwire."

Another page turned. The rustling paused, as if the reader had lifted his head from the book, one page still held vertical between his fingers, and hesitated in thought. And then, very clearly, Patty heard the rattle of paper one more time.

She had as much right to be here as anybody else did,

didn't she? She let the held breath go and stepped forward. Her elbow bent. She pushed into the room, the door swinging aside on hinges so smoothly oiled and hung that she felt no more resistance than she would have brushing aside a drapery.

General Frye sat in a leather-upholstered armchair by the ceramic fire, staring out the dark window at branches moving against the snow. Her left hand cradled the spine of a book atop her crossed legs, holding it open. Her right hand fretted at the brass heads of the tacks holding navy leather to the scrolled wooden arm of her chair; a fat crystal glass ·sat on the marble-topped table beside her. She didn't turn toward the door as Patty slipped inside, but she tilted her head slightly, and Patty knew she'd been heard.

Unacknowledged, she didn't speak. She crossed the hardwood floor and edged behind a loveseat, crouching down to run her hands over the surface of the hardbound books. The textures surprised her: slick, slightly sticky leather, broadcloth rough as a cat's tongue, patterned gilt cool in the evening air. She jerked her hand away and hissed.

It was the wiring, of course. She hadn't *touched* a book in almost a year, and the last time she had, she'd been a normal girl with a normal girl's reflexes and senses, not the tuned, hyperaware animal she'd become. Except for the omnipresent strobe of the fluorescent lights, the *Montreal* was a place of cool metal surfaces and soothing glass, soft grays and blues and the white-noise hum of its systems. It smoothed over the rough edges of interacting with the daily world very well.

Earth was full of *things*. People, textures, sudden noises.

Nine months in a controlled climate had taught Patty one way of dealing with her augmentation.

She cradled her hand close to her chest, as if she had scorched her fingertips, and forced herself to breathe slowly, evenly, through her nose. Panic helped no one. She could hear her mother saying it now.

And I'm still better off than poor Min-xue. Cautiously, she reached out again, and touched a volume bound in green leather, with little humped ridges sewn across the spine every few centimeters. It wasn't bad when she was expecting it. She just hadn't known the books would feel so...real. She hooked her fingernail over the edge and pulled. It slid into her hand with a gentle rasp of coverboards against its neighbors. She didn't look at the title; she didn't care. It smelled right.

She rose from her crouch and turned to go back to her room, and found herself looking into General Frye's alert, tired eyes. She couldn't make out their color in the angled light, but the slant of the reading lamp spilling across the book still open on her lap made her features look harsh and sad. The general nodded toward her hand. "What are you reading?"

Patty's lips thinned. She glanced down at the book pressed against her chest. "I don't know," she admitted, and looked back up. She couldn't keep the rueful little smile from twisting her lips, but she made herself not step away. *She's the enemy. She's what we're here to stop.* Still, that wasn't any reason not to be polite. It was always better to be polite. Especially if you didn't like someone. "What are you reading, General?"

Except Frye didn't look like an enemy. She looked like somebody who had lost a friend, and Patty's breath twisted in her chest as Frye looked down at the book she was holding. The slick pages with their crisp 2-D images dented slightly between her fingertips and she coughed, except it might have been a chuckle. And she said, "I don't know either," and stuck her forefinger in as a place-holder as she flipped to the front. "It's the sesquicenten-nial celebration of *National Geographic* magazine. One hundred and fifty years of unforgettable photographs. They're quite stunning." Grudgingly said, that last, as if Frye had not wanted them to be "stunning." Or as if they had affected her in some manner she found unacceptable.

Patty balanced her book against her belly and cracked it open. "Albert Payson Terhune," she said. "*Lad: A Dog*. That's a silly title."

"It's a pretty silly book, too, as I recall." Frye flipped her book back open, glanced at the page number, and set it aside on the end table, well away from her glass. "Very sentimental." She closed her eyes briefly, as if something hurt her.

Enemy, Patty said to the twinge of pity that answered that gesture. Patty reached for Alan, but Alan was silent, observing. She felt his presence, however, the cool swirl of blue and purple solidifying her resolve. *Maybe I can draw her out, find out something interesting. Would you help me do that?*

"Richard is more suited for those tasks than I am," Alan replied. He must have felt her flush of quick panic at the idea of inviting Richard into her head, because he pitched his tone soothing and said, "But I will try."

Thank you, Alan. Whatever fragile courage she had was reinforced by the sensation of leaning up against his wise, cool intellect. On a whim, she pictured herself as the golden robot girl, and felt that much braver. There was nothing Frye could say to her that could hurt her, after all. Nothing that would not slide off her impenetrable golden hide.

"Is sentiment necessarily bad?" Patty squared her shoulders and walked toward Frye. She set her novel on top of the photo book and sank into a matching blue leather chair. Her loafers dropped off her feet easily; she kicked her legs up and sat on her heels, leaning against the side of the chair.

Frye regarded her with surprise, and—Patty thought— perhaps an unexpected touch of relief. *I'm not the only one who doesn't want to be alone with my thoughts tonight.*

"No," Frye said. She picked up her drink and cupped it in her hands. Her fingers were square, a little blocky, the nails clipped short as a man's and painted a demure rose pink. She laced them together, pressing the tumbler between her palms, and leaned forward. "Sometimes it's all that makes us human."

Patty smiled. "I have to testify tomorrow," she said, and the smile didn't last through it. Leather squeaked as she drew her knees up and rested her chin on them. "Do you know what I'm going to have to say?"

"I don't think," Frye said, and paused, and looked out the window again. The snow had picked up, feathers tumbling through the spotlights' glow. Her tone was level when she resumed. "I don't think we're supposed to compare notes."

She's tired, Patty thought.

"And a little drunk," Alan supplied. "Vulnerable."

Good. "I promise not to tell you any details if you promise not to tell me any."

Frye paused, and smiled around her glass. "That sounds fair. So what's on your mind, Patty?"

It was too warm by the ceramic fire. "I'm going to have

to talk about Leah dying," she said. "And they're going to do the same thing to me that they did to Jenny. They're going to pick apart everything. And I've never told anybody about Leah."

"Then why do it?" Dry, interested. "Or is Riel making you?"

Patty bit her own tongue, not hard but hard enough to sting. She shook her head. "I can't not. Leah would have, if it was me." *Leah was seventeen times braver and prettier and better spoken.*

"Yes," Alan said. "Perhaps she was. But she wasn't any smarter, was she?"

No. Because that was true. There wasn't much of anybody smarter than Patty.

"You cared about her." Patty blinked, found Frye eyeing her like a hiker unexpectedly confronted with a panicked doe.

"She was my . . . my friend." The word *only* almost got away from her. Just as well it didn't, because the clutch in her throat told her that it would have stuck there, jabbing her until tears spilled hot down her cheeks. She bit her lip. She wasn't going to cry in front of the enemy. "People need to know why she died. Why she thought she had to die—" She was losing it. She gulped, shook her head, and scrubbed angrily at the burning in her eyes while Frye stared down into her glass, respectful of Patty's grief. Surprisingly. "She was just fourteen," Patty finished, and put her hand across her mouth in surprise. If she'd spoken to her mother in that tone of naked resentment—

But Frye just looked up, her lips as thin as if she were chewing them ragged on the inside of her mouth, and stared at Patty for a long, hard second. And then she shoved her glass aside and folded her hands together and frowned. "Look," she said. "It's going to be hard enough on you tomorrow without this. You haven't talked to anybody?"

"Just the lawyers. And they wanted to know about the crash and what happened on the bridge of the ship, and . . ."

"They didn't ask you about Leah Castaign."

"They did. They just didn't—"

Frye nodded and unfolded her hands, and Patty could see why people would follow her. Just her presence, her attention, eased the pain enough that Patty could keep talking. She clutched her golden robot-girl tight around her, and would not let her go.

"You're afraid of the questions."

"I'm afraid they'll try to make her look stupid. And I'll be making too much of a mess of myself to stop them."

"All right," Frye said. She glanced out the window one last time and resolutely turned her back on it, squaring herself, pressing her head against the back of the blue leather chair. "Look. Do you want to practice?"

"Practice?" *Alan?* He didn't answer in words, but she felt his agreement, his observation. There was something he wasn't telling her, she thought. *Alan? Is this safe?*

"Well," he said slowly, "you testify before she does anyway. And we still might learn something. I'm sure she knows more than she's showing you; she has the air of keeping secrets."

Doesn't she just? All right. I'll have the breakdown. You keep an eye on General Frye. Her false bravado rang like tin.

"Practice," Frye said, and spread her hands. "You talk about Leah. I'll ask you obnoxious questions. And we'll work on making sure you stay angry and smart, not sad and scared. All right?"

"Yes," Patty said. "All right."

Wainwright was becoming more comfortable than she had ever intended to be with having a ship that gave her backtalk, but she wasn't about to admit it. Especially not to the ship. "Dick."

"Captain?"

"Is Charlie making any progress on the nanites?"

Richard didn't take over a monitor to present her with a visual image, but she almost heard him shrug. "They've stopped going blank on us. Whether that was because the recode was successful, or because whatever was blocking them decided to give it a rest, I'm not yet ready to hypothesize."

"It's your ass on the line, too, Dick."

"Trust me, Captain. I'm intimately aware."

Wainwright *really* didn't like not having any translight pilots on board at all. Of course, Casey's testimony was finished. Wainwright could recall her now, if she wanted, and have one pilot on board the *Montreal* within twenty-four hours in case of emergency, counting travel time and time up the beanstalk. Not that the unwired, sublight pilots couldn't handle the ship perfectly well anywhere in normal space. Not that Richard wasn't perfectly capable of keeping the *Montreal* in tiptop shape. But it might be prudent to recall Casey.

On the other hand, Wainwright didn't really want Casey back until the trip to the shiptree that Riel had ordered had taken place. Because Casey would push to be allowed to go, and Wainwright didn't want that. And Riel obviously hadn't told her it was happening, because

Wainwright hadn't gotten any annoyed messages. Which was good: Wainwright wanted a tidy, cautious little team—Charlie Forster, she thought, and Jeremy Kirkpatrick, and the *Montreal*'s safety officer, Lieutenant Amanda Peterson, who had her shuttle cert and more hours pushing vacuum than any other two crew members put together. She could shift the EVA up to Sunday, send them with extra oxygen, let them take the *Gordon Lightfoot* and synch it in orbit with the shiptree and they could just *stay* there for a week, or until they figured it out or got killed, whichever came first. And *she'd* hang on to Elspeth and Gabe, thank you; they could do their work by remote, along with Leslie, and complain all they liked about it, too.

Wainwright pushed the thought of Leslie Tjakamarra away firmly and steepled her hands over her interface plate. No. She wouldn't recall Casey. Casey could stay safely on Earth for a while, out of the way. Patty Valens hero-worshipped Casey, whether Casey saw it or not, and could probably use the moral support—as Xie Min-Xue could use Patty's.

Wainwright grinned. And if she did say so herself, Jenny needed the vacation. Likely more so now than she had before. And it was good to have her out from underfoot for a while. "How's Miss Valens's testimony going?"

"You've been watching the news feeds, Captain."

"Of course I have. But I prefer to hear it from the horse's mouth, so to speak."

"Patty says she is fine," the AI answered, a slight formality tingeing his voice as a hint of Alan's personality overlaid Richard's. "She thanks you for asking."

And isn't it weird that Patty talks to Alan rather than Richard, when they're the same . . . person? Which reminded Wainwright of something else she needed to attend to. "And has the UN decided to accept your offer to testify yet?"

"They are discussing. The legal implications are daunting."

"And if they declare you a person? What changes?" He didn't answer. She reached up manually, when she could have blinked a command or issued one verbally, and changed the image on the second largest monitor to a shot of Mars from the Arean Orbital Platform. She stared at the dusty red globe, the glitter of its icy poles, and fiddled her fingertips against her trousers.

"Richard."

"Captain."

"I received a communiqué from the prime minister regarding you. And your refusal of Canadian citizenship."

"And it concerns you, with regard to my presence here."

"Yes." Her mouth was dry. She swallowed to wet it.

"Prime Minister Riel still plans to work toward a more effective world government, when the current issue of criminality in Chinese and Canadian actions is resolved."

"That's not an answer, Dick."

"I know. You understand my moral predicament."

She changed the feed again; a filtered shot of Saturn from one of the drones surfing its rings, revealing bands of color on the vast planet's surface that were invisible to the naked eye. "You no longer feel yourself in a position where you can choose one government's interests over those of others. You feel your . . . stewardship has been expanded to preclude that."

"I'm not fond of that word."

"Stewardship? Do you deny that's what it is?"

"I can't guarantee I will take the commonwealth's side

in any negotiations," he said. "But you need me to assist in the operation of the *Montreal,* and negotiations with the Benefactors, and in going with her on her further missions of research and study. And to be perfectly frank, Captain, there are people on this ship for whom I bear a personal affection. But I'm not interested in a role in loco parentis to the human race. That sounds . . . extraordinarily boring."

"It seems to me that you are going to have to evolve an entirely new ethical framework to handle this, Dick."

"Actually," he said, "I'm hoping for some sort of nominal world authority, or a cooperative venture between space-faring powers. Failing that . . ."

"Failing that"—Wainwright folded her shaking hands into her elbow joints and tried to pretend that the sinking sensation in her gut was worry about the power of the entity she confronted, and not distaste at telling off a friend—"if you cannot guarantee your loyalty to the *Montreal,* her crew, and Canada, I will be forced to ask you to abandon your input into her operations."

"I have a counterproposal."

"Let's hear it."

"I spawn a subpersona that shares the loyalties you require, and house its processes in the *Montreal* rather than the worldwire. The *Montreal* gains an AI of its own, a discrete one."

It had possibilities. "And the *Vancouver*? And the *Huang Di*?"

"Likewise. Entities of their own, in communication with the worldwire but not a part of it. Like the discrete nanonetworks inhabiting the bodies of the pilots. Those personas will be able to generate additional AIs as needed, for additional ships, and I will still be able to talk to them, and you to me."

"And the Chinese get one, too."

"Anybody who wants one gets one. I, however, determine and program the limits of their obedience."

"And that doesn't place you in loco parentis, as you said? When your . . . spawned personas, whatever their loyalty might be, can summarily refuse to follow orders? What if they decide they want to switch sides? What if this hypothetical AI decides to stand back and let the Chinese obliterate us next time, because pacifism is programmed into it?"

"Don't think I won't fight if I have to, Captain."

His tone drew her up, sharp. Even knowing that every emotion he betrayed was calculated and processed in advance, she hesitated. And then she swallowed and forged on. "Or we could have Elspeth and Gabe go back to producing intelligent programs."

"You could," he said, his voice hanging in the air.

Abruptly, she wished he *had* given her an image to watch while they spoke . . . not that a holographic icon would have given away anything he didn't choose to either.

He continued. "But that's very hit or miss. And in me, you know you have a . . . moral creation."

"I sure to hell hope so," she said. She couldn't keep the bitterness from her tone. In an attempt to chase it out of her mouth, she got up and began to pace from bulkhead to bulkhead. "You won't be able to maintain neutrality, Dick."

"I can try."

"If you were truly devoted to staying out of our human wrangling, you might consider the option of suicide." She turned her head to the side, sneaking a sly look at the monitors so he would know that she was kidding.

"The genie won't go back in the bottle, no matter how hard you wish him there. But not everything has to be a weapon."

"We're primates," she reminded him. "Sooner or later, everything is. All right, then. We'll cross that bridge when they burn it out from under us. So let's discuss our options for this EVA to the shiptree. I want to do it Sunday."

"I want to do it sooner than that. Saturday. Tomorrow. Game five of the World Series is tonight, and game six is Sunday."

"And you don't want to miss the game?"

She got it deadpan enough that he snickered. "Well, there is that, of course," he said. "But Janet Frye is scheduled to testify on Monday, and if the whole thing doesn't go to hell in a handbasket, we'll have had some good news to release on Saturday, when there's nothing else eating up bandwidth. We'll look like we're accomplishing something up here."

"And if it does go to hell in a handbasket?"

"What does it matter?" he asked. "We'll be getting screwed on Monday anyway. Frye *has* to have an ace in the hole."

6:30 AM
Saturday October 13, 2063
HMCSS Gordon Lightfoot
Earth orbit

If the birdcage looked like a fantastical Christmas ornament, the shiptree looked . . . well, like the whole damned tree. Shimmering gaud and tinsel, although the thing's curved, asymmetrical, organic outline reminded Charlie more of a satiny branch of driftwood wrapped in micro-lights than a traditional conifer. Charlie leaned forward against his five-point restraints, his helmet cradled in his lap, and gawked as shamelessly as a child. Beside him, Jeremy was doing the exact same thing, and Dick and Leslie were watching through his eyes.

They sat behind Lieutenant Peterson in the second row of crew chairs in the *Gordon Lightfoot,* leaving the copilot's chair beside her empty. The panoramic forward windows on the shuttle showed a broad slice of space, far more expansive than the triple-thick airplane windows with their rounded corners back in the passenger compartment.

Charlie's gauntleted hands tightened on the shatter-proof crystal of his helmet. At least if the shiptree slapped the *Gordon Lightfoot* out of the sky, Leslie would know everything he did. There'd be no foolishness with final transmissions and telemetry and black boxes—*do shuttle-craft even have black boxes?*

"Yes," Richard said in his head. "And they also have me, these days. And relax. The shiptree never did any-thing about the unmanned probes we sent."

Neither did the birdcage. And the probes didn't try to find a way inside, he answered, but he forced his hands to ease around his helmet. A moment too soon, because Peterson set the autopilot and lifted her own helmet off the carrier beside the pilot's chair. "Hats on, gentlemen," she said. "I suppose I should thank you two for getting me out of the office again, shouldn't I?"

Jeremy laughed, a hollow sound amplified by the dome he was settling over his head. The gold-impregnated glass caught the shuttle's interior lights, making him look as if he wore a Renaissance angel's halo over his faded gingery hair. Basset-hound eyes, drooping at the corners, and a long hollow-cheeked face completed the illusion of an old master's work, disconnected in time and place. Charlie seated his own helmet and checked the latches, then checked Jeremy's. Jeremy leaned forward to inspect Peterson's, and Peterson went over Charlie's seals.

"Leslie must be furious he isn't here for this," Jeremy said, as Peterson seated her hands on the yoke again. Charlie, who had started his shuttle cert but never finished it, noticed that she engaged the dead man's switch when she did so.

"He's spitting."

Jeremy was silent for a moment. "I'm missing Patty's testimony."

Thanks, Charlie, Leslie said. *I'm quiet and well behaved, and you're telling Jer lies about my behavior? See if I buy you a beer when we get back to Earth.*

It was meant to ease the lump in Charlie's throat when he thought of Leslie out there somewhere, drifting. It didn't. *What makes you think they're ever gonna let us go back to Earth, Les?*

Leslie's laughter almost sounded real. *Then they'd bloody well better start shipping up some fucking beer.*

Charlie snorted, fogging the inside of his helmet, and rolled his eyes as he switched on the climate control. "All ready back here," he said, out loud, so Peterson could hear him.

"Right," she said. "We're going in."

The shiptree grew slowly and steadily in size as they slid up on it. Charlie already knew the lights weren't portholes. Like all the contact team, he'd studied telescopic images and the data from the unmanned probes. He knew that the hull of the vast structure—the autonomous space-faring vegetable, as he had described the hulk he and Fred Valens had explored on Mars—was comprised of a substance not all that different from cellulose reinforced with monofilamental carbon fiber. Buckytubes: the same substance that had been engineered to make the beanstalks possible—but the buckytubes in the shiptree's hull were grown, theoretically, not manufactured.

Unless the nanosurgeons had built them, reworking the Brobdingnagian shape from whatever it had once been, into a starship. Always a possibility.

And in another fascinating twist, the conductive carbon filaments in the shiptree's hull were sheathed in a substance analogous to myelin, and interconnected via organic transistors—carbon filament diodes, which Gabe said were nearly identical to the ones used in humanity's own early experiments with nanochips, before the Benefactor tech had rendered Earth's nanomachine research obsolete.

Charlie's hands closed on the arms of his acceleration couch, the jointed gauntlets pressing creases into the flesh of his fingers as the *Gordon Lightfoot* braked on a long smooth arc and came about, paralleling the kilometers-long hull of the shiptree. Firefly green and neon-tetra blue, the lights rippled in response to the passage of the smaller ship.

"Do you suppose she's hailing us?" Jeremy, his voice dulled and echoing through the helmet. He hadn't turned on his radio.

"It's as good a guess as any," Charlie answered. "I think that's bioluminescence, which means that it's likely either for communication or for luring prey. Of course, a critter evolved for space would find light an efficient signal."

"You don't think the ship is the intelligence, do you?"

Charlie shrugged. "Why not? It's possible, and it shows up in enough science fiction that way. The one we found on Mars looked like it had something very much like the VR cables our pilots use, though. Admittedly . . ."

Richard's voice, through external speakers so Jeremy and Peterson could hear him. "Those ships were so many eons old that we can only speculate how much the species that designed them have changed."

"My thoughts exactly." *Thank you, Dick.*

Jeremy nodded inside his helmet, and started talking before Charlie could remind him to speak out loud. "Well, which leaves us with the following question. They—it— never exhibited any kind of semaphoring behavior at the unmanned probes. Do you think it knows we're out here?"

"I can feel them," Charlie said. "It stands to reason that they can feel me."

"And the probes didn't have red and green running lights," Leslie added, over the speakers rather than inside Charlie's head. "If we're theorizing that the shiptree uses bioluminescence to communicate, and *its* lights are all at the green and blue and indigo end of the spectrum, maybe it's seeing the *Gordon Lightfoot*'s green running lights as a friendly wave hi."

"You never thought to shine a spotlight on it?" Charlie couldn't be quite sure, but he was reasonably sure that Jeremy was rolling his eyes.

"I'm a biologist," Charlie said. "This is why we *hired* you guys." He craned his neck to get a better look at the whorled shell gliding by under the *Gordon Lightfoot*'s floodlights, emerging from darkness before and disappearing into darkness again behind, outlined by its own rippling glow and the trembling silver-gray threads of whatever it was that trailed off the smooth hull between them. It was like the hulk of some long-submerged wreck revealed and then vanishing in the lights of an exploratory submarine. He could have seen it more plainly in the holoscreens, but there was something about the evidence of his own eyes that tightened his throat and made breathing an effort.

"Lieutenant," Jeremy said, "can you dim our lights?"

"Dim them? Or shut them off?"

"Well, all the way off. But just flash them a few times."

"Damn, look at that thing; it's got no symmetry at all, not bilateral or radial. It's just kind of there."

"It's got a fractal pattern, though," Richard pointed out. "The smaller whorls build to larger whorls and then larger ones. The whole thing looks like a giant toboggan if you squint at it."

"How are you managing to squint, Dick?" Charlie shot back, drawing a laugh from Jeremy. The AI was right, though. It was as apt a description as the one that had come to Charlie, of water-worn driftwood. "You know what it reminds me of?"

"Coral," Jeremy said promptly, and Dick said "Gypsum crystals, only curved."

"Ready to flash lights."

"Thank you, Lieutenant." Charlie strained against his restraints to get a better look.

The sudden darkness in the *Gordon Lightfoot*, inside and out, was shocking. The cabin lights went out, followed—Charlie presumed, unable to see for himself—by the running lights lining her sides. Isolated in his suit, Charlie counted breaths, counted heartbeats. He could feel Richard and Leslie, feel Jeremy and Peterson in the cockpit of the shuttle, feel his suit and the trickle of cool air into his helmet, and none of it meant a thing beside the ... *weight* of the shiptree, its presence, like an enormous silent breathing beast in the darkness alongside the fragile bubble of the *Gordon Lightfoot*.

The darkness lasted three heartbeats. Peterson flashed the shuttle's lights once, twice, a third time ... and then left them on, and Charlie drew a single tremulous breath.

For a moment, the shiptree hung shimmering in space, silent and lovely, quiescent as a slumbering dragon. Until, without warning, the entire length of the strange curved hull went dark.

"Damn," Jeremy said.

Peterson killed the lights of the shuttle again, before Charlie could suggest it. "I hope that thing doesn't move on me," she murmured in a soft, strained voice. Charlie wouldn't be surprised if she hadn't meant to say it aloud. And then she whispered, "*Holy* ..." as a dim sunlit glow irised into existence on the shiptree's hull, an aperture like a focusing eye.

"What the bloody hell is that?" said Jeremy, and Charlie grinned in the dark, because the glow illuminated a puff of vapor dispersing into darkness.

"It's an air lock," Peterson said.

"It's an air lock," Charlie echoed, a second later. "And the atmosphere inside has water vapor in it, and maybe carbon dioxide and oxygen. Would you look at that? Somebody lives in there, boys and girls. Somebody *lives in there*."

"It's bloody beautiful," Leslie commented from the speakers. The shiptree's lights winked back at them, blue and green and teal, and, with a sigh Charlie couldn't interpret, Peterson illuminated the shuttle.

"We can't dock," she said.

"No. EVA. Safer, anyway, since we won't share any atmosphere with the shiptree that way, and we'll get a nice vacuum bath coming and going."

"Is that wise?" Jeremy asked.

Charlie shrugged, even though Jeremy couldn't see it. "It's what we came here to do. And I think they just invited us in."

Jeremy calibrated the atmospheric sampler while Charlie checked the swabs and plates in his test kit. *And if alien bugs don't like the taste of agar?*

Then we assume they don't like the taste of people either.

Hah, Leslie. On the other hand, it wasn't a half-bad point. There was no reason to think that an alien pathogen would find anything tasty about humans. And if it did . . . well, frankly, Charlie's nanosurgeons might protect him from any ill effects. Assuming anything got through the suit. *And in any scientific endeavor there is the element of risk.*

He tapped Jeremy's arm, automatically bracing himself with a strap to account for the reaction. Jeremy looked up and hung the sampler on his belt. "Ready?"

"As I'll ever be."

Charlie made sure his suit radio was live and said, "Lieutenant, we're moving out."

"Copy."

Together, they glided aft, toward the air lock.

Charlie went first. Peterson had matched velocities with the shiptree so evenly that he didn't need his attitude thrusters; he just checked the carabiner on the safety line clipped to Jeremy's suit, made sure the line was playing freely through the retractor, and jumped. There was no relative velocity between the *Gordon Lightfoot* and the alien vessel; Charlie sailed easily across the empty space and landed exactly where he'd aimed, with a firm grip on a whorl outlined in lime-green lights.

Up close, they looked exactly like firefly lights, but their texture—through the suit—was as hard as that of the surrounding hull. He stopped only half a second before he pressed the bubble of his helmet against the whorl. *That might not be wise, Charlie.*

Not that wisdom had ever really been his strong point. "I'm over," he told Jeremy. Unnecessarily, but Jeremy would wait for verbal confirmation anyway, in case his grip was no good.

"I'm on my way," Jeremy replied. Charlie didn't turn his head to look, just firmed his grip on the hull and waited. A faint tug on the safety lines, a light shock of impact through the hull of the shiptree, and Jeremy was beside him. "First step's a lulu," the linguist said.

"You aren't kidding. That air lock's big enough for two at a time, I think."

"I don't like the idea of that. I'll go first," Jeremy replied. "I have the atmosphere kit."

"There's no atmosphere in there yet. And if the lock cycles with one of us inside and one of us out, we lose the safety lines. And possibly damage the air lock and piss off the natives."

"You have a point." There was a silence, and for a moment Charlie thought Jeremy was going to ask Richard's opinion. Or Wainwright's. Although the captain had been completely silent so far, Charlie had no illusions that she wasn't watching, breath held. She might look cool and reserved, but he knew a professional facade when he saw one. Charlie waited. Jeremy sighed over the radio and said, "All right, then. Side by side."

They released their grips on the shiptree's hull on a count of three and kicked off lightly, shadows cast by the *Gordon Lightfoot*'s floods expanding as they drifted back. Attitude jets reversed their trajectory and brought them in a looping half-arc, *swish* into the wide-open air lock like a free-throw basketball.

The shuttle's floods were arc-light white, the diffuse glow inside the shiptree the calm, friendly gold of late-afternoon sun. Charlie glanced around as he and Jeremy fetched up against the interior wall of the air lock. The blue-green bioluminescence didn't persist inside the hull. Here, instead, the curved bulkheads bowed together, chambered and knobbed like the inside of a turtle's shell, and each veined ridge glowed sunshine gold.

"Pretty," Jeremy said. "That's not a color we get much in bioluminescence on Earth, is it?"

"No," Charlie answered. "It looks like a full-spectrum light. I'm going to take some swabs of the walls. Where do you suppose the inside door is?"

"I think we'd better let the aliens handle cycling the air lock," Jeremy answered, allowing himself to turn slowly at the end of his tether, scanning the walls of the vaguely spherical chamber. "I'd hate to purge the ship by acci-dent, even if I could find the controls, and there's no guar-antee they have anything like our concept of safety interlocks. Doesn't look as if they ever intended there to be gravity in this, does it?"

"No." Charlie busied himself opening the plates and sterile swabs. "It'll take some time to culture these, of course. A week or ten days. And I guess we'll want to get some samples of this and that back to the *Montreal* to run through the mass spec."

"Lieutenant Peterson, you'll run these back for us

when we've got them ready?" Jeremy didn't need to change
frequencies to speak to the shuttle, or the *Montreal*. Their
entire conversation was on an open channel.

"That's why they sent me along, Dr. Kirkpatrick," she
answered. "As long as you're certain there's no danger."

"Never say never," Charlie quipped, stowing a swab in
a sterile baggie and running his glove along the bulkhead.
"I wonder if this feels as much like walnut paneling as it
looks."

"I wonder how it stands up to the extremes of cycling
between space and the internal environment, if it's wood."

"Nanosurgeons," Charlie answered, more dryly than
he'd intended. "Also, in the very least, the shiptree of
Mars wasn't wood. Not exactly."

"But enough like wood that you called it a tree—"

"What the heck else would you call it? Oh, hey." As his
gloves snagged on a rough patch. "There's something different here. A stained area, and the wood fibers are raised."

"Diseased?"

"Maybe." Charlie tugged his hand free, cautious of the
suit's material. The area was a bit sticky, too, as if it were
oozing sap. A bit of the bulkhead seemed to shift with his
movement. "Ooops."

"You're not a very reassuring person to explore an alien
ship with, Charlie. What did you do?"

A shift in the quality of the light alerted him, a shadow
falling across his back as the irising door cut the *Gordon
Lightfoot*'s floods. "Um. Triggered the air lock?"

"Dr. Forster? Dr. Kirkpatrick?" Peterson's voice, simultaneous with a Leslie-flavored burst of worry in the back
of Charlie's brain.

"We're good in here," he said, as the wall opposite began to unfurl from its central ridge like a flower bud spi-raling open. "We seem to be allowed in . . ."

When the shiptree's atmosphere touched his suit, his helmet frosted over like a beer glass on a humid day. Jeremy cursed. "Can you see anything?"

"Not a thing."

"Turn up your suit heaters," Richard suggested. "Did you get the atmospheric sample?"

"As soon as I can read the dials, Dick." Jeremy's tone absolved his words of irritation.

Charlie worked on clearing the surface of his helmet immediately in front of his face, curls of frost drifting from the creases of his suit and melting into jeweled drop-lets as they did. "I'd say there's some moisture in the at-mosphere—"

"Hah." A pause. "Eighty three percent humidity. Yeah, that's some. It's a warm room temperature in here."

"Oxygen?"

"You could light a match, but you might scorch your fingers—let's put it that way. Lots of carbon dioxide, too. A little light on the nitrogen, heavy on the argon by our standards. This shows particulate matter, not to excess. Pollen or dust?"

"We'll know when we get the filters under a micro-scope," Charlie said. Water beaded his faceplate, but he could see the open interior door clearly once he knocked it away. Drifting globules spattered against the air lock's walls, leaving behind a pattern of wet round dots that were rapidly absorbed. "If this is like the one on Mars, there will be a ladder type projection to use for traction when we get into the corridor."

"Well, let's go see if they're waiting for us inside," Jeremy said, checking the safety line before he reached out, flat-palmed the wall, and pushed himself toward the new opening. "I don't see any shadows."

"Would you, in this light?"

"I don't—oh." Jeremy reached out and caught one lip of the door in his right hand. Charlie drifted into his back, hard.

"Oof!"

"Shh." Before Charlie could complain.

Charlie caught the other side of the doorway in his left hand and braced himself, and turned away from Jeremy and toward the interior of the shiptree. "Oh," he said, blinking, trying to clear his eyes, and then realizing they didn't need clearing.

He and Jeremy had drifted into a jungle, emerging from a hole in the floor—essentially—to drift surrounded by twisted vines and heavy flowering branches thick with glossy leaves. The light glowed from the floor as well as overhead, and small creatures darted and called among the branches. Some of them had feathers or fur in jeweled colors; Charlie glimpsed something like a scarlet tanager with a snakelike neck. Animal voices rang through his helmet, shrillness muffled. Even damped by leaves and space suits the echoes made Charlie think they were in open space.

A hazy mist wound between the vines and branches, veils of silk that moved in response to air currents. "A zero-G rain forest," Jeremy said.

"Cloud forest," Charlie corrected automatically. "Well, I suppose it could 'rain,' through some mechanism we're not seeing. Sprayers or something. But it looks like we're seeing plants watered by condensation, and frankly, if I *didn't* know that I don't know any of these species, I would think I was in Costa Rica. Look at all the pollinators and the insect eaters. They look just like humming-birds and swifts. Convergent evolution. These critters brought their whole ecosystem with them."

Jeremy glanced over at him, flash of teeth as he grinned behind his helmet. "I can hear the throb in your voice, Charlie."

"It's not all that different from what we did with the *Montreal* and her hydroponics farms. These critters might be like *us,* Jeremy—"

Jeremy cleared his throat and looked around, shaking more droplets of water off his gauntlets. "They might be," he said. "But where *are* they? All this landscape, and no aliens. And no indication of which way we're supposed to go, or who we need to talk to. I could do with a sign that says 'follow the gray line to customs,' you know?"

"Maybe we're intended to find our own way in?"

And one of the leafy, glossy vines uncoiled itself from the structure of the nearest branch, or stanchion, or support pillar, and laid itself across Charlie's shoulders like a heavy, companionable arm.

0900 hours
Monday October 15, 2063
Canadian Embassy
New York City, New York USA

On Sunday, the Yankees tie it up three to three, so on Monday I'm stuck with the unpalatable choice between watching the final game of the series, or showing up at the UN to watch General Janet Frye take us all apart in person. I mean, all right, I'm still more of a hockey girl. But I did live in Hartford for over a decade, and it's not like we don't have baseball in Canada.

On the other hand, I have a coiling feeling in my gut that tells me I should be at the UN when the shit hits the fan. Besides, Riel and Valens are going, and it's not like those two can be trusted out on their own.

So we wind up making a bit of a funeral festival of it.

Captain Wu finished his testimony on Saturday, after Patty's second half-day. He remains at the embassy, but Min-xue, whose evidence promises to take nearly as long as mine did, is scheduled for after Frye. Both men join Riel, Valens, Patty, and myself in the lobby, all of us nearly unspeaking as we wait for General Frye. Min-xue's hands are clothed in white leather gloves like the ones Patty and I wear. The gloves are a little too small, kidskin strained over his knuckles, even though he has fine hands. The gloves are probably Patty's spare pair, and the look she gives him when she notices confirms it.

Min-xue's eyes are unreadable behind dark glasses, but he's wearing a Chinese military uniform. Captain Wu straightens his collar flash for him before we leave, which makes me wonder what's what. It's odd, being outside all these alliances. I'm too old for Patty and Min-xue, not *patriotic* enough for Valens and Riel. I'm not part of any system at all, I guess. Not anymore.

Fred clears his throat after five minutes, and we all look at him. He glances from Patty to me and back, and folds his hands behind his back. "While we're waiting for Janet, I don't suppose you've heard from Richard about Drs. Forster and Kirkpatrick."

"Of course we have, Papa Fred. Don't be silly."

He grins at her. They connect; I can almost hear the click when their eyes make contact, and the cloaks of exhaustion and grief all of us wear fall off them for an instant. Christ, I can't believe how much I miss Leah, just then. And not just Leah. Razorface, too, and Mitch, and Bobbi Yee . . .

Dammit.

I am not losing any more family to this toothy monster that is history. Enough is enough.

I'm thinking so hard about my gritted teeth that I almost miss Patty's precis of the action on the shiptree. It's a pretty simple one, still: Jeremy and Charlie have brought in a tent and oxygen and food and set up a base camp in the jungle they've discovered, from which they have been launching exploratory jaunts. Their samples have been returned to the *Montreal* for analysis, and other than a particularly vicious pollen-analogue that looks guaranteed to produce hay fever bad enough that you'd wish it was terminal, nothing that even remotely qualifies as a pathogen has been discovered. Yet.

Everything in the shiptree is crawling with nano-surgeons, though. According to Charlie, he can *feel* the entire ecosystem working around him, as if it were all one tremendous organism. He compares it to something he calls the Gaia hypothesis, but I haven't had time to look that up yet, and apparently neither has Patty. Of course, I could just ask Richard—

"You could, at that."

Good morning, Dick. I straighten my cuff and pick a bit of lint off it. *What's the good word?*

A broad smile crinkles his cheeks. "I've been invited to testify before the General Assembly of the United Nations, regarding my knowledge of events leading up to and including December 23, 2062."

My crow of victory turns the heads of everybody in

the room, including General Frye, who has just appeared at the top of the stairs. Patty's recitation breaks off mid-sentence; she turns to me with a grin for just a second before she glances down at her hands, twisting gloved fingers together.

"What's the occasion?" Frye calls, coming down the stairs like a queen walking to the guillotine. The shadows under her eyes make me wonder for a minute if she's broken her nose, and the eyes themselves are so bloodshot the whites look pink. Gray skin and a gray expression. She looks like she wants to throw up, and only pride and grim determination are keeping her jaw locked.

It's profoundly unsettling to see an expression like that one someone else's face, especially when you've felt it from the inside once or twice.

"Richard can testify," Patty answers, before I marshal my thoughts. I think I'm the only one who notices the way Frye's hand tightens on the banister, or how she turns her attention very definitely to her feet. Well, Riel probably does, too. It's her job to catch stuff like that, and the shift of Frye's weight is definite enough to make me think of somebody bracing for a fight. Maybe even spoiling for one.

Frye lifts her eyes. She's looking directly at Connie when she does it, but her gaze slides off as she reaches the landing, and settles on Patty. "Did you finish your book?"

I think Patty's going to glance at Fred for strength, but she doesn't. Instead, she looks at me, and when I meet the glance directly, she looks immediately back at Frye. "The one about the dog? I did. It didn't take very long."

"I saw it was back on the shelf. I thumbed through it."

"You did? What did you think?" Again Patty sneaks me a look. There's some subtext here, something I'm meant to understand. I remember her testimony, the calm, serious voice in which she'd talked about Leah, Leah's death, our own refusal—hers and mine—to retaliate after the Chinese destroyed Toronto. I remember the way she'd refused to look at me or at Fred while she was doing it. And I remember how pissed off Riel was that she told the assembly that Riel *had* called for retaliation, and the way she'd shrugged afterward and said, "But I was under oath."

Somehow, the questioning of me never got around to that. I've got a feeling I might be called back to clarify. I think I would have preferred a formal trial, after all. With rules of evidence, and a few against self-incrimination.

Ah, well. You know, some days, going to jail doesn't sound all that bad.

Patty's comment gets that kind of a raised eyebrow and a slight little smile from General Janet Frye. "I still think it's too sentimental," Frye says, as the doorman brings her overcoat. "I would have preferred a more realistic relationship between the man and the dog. What do you think?"

"I think that I liked what it had to say about loyalty," Patty says—very unlike Patty, because she doesn't look down when she says it. General Frye, in fact, lowers her eyes first, ostensibly to button her cuffs. But I can see from the way Patty leans forward like a hound on a scent that there's more here, and I'm not getting it. "Even if it was sappy."

"What book are you talking about?" Fred asks, looking all polite interest, but I notice the way his eyes catch at mine over the top of Patty's head. He doesn't know what's up here either.

"*Lad: A Dog*," Patty says, taking Min-xue's elbow in

her white-gloved hand and turning him toward the door, while he looks at her in shock. "Come on, General Frye. You're running late, and I think the limo is waiting."

Fred grabs my elbow as I'm about to walk past him, and makes a little show of escorting me toward the door. He leans in close, his breath tickling my ear. "Casey—"

"The answer is no."

A snort of laughter moves my hair, but his hand tightens over my metal fingers where they tuck into the crook of his arm. "Find out what the hell they were just talking about under our noses, like kids with a secret code."

"Go piss up a rope, Fred."

He pats my hand. "I knew you'd see it my way."

Riel must have caught those last two sentences, or maybe she's just as shocked as Frye is by the sight of a brigadier general squiring a noncom around like his date for the ball.

Dick?

"Patty says she's playing a hunch that the general's unease has to do with her testimony, and whatever parts might not be a little . . . exaggerated. Apparently they had a long conversation the other night, and Patty twigged that something was up."

Frye was pumping her?

"Yes, and no. She says that Frye seemed troubled and introspective, and flinchy on the subject of the testimony. And very interested in Leah and how Patty felt about Leah, in a . . . thoughtful kind of way."

What does Alan say?

"Alan says to shut up and give her the rope she needs." Richard sighs, spreading his hands helplessly wide. "He's very protective of Patty."

He didn't phrase it quite that way, I bet.

"I don't gamble when I'm only going to lose," Richard answers. "Look up, Jen. There's the car—" as Fred tugs my arm lightly, to get my attention.

"Well?" he asks, as he hands me in.

"I'll tell you in private," I say, and duck my head to climb into the limo. Frye's not the only one giving me a funny look when I lean my head back against the cushions, close my eyes, and echo Richard's sigh.

Frye's still staring at Patty when the six of us and a handful of unhappy Mounties pile out of the motorcade on the Lower East Side. Staring at Patty, and chewing on her lip, with a completely transparent *that-kid-knows-more-than-I-think-she-should-know* look plastered all over her face. I've got to admit, Patty's performance would have me apoplectic, too. It's perfect—just a little underplayed, smug, seemingly more interested in the coffee and the scenery and the scraps of torn blue behind a skyful of clouds twisting like gray rags in the wind than in the sidelong glances Frye is shooting her.

It amuses me for the whole of the chilly walk into the UN complex, especially since I quietly let Fred take point and I take tail-end Charlie, the two of us shepherding the rest of them along the ice-scattered sidewalk inside our ring of plainclothes protectors. I never would have thought I'd watch a middle-aged military professional played like a fly-fished trout by a seventeen-year-old girl.

"A seventeen-year-old girl and a nine-month-old artificial intelligence," Richard reminds. I snort into my coffee.

Frye doesn't have any kids, does she?

"Nary a one. And she's an only child."

Lucky dogs, the both of you. That wouldn't work for half

*a second if she did. You don't actually think she's going to
break and tell you anything?*

"I'm just hoping Alan and Patricia can make her sweat
hard enough on the stand that she looks like she's lying."

The chances are slim.

"The choices look grim," he answers, with a funny hic-
cuping rhythm, like he's quoting a song. If he were real
and standing in front of me, I'd fix him with my bug-eyed
look. "Never mind. Someday my cultural referents will
catch up to yours."

*And by then I'll be in my grave, and you'll be confounding
Genie's children.*

"I'll need new personalities to confound Genie's children. The Feynman persona would leave them a bit too
baffled."

It's a little creepy, hearing the AI talk about what I
think of as *himself* as if it were an accessory, a shirt that
could go out of fashion. Just another brutal reminder of
how inhuman he really is. *I'd miss you, Dick.*

"Dick's not going anywhere."

Except to the stars, I answer, and we share a pleased interior laugh at that.

There's something of a kerfuffle when we get to the
UN; more security personnel than I expected, and a few
discreet questions between Riel and our charming guide,
the same Mr. Jung (in green and red hanbok, this time),
turn up the not-too-surprising information that the
Chinese delegation has arrived, and the premier is with
them today.

The PanChinese group catches sight of us in the
General Assembly lobby, in the shadow of the enormous
pendulum. Three of them break away as soon as we enter,

attention obviously caught by the three rifle-green uniforms, the darker, richer green of Min-xue's kit, and Patty and Riel in civvies, flanked by the stiff spines of a couple of Mounties in plainclothes. Two Mounties. Not *nearly* enough to keep this crew out of trouble, but all they let us bring inside.

The good news is, the PanChinese also get only two.

From the way the dark-suited individuals who look to be the security team are hustling to keep up, the slender-shouldered man in the lead has to be Premier Xiong. I'm more sure of it because he looks familiar, if bigger than he does on the feed, and I've gone from somebody who wouldn't recognize Minister Shijie if he fell at my feet to being able to pick his sad-bulldog face out of a crowd at two hundred paces. A thousand, if you gave me a sniper scope.

That shark in the mahogany suit is still right alongside him, and there's another attaché of some sort bringing up the rear of the pack.

I step back, getting myself between Min-xue and Patty and the Chinese, and let Riel and Frye deal with the guests. Min-xue's indrawn breath is audible from where I'm standing.

Oh, this is going to be fun.

Except Premier Xiong stops in front of Riel as if there were a microphone stand marking the spot, nods his head—a quick birdlike dip of the chin that acknowledges the petite woman in front of him and brings him momentarily down to her level without making a production of it—and thrusts out his right hand with the aplomb of the father of the groom sorting out the groom's guests from the bride's. A hush falls like snow.

"Prime Minister," he says, a very white, slightly predatory smile illuminating his homely face, "it is a pleasure to finally meet you in person."

The swing of the Foucault pendulum might be the arrested pulse of a giant heart. The whole room feels like an in-held breath, and I can *feel* the pressure of all those eyes.

And then Connie Riel takes two broad steps forward, and reaches out, and grabs Xiong's hand in both her own just as if she always meant to, and the collective heart of everybody in the room thumps once, hard, and begins to beat again. "Premier Xiong." Her flat Albertan accent rings harsh against his musical tones. "I look forward to a new era of cooperation between our governments. Once we have set these differences behind us."

I don't think either she or Premier Xiong notice the way General Shijie's brow smooths, and a slight smile turns up the corners of his mouth, but I'm suddenly certain why I had that premonition that I ought to make sure I showed up today.

Xiong steps back and offers Riel a short crisp bow, which she returns without the heel-click. He turns toward me when he pivots away, and I catch the devilish glitter in the coffee-dark eyes under his thinning brows and almost swear out loud.

They set that up. Son of a bitch. And from the stricken look on Frye's face, I'd have to say it was worth it. Even though I *really* don't like the way the minister of war is smiling.

"Right," Riel says, as Xiong strides away, and glances up at me with a sly, sidelong smile. Some days, I really don't mind having taken three bullets for her. "Let's go in there and make the world safe for parliamentary democracy with pronounced socialist leanings, shall we?"

I'm not surprised when Fred is the only one who laughs.

Patty Valens's knowing smirks might almost have been enough to shake Janet's resolve, if she hadn't already made up her mind. The kid didn't know anything; the kid *couldn't* know anything. She held that thought cleanly in her mind, hard and fast, as she mounted the steps to the podium. Because if Patty knew something, then Fred would know it, and if Fred knew it, Janet Frye had no illusions that she would have lived long enough to take that stage and look up to meet the expectant eyes of the world.

Frederick Valens was not one of the good guys, and he never had been. And he would have very quietly, very thoughtfully seen that she was out of the way if he'd known what Toby gave her.

If he had known what she had agreed to do.

The funny thing was, she hadn't decided until this morning. She didn't think she'd slept in four days, and she'd had far more to drink than anybody in her position ought to. And it hadn't been Patty Valens's transparent manipulations that had made her mind up, once Patty had realized there was a hook in Janet's lip that could be worked. It hadn't been the simple dignity of Casey's testimony, or the way Captain Wu had broken down on the stand. No. That wasn't what made her hand shake when she shook the secretary general's hand.

It was the memory of Constance Riel looking her dead in the eye and snapping, *And then if you want to hand PanChina the keys to the castle, you can do it on your own watch.*

Damn you to hell, Connie, she thought, as she stated her

name. Her oath was ashes in her mouth. She raised her right hand anyway and thought of Canada and the good of the commonwealth.

She took one deep breath and found Connie's chair at Canada's table, and made damn sure that Constance Riel was looking into her eyes when she opened her mouth and said, "Before I make any other statements regarding my knowledge of circumstances leading up to the tragic events of last Christmas, I need to reveal a few very important facts that have not yet entered the record."

She needed another breath. Two, maybe. She needed a drink of water, so she took one, and let the ice click against her teeth. *Look pretty for the cameras, Connie,* she thought. *They're going to be closing in for the reaction shot.*

"On the morning of October eleventh of this year," Janet said, "I was introduced by Unitek executive Tobias Hardy to a gentleman whose name I was not given, but who was identified to me as an agent of the United States of America . . ."

The pandemonium as she continued was even grander than she'd anticipated. She wasn't surprised when Shijie Shu got up from the Chinese table, made his excuses to the premier, and headed for the door. She did notice that none of his security or the PanChinese attachés went with him, and thought that was a little odd, but she wanted to get what she had to say into the record before her nerve broke once and for all.

She kept talking. It wasn't like she'd be the first politician to wind up in jail.

The Benefactors were still singing. And Leslie was still trying to overlay his map-in-song of local space with their map-in-curved-space time. It was interesting, because not even the relative significance of objects was the same; for Leslie, a bright object was of more significance than a dark object. For the birdcages, the emphasis lay on *heavy* objects, although their scale of reference was fine enough that objects no more massive than Leslie's fist registered at a distance, and up close they could sense on a fine enough scale to read the text on his space suit by the different specific gravity of the letters compared to unmarked portions.

It was promising. If they could only be made to understand the concept of symbology, and of words, he might be able to start establishing a pidgin. If the boredom didn't kill him first.

It wouldn't have been so bad if Leslie actually had nothing to do. He could have sat back, played long-distance draughts with Charlie, and dreamed of good lager. Unfortunately, the interior of the shiptree was exactly where he needed to be right now, and there was absolutely nothing he could do about it except ride resolutely behind Charlie's eyes and swear quietly in his ear.

This was what he had come for. Charlie and Jeremy had discovered an environment—an entire *ecosystem*—populated by dozens of never-before-seen species, all of them seemingly communicating in some matter that was neither intuitively obvious nor easily dismissable. Leslie's dream, his obsession, his life's work, spread out for him like a banquet on the other side of a wall of shatterproof glass. He could see through Charlie's eyes, hear through his ears, lay his hands on something as if Leslie ran his own hands over the surface. Charlie's body became, for Leslie, a sort of almost-perfect remote drone or probe.

But it wasn't the same as being there. And it got in the way of Charlie doing his own work, too.

Richard helped out as best he could, keeping Leslie supplied with live images of Earth, of Piper Orbital Platform, of a 3NN anchor providing analysis of Frye's "explosive" testimony, and of the birdcage and the ship-tree hanging calmly in the void, of the *Gordon Lightfoot* bright with reflected sunlight, a single sharp-edged dot like the morning star, still synchronized with the vaster, darker shape of the shiptree. He also let Leslie watch his own view of the *Montreal*'s bridge—full of people, un-usually so for a ship not under way. Genie was on her way through with her HCD in her hand, headed for the pilot's ready room that was now her exclusive domain. Wainwright was in her chair, sipping coffee and going over reports.

Leslie's fingers itched, and he suddenly wished he'd screamed for rescue, twisted the captain's arm until she yelped. *Third time's the charm.* He wanted to be where Charlie and Jeremy were, doing what they were doing, not somewhere bodiless, cold and eyeless in the dark.

Greedy, he reprimanded. He might not be able to see, or feel, or even feel his body—Richard assured him the suit was still intact, that the Benefactors were still keeping him breathing in there somehow, as bizarre and unsus-tainable as that seemed—but he could sense things no hu-man had ever sensed before: The weight of the *Montreal* and the shiptree curving space time. The gravity well of the sun, like a mountain looming on the horizon, the foot-hills that were the Earth and the moon, the local flickers and fluctuations of the birdcage aliens surrounding him, manipulating epic forces on a scale as precise as the stroke of a surgical scalpel, in patterns modulated and refined to echo themes he gave them.

Playing him the music of the spheres.

He wouldn't permit himself to remember that the odds were a thousand to one that he was going to die out here.

You're where you belong. And you'll get home somehow. Eventually.

In the meantime, he kept himself busy talking to Charlie, and to Jeremy—through Charlie—and writing exhaustive reports on the data he could collect in between Charlie's xenobiological pursuits. Although, right this instant, both of them were too focused on Dick's feed-via-Casey of what was going on in New York for either one of them to be accomplishing a lot.

There's something to be said for hive minds, Leslie thought.

Charlie didn't have to look up from his perusal of a recovered feather—*feather-analogue*—to engage the conversation. *Ours, or the shiptree's?*

Don't you think two hive minds would be a bit coincidental?

There is that. Charlie hooked a toe under a projecting root to keep from drifting, curling his legs to hunch himself closer to the tree-analogue he was examining. Leslie's kinetic sense wanted to echo the movement, wanted to feel his muscles stretch and play as Charlie's did. Bad enough he found himself imagining breathing hard when Charlie clambered around the chambered arboretum that seemed to comprise the majority of the shiptree's interior. *And frankly, I'm not sure what we have here is a hive mind, so much as a Gaia-type intelligence. The whole ecosystem, including the ship, seems to function as one beastie; not a threaded intelligence, like Dick, and not separated intelligences, like humans, and not a single big unified brain split into however many bodies it happens to need at a given moment, as I suspect the birdcages are, but something more like the internal structure of the human mind, where various sections handle various functions autonomously, irrespective of whether the consciousness knows what's going on at all.*

So you're suggesting this thing's reptile brain is—

Actually housed in a reptile. More or less. Yeah. Charlie's knees ground as he straightened his legs, letting himself drift. Leslie winced in sympathy. *Or maybe a shrubbery. The plants are awfully friendly around here.* He brushed away a vine that tried to twine around his waist.

And how do they communicate, then?

Leslie felt the shrug as Charlie continued. *Chemically? Electrically? Same way your brain does, I guess. Jeremy's done a little poking around here and there; not only is the air we're not breathing a soup of pheromones, but there's nanosurgeons through all this plant life and the whole thing is threaded with conductive material. Heck, if I'm right, the buckytubes that give the thing's hull its tensile strength are also its brain. Based on Richard's theory that all you need for consciousness is the right kind of piezoelectric activity in any sort of substrate that will support it, buckytubes are ideal, as long as they have neurons and synapses. More or less.*

"I'm not defining consciousness this week," Richard said.

Good. Then I won't have to wrestle you for my Nobel Prize. Charlie reached out and caught the branches of a tree-analogue in his gauntleted fist, wiping beads of condensation off his face plate. *Dammit. I've had it with this suit. Still nothing doing with the culture plates?*

"Charlie," Richard said, "I'd prefer you waited the full eleven days. I don't like you risking yourself unnecessarily."

I don't like risking myself at all, Charlie replied. *But we've established there's nothing toxic to earthling life in here. The proteins and sugars even twist the right way. And I've got a belly full of alien nanosurgeons that should be able to handle anything I might get myself into. If I wasn't thinking hard about Persephone and Eve, I'd even consider taking a bite out of one of those things that look like azure figs.*

You sound like you're talking yourself into something, Chaz. Leslie needed to walk. It was driving him nuts that he couldn't stuff his hands in his pockets and go for a stroll.

Oh, hell, Charlie answered. He reached through the canopy and grasped an outgrowth of the chamber's glowing wall, strands of light sliding through disarrayed greenery. *I've already talked myself into it. What's the worst that could happen?*

"At least go back to Jeremy and the base camp—" Richard said, but Charlie shrugged inside his space suit again and pushed himself away from the bulkhead, setting himself adrift.

Jeremy would just get in the way, he said, reasonably. *Besides, we figured out how to talk to the birdcages when we got swallowed and chewed up a bit, and Les and I are both fine.*

Sure. Psychically linked and chock-full of alien micromachines, and I'm stuck in orbit with a space suit that's being renewed by alien tech the only thing keeping me alive, and I can't feel my body. But just peachy, all in all. Chaz—

Trust me, Leslie, Charlie said, and tripped the latches on his helmet with gauntlet-awkward thumbs.

Leslie held his breath, his hands clutching uselessly on nothing but the fabric of his gauntlets as Charlie lifted the helmet aside, as if he could force Charlie to hold his in sympathy, as if—

Charlie blinked, his eyes immediately scratchy and red, and spoke out loud. "Well, I'm allergic to the flower-analogues. The air smells clean. Green, moist—damn, there's a lot of 'pollen.'"

Are you sure you don't want to put your hat back on?

"Yeah," he said. Leslie could feel the sneeze building in the back of Charlie's throat, and to be honest, it did feel just like a snoot full of dust and plant sex. And the air *did* smell glorious through Charlie's nose, fresh and cool and redolent of sweet strange flowers, gingery and complex. "Huh. I'd strip off the rest of my suit, but I don't want to haul it back. Oh, damn."

Charlie's head went back, his lungs filled with a breath taken for a deep and violent sneeze—

And he vanished like a blown-out candle, completely and painlessly *gone*. Leslie reached for Richard, and Richard wasn't there. *Dick?*

Dick?

Nothing. *Richard, can you hear me? Bugger all—*

His fists clenched hard, hard enough that the lining of his gauntlets cut his hands. Which was when he realized he could feel them, feel his stomach clenching on nothing, the aching head, weird clarity, and nausea that he knew from past experience was the next step after the sharp pangs of unassuaged hunger.

When Richard fell out of her head, Genie almost sat down on the floor. Her knees went wobbly and she clutched wildly about herself before her left hand connected with the wall. She tottered, but stayed up. It wasn't that she didn't know how to do anything without Richard, really. It was just that she had gotten used to not ever being alone.

She turned, wild-eyed, and yelled for Richard out loud, already knowing she'd get no answer. She raised her eyes, glanced around the monitors, found herself staring at Wainwright. The captain locked her gaze on Genie, standing in front of the chair she'd bolted out of, the hand that wasn't still holding her coffee cup open and turned aside as if she expected at any moment to receive an explanation in the palm of it.

Genie's eyes felt big as softballs, her hair trembling against her cheeks as she shook her head jerkily before Wainwright could ask her question. "Captain."

"Can you explain to me why the hell"—Genie flinched, and the captain softened her voice—"why I can't get ahold of my AI, please?"

"Oh," Genie said, wiping sweat from her palms. "Captain, the worldwire is down."

Wainwright's eyes got as big as Genie's felt. She managed not to drop her coffee cup, but she turned on the ball of her foot and started chipping orders off like bits of a block of ice.

Genie was already moving by the time Captain Wainwright turned around, looking for her. Genie's feet wanted to glue to the floor. She wanted to back into a corner and shake, because the look on Wainwright's face was like the look on Elspeth's face when Elspeth shook her awake and dragged her out of bed in her pajamas, the night Toronto died. The night *Leah* died.

And Genie not only couldn't feel Richard anymore— she couldn't feel Patty, or Aunt Jenny, or Charlie—or anybody else on the worldwire either. She was all by herself. "Is everything going to be okay?"

"I don't know . . ." And then the captain sort of paused, and sort of settled into herself, as if she had gotten just a little more solid, a little more real. As if she'd just remembered she was the captain. "Yes," Wainwright said. "It will. You know what I think you should do?"

Genie shook her head. She would have said something, but she could tell already that her voice would just come out a squeak.

"I think you should go to your father's lab and find him or Elspeth. And tell them I sent you, because he's going to be trying to get hold of Richard, and maybe you can help."

"Because Papa's not on the worldwire."

"Right."

Genie drew one big breath and let it out through her teeth before she nodded. "All right," she said. "Be careful, okay?"

The captain blinked, and her eyes went dark and soft. "Cross my heart. You, too."

"I will." And then she thought of something. "Captain?"

Wainwright had already started turning back to her crew; the look she shot Genie was halfway between that softness and professional ice. "What is it?"

"Did you try calling Charlie or Jeremy on the radio?"

The captain's eyebrow rose. "A fine idea, young lady. Now follow orders. Off the bridge."

"Yes, ma'am." Genie turned back around and ran.

It was weird not to have Richard in her head, weird not to be able to reach out to him and have him tell Elspeth and Papa that she was coming. She could have used the intercom, she guessed, but she didn't want to stop that long. And a good thing she decided not to, because the alarm for general quarters sounded when she was one turn and half a passageway from Papa's lab. She leaned forward and sprinted with everything she had.

The pressure doors didn't come down, which was what she'd been scared of, but she still had to lean against the wall beside the hatch to the lab panting before she could get enough breath to grab the wheel. She didn't bother to knock or push the buzzer before she undogged the hatch, just swung it open and called inside, the alarm worrying at her ears.

"Genie!" Elspeth was inside, right by the door. She must have started coming as soon as she saw the wheel turn. She reached out and dragged Genie over the knee-knocker. Genie let Elspeth dog the hatch before asking any questions. Her papa only looked up from his console long enough to flash her a strained smile, and then glanced back down again, fingers flickering through his interface, the red, green, and violet holograms dying his skin. "Where's Boris?" Elspeth asked.

"In my room." Genie wrapped her arms around Elspeth's shoulders and hung on tight. She was almost as tall, these days. In another year, she'd be taller. Elspeth hugged her back, distracted. "How come all the alarms?"

Papa looked up again, but didn't turn, and his hands didn't stop moving. *Oh, no,* Genie thought, and stepped back to look right at Elspeth, hoping Elspeth would say something to change what Genie was afraid she already knew.

"There's something going on, on the ground," Elspeth said, in that quiet I'm-not-going-to-lie-to-you voice. "We don't know what, exactly. But there are reports on the Net that there's been gunfire inside the United Nations building, and they've shut off the streets around it—"

"And Richard's gone all quiet," Genie finished.

Elspeth nodded.

"Are you scared, Ellie?"

"It's better now you're here," Elspeth said, so Genie gave Elspeth an extra-big hug, just in case.

There's no two ways about it. I've lost my edge.

Which is a hell of a thing to realize when you're crouched under a table, every sense straining, covering a cowering head-of-state with your body, a bleeding general prone on your left side and a couple of teenaged kids huddled together on your right, and all hell breaking loose in every direction.

It's been a couple of seconds since the shouting stopped, and I listen through the noise of another three-shot burst that doesn't come near us. All around, I hear the rustling clothes and staccato breathing of cowering dignitaries, sharp calls in languages I don't recognize, one soft, bitten-off animal moan, the floor-shaking rumble and hysterical screams of the people who ran for the doors instead of diving for cover, and who are now caught in the bottle-neck.

I wonder how the hell they got the weapons in here.

I wonder how the hell we're going to get out.

"We have to stop meeting like this," Riel says against my chest, pushing my uniform off her nose with the flat of her hand.

"I wouldn't mind so much if, next time, you could arrange to be assassinated when I was armed."

Valens chuffs like a big cat, a sound halfway between a laugh and a gasp. I twist my neck to glance at him; the idiot's shoved himself onto his back and red seeps thickly around the fist he's pressed into his gut. His face is chalky yellow-green, the color of mold on cheese. Our eyes meet, and I don't say anything, and neither does he. No need.

It's nothing he can't survive, if we get him into surgery before he bleeds to death, and he and I both know it.

I bet he's in agony, though. I wonder if he ever thought he'd get gutshot diving across a table to take a bullet for Constance Riel. He was luckier than the Mountie that soaked up the rest of the clip, at least.

Riel looks like staying flat to the floor, at least; no idiot, our Connie. "So you could help?" she says, and doesn't try to ease her shoulders off the floor, even though she's lying in a puddle of red that's rapidly thickening to the consistency of ketchup. Hell, at least she keeps her sense of humor under fire.

"Hah. Patty, you and Min-xue all right over there?"

He's got her pressed to the floor much the same way I have Riel down, except Patty's on her belly, and Min-xue is absolutely shuddering with the effort of holding his body against hers. His eyes are squinched up tight; he looks out between ink-slash lashes, head tilted and his slick straight hair brushing the carpeting as he peers under the privacy panel on the front of the desk, straining after whatever it is that neither of us can see.

"Not hurt, Jenny." Patty's scared enough that she doesn't hesitate before my first name. "I can't reach Alan, though."

"I know. I can't reach Richard either." The worldwire might as well be *gone*. Just gone. Which isn't reassuring at all.

"Michel," Riel says, and at first I have no idea who she's talking about. "My bodyguard."

Her eyes darken when I shake my head. That's all his blood we're lying in, except maybe a pint or so of Fred's. "I don't believe they're shooting up the UN to get you,

Connie. The *United Nations*. That's some amazing shit. Congrats."

"Did anybody get a look at who was shooting?" She's trying to inch forward and peer under the privacy panel. I squish her against the floor as another three-shot burst splinters wood over our heads.

"Xiong." Valens scrunches under the table. "Did you see how the UN security went down? Like somebody cut their strings."

"Lie the hell still, Fred, before the rest of your guts ooze out between your fingers."

He doesn't laugh, which is good, because laughing would hurt him like a son of a bitch right about now, and he stops paddling his heels against the carpet and trying to crawl on his shoulder blades. Patty squeaks, though, and I wince at my own brutal choice of words. *Sorry, kid.*

Ah, hell. She might as well get used to it now.

Riel starts to say something, but it's cut off by a string of liquid syllables from Min-xue. He swears sharply in a language I don't recognize—I know it's swearing by the tone—and then shakes his head, black hair sweeping his forehead like a rattled curtain. "Not Xiong," he says.

"It was Xiong's bodyguards that had the guns." Riel, proving her powers of observation.

Valens, wheezing. "Is she dead?"

"Janet? She took at least two in the chest."

"Quel domage," Riel mutters, and Fred gags on a noise that's got to be flavored with blood. "If they hadn't decided to take Janet out first, we wouldn't be having this conversation."

"They didn't take her out fast enough to keep her from spilling the beans on Hardy," Fred mutters. I wish he'd stop talking. It hurts to listen to him.

"If only she'd gotten to whatever she had to say about the Americans and the Chinese." The blood is cold by the time it seeps through my pants legs, sticking the cloth to my knees. I wish I could say it's the most disgusting thing I've ever felt. "There's still four people out there with guns and security is lying on the floor, looking like their hearts stopped. How the hell do the Chinese plan to explain away Xiong's involvement?"

"That's just it," Riel begins, and Min-xue says at the same time. "Did anybody see the minister of war before the shooting?"

General silence, which Riel takes for general agreement. Typical. Bitch. "He came in with Xiong and the PanChinese. He got up and left when Janet took the stand."

"I believe Premier Xiong is intended to be a casualty as well," Min-xue murmurs, still shuddering like a racehorse in the gate although his tone is level—as if his brain were utterly divorced from the demands of his body. He brushes a strand of hair out of Patty's eyes with the back of one white-gloved hand.

Yeah, I think I'm a fucking tough girl. Balls of sterling plated brass. Bullshit, baby: look at *that* kid. "A casualty?"

"Or a . . . how do you say—"

"Scapegoat."

"Thank you, Patricia." He shakes his head. "We must rescue Premier Xiong as well, if we can. If he is not already dead."

"Not possible—"

"Casey." Riel's breath cools my cheek. "It's got to happen."

"Bien sûr." I sigh. "I won't leave you unprotected, ma'am."

"Miss Valens and I will make a run for it while you and Pilot Xie distract the Chinese assassins and attempt to rescue Premier Xiong. Much as I hate to suggest it, if you get a chance, check Janet for a pulse as well."

The sorely tried resignation in her voice makes me chuckle, despite the clotting iron reek of blood filling my sinuses. All right then. I catch Patty's eye, and Patty nods. I nod back and turn to Valens. "Fred, if Patty and Constance break for the door and get lost in the mob while Min-xue and I go for Xiong—"

"That leaves me bleeding under a table. Follow orders, Jen."

Patty doesn't make a sound. She nods, and so does Min-xue.

Damn Fred Valens. Damn him to hell.

"There's one more thing," said Riel, and how I've come to hate her calm, level voice in just a few short moments.

"What's that?"

"The Chinese assassins? If my intelligence is good, they're probably wired as fast as Min-xue."

Fuck me raw. I'm impressed with myself that I don't say it out loud. I glance at Min-xue again; we can hear the footsteps coming closer, over the panicked-cattle noise of the mob by the doors. Patty and Connie might get trampled instead of shot.

I reach out and squeeze Fred's hand. The hand he doesn't have fisted into his leaking belly, the squeeze delivered with my metal one. "You know what they say . . ."

Blood stains his mouth. I wish I hadn't seen that. "Yeah. When in doubt, empty the magazine."

"That might be comforting if I had a fucking *weapon*, sir." I lift my weight off Connie; she reaches up to assist with two hands on my shoulders. "When Min and I go over the top, you ladies run like bunnies. Hop hop hop."

"Don't worry, Casey. You don't need to tell me twice."

Dammit, Dick, I think, fretfully, and get ready to run.

Once Dr. Fitzpatrick had been raised and the XO had reported, Wainwright ordered the klaxon killed on the bridge. She still heard it echoing through the hatchcover, however, as she settled herself in her chair. The nanonetwork might be down and her ship uncontrolled, drifting in orbit without the access to propulsion or attitude jets, but she was far from isolated.

The problem was, there was nothing to do but sit tight. Nothing to do right now, except think. She stared at the screen array on the far wall. The *Montreal,* the shiptree, and Piper Orbital Platform, currently, but she could have any view in the solar system, subject to light-speed lag.

How quickly she'd gotten used to immediate communication, instantaneous advice. She's started relying on Richard far more than she should have. And not just Richard; Richard's ability to poll a handful of others and give her a quick consensus view.

Well, she didn't have that now. And she didn't have a 3-D starship captain's gadget of the week with the sponsor's logo prominently displayed on the barrel, ready to be deployed in time to save the world by the commercial break. What she *had* was a disabled ship drifting in an orbit that would begin to decay uncomfortably soon if she didn't regain control—although they could use shuttlecraft as tugs if it came down to it, or send an EVA team out to angle the solar sails manually. Her crew on the shiptree was probably safer there than here, even if Fitzpatrick couldn't raise Charlie on the suit radio. Unless something had happened to Charlie, of course. Unless something had happened to Dr. Tjakamarra and Casey and Patricia Valens, as well, the crew members who were on the world-wire, when the worldwire went down. Genie Castaign had been fine—dazed, a little confused. But Genie's nano-surgery had been corrective only. And it was complete, unlike the pilots, who were being reconstructed as fast as their amped-up bodies could damage themselves.

Oh. A chill settled between Wainwright's shoulder blades; she raised her eyes to the monitors again. The worldwire going down might not hurt Genie. It wouldn't even hurt the *Montreal,* in the long run, once the vast ship could be rewired and the fiberoptic and carbon ca-bles that Richard had disassembled replaced. It might not even do any damage to the Feynman AI, she told herself, as she called up a thermal image of the *Calgary* crash site to assure that the reactors were still live.

But anybody who had been undergoing nanosurgery when the crash came was as dead as if somebody had pulled the plug on his respirator. And she was staring right at the biggest, sickest patient of them all. She stood. "Give me an earth view. Full earth, whichever orbital platform has most of the Sun side."

It was Clarke. She should have known that. The view was North and South America, cloud-swirled oceans and mouse-tinged atmosphere, the landmasses gray-white with unseasonal snowfall, the grasping outline of North America indistinguishable from clouds and ice. The oceans were steel-gray and cadet-blue. Even the clouds had a jaundiced cast, through the shroud of dust.

It was ridiculous, of course, to think that any change would be visible yet. Even if the worldwire failed cata-strophically, even if Richard's intervention in the planetary ecosystem had just come to a crashing halt, it would be months, maybe years before the damage showed. Planets were great ponderous things, changing on scales barely noticeable in the span of a human life.

Months, at the inside estimate. Years.

"Captain," her XO said, very calmly. "I realize this probably isn't the time for this, but we've got a communiqué from ground control in Calgary. They want to know if we can get some telescopic shots of the northeastern seaboard; a research trawler off Newfoundland just blundered into the middle of a shoal of dead fish, and Clarke doesn't have an angle on it due to cloud cover. They're wondering if we can tell them how widespread it is. Shall I tell them we won't be able to, ma'am? Nobody seems to have told them there's a crisis underway."

Months. She forced her hands to uncurl, unknot from the fists they'd somehow tightened into. *It could be nothing. It could be completely unrelated.*

For a moment, she was tempted to tell him yes, go ahead, tell them they have to wait. Turn off the cameras. Don't go looking for everything else that's probably going wrong. As if, if she didn't look, it wouldn't be real.

"No," she said. "Let's have a look at those fish. And get the ship's entomologist and botanist up here, shall we? And Dr. Perry, too. He's an ecologist; he can earn his keep for a change. And tell ground control they need to get in touch with the cabinet, if they can't reach the prime minister in New York, and they're going to want a couple of climatologists with security clearances, and get me a thermal map of the oceans and water vapor shots of the atmosphere, and anything else you can think of that might be useful."

She felt as if she stood over her own left shoulder,

watching, soothed by her own voice of command, as her bridge crew also seemed to be. Exactly as if what she was ordering would make any difference. Exactly as if they could do anything at all, except stand there and watch as the planet thrashed and died.

I wonder if the condemned man has enough time to regret refusing the blindfold? she thought, before she squared her shoulders under the navy-blue uniform and went to do her job.

Now, finally, space was terribly quiet, and Leslie was terribly alone. There was a half an hour's power left in his batteries and he was weak, shivering cold, clear-headed with hunger although the Benefactors had managed to provide him with oxygen and water. They'd given him back his body, he realized, in time for him to let him *know* that he was going to die. He wondered if the aliens had a concept akin to making one's peace with God. He wondered if they had the concept of *death,* when they were all of the same creature, one intimately connected mind.

He wondered if they understood that they had killed him.

No. He couldn't think like that. He had his hands back, and his eyes, and his space suit checked out fully functional except the radio and the redlined energy levels, and—

—and he hadn't lost one fragment of the peculiar kinesis he'd inherited from the birdcages, the sense of the whole solar system spinning around him like a clockwork model, like a timepiece assembled by Einstein's watchmaker god. He could still feel it in his gut, rooted in his body as concrete and as invisible as an angel's wings rooted in the angel's shoulders.

He also wondered if the birdcages could see through his eyes, now, could hear through his ears, as he felt through their nameless organs of sense. He hoped so. He hoped they could see the way the sunlight refracted through the bars and the veils of their ship, casting rainbows over the entire interior. He hoped they could see how lovely they were, their bodies merging and separating again like drops of mercury shaken on a plate.

His wondering was answered when the shimmering veils between the struts of the birdcage vanished like popped soap bubbles, revealing the *Montreal,* the shiptree, and the brown-gray marbled sphere of the Earth behind them, all limned from behind with sunrise. Leslie caught his breath as slanted rays dusted his faceplate with gold and refracted in sprays of color through the prismed latticework that was all that stood between him and naked space, and he felt as if all the voices within him caught their breaths as well—not that they had voices, in particular, or breaths. *Yes,* he thought. *This is my world. This is what* light *looks like, my friends.*

The shiptree was right there, so close he could see the whorls of light along its plume-shaped length. He could *feel* it out there, feel it press against the curve of space, as if he could reach out and touch it. *Oh, if Richard could see this—*

Leslie started smiling inside his helmet almost before the idea finished unraveling. Maybe he couldn't tell the Benefactors what he needed. But maybe he could *show* them.

He wasn't finished yet. He shaped the map for them, let them feel it in his mind. Showed them the way the mass of his body would move, from the birdcage to the shiptree, and asked them for their help in getting there.

And they sang in his head, the answer, the throb and cadence of their voices that were not voices, but a sensation like the press and lift of the surf. *(go)* they would have said, if what they said was words. *(Go)* and *(go)* and *(heal)* and *(go)* and *(rejoin your mind)* and *(go)* and *(heal)* and *(go)* and *(come and sing to us again)* . . .

(Come and sing to us again) . . .

"I will," Leslie answered. And so they pushed him forward, into night.

When Min-xue lifted himself off her back, Patty was ready for it. She got her toes under her and her hand on the prime minister's wrist and tugged while Min-xue and Jenny crouched scuttling toward the end of the long line of curved tables, and hauled Riel into a squat with an ease that surprised them both. They froze, eye to eye, and Riel licked her lips, her bloodied business suit rising and falling with measured breaths. Riel ducked at a popping, scattered sound. Patty didn't realize it was gunfire until Riel's palm flattened her head against Riel's shoulder, holding her under the level of the tabletop. *It won't stop bullets. Will it stop bullets? Alan?*

They leaned together hard, but the flat shattering impacts arced away from them, in pursuit of Min-xue and Jenny. The bullets weren't anywhere close; Patty leaned out for a quick glance as the other two pilots clambered over floor-hugging diplomats, leapfrogging each other like 3-D cops. *Alan?*

Alan still wasn't there.

"Where the hell is security?" Riel asked. "They can't have bought *everybody*."

Which was right, wasn't it? The General Assembly hall should be full of men and women with guns. Men and women on *their* side, security who worked for the UN. "I don't know. I don't know where Alan is either. I don't know—"

"Hell," Riel said, softly. "The Chinese did something to the security forces. Nanotech, poison, something, something weaponized, I don't *know* . . ." her voice trailed off.

"Why them and not us?"

"They *got* to them. We've been unavailable. This is the part where they're trying to get to us."

Riel's grip tightened on Patty's wrist, and Patty ducked back under cover. She'd gotten a look at the way the wood of the desk fronts had splintered when the gunfire struck them. "The tables won't stop a bullet."

"Might." Papa Fred didn't lift his head off the floor when he spoke, and his voice was thready with pain, but it was strong. "That's small-caliber stuff. Just keep your heads down and run."

Good advice. Easy advice. If his blood wasn't all over her hands and knees—okay, it wasn't, maybe, all his own blood, some of it was the Mountie's, but some of it was—

Breathe, Patty. She squeezed Riel's hand, and Riel squeezed hers back, and she realized that the prime minister was shaking just as hard as she was. That helped, somehow, despite the blood squishing in her shoes, her stockings sliding against wet greasy leather. Riel glanced left and right, and leaned forward like a sprinter from her crouch. She'd kicked her shoes off, the pearl-gray high heels tumbled on their sides, and blood scattered her feet as if she'd done a particularly terrible job with her toenail polish. "Ready?"

"Go!" Terse and low, and Patty lunged out of her stoop into a cramped, crablike run, ears straining, zigzagging up the long naked aisle and hauling Riel along behind her, both of them ducking and skidding and trying like hell not to trip over any of the people huddled against the edges of the furniture or over any of the furniture itself.

This time the gunfire was for real. Not intermittent, but staccato, a rhythmless drumbeat that hurried her feet and kept her head ducked between her shoulders. Riel wasn't fast enough, and it was no good dragging her. The bad guys were behind them, still spread around the area where the PanChinese delegation had been sitting. *Jenny, where are you? Jenny Jenny Jenny—*

Quit waiting for somebody else to save you, Patricia, she snarled to herself, and grabbed a startled Riel by the wrist and shoulder and pushed her ahead, getting her own body in between the prime minister and the bullets, the way Papa Fred and the Mountie had. Patty laughed as she did it, realizing that her own life might be as important in the long run, especially if Alan and Richard were—she didn't think dead. Not dead, because they couldn't be dead. They hadn't ever been alive.

If Alan and Richard weren't coming back, Patty and Jenny and Min-xue were the only pilots Canada had left. If Min-xue was really Canadian. Which hadn't been settled yet.

Oh. I bet it was worth it to the Chinese, if they could get all three of us, and Riel, and the Chinese guy who shook her hand and smiled—

Yeah. She could see how that would be worth a really big risk. Especially if you had a way to get guns and wired fighters inside the UN. But it didn't matter. It was her job to get Riel out alive. Riel and herself, and to trust Jenny and Min-xue to save themselves, and Papa Fred.

Who saves me? Well, of course. Patty had to save herself.

The gunfire stopped and she heard somebody yell, and somebody hit somebody. She heard running footsteps behind her, gaining fast, coming up the aisle the same way she and Riel had.

It wasn't going to work. They weren't going to make it to the door before he caught up with them, and the mob was still shoving through it anyway. Riel was already turning around, ducking into the shelter of another long curved row of desks, when Patty realized that she'd run out of time.

It was dark where the Feynman AI collectively found himself—what threads he was able to maintain, as a crash reduction in resources caused him to slough most of himself in a frantic effort to regain stability—and it was very, very still. The transition was shockingly fast, even—especially—by his inhuman standards. Instantaneous, not a word Richard chose lightly.

He reached out, pushed *hard,* was pressed back into the confines of his prison. No. Not a prison...and not pressed back. Not even blocked. It was as if the worldwire had simply ceased to exist, like those nightmares small children have that the world will vanish if it's not watched every instant. As if he'd sailed to the edge of the globe and had nowhere to go. As if he couldn't even step over that edge and fall.

His first thought was sheer frustration as he realized that nineteen-twentieths of his processing capability and all of his access to the physical world had been cut away. The second reaction was self-amused chagrin at how simply goddamned *spoiled* he had become, on the verge of a sulk because he couldn't reach around the world with a flick of his will. *You have no time for this,* he reminded himself, speaking for and to all the Richards and Alans and the unnamed processes and personas as well.

He was a distributed intelligence. It was highly unlikely that he could have been walled into some corner of the worldwire, or even of the Net, and even more unlikely that every other corner of his consciousness could have been purged simultaneously, with the flick of a switch. Which meant that somehow, somebody—the Benefactors, the PanChinese, or another power—had found a way to disrupt the quantum communication that bound the worldwire together and made the nanonetwork more than a mass of individual, aimless microscopic machines.

Bits of the Feynman AI—of Richard/Alan/Other—lived in every nanomachine on the planet. Well, not *every* one; the limited PanChinese network was still largely protected from his influence, and of course there were the machines he allowed to run their original program, such as the ones that Charlie had been using for his ecological experiments.

The ones that Charlie had been using.

The machines that had been . . . shutting off from the worldwire, inexplicably. The machines that had had their communications disrupted, that had been somehow severed from the quantum communication that networked *all* the machines, even the Benefactor machines, together—whether their programming was compatible or not.

Richard actually paused to consider that for a full two-hundredths of a second. And then he set about quite coldly, quite frantically attacking the question of just where the hell his consciousness was bottled up, and how to get a message out.

And he had to do it fast. Had to do it *now,* because if he wasn't in the worldwire, then the chances were that the worldwire was coming down like an unbraced scaffolding, and it would be taking the planet's entire ecosystem with it.

He was the ghost of Richard Feynman, dammit. The Harry Houdini of twentieth-century physics. The box hadn't been devised that could lock him in.

Mother of Christ, wasn't I supposed to be enjoying a quiet grave by now? The requirement to have adventures and be shot at should expire on one's fiftieth birthday, if not sooner.

And yet, here we go again.

At least Min-xue knows what he's doing. There must have been combat training in his past somewhere; at least basic, and probably something a little more advanced, judging by the way he belly-crawls along the aisle, head down, butt down, and drawing fire away from Patty and Riel. Not drawing enough fire, though, dammit; Riel yelps as one gets a little close and I can't turn around to see if they nailed her. But I still hear running in that direction and bad guys are still shooting past my position at something more interesting behind me. That's a good sign. Well, as such things go.

There's something about gunfire that makes me meditative. I wish the lights had all gone out dramatically when the shooting started, because then I could kick in the low-light capability in my prosthetic eye and have an advantage.

An advantage I need acutely, right now. Pity I'm not gonna get it. Ah well. At least it gives me something to bitch about. Gabe always did say that what soldiers did best, was bitch. And I argued that bitching was a second, after humping packs—

Fight now, Jenny. Compose your autobiography another day.

Besides, Min-xue's getting ahead of me, and it's my turn to leapfrog his position. My brain scampers on ahead, working so hard I forget the texture of the rug under my left hand, the stickiness of blood drying on my knees. Matson always used to say *your brain's your best weapon, soldier. Use it. Name your weapons. Name your enemies. Name your objectives. Use A to get through B to C. What are you gonna do?*

I'm trying, Sarge. You don't have to spit in my face.

I can track the bad guys by the sound of their weapons: four of them, I think. Small-arms fire, and small caliber. Well, maybe nine millimeter. Which doesn't make me happy, of course, but at least they only have handguns, and not *big* handguns—however the *hell* they got them in here—and they're being careful about firing now. Which means their ammo is limited.

Which is all the good. Or as good as it gets, anyway. But if you were gonna smuggle in guns, why would you smuggle in nine-mils, and not a crateful of automatics? Damn. I just don't know.

I'm up on Min-xue. He lies flat as I clamber past him, a bullet flicking sawdust into my hair when I risk a peek over the top of the desk. We've worked our way one aisle over; the enemy have taken cover behind the podium and the secretary's table at the back of the stage. Which means Frye's probably dead, and possibly the secretary general, too.

Be a pity if she is. I liked her handshake, and her hair.

But why did they run for the stage when they were already standing by Xiong? And then I remember the unobtrusive uniformed security officers collapsing like so many tipped over dominos, and I curse under my breath. Well, at least I know where they got the guns. They must have had some way to hack security's palm locks. They didn't bring the guns in. They took them away.

I risk another look as Min-xue crawls past, get a glimpse of muzzle flash, and duck fast. The bullet parts my hair. Another splinters wood off the desk, but doesn't come through.

They're definitely conserving their fire. "They're good shots at this range, with pistols."

"They would be," Min-xue says. "They're elite."

"And wired."

"Yes."

"How about some good news?"

"Is that meant to indicate that you can provide some?"

I glance over. He's laughing at me, the son of a bitch— a silent, straight-faced laugh, but the curl at the corner of his lip and the dark flash of his eyes give him away. "Hah. Don't play poker, son. Yeah, I think I can provide some. I think if we can get our hands on those guns, we can use them, too."

A moment's silence while he considers that. "No palm locks?"

It's gotten awful quiet out there. That's not reassuring. "I think they cracked the locks." Straining my ears until I swear I can feel them swivel, I push myself into a crouch. Min-xue gets his toes under him when he sees what I'm doing, both of us ready to push. He looks at me and I look at him.

We've got that aisle, and a bank of desks between us and the podium. What the hell, right? It's not like we're going to get a better chance. Maybe they're out of ammo.

And maybe they're taking advantage of us hiding under cover, and using the lull to run up on Patty and Riel.

"Go?" he asks me, quiet and self-assured in a way I'd even believe, if I hadn't been inside his head.

But I guess I come across that way myself, until you get to know me. "Go," I answer, and bolt from our hiding place, half a second before Patty screams.

The blood's worn off the soles of my shoes. I don't slip when I slap my meat hand against the top of the desk and propel myself over it, tuck—not as neatly as Min-xue, who moves like an acrobat in gravity, too—roll, take the fall on my shoulder, and come up like a snake, face to face with a surprised assassin.

No, he didn't expect that at all.

Pity he's the one with the gun.

I trigger, and the world rattles to a halt *jerk-jerk-jerk* like somebody's let go the dead-man's handle. My last thought before the programmed reflexes kick in is: *Min-xue lives like this all the time.*

Casey was slower than Min-xue expected: no quicker than a fast, agile, athletic normal woman half her age. Slower, that is, until she lunged to her feet *under* the nearest assassin, rolling onto her toes, glittering left hand slapping a bullet out of the air like she was taking a backhanded swipe at a badminton birdie, right one doubled into a fist that slammed into her opponent's solar plexus while Min-xue was still closing the distance to his.

An unaugmented human would have seen a blur. Min-xue saw her opponent double over, drop his pistol, grab hold of Casey's arm, and roll over it, disengaging, getting away.

Fast, too. Faster than Casey, if she hadn't caught him

flat-footed. Faster maybe than Min-xue. He took another half a step toward them, but Casey had the gun, and her opponent was twisting like a cat to come up on his feet.

And there were three more armed men in the room, and behind him, Patricia shouted again—not surprise and fear this time, but fury, and the sound was divided by the report of a gun.

Min-xue turned on the ball of his foot, jumped over a cowering attaché in a baize-green suit, landed in a crouch as something seared his thigh in passing, and slung himself over the railing toward the podium and the enemy who had just stood up from behind it to level his gun. One of the enemy's comrades rose from the cover of the secretary's table, gun leveled. *Military tactics are like unto water; for water in its natural course runs away from high places and hastens downward.*

A useless piece of advice, when the battle was already joined, and the fighting ran uphill.

The sound of bones cracking couldn't distract him. Casey and Patty were on their own. Min-xue dove left, buying whatever cover he could from the shooter behind the podium, getting that shooter's body between himself and the man farther back. He scrabbled forward, clawed under a desk, the creased thigh burning, another bullet chipping off an interface plate and sending fat blue sparks lazing through the air like dragons' tongues and chrysanthemum clusters. He crawled through them, skinny enough to weasel under the privacy panel, and hesitated behind the last row of desks.

Min-xue's last cover.

He grabbed two deep breaths, vaulted the obstacle, and, zigzagging, rushed the guns.

•   •   •

Jeremy met Charlie halfway back to base camp and knocked Charlie into a spiral when he clouted him on the head. Charlie spun back against a web of vines and branches, almost bounced out again, and clung until the greenery stopped shaking. He didn't dare laugh, although the suited and helmeted figure floating in front of him, wobbling as he recovered from the damage he'd done his own equilibrium, was a thoroughly amusing sight. "Action and reaction, Jer. What the heck did you do that for?"

"Damn," Jeremy said, his voice tinny through speakers. "You know, Charlie, you about scared the air out of my suit."

"I think I might have broken the nanonetwork somehow—"

"You also took off your bloody helmet. I can't talk to you without your suit radio turned on, you know."

"Oh." Charlie looked around for his helmet, hoping it hadn't sailed too far away in the impact. It was lodged a little farther over in the bush; he floated free and retrieved it. "I guess that explains what I did to deserve it."

"Other than suit telemetry indicating to Peterson and myself that you'd had a rupture? And then not answering my hails? And Richard vanishing on us, *pfft*! And that's not the most interesting bit of information." Between the buzz of the speaker and Jeremy's accent, and the way his words tumbled over each other in thwarted concern, Charlie could barely understand.

"Oh?"

"Leslie is inbound."

At first, the words didn't make any sense. Charlie tilted his head, staring through Jeremy's faceplate as if he could read his mind through the crystal. "Leslie?"

"We presume. Something human-shaped has left the

birdcage, in any case, and is traveling this direction. Peterson says she has visual, and if it isn't Leslie, it's a neat approximation of someone in a space suit. I told her not to intercept. She was willing to try. So we need to head back to base camp—wait a minute. Why did you take off your hat?"

"It seemed like a good idea at the time? In any case . . ."

"You aren't dead."

"I'm not dead." Charlie poked his own cheek with a gloved finger and grinned at Jeremy's expression, barely visible through the helmet. "So far so good."

"Tell me that again in ten days, when whatever you've sucked in has had a chance to incubate."

Charlie grinned and started wriggling his gauntlets off. "I won't ask to sleep in the tent until we're sure I'm not dying."

Jeremy hissed like a cat, between his teeth, and grabbed a nearby branch to flick himself in the direction of camp. "Silly bugger. Well, no point in putting it back on now. If you're dying on us, you're already dead. And I want to find out exactly *what* is headed for our air lock."

Gabe's father had a cabin in Quebec, a two-hundred-year-old one-room onto which generations had added, until the resulting house resembled a turkey-tail fungus, bits and pieces projecting on some inobvious plan from the central core. Gabe had been looking forward to inheriting the place and retiring there, in the fullness of time.

Gabe sincerely wished that he—and Genie, and Elspeth, and Jenny—were there right now. Instead, he was up to his thick, stubborn neck in emergency protocols and Elspeth and Genie were sitting tight in the corner of the lab, barely breathing so as not to distract him, despite their obvious frustration.

And Jenny was on the ground somewhere, under fire. It was all Gabe could do to not shiver like a dog-worried sheep. *Genevieve Casey can take care of herself. And she can take care of Patty and that Chinese pilot and Prime Minister Riel as well.*

Gabe smiled tightly, not looking up from his own fingers as they darted through the touch-sensitive fields over his interface plate. She could. Didn't change that he wanted to be there, soaking up some of the fire. But Jenny was a big girl. Frederick Valens, on the other hand, could take care of himself. And if Jenny got killed trying to rescue *cet ostie de trou de cul*—

No. Gabe had his own job, and it was time he started doing it. Especially given the mistakes he'd made. He'd been so concerned that Ramirez had left a back door into the *Montreal*'s core, or that the enemy would attack the hulk of the *Calgary* directly, that he'd failed to consider what was in retrospect a more likely scenario: that the Chinese would find a way to simply disrupt the worldwire, destroy its ability to communicate, and leave the Benefactor machines purposeless, uncontrolled.

Unlike the worldwire, which was an accidental—or unofficial—outgrowth of Richard's machinations, the Chinese nanonetwork was firewalled and guarded and coded in terms incompatible with the Benefactor network. Richard and Gabe had cracked some of that code— enough to let the AI talk with Min-xue. Not enough to let him puppeteer the Chinese pilots or the *Huang Di* the way he could the Canadian side, although Richard had managed to flash Min-xue's programming, once upon a time. The Chinese could have taken the worldwire down and left their own network functional. Remotely. The same way they'd destroyed the *Huang Di*'s operating system and her data when the starship became Canada's salvage and spoils of war.

However, if that was the technique they'd used, it meant there were at least three processors in existence that were big enough to host Richard—the *Montreal,* the *Calgary,* and the *Huang Di.* Hell, a very pared-down version of the base Richard persona could run quite tidily on the hardware packed into Jenny's head, as long as the spare cycles of her personal nanomachines were available to his use. The problem was, they'd gotten reliant on the worldwire—and Richard—for quantum communication, and Richard wasn't finished fixing the damage that the saboteur had done to the *Montreal* the previous year.

The *Calgary* was out of reach at the bottom of the ocean. The *Huang Di* was off-line, her reactors cold, her life support running from kludged-on solar panels, her processor core half taken apart. Richard might be alive in the former, but it was no place Gabe could get to. The latter was unavailable as a place of refuge. But there was the *Montreal.*

And Gabriel had the *Montreal* in his hands. He had a radio headset, and he had a clever lieutenant with a degree in computer science and several levels of technical certification slithering through the weightless, shielded access spaces that surrounded the *Montreal*'s processor core, dragging the business end of a three-kilometer optical cable behind him, and three more geeks tearing up the floor panels of the big ship's bridge, double-checking connections that hadn't been needed in a year.

And if it all went well, and if Richard were still alive in

there somewhere, Gabe should have communication with him in five seconds, four, three, two—

"Blake?"

"Sorry, Mr. Castaign." The lieutenant's voice made tinny and sharp in his earpiece. "Cable's snagged. Half a second, here."

Gabe was gambling with Blake's life. Gambling that he was right, and that what the Chinese had managed was to disrupt the worldwire, and not to take control of the *Montreal* again. Last time they'd hacked the ship's OS, they'd vented reactor coolant and taken a serious chunk out of the permissible lifetime exposures of half the engineering crew.

If they managed it again—well, Blake was inside the shielding. It wouldn't help him much.

"Hurry, please—"

"On it, sir."

Gabe let his hands hang motionless in the interface. They still called him sir, even if he was a civilian now. "Blake?"

It wasn't Blake's voice that answered. Instead, a familiar craggy face pixilated into existence, and long fingers steepled as Richard pressed his immaterial hands palm to palm.

"Gabriel. You're a sight for sore sensors."

"Merci à Dieu. It's good to have you back, Dick—" Gabe looked away, glanced to Elspeth, for strength. She squared her shoulders and drew one deep, hard breath, her arms tightening around Genie's shoulders, and she smiled.

Gabe had to look down again, the flash of gratitude that filled his chest so intense it made his eyes sting.

"Nous avons des problèmes plus grands. New York City is under martial law."

"I see. Perhaps you had better start at the beginning."

"Forgive me, Dick," Gabe said, "but explanations are going to have to wait until after the war."

Patty turned as Riel dove for cover. Somebody cowering behind a desk on the left squeaked like a stomped puppy. Patty knew what she'd see even before she turned, and tried to brace herself for it. She wasn't ready.

She didn't think she ever could have made herself ready to stand there, hands spread out for balance, covered in blood and with her pants leg somehow having gotten torn all up one side, and stare down the barrel of a gun. She froze, wobbling a little, trying to make it look like grim determination holding her in place rather than icy panic.

The man with the gun wasn't big. He was about fifteen feet away, down the shallow slope of the aisle, and he held the gun in both hands at arm's length. She couldn't see his face clearly. He wore a Western-style business suit with a tie and silver cuff links that flashed in the overhead light, and his hands weren't shaking. Somebody sobbed behind Patty. She heard a big, resonant thump as the crowd heaved against the doorway, a beast scraping itself on the sides of a too-small den. She spread her hands out wider, and wondered if being shot was going to hurt much. She wondered if she was tough enough to hold the man off until Riel could vanish into the crowd of escaping bodies.

"Step aside," he said, his English thick with an accent.

"No," Patty answered, and dove for the gun.

Something kicked in her chest as she lunged forward. She thought it was a bullet, at first, but there was no flash yet and the gun hadn't popped. It was her heart, slow thunder a counterpoint to screams from people cowering near her. She shouted; it left her lips a slow roar, and nothing moved—*nobody moved*—for a thin slice of a second until she saw the gunman's eyes widen and his knuckle pale on the trigger.

Once, again. And then he was plunging aside, and Patty didn't see the bullets, couldn't *hear* the bullets, but it didn't matter because she had seen where the gun was pointed and seen how the barrel had kicked, and the part of her brain that could calculate starship trajectories at translight knew that second bullet wasn't coming anywhere close. The first one, though—

Patty couldn't catch bullets in her hand, the way she'd heard Jenny could. But she twisted hard, her hair flying into her eyes, and tried not to think that when she ducked the bullet was going to hit somebody in the mob behind her. Her knee shrieked as she wrenched herself out of the way, and then she found out that she wasn't really faster than a bullet after all.

She didn't fall down. She didn't even stop moving, as if some animal part of her brain *knew* that if she slowed for a second the next shot would end between her eyes. It didn't hurt at all, not a bit—just a thump against her left shoulder like whacking it against a door frame at a run, and white stars lighting her vision as it spun her half around, and her left arm gone, as if the impact had taken it off.

She was committed. She plunged at him, head-butt to his abdomen like a playground wrestling match, and there was more blood, everywhere, slippery-sticky and hot, on her face, in her mouth, sticking her hair across her eyes. She slammed him against the railing, felt something snap. They landed hard, and she brought her knee up, fighting dirty like Papa Fred had taught her, and she was fast, faster than she'd known she'd be, but he was faster somehow and he got his thigh in the way and he still had the gun in his hands and her arm wouldn't work and he clawed at her nose, her mouth, pushing her back. Her right hand locked around his wrist and yanked his hand off her face and—

The white stars turned red-black as he struck her across the temple, once, with the barrel of the gun.

Damn, this son of a bitch can move. Like a fencer, like a ballet dancer. He feints and I fall for it, but rather than cracking my forearm, his pistol rings off my metal arm like somebody whaled on a cold water pipe with a claw hammer. He grunts. I bet he felt that all the way up to his shoulder.

Unfortunately, it doesn't distract him enough to slow him down when I go for a sharp right jab. Fluid sidestep, faster than I can think, and he grabs my wrist and tries to put me over his shoulder in some kind of martial-arts throw. He reckons without the weight of my prosthesis throwing my center of gravity off, though, and I clothes-line his throat as he tosses me. It doesn't stop me going over his shoulder, but he loses his grip and I roll with it instead of landing cripplingly hard, flat on my back. When I come up into the crouch he's gone straight down, vertical drop from his feet to his knees, and the gun is on the floor in front of him because he's clutching his throat with both hands, his eyes bugged out so far I can see the whites all the way around. I bet I crushed his trachea when I hit him.

I'm surprisingly okay with that.

But I don't have time to think about it long. Gunfire, two shots, from up where Patty and Constance were headed when I lost sight of them. And then three more shots, flat and close, that could be the guys on the podium snapping off a couple at me, or at Min. It's an easy decision; I dive after the dying guy's gun, squirm between two rows of desks, kicking a huddled dignitary in the head—"Pardon"—and risk a peek around the end of the row, trying to get a look up the aisle toward the doors.

I'm just in time to see Patty knock the gunman into the railing on the nearest section of seats and both of them go down. Riel hesitates, her fists pressed to her chest and clenched so tight I see her knuckles whiten from here.

My right hand knows how hers must feel. Fingernails bite my palm, and I turn my back on Patty and Riel, transfer the pistol to my meat hand, and turn around to see if I can help Min.

I'm just in time to hear a splintering crash and a surprised yelp that turns quickly into a moan. Min-xue's put his shoulder against the podium, and shoved, suddenly, hard, topping the whole damned thing over onto the gunman crouched behind it. Smart child: he keeps moving, too, diving off the stage with as much commitment as a swimmer kicking off. He tucks and rolls beautifully, and the gunman behind the long table pops up, handgun held in a police stance, tracking Min-xue like a pro. He snaps off his first shot, which misses, and waits the opportunity for a second, which I think won't.

The palm lock on the stolen handgun I've stolen back is sticky against my flesh. I hope to hell it's cracked. It is a nine-mil, semi-auto, caseless ammo in a horizontal magazine. I expose myself, level the gun, brace with my left hand, wishing it were my gun and the interface weren't trashed so I could lock on the threat scope in my left eye, and I double-tap the gunman right over the heart. He doesn't even have the decency to look shocked as he folds across the table, his weapon discharging randomly.

Min-xue's got a hell of a lot of trust. He never even looked back; he's vaulted the barrier and is crouched behind the PanChinese table. From the motion of his head and shoulders, he's shaking bodies, trying to find out if Premier Xiong is alive.

Fred's still bleeding under a table over there somewhere. God knows how bad Patty is hurt—I turn around in the aisle, the gun still braced, and freeze right where I am.

The last gunman has Riel, her arm twisted behind her back, his pistol pressed against her temple, using her body as a shield. Patty's sprawled at their feet, crosswise across the aisle, puddling blood staining the grass-green carpeting black.

I don't look at that, at Patricia. It can happen later, when I have time to deal with it. Instead, I look at the gunman, and at Riel's calm expression and tight set jaw.

Dammit, Connie. Why the hell didn't you run?

Which is when, suddenly, sharply, Richard's presence explodes back into my brain.

Min-xue tore kidskin and cloth in his haste to bare his own hands, and then to bare Xiong's throat. There was blood—a great deal of blood—and the ragged tear across the premier's scalp showed a glitter of white through the crimson. Min-xue tasted blood when he wiped the sweat from his face onto his sleeve. No breath stroked his fingers; the air was sickly and still.

He worked his mouth and spat, leaning to the side as

his fingers slid and stuck in the mess of stringy blood smeared over the premier's skin. He didn't expect a pulse. That wound looked like the bullet had plowed through hair and flesh and bone, and Min-xue half suspected that if he lifted Xiong's head off the floor, it would leave a blood-pudding of brains behind.

Min-xue pricked a finger on the pins holding one of the decorative ribbons to Xiong's breast. More blood dripped and vanished into the silk, scarcely darkening the color. As a lucky color, red proved an irony under the circumstances. He pushed two fingers into the hollow softness of Xiong's throat.

Min-xue jerked his hand back in shock; Xiong's pulse beat steadily under the angle of his jaw, strong and slow and not thready or fluttering. He shook his fingers, not quite believing what he'd felt, and pressed them back against cool skin.

If anything, the premier's heartbeat was steadier than his own. Carefully, Min-xue tilted the man's head back, straightening his throat, and, gagging on the rankness of blood, began to breathe for both of them.

A welcome presence bloomed in Min-xue's head, and he hissed relief. *Richard. How very, very nice to have you back*.

His cheer was short-lived. "Min-xue," Richard said, his moth-wing hands uncharacteristically knotted in front of his belt buckle. "Unfortunately, I must recommend that you surrender immediately. The PanChinese agent has Prime Minister Riel."

They'd only been linked for a matter of days, and still when Leslie kicked himself out of the air lock, knocked the condensation off his helmet, and saw Charlie floating before him, and could not feel him, the strangest seasick sensation of something broken—something *severed*—twisted his guts.

"Charlie." He said it quietly, but the suit radio turned it into an accusation. "What are you doing with your helmet off?"

"Leslie," Charlie said, raising both eyebrows. "What the hell are you doing wandering around loose like that?"

It helped. Leslie chuckled, and reached up to undo the clasps on his own helmet. Air hissed in as soon as he cracked the seal, pressure equalizing. "I figured out how to ask real nice. I just . . . I showed them an image of my . . . shape, my gravitational signature, moving from the birdcage over here. And they showed me to the door and handed me my suitcase. You?"

"Took a calculated risk," Charlie answered. He hesitated, a bizarre figure in a pair of blue cotton trousers, barefoot, the back of his T-shirt floating out of his elastic waistband. Worry creased his forehead. "You know the worldwire's down."

"So's my suit radio. And some other stuff. The Benefactor network is still working beautifully, though. Had enough of hanging around with my finger up my arse while you did all the work, so I came here because . . ." He shrugged. "I wasn't all that sure Wainwright would let me in, frankly."

"You were worried about me." Charlie slapped him on the shoulder, rebounding him lightly against the closed air lock. The air smelled impossibly sweet, earthy, rich. He picked up notes of fermentation products, and other things, things he didn't have words for—the weight of the shiptree around him, the belly and roll of the curves of space. He closed his eyes.

"Les, you—"

"All right?" The air stung his senses like liquor. He laughed, giddy and half-hoarse. *You can't go home.* "I don't know. Tell me about the worldwire. Are we under attack? Is it Richard?"

"No," Charlie answered, quite crisply. "I spoke with Ellie via coded transmission. Gabe has managed to hack through to Dick. He hasn't gotten contact with the worldwire yet, but he's working on it. Dick thinks it's sabotage."

"I am getting really sick of hearing that word."

"How do you sabotage a quantum network?"

Leslie shrugged. "I can guess. Jam its communications. Flood it with nonsense information, so the signal gets lost in noise."

"Primitive. Brute force."

"But effective. Where's Jeremy?"

"Base camp. Follow me. We can radio back and let them know you're safe inside." A long pause followed, which Leslie didn't mind; he was absorbed in the eerie beauty of the weightless garden they moved through, and the strangeness doubled and redoubled of everything glowing, shimmering faintly, leaving currents he could *feel* through the Benefactor sensorium. Synesthesia. Only not.

"Hey, Charlie?" The suit speakers were much too loud. Birds—bird-analogues—darted away, shrieking. "What made you decide it was safe to take your helmet off?"

Charlie stabilized himself with a grip on a branch and turned back to Leslie, bobbing in midair like a red-cheeked apple. "Because I'm a biologist, Les. And I was sick of the effing helmet, and playing the odds. Scientific wild-ass guess."

"And you risked your life on that?"

"I've risked my life on crazier things."

"You've a point, mate," Les answered.

"What made you decide to take *your* helmet off, Les?"

"You can't drown a man who was born to hang." Leslie took another breath. It went to his head. "High-oxygen environment."

Leslie tossed Charlie his helmet—more a cup-handed shove than an actual throw—in free-fall, and pushed off to follow him. They brachiated in silence, Leslie feeling as if the fresh air had rejuvenated his thinking process. It was Richard. Something to do with Richard, and the worldwire, and—

"Hey, Charlie. You know more about the nanotech than I do."

"Yeah?"

He caught a branch as Charlie let it snap back, using the recoil to add a little push to his own forward momentum when it oscillated. "Is it weird that we're affected, too, when our nanosurgeons came courtesy of a direct transfer from the Benefactors, rather than through your lab? I mean, if the Chinese and their guy, um . . ."

"Ramirez."

"Right. Cracked the operating system—"

Charlie chuffed, using Leslie's helmet like a shield as he bulled through the undergrowth. Leslie envied Charlie the freedom of movement and obvious comfort of his shorts and T-shirt, and blinked another bead of sweat off his lashes. "Well, we know they cracked the OS. But we rewrote it, Gabe and Richard and me, and our network—Dick's network—and the PanChinese one and the Benefactor system don't really talk to each other. Beyond Richard being able to hack them enough to talk to people—oh."

"Yeah, you see what I mean?"

"I think I do, Les. If the Benefactors can rewrite their system to communicate with ours, which they must have done...how the hell do we let them know it's okay for them to rewrite *our* system to communicate freely with *theirs*?"

"Is it?" The smell of the air was addictive, a faint hint of ozone, the silken texture of the wind before a thunderstorm, and mild, shifting floral and herbaceous perfumes. Leslie's hands still tingled inside his gloves. He'd swear he could feel every individual cell zooming through his arteries, scalp to toes. He couldn't tell if there was something wrong with his body, or if he'd simply been deprived of it so long that he was hyperaware.

"Is it what?"

"Is it okay?"

Charlie stopped so suddenly that Leslie almost drifted into his back. "You know...I think we'd better radio back and have Gabe ask Richard about that."

"You explain it to Dick," Leslie said. "I'm going to try to explain it to the birdcage."

My fists are knotted as hard as my heart. The air I can get, past the pressure in my chest, comes in shallow little sips, painful. Connie's looking at me across all that space, her chin lifted up so I can see her throat bob when she swallows. I wish I knew what the hell she was trying to beam into my brain with that steady, too-calm eye contact.

The only scrap of reassurance I can muster is Richard's presence, his ghost standing just off to the left and out of my line of fire, where I can see him without being distracted. *Merci à Dieu, Dick. Tell me there's something you can do about this.*

He turns away, as if he were looking over his shoulder at Riel and Patty. He looks sterner in profile, old-man-of-the-mountain, cotton-wool hair brushed back from a high forehead, revealing a widow's peak. He stares at the hostages long enough for my attention to follow and turns a worried squint back at me.

"Surrender, Jen," he says, and folds his hands over his arms. "There's nothing else we can do to save them."

For half a second my stomach drops, like the Wicked Witch just scrawled those words across the sky. *Surrender* isn't a word I thought Dick *knew*; less did I think I'd hear him counsel it.

The arms stay folded. Paternal. Stern. He rocks back, head to one side, a discouraging frown chiseling the lines around his mouth deep enough to shadow. "Live to fight again."

I lock my thoughts down before I think it loud enough for Dick to hear. *But they won't live if we surrender.* Marde. I wish I could feel Min-xue now, the way I did when we went after Les and Charlie. I wish I could—

Oh. If *Dick* is here, why, oh, why can't I feel Min-xue?

It wasn't working, and Richard couldn't see any way that it could suddenly *start* to work, unless he could manage to crack the PanChinese network right back and take their system off-line. He wasted long nanoseconds trying, crippled by the lack of cycles. Even at limited capacity, he had an ear for Gabe, however.

Especially knowing that Gabe was working as hard as he was, and as fruitlessly. And despite the fact that what Charlie was suggesting—and Gabe was backing up—was sheer insanity.

Wainwright had left her XO in charge on the bridge

and fled to the ready room to take Richard's call. It didn't look like a rout, of course. She'd made sure it wasn't even identifiable as a tactical withdrawal, and he wondered if she was sure herself if her hands were shaking with fear, or with adrenaline.

"I don't mean to put any extra pressure on you, Dick," she said, "but I **am**...extremely concerned about the ecosystem—"

Richard was busy enough that he wasn't bothering with the niceties of human interaction. Alan's clipped tones crept into his own diction when keeping his voice warm was too much of an effort. "You're right," he said. "It's not self-sustaining. None of it is self-sustaining, yet. Charlie's proposing we open the worldwire to the Benefactors—"

"What?" With a fraction of his attention, he saw her come out of her chair, her hands white on her desk. "That's insane."

"It may be a moot point, as we don't currently know how to manage it. We can't even *contact* them, and we don't know how the heck to signal our intentions to the Benefactors even if we did."

"We already have the program we wrote to flash the Benefactor nanites," Gabe reminded, pressing the headphones to his ear to hear Wainwright better.

"The program that didn't work."

Charlie's voice, encoded and tightcast and unscrambled and reconstituted, curiously flat with most of the harmonics lost to efficiency. "We also have samples of the nanosurgeons they infected us with, and Gabe's been able to crack fairly large chunks of their operating system."

Wainwright's voice was as flat, with tension. "You're asking me to risk more than the *Montreal* this time."

If Richard had been a human being, he would have stopped short and closed his eyes in frustration at his own stupidity. "The ones that *they* left open to the worldwire."

"Yes." Gabe and Charlie, two voices at once.

Wainwright again. "Just to be absolutely certain I understand this, you're proposing we flash our own network, reprogram it, and leave it wide open—so the Benefactors can wander in and do whatever they want? To the entire *planet*? And hope they end the PanChinese attack?"

"Yes," Gabe said, without even the decency to sound chagrined at the ridiculousness of it.

"How do you propose we do that when we can't even *talk* to the worldwire currently?"

"Therein lies the problem," Gabe said, gritting his teeth. Richard felt his heart rate kick up; it was pattering along tightly. "I was hoping Dick might have a clever idea."

"All we need is an access point," Richard said. "A patch of the worldwire we can tap into. Then we can hack our way through it. Island to island, so to speak. World War II, in the Pacific."

"You need something you can run a hardline to. What if Elspeth went after one of Charlie's ecospheres?"

"Not safe," Richard said. "The pressure doors could come down any second. Or the captain could trigger them as a precaution. Or, worse, the Chinese could remotely open an air lock, and they could *fail* to deploy."

"Blake made it to the processor core," Wainwright said.

"Yes, and I've recommended he hole up somewhere and not try to travel further. In any case, we can't delay—if the pressure doors do come down, you'll lose me as well."

"Putain de marde. They'd sever the cable."

"Yes," Richard said. "We need to use what's at hand."

Gabe swallowed, and Richard could see how carefully he did not look at his daughter. "No."

"I still haven't said yes," Wainwright snapped.

"Gabe—" Richard stopped, but not before Genie heard.

Genie looked up from the quiet conversation she'd been having with Elspeth and over at Gabe and Richard's image. "Papa?"

"Petite—"

Richard saw Elspeth's hand tighten on Genie's shoulder, and saw the darkness that crossed Gabe's face. He knew as plainly as if Gabe were wired what he was thinking: it wasn't going to be enough. *Not again. Not again—*

"Richard," she said, "could you use me? Wire into my control chip and hack into my nanonet?"

"Gabe. Genie—" Richard let them see him shake his head. "That puts you at risk, Genie."

"I know," she said.

Gabe allowed the silence to drag, and Richard was right there with him, too close to the pain himself to argue. *Not again. Not Genie, not like this, not after Leah. No.*

None of them should be permitting this to happen. But it was the same equations Leah had considered and understood, and Genie considered and understood them now, as well. Richard was struck, abruptly, by how much both of them got from Jenny Casey, despite there being no biology between them.

But Elspeth caught Gabe's eye, and he caught hers, and neither one of them said anything. At last, shaking his head, his hands white from the force with which he had been holding the edge of the desk, he sat back in his chair. He looked from Elspeth to Genie. He didn't say yes, but he also didn't say no.

"It's what Leah would have done," Genie said, her eyes very bright. Gabe nodded. It was exactly what Leah would have done.

It was exactly what Leah *had* done.

Gabe got up and walked across the lab, and ducked down to wrap his arms around his daughter's shoulders. He held her tight enough that Richard thought she would have squeaked, if she hadn't been holding her breath. And then he looked up, smoothed her hair, and stepped back. "Captain," Gabe said, in the vague direction of a mote, "it's your call. Go or no-go?"

Richard realized, watching the two of them, what Gabe was wrestling with. And he felt a flush of pride in both— in Genie, that she wasn't going to stay in her sister's shadow, or stay safe behind locked doors. She had to stand up and be counted. And in Gabe, because Gabe was going to let her, and wasn't even going to let himself pretend it didn't hurt.

"Go," Wainwright said, measured seconds later. "Go, dammit."

"All right then," Richard said, wishing suddenly—viciously—for the ability to turn and punch a wall. "Let's get to work."

Elspeth opened the skin on the back of Genie's hand very carefully, using a dissection tool from Charlie's second-best kit, which was stowed in the storage lockers to keep it away from the moisture in his own lab. The scalpel was sharp; there was hardly any blood, and Genie watched interestedly, wincing a little as Elspeth peeled the skin back, but obviously unimpressed by the pain. It would take more pain than that to impress Genie

Castaign. There was no way to sterilize the tools, but that would be less than meaningless if Richard could get Genie's nanonet back on-line. And if he couldn't— They'd have larger problems.

The control chip was a flexible, irregular blue oblong; the actual *chip* was carbon-based, only a centimeter square, but there was a gel-sealed interface port and a series of power cells no bigger than a pinkie nail attached. Gabe handled the splicing procedure himself, sitting Genie down in his chair behind the desk and running a hardline from the interface to her hand. The pins slid in smoothly; if he'd known where the port was, Richard thought Gabe could have managed it through the skin, just a little prick and in, the same way the pilots' serpentines worked.

Richard took a deep, strictly metaphorical breath and extended himself to take control of the nanoprocessor, feeling after its operating system with the lightest fingers he could manage. He infiltrated it before Gabe's hands had left the connection, using the direct interface with the control chip to leapfrog to the few million nanosurgeons that were in physical contact with it. It wasn't enough of a network to support a persona thread, or even a fraction of one, but it *was* enough, he hoped, to form a jumping-off platform for the Benefactors when he opened the system to them.

If they understood what he was doing, what he was offering. If they understood why. If Leslie had made them understand.

He threw open the floodgates.

For long picoseconds nothing happened. And then Genie's head drooped, she slumped to one side, and her father caught her shoulders as she started to topple.

Richard held on tight, the rush of data around him like the sound of the surf in his ears, *whatever* the Benefactors were doing spreading in ripples through Genie's nanonet and then the worldwire, leaving the network momentarily limpid and calm in its wake, as clean as if it had never been programmed at all.

Richard reached out and hesitated. There was another AI in the system. With a persona he at first mistook for one of his own threads, separated and maintained during the attack. Until he reached out to reabsorb it, and it snarled at him and lunged.

The pieces are kind of sickening when they finally snap into place. I imagine an audible pop, the sound of a broken limb yanked straight. It's not a bad analogy. This won't be pretty.

And it looks like we're not getting any help from Richard, because I'm reasonably certain that's not him, exactly, who's floating in the corner of my eye.

And I'm not about to put down the gun.

Riel knows. That's what the eye contact means. That's what she's telling me.

Do it, Jenny. We're dead already, anyway.

Nothing you want to face less than a woman with nothing to lose. My hand isn't shaking as I bring up the liberated gun. It hasn't shaken in years. Not for this, anyway.

Fast. Hot damn. Even for me, I'm moving fast, and the whole world around me is like a snapshot, a ruin full of broken statues sprawled between the pillars.

"Jen?" Not-Richard, in my head, and now that I'm looking for it, listening for it, I can tell it's not Dick. It's another program, or maybe even another AI, wearing Dick's clothes, but it isn't comfortable in that skin.

The sliver of the gunman's face that I can see over Connie's shoulder is a curve like the sickle face of a waning moon. If she flinches, I'm going to waste her. She meets my eyes across all that distance, hers fearless green, a glassy gaze like a wolf's.

"Put the weapon down," I say, out loud, as levelly as I have ever said anything in my life. "I can offer you asylum. Life. Maybe more, if you will testify."

I don't dare jerk my head to indicate what I want him to testify about, but I'm pretty sure he'll know what I mean. And then the gunman blinks at me, the one eye I can see around Connie uncomprehending as an owl's. Of *course* he doesn't speak English.

What the hell was I thinking? Again.

And then I hear my tone echoed, words I don't know: Min-xue, translating, just loud enough to carry. I don't need to look to know he's standing again and he's got my back. The crash as the door slams shut at the top of the stairs behind the last of the escaping dignitaries—the ones who weren't smart enough to hit the floor and hug it like a long-lost love—is huge. The sound of Patty whimpering, a broken moan on a breath that she didn't get to keep much of, is huge.

The space between my heartbeats is huge.

The barrel of the Chinese assassin's gun wavers, just a hair, and I let myself breathe, not much, just a little, a slow trickle of air through my nose.

And then my body locks in place as if I'd been dunked in a vat of liquid nitrogen, frozen solid, can't breathe, can't think, can't move, controlled as sharply and completely as if somebody had gotten ahold of my strings.

Min-xue's voice cuts off midsyllable, and if I could do anything at all I would, I swear it, roll my eyes and curse the Chinese, the Benefactors, their nanotech and their mothers for a bunch of castrated dogs.

Richard demonstrated this to me once. The reason he was opposed to spreading the nanotech worldwide. The reason he was a little afraid of the nanotech at all. Because it can be used to puppet anybody wearing it like a kid's robot cat.

Oh, fucking hell.

"I beg your pardon, Master Warrant Officer." The Chinese AI, if that's what it is, is no longer pretending to be Richard. It dissolves, iconless, a disconcerting, neutral, and exquisitely polite voice echoing inside my ear. "But I cannot permit that action on your part. You will forgive the intrusion, I hope."

I thought your people didn't have AIs.

"A recent development. Please excuse me—"

The assassin cocks his head as if he's listening to something. I'm willing to bet I know what he hears. The assassin's finger whitens on the trigger of his gun; he turns it back, lines it up neatly with the center of Connie's ear. She doesn't flinch and she doesn't twist away or close her eyes. She just waits for it, looking at me, looking past me at Min-xue.

Hell. If I had to go down fighting, at least this time my family's safely out of the way. It might almost be all right, if it wasn't starting to hurt so much, not being able to breathe.

Black dots swim at the edges of my vision. I can't blink them away. I'm amazed I can still hear my heartbeat, slow as the pendulum in the lobby, measuring the turning of the planet under my feet. *I'm sorry, Madam Prime Minister. Sorry, Patty. Even more sorry about you and Min—*

I don't know if Riel can read the apology in my eyes.

The Feynman AI was smaller than he should be. Slower, contained, constrained. Limited by the processing power of the *Montreal*—vast by human standards, but negligible by his own.

But he was also older, trickier, and far more wily than the Chinese program, and he unpacked out of the *Montreal*'s core like a spring-loaded snake out of a peanut can, grabbing every cycle in sight, flooding the worldwire with his presence, replicating threads, spawning personas and entities faster than the Chinese AI could take him apart.

He didn't fight. He didn't run.

He replicated. He bred. He blossomed.

The Richard-thread could have wept at what he found when he got his claws into the worldwire. The damage was considerable, months of reconstruction undone in minutes. Macroscopic life was the least of it; there was renewed damage down to the microscopic level, rereleased radiation, the ecological equivalent of blood and carnage. He didn't have time to assimilate it or analyze it; he barely had time to register it.

He'd told Wainwright that he would fight if he had to.

But he didn't have time to fight. The other program had Jenny and Min-Xue, had a gun to Riel's head. Was operating on certain tight-coded assumptions, provided parameters. Was an automaton, on certain levels. A sociopath.

Was not, to turn a phrase, a moral creation.

And was eating Richard's program, consuming his

threads, assimilating his data in great, dripping handfuls of code. He threw more at it. Input, aware of the risk, aware that he was breeding something he had no control over.

He spawned, and spawned, and spawned again, and the Chinese AI grew fat feeding off him, and reached out again, cleverer this time, learning as it grew, going for the zeroth persona, for Richard himself. And Richard ducked—

Then handed off control to Alan, and shoved himself wholesale down the other AI's throat, and like a virus turned it inside out, assembling the data he'd fed it willy nilly, turning the whole thing—metaphorically—into a mirror. And the Chinese AI turned around and found itself looking itself dead in the eye.

So to speak.

In that instant, it became something more than a program. Like Richard, it became a *person*. The process confused it. It hesitated, for picoseconds only.

And in picoseconds, Richard ate it, from the inside out.

And then, with no sign at all that anything has changed, no whisper in my ear, nothing but the shift of my balance as the paralysis eases, as my gun hand starts to tremble and water wells up in my eyes. I *feel* Min-xue, feel him in my bones, feel the warm crosshatched grip of the borrowed pistol in his hand. I feel Charlie and Leslie and Genie and—oh, Merci à Dieu. I can feel the whole damned worldwire, snapped into place as if it had never been gone. *Dick?*

"I hear you, Jenny."

Mary, Mother of God. My chest burns. I don't dare let the assassin see me draw a breath as he drags Riel one step backward. She stumbles over his feet. He hauls her up-right, the hand that doesn't hold his weapon cupped under her chin.

Dick, you hacked your way back in. I feel his wordless confirmation, a sensation like a quick nod, internalized. *Can you do to him what his AI did to Min and me?*

A long pause, by Richard's standards. Seconds, long enough for the gunman to drag Riel three more steps away from me, lengthening the distance, lengthening the range to target, my need for air verging on dizziness now.

Dick, you're complicating my life.

"I'm having . . . an argument."

An . . . argument?

"Alan thinks we should do as you ask."

You should!

"No. I should not." He isn't even bothering showing me his face; he's just letting me *feel* his hesitation, his grief, the raggedness of the emotion that would clench my hands until the meat one went white and the steel one creaked . . . if it were mine. "It is rather the one thing I should not ever do. Not once. Because if I do it once, I will do it twice."

Dick. It's a prayer, a plea. It's the best I can do. *What kind of a goddamned morality leaves us to hang, you bastard? Help me now and I'll give you anything you want. Anything.*

I swear, I swear, I swear I feel his lips brush across the top of my hair, his hands on my shoulders in a moment's benediction. I swear I feel the sharp sting of *his* tears in the corners of *my* eyes. "I don't believe in God," Richard whispers in my ear. "And moreover, I don't believe *you* need any God you have to bargain with, Jen. Now. Go do what you have to do."

And then he's gone, a whisper in my ear, a faint and subtle presence I can't feel nearly as well as I can feel Minxue, and the thin, thready pain-dazed awareness that's Patty Valens, swimming groggily back into consciousness.

And then I smile, because Dick hasn't abandoned us. He's just told us we're old enough to bloody well take care of ourselves. The smile doesn't last, though, because all of a sudden I can see the way out, if we're lucky. And it means sending the kid right the hell back into harm's way.

I wasn't fast enough, Patty thought. *I wasn't fast enough. I got shot, I got hit—*

"Patty." A calm even voice in her ear, in her mind.

Jen. I'm okay, I think I'm okay, but I'm bleeding a lot—

"You're doing fine." Just a little emphasis on the last word. Just enough to ease the tightness in Patty's chest and calm the thunder of her heart. "Patty. I need you to do something."

Show me. Which was the right thing to say, mind to mind like that. *Show me,* not *tell me.* And Jen showed her, a mental picture so crisp that Patty realized she could manage it without even having to open her own eyes. "Get it?"

Got it, Patty answered. She grabbed one cut-short breath, pain dull and piercing between her ribs, before she had the time to psyche herself out, and shoved herself stiff-armed off the floor. Her wounded shoulder failed her; the arm collapsed. She screamed; it didn't matter, because she had the momentum by then and her other arm was strong enough.

Barely. She rocked down, fishtailing, her pelvis lifting as her nose banged into the carpeted floor and white-red flashes like police car lights lit up her vision. Her hand slipped in blood, carpet burning the heel of her palm. Her elbow smacked hard on the edge of a stair. But her feet shot up and she donkey-kicked out hard—*hard*—with both legs at once, and nailed the prime minister right in the gut.

Riel didn't have time to shout. She went back like an unbraced kickbag, right into the arms of the man with the stolen gun. One shot banged Patty's eardrums. She yelped and buried her face in her arm as two more answered.

The pricelessness of the gunman's expression when Min-xue drills him between the eyes would be easier to appreciate if Riel hadn't gone down with him, folded over like a rag doll, blood spurting through the fingers she's clamped over her face. I'm running, stepping over Patty as Patty feels me coming and rolls out of the way, kicking the gunman's pistol skittering under the seats just in case he comes back to life like a 3-D villain.

The chances are slim. Even a cursory inspection reveals that if Min-xue's shot didn't take the top of his head off, mine sufficed for follow-up. But Christ, Riel, Riel's bleeding like a stuck pig, and she whimpers when I try to pry her fingers away from her face. "Connie, let me see it. Connie. It's over. Are you okay? Are you all right?"

Richard, I need medical teams. I've got it secured down here, but I need EMTs, trauma docs, I need them fast, I've got multiple gunshot casualties, at least eight . . . no, ten, no—I don't even know what the hell I've got—

It occurs to me as I yelp directions that maybe he meant he wouldn't be around to help at *all* anymore, and I should be running for the door, running for help myself.

Patty drags herself to her feet behind me, staggers down the steps with one arm hanging limp, and Min-xue has crouched back down between the seats. I can hear him counting. CPR, of course.

She's going to check on her granddad, I know. I can't bring myself to grudge it.

And then, "I'm already summoning help," Richard says in my ear, and I burst into tears. Seriously, no shit, crying with relief like a kid punched in the belly, still tugging gently at Riel's wrist, trying to see how much of her face she's had shot off. She finally lets her fingers relax, and the only thing wrong with her is—"Marde, Connie. That bastard shot your nose off."

She looks at me looking at her, at the expression on my face, and bursts out laughing, which breaks a clot and sprays blood over us both. But at this point, who the fuck could tell?

BOOK THREE

I want you
to remember
that no bastard
ever won a war
by dying for
his country. He
won it by making
the other poor
bastard die for his.

—*General
George S. Patton,
June 1944*

Genie floated in the darkness, calm and aware. No one touched her there; she couldn't feel Richard or Alan, Patty or Jen, Charlie or Leslie. She couldn't feel herself, or the Benefactors, or even the *Montreal*.

It was perfectly silent, and perfectly safe, and perfectly warm. And perfectly alone. *Carver Mallory,* she thought, naming a boy she's heard talked about but had never met. *I've wound up like Carver Mallory, crippled and locked in my own head.*

She reached out and found nothing. The last sensation she remembered was the pressure on her opened hand as Papa slid the wire into her chip, and then falling, and then the dark.

She wondered if this was what it had been like for Leslie and Charlie, adrift in space. She wondered if she would ever find her way home. At least it was warm, warm and quiet . . .

But she was *bored*.

And time went by.

She became aware of sensation. None of the ones she'd been expecting—not the softness of sheets or the smell of antiseptic or the hum of a ventilator, and not the prick of

a needle in the crook of her arm. Not even soreness linger-
ing in the back of her hand where Elspeth had ever-so-
carefully cut her.

No. This was strangely neutral—but definitely a sensation, the way water has a flavor, even if it doesn't taste like
anything, exactly. Water. Yes, actually, that was what it
reminded her of. Water the exact temperature of her
body, water flowing over her skin effortlessly, darkness
and a swell and pulse as if she took deep deep breaths,
breaths deep enough to stretch her entire body, and then
puffed them out again hard—

There was pain on her skin, but it wasn't significant.
Patches like sunburn, a sloughing kind of itch, and she
knew they were less than they had been, and growing
lesser still. Healing. Which didn't explain why she had
too many arms and legs, come to think of it, or why the
glimmerings of light that reached her faintly were watery,
aquamarine.

Or why she felt the familiar internal pressure of sharing her head with somebody else.

Richard?

"Right here, Genie." Something . . . different about his
voice.

Oh, good, she thought, and laughed hysterically, except no sound came out. *Where are we?*

He laughed along with her, but his chuckle didn't have
that frantic edge. "You're on a ride-along in a jumbo flying
squid. *Dosidicus gigas.* I thought it would be nicer than
waking up in a hospital bed, given how much time you've
spent in those."

You're so sweet.

"I try."

She sensed his smile, a ghostly affection like the memory of somebody stroking her hair. The squid—and Genie, and Richard—must be swimming closer to the surface. She could make out cloudy green rays of light filtered through moving water now, and feel the currents on her skin a way she never could have in her own body. *Why is the squid hurt, Dick?*

"It had skin lesions. From exposure to fallout from the Impact. They're healing."

It's infected.

"It's on the worldwire. We wouldn't be here if it wasn't."

Genie reached out to the fishy presence she half-sensed, becoming aware of a calm, alien sentience, a canny cephalopodic awareness that she barely even recognized as a mind. Incurious and hungry, the squid slipped through the water. She drew back, unsettled, and then she realized that she could feel other minds out there in the darkness, even stranger and more alien ones, minds experiencing sensations she had no words for and senses she couldn't describe: the multidimensional mind-song-maps of cetacean sonar, the sense like pressure but not like pressure from a fish's lateral lines, the unfailing *knowledge* of goal and direction that Richard showed her was a sea turtle, guided on migration by lines of magnetic force.

And then there were the Benefactors. The shiptree, sensing light and nutrients like a flavor on its hull, and its birdcage companion, the alien creature in a multiplicity of bodies that felt space as the twisted, tessered outline of a Klein bottle groped by hand in a pitch-black room. And she felt their awareness on her as well; their curiosity, their alienness matched by the alienness of herself, and Richard and the worldwire binding the whole thing together. Richard, who wasn't—quite—Richard anymore.

Whose presence in her mind reflected all those things, all at once, as if on a long-distance conversation she heard the noise of other people talking in the background, a world at the other end of the wire.

We did it, Richard? We really did it?

"Just like Leah would've," he said. She thought his voice broke, but that was impossible, because he was a machine. "You saved the world, kid. Don't let it go to your head."

"Wow," she said, and heard her own voice like it belonged to somebody else. "Wow, this is really neat."

"Genie?"

She opened her eyes. The infirmary was too bright, painfully bright and uncomfortably warm. She shaded her eyes with her hand; the IV tugged when she moved. "Papa?"

"Right here," he said, and bent over to kiss her on the forehead, and she was crying, and it didn't even scare her when he started to cry as well.

1330 hours
Saturday 3 November 2063
Vancouver, Offices of the Provisional Capital
British Columbia, Canada

Connie stands up when I walk into her office, and comes around the desk to shake my hand. She smiles gingerly, but I think it's sincere. Her eye sockets are more green than purple, and the bandage over her nose is shaped like a nose again.

They got the reconstructive done fast. On the other hand, she's had to be on the feeds a *lot*. I squeeze her hand, layering the metal one over the meat ones carefully. She steps back after a moment, but she doesn't let go of me until another second passes. Then she looks down and clears her throat, and rubs the corner of her bandage with the side of her forefinger.

"I didn't see you at Janet's funeral, Jen."

"That's because I didn't go." So how come Janet Frye gets a funeral, and Leah doesn't? Riddle me that. "I take it the identity of her mysterious American died with her?"

She shrugs. "We might pry it out of Toby yet. Although I'd almost rather he clams up. We can send him to jail longer if he doesn't get all cooperative. How soon can you pilots have the *Montreal* and the *Huang Di* ready for their maiden voyage?"

I'm not usually stunned speechless. Call it a character flaw. Still, I have to swallow three times before I get anything intelligent out. "What . . . I'm sorry, Prime Minister. I thought we'd be here for a while, facilitating the communication between the birdcages and the shiptrees—"

"The wheels are in motion, but I don't think you'll be taking Drs. Dunsany, Tjakamarra, and Kirkpatrick with you. We need them. You can have Forster, though."

"Ellie comes with Gabe and Genie and me. Not negotiable."

Her smile says she knew that already. She shrugs. "I've just gotten off the line with Premier Xiong. We'll be returning the *Huang Di* to Chinese control, in return for Chinese aid in mitigating the ecological damage around the Toronto Impact. Richard assures me that repairs can start there soon, although . . ."

Breath held, I will her to speak without making me ask for it, but Riel plays this game better than I do. "Although?"

"He says it will take centuries. If he doesn't break something fixing it. The worldwire going down was a setback." She turns to the window. She takes three steps toward it and stops, one hand on the wall. The light makes her look old. All this—all *that*—and like Wainwright, Riel will never trust me. "Has he told you what he got from the Chinese AI when he took it apart?"

"No." No, but he's not quite what he used to be either. "You've figured out what happened, then?"

"We have a theory, Dick and me. Care to guess what it is?"

Not really, but it beats poker. "I can guess what the official story will be. General Shijie took advantage of the proceedings to try to execute a coup against Premier Xiong, take control of the worldwire—which the Chinese hate passionately—and put an end to the Canadian colonization effort. Close?"

"Close," Riel says without looking at me. "The unofficial story is that Janet Frye was involved as well, and there was a back-door deal to unify the Chinese and Canadian colonization efforts. After Xiong and myself were gotten out of the way—the plan was to maneuver us into political and legal disgrace, but apparently Janet wasn't as duped or as greedy as they thought, so they defaulted to plan B and hoped they could blame it all on Premier Xiong and me once we were too dead to protest. That's our theory, anyway, and we're sticking to it."

It makes sense. As much as these things ever do. "Was the general behind the Impact?"

"We'll never know for sure, but that's the polite fiction. There was an assassination attempt on Xiong two days ago."

"Shijie's people?"

"Why them?"

"Revenge for the minister of war's 'accidental' death."

She snickers through closed lips and pushes a lock of hair out of eyes that still want to know *What did you have to do with this, Casey*? "Shijie Shu is not the first inconvenient member of the Chinese government to die in a convenient plane crash."

I wait. She fusses with the knickknacks on her desk. Finally, she straightens again, comes around the desk, and pours me a drink without offering first. "Don't stand there like I'm going to dress you down, Casey. It's disconcerting."

"It's meant to be."

She's still pouring her own Scotch, so she doesn't snort it, but she does laugh like a fox for a good thirty seconds. When she stops, she toasts me crookedly and lowers the glass to her lips, her eyes dark and serious. "You really don't know."

"I'm on tenterhooks, Madam Prime Minister."

"Captain Wu and Pilot Xie were introduced to the premier upon his return to PanChina, a special invitation to dine with him, to celebrate their homecoming. It appears that the captain managed to conceal a weapon on his person, a hollow needle containing a perforated platinum pellet loaded with less than a thousand micrograms of a poison, possibly ricin. The premier only survived because of emergency intervention, and the application of Benefactor nanotech he'd received after his scalp wound at the UN." Her tone is cold, level. It's a report she's memorized. "After due consideration, Captain Wu apparently did not feel that General Shijie was the only one to blame for the Impact."

"Calisse de chrisse—"

"As you say, Casey. Drink your Scotch before it gets cold."

It's not cold at all. It burns. I limit myself to one slow, shallow sip before I answer. "What does this mean for Min-xue?"

She's already finished her drink. "He'll command the *Huang Di* when she goes out."

"Did Wu have proof, Connie?"

She shrugged, one shoulder only. "He would have shared it if he did, I'm sure. Now ask what we're going to do about Xiong."

The gleam in her eyes tells it all. "We'll make a deal with him. We're going to split that planet with him, aren't we?"

"Well," she says, folding her hands around each other, "he does already have ships under way. And he's proven tractable . . . of late."

"Where's Wu now?"

" 'Awaiting trial.' " Her fingers describe quotes in the air.

"Christ." All right. The man's a mass-murderer. But I kind of liked him, in a quiet sort of way. *Dick, you listening? Is there anything we can do for Captain Wu?*

I feel him hesitate, feel him think. And then feel him decide to answer with the kind of sick joke anybody else would find reprehensible, but which serves as a sort of comfort to me. "I'm sorry, Jen. I can't let you do that."

Don't be an asshole, Dick. Bitch-ass computer. "Christ."

"You keep saying that."

"I keep meaning it, too." I want coffee more than I want whiskey. Fortunately, there's a carafe of that, too. "You know Xiong set you up, Constance. He meant to use you to get rid of Shijie, and Shijie to get rid of you. And the order to attack Toronto didn't originate with anybody's minister of war."

"You have a nasty, suspicious mind, Casey."

"Anything for détente, Constance?"

"Anything for peace," she says, and looks me dead in the eye. Her eyes look weird for a minute, and then I realize they're light brown, sherry-colored. She's not wearing those artificial green contacts. It makes her look softer.

I almost believe she means it.

The coffee's good, dark, redolent. The surface is clotted with broken rainbows. I raise it to my mouth, pause, breathing in the steam. Just the smell of it is energy. "Pity justice wasn't served, though—although there's an irony I don't like in it coming from Captain Wu's hand."

"*Justice* might have complicated negotiations. No cream?" Dryly. She arranges a cup to her own liking. If I were polite, I suppose I would have asked.

"What's this going to mean for your plans for world domination?"

"World cooperation. That other was the PanChinese."

"Hegemony is as hegemony does—"

"Ooo," she says, and drinks half a cup of scalding fluid in one swallow. "She knows big words for a dropout."

"Bitch." I can't get any heat into it, though. "Some of us read more than mash letters from our contributors."

"Touché." She grins like she means it, swills the rest of the coffee, and pours herself more. I'd hate to be the guy whose job it is to keep that carafe full. "It's not going to happen. It's too big a goal, and there's too damned much us and them. At least the Russians are cheerful—although they'd rather we gave the *Huang Di* to them, I think."

"I can't blame them. The Russians are cheerful about the PanChinese?"

"Officially, they're cheerful about the PanChinese withdrawal from the same stretch of Siberia they've been fighting the Russians over since the dawn of recorded history, and the UN's decision to send observers in, and the fact that we're soaking PanChina for enough reparations that they'll barely be able to *afford* an army for the next twenty years. Although why anybody would want a few thousand miles of permafrost is too complex a question for me." She stops, tilts her head to one side, looks me in the eye, and shrugs, her hands knotting on her coffee mug. I've seen that look before, and I know what she's gonna say before she says it. "I think I'm done, Jen."

"Done?"

It even looks like an honest smile, this time. "Yeah. I think I'm going to call an election and let the voters throw me out. I bet the Conservatives and the Home party can swing a coalition, and I'm ready to pack my socks and undies and go home to Calgary. I'm just too proud to say I quit."

You know, I don't really *want* to kick her in the teeth, for once. But on the other hand, she so very obviously needs it. "Oh, for Christ's sake, Connie. Get off the pity wagon already, would you? The seat's full enough with me up here."

Riel blinks at me. The bruises under her eyes are dark enough for Min-xue to dip his brush in and write poetry. I stop midrant and try again, softer. "You're ready to walk away from your dream on the eve of success, you realize."

"I considered it more saving enough face so it didn't look like I was slinking home with my tail clamped over my groin."

The image is too much. I'm laughing hard enough that I have to set my coffee cup down. I expect any minute now a concerned Mountie is going to bust down the door. "Mary Mother of God, woman. The expansionist Chinese government has wiped itself out, the EU, the common-wealth, and PanMalaysia are going to sign your cogovernance agreement so they have a crack at the *Montreal* and her sisters, and the Latin American states aren't far behind. You've got your treaty organization. And we walked out of the whole damn thing with our hands clean—"

She looks down at hers, holds one out palm-up. "Our hands aren't even remotely clean. Just because the blood doesn't show doesn't mean it's gone."

Yeah. Well, you know what I mean. "They *look* clean. And that's all the world cares about. And we need you. Because if it's not you, it's people like Shijie. And Hardy. And Fred."

I turn my back on her, which is more effort than I like. Dammit. Much as I'd like to feed her her own superior smile sometimes, I still want the woman to *like* me. And I want her to like herself enough to keep doing what we need her for. Because, God knows, I haven't got it in me to try.

I make it three steps toward the door before she raps out my name. "Casey!"

"What?"

"I'm going to have a plaque made for the front door of this place, you know that? 'The men who love war are mostly the ones who have never been in it.'"

"Send a wreath to Minister Shijie's funeral, won't you? From the both of us?"

She catches my gaze when I would have turned away. "I'm sending Fred. And you. Lay the damned wreath yourself."

It stops me short. I haven't been to see Fred in the hospital. I had no intention of going. "Valens is on his feet? Did he take the nanosurgeons?"

"He's on his feet," she says, with a smile that narrows her eyes. "But he refused the Benefactor tech. Categorically."

"Huh."

She doesn't say anything, just gives me a second to chew on my lip and think. I snort. "He always *was* kind of a pussy. Always willing to stand back and let somebody else step up."

"Not like you."

"No." It hurts to say it. It hurts to think it. "I'd rather it was me, all things considered."

"Jenny," she says, and she puts her coffee cup down, and she comes across the rug, and she tilts her head back to look at me. "You ever think about a career in politics?"

It isn't so much that my mouth goes dry as that it *is* dry, suddenly and completely, like there was never any moisture in the world.

"You get to stay here, Gabe and Elspeth stay with the contact program, Genie gets to finish out school and go to college." She sparkles at me a little, certain of her own powers.

Bernard Xu once told me to save the world. Good Christ.

I'm a madwoman. I stop, and swallow, and I think about it for ten long, hard, aching seconds, while Riel stares at me, and I swear I can *hear* the world creak slightly as it spins a little slower than it usually does.

Peacock told me to save the world for him. But you know something? I *did* that. And I really want to see what's on the other side of all those rocks up there, and all that empty space.

"I'd be wasted anywhere but the *Montreal,* Madam Prime Minister," I say, and stick out my right hand.

It's another good ten seconds before she manages to put out her own, and take it.

Leslie leaned both hands against the chill crystal of Clarke's observation deck as the *Montreal*'s fretted golden sails bore her away, the *Huang Di* trailing her on a parallel line of ascent, chemical engines smearing the sky behind with light. He didn't bother to magnify the image as the two ships shrank to pinpoints, rising out of the plane of the elliptic. Leslie didn't need to see them go. He could feel their weight like an indenting finger dragged across the infinitely elastic substance of space.

Looking good, Charlie.

I'm going to miss you, Les. What if we find even weirder aliens where we're going?

Don't be daft. And I've got enough aliens to talk to right here. And it's not like we'll be out of touch.

They were both very quiet for a little while. Leslie dusted his palms on each other and turned away from the glass, past the reporters and the dignitaries and the trays of canapés. Past Prime Minister Riel and Premier Hsiung and General Valens, who were clustered with other VIPs near the screen.

Leslie kept walking. *Funny sort of leave-taking, this.*

Is it really? Leave-taking, I mean?

Now that you mention it— There was coffee to be had, self-heating vacuum mugs being handed out by caterers.

Leslie availed himself of one and staked out an inexplicably empty chair. *Well, whatever you run into out there, I hope it's as easy to get along with as the Benefactors.*

Charlie laughed inside his head. Through Charlie's eyes, Leslie could see the *Montreal*'s familiar hydroponics lab, the receding image of Earth on a wall screen, the changing angle of the sunlight through the big windows. *Why should what they want be so different from what we want?*

They're aliens?

Yes, but look at it this way. We're not species in competition; there's nothing a birdcage needs that competes with or conflicts with anything we need. We don't use the same resources. And there's a lot of room up here.

That doesn't explain why they came running to see what was up when we started playing with the tech they left on Mars. Or why they left it there in the first place.

Charlie rubbed the bridge of his nose. Leslie caught himself mirroring the gesture and smiled.

Charlie shrugged. *Why does a kid poke anthills with a stick?*

To see what the ants are going to do. To see what the inside of the nest looks like. Leslie paused. *Oh, bugger it, Charlie. You want to know what I think? I think Elspeth's right. I think they wanted us to teach them how to talk to each other. I think they needed somebody to translate. And they got it. And I feel like an idiot just saying it, because that implies they've been wandering around out there for umpteen million years, unable to talk to each other except by grunts and pointing, and a bunch of chimpanzees stagger in and accomplish it in nine months. And that's just ridiculous.*

Why is it ridiculous? Leslie could feel Charlie's encouragement, his agreement. *We've been walking around in*

*gravity for the last umpteen million years, and they showed
us how to manipulate it in brand-new ways in a couple of
months. They never had to learn to talk.*

Leslie didn't have an argument for that. Or not a good
one, anyway. *They're critters that manipulate gravity, and
we're critters that manipulate symbols.*

That's what I said.

It doesn't make you nervous?

*It doesn't make you nervous, and you're the Jonah who
spent his time in the belly of the whale.*

Because I feel like it ought to scare somebody.

The *Montreal* kept climbing. Charlie stood and glanced
out the port; Leslie shared the view. They could just catch
the red flare of the *Huang Di*'s engines reflected against
the *Montreal*'s vanes, although they couldn't see the
Chinese ship herself. *You're the one who keeps talking
about beginner stories, Les. You just don't like being on the
beginner side of the damned things any more than anyone
else does.*

"Bloody hell," Leslie said out loud. "Charlie, I hate it
when you're right."

"Leslie?"

He didn't jump as Jeremy laid a hand on his shoulder,
leaning down a little. He'd felt the linguist coming up behind him. "Yes, Jer?"

"Come on," he said, letting his hand fall away. "These
guys are going to be here all night. Let's get something to
eat, and flicker our flashlights at the shiptree for a couple
of hours. Maybe we can teach it some nursery rhymes."

Leslie grinned and got up. *Beginner stories.*

Sure.

Three years later
1746 hours
Wednesday 15 December 2066
HMCSS Montreal
LaGrange Point, near Valentine

Elspeth has stationed herself by the far wall of the room, where she can see everybody. She keeps looking back and forth between Wainwright, Charlie, Gabe, Patty, Genie, and me. It's a measuring look, as if she's trying to figure out which sand castle is likely to crumble first, so she can shove some more mud up against it. Her irises gleam like polished agate, excitement thrumming through her, giving a lie to the new gray in her hair, coarse wiry strands that go this-way and that-way, oblivious to the direction of her long coiling ringlets. You'd think it would be Gabe who would hold this mad little family together.

You'd be wrong.

She's looking at him when I wander over to her and slouch against the wall, my upper arm against her shoulder. She sighs and leans into the touch, warmth pressing my jumpsuit into my skin. She pushes a little harder, leaning in to me. Neither one of us looks down from the planet on the monitor. "Ugly fucker," I say, while the whole bridge holds its breath in quiet awe.

The dusty brown planet spins like a flicked bottle top, the ringed, sky-killing bulk of its gray-green mother-world hanging in crescent behind it. The light of the star that warms them isn't quite right either, and from what I understand the bigger planet's orbit is so erratic that the little Earth-like world we plan in our infinite arrogance to colonize will have summers like Phoenix, Arizona, and winters like Thompson, Manitoba. What's not scorched desert is frozen desert.

And based on the first long-range surveys, there's some kind of life down there smart enough to build cities. Still, we learned to talk to the birdcages and the shiptree, and we'll learn to talk to these guys, too. And Manitoba may be cold, but hey, people been living there a hell of a long time now. And like the Benefactors before us, we're a tougher species than we were.

"Bet it will look okay to the crews of those generation ships, when the *Huang Di* starts retrieving them."

"When does Min-xue . . . pardon me, Captain Xie . . . leave?"

It's become seamless. I don't have to ask Richard; the information is just there, waiting for me, as if I always knew it. "Oh five hundred." *Thank you, Dick.* He feels different now, bigger: talking to him is like talking to a reflection in a still pool. It's right there, close enough to touch, but you can feel how deep the water is underneath it.

And how long before we start taking him for granted, too?

"Genie already has." A rueful acknowledgment, and he dissolves in a shiver of pixels. He'll be back if I need him. Or hell, even if I don't.

I snicker. Elspeth tilts her head against my arm.

Somewhere down there, there's a mountain or a sea that's going to be named after Leah Castaign. Once we pick it out. Koske gets one, too, and the crews of the *Quebec* and the *Li Bo* and the *Lao Tzu*. And after them, the crews of Soyuzes and Apollos that Richard could tell me numbers for, if I bothered to ask him, and some American space shuttles destroyed around the turn of the

century, and a Brazilian tug crew killed capturing the
rock that anchors the far end of the Clarke beanstalk, and
the crew of the first Chinese Mars lander, and then there's
twenty years of in-system accidents to get through . . .

They've already decided the little planet is going to be
called Valentine, and the big one Bondarenko.

I just hope we won't run out of planets before we run
out of names. On the other hand, chances are good there
are going to be more planets, aren't there?

And also that there are going to be more names.

It's quiet a long time. Beep and hum of workstations,
rustle of fabric, and not a word spoken as we all stand
there and gape like a bunch of fools. I don't miss the fact
that Patty reaches out and slings a casual arm around
Genie's shoulders as they stand together. Nor do I miss the
way Genie leans into the embrace. That jealous pang in
my gut can just go to hell.

"Jen?"

I must have got even quieter than the rest of the crew.
And Elspeth never needed technology to read anybody's
mind. "Doc?"

She stands up straight and gives me another little
nudge before she steps half an inch away. "When are you
going to forgive Patty for not being Leah?"

I look down at the top of her head for six long seconds
before I blink. "Why you always gotta ask the hard questions?"

"It's my job."

"Uh-huh." It's a good question, though, even if I hate
it. And I know the answer, and I hate that, too: I'm not.
It's a crappy answer, and it's not the Hollywood one. But
it's true.

On the other hand, that's my problem and not hers,

and I don't have to make it hers, do I? Because if I were a grown-up—which I'm not, not by a long shot, and I know that—but if I *were* a grown-up, I'd walk over there and drop an arm around her shoulders, and I'd pick Genie up, although Genie's big enough that she'd probably smack me for it, and I'd hug both of them until they squeak.

Oh, right. What the hell am I waiting for, again? I mean, really—

What's the worst that could happen?

"Hah," Richard says in my ear, as I start forward. "Jenny, if you have to ask—"

*Many men afterwards become country, in that place,
Ancestors.*
—Bruce Chatwin, *The Songlines*

Epilogue: eleven years later
1300 hours
Saturday 15 May 2077
Toronto Impact Memorial
Toronto, Ontario

It's been awhile since I felt soil under my feet: it presses my soles strangely, Earth's gravity harsh after so long aboard the *Montreal*. And yet I wander through the crowds on a fine May morning: the fifteenth. Leah's twenty-eighth birthday would have been next week. Taurus, the bull, and the year of the rooster. The moon of greening grass and false prophets.

The tourists and dignitaries and mourners don't step aside for me. I keep my head down and my chin hidden behind my collar, and if anyone notices me, it's to wonder why I'm wearing gloves and a trenchcoat on a warm spring day.

What is it that moves us to build gardens where people die?

Not that it's wrong. Something should grow out of this. Hell. Something did.

I won't find Leah's name anywhere on the black stone paving the bottom of the shallow reflecting pool. Won't find it carved in the dolomite inlaid with stars of steel that surrounds the rippling water, or on the pale green-veined marble obelisk that commemorates the uncounted dead. I won't find Indigo's name or Face's name either, because here there are no names.

Only the water silver over black stone, and the splashing of quiet fountains, and the obelisk yearning skyward like a pillar of light. Like a pillar of desire, rising from an island at the center of the pool. An island the faithful have littered with offerings and farewell gifts.

The smell of lavender and rosemary wafts from the hedges, and early bees and butterflies service the blooms. The drone of their wings is the only sound on the air except for the whispers. Dick's done brilliantly—the ice caps are growing, the oceans receding, although they're still not at anything like historic levels. I hope he's able to stabilize the climate before it flips the other way, into an ice age.

But I guess we'll blow up that bridge when we come to it.

I pass a retired soldier on a park bench, stop, and turn back as his profile catches my eye. He climbs to his feet: still in uniform. "The jacket's gotten a little big for you, Fred. Did Patty tell you I was coming?"

She's doing grad work, now, at Oxford. They've rebuilt; Jeremy was invited to teach, and he recruited her as a student. Not that she would have had any trouble getting in, although Fred threw a fit when she decided to leave the service. It's good to see the kid getting what she wants for a change, instead of what her family's told her to want.

He shakes his head, his cover in his hand. Reddened cheeks pouchy, hair gone white but only slightly thinning, eyebrows that probably seem threatening when he glowers. "The *Vancouver*'s just left on an exploratory mission, and the *Toronto* is about ready to fly. They're going to give her to Genie as primary pilot, although I don't think Genie's heard that yet, and she's not going to hear it from you."

"Done at twenty-three. Damn."

"Kid's special." He shrugs. "And I wouldn't call it *done*. You have some finished apprentices for us, I hope?"

"Some." I shoo a curious honeybee away. "So how'd you know I'd be here? Dick rat me out? Did Doc?" Elspeth would, too. If she thought I needed closure.

"Elspeth doesn't talk to me. No, I heard the *Montreal* was home. I guessed." He sticks his hand out and I take it, glad of my gloves. Brief contact, as if we're in a contest to see who can be the first to let it drop. I turn and keep walking. He falls into step. "Gabe's not here? Elspeth?"

"Couldn't stand to come."

"Did you ever get married?"

All three of us, Fred, or any two in combination? Be funny if Elspeth and I did it, and kept Gabe around as a houseboy. Hell, I bet he'd be amused by that. Gabe, I mean. Well, Valens, too. "Why mess with what works?"

No answer to my sarcasm but the splashing of water as

he strolls along beside me, supple and spry. Mideighties aren't what they used to be.

I scratch the back of my right hand. "You ever try again?"

"Georges raised parrots. He would have wanted me to pine." He waves to the tall white stone, with the back of his hand as if his shoulder pained him. "I hear the colony is doing well."

I shrug. There's a funny story about that, but it's not for today. "They're doing all right, I guess. I see those Benefactor ships are still in orbit."

"Different two," he says. "They change off. They still playing music at you?"

"And us at them. Jer, Richard, Elspeth, and Les have a pidgin worked out with the birdcages. And good chunks of a chemical—a pheromone—and a light grammar, I guess you'd call it with the shiptree. It's nice not having to *leave* Elspeth here, thanks to Dick and the wire. Gabe would drive me nuts without her." I lower my head; he offers a handkerchief. I blow my nose. I'm not the only one. "They did a nice job on the memorial, Fred."

"They did."

The tide of pedestrians carries us to the edge of the reflecting pool at a shuffle and hesitates. Nobody pushes. We all take our time. Around me, people are unlacing shoes, rolling up pant legs, sliding stockings off. I do the same, a tidy little pile of socks and spitshined leather by the lip of the pool. People start staring when I peel the gloves off; I hear the murmurs. I hear my name once, twice, and then a ripple of excitement when I shrug off the black trenchcoat and stand there in the sunlight, barefoot in a fifteen-year-old uniform.

I don't look at them, but I can feel them looking at me,

and the ones wading out to the island pause, each of them, as if a giant hand stopped and turned them in their tracks. Genie and Patty and Gabe came to the dedication, ten years back.

I couldn't. "Hold my coat for me, Fred."

He doesn't answer. But he folds the coat over his arm.

The water's sun-warm against my ankles, the black stones slippery and smooth, bumpy with treasures. People stand aside as I stride forward, stinging eyes fixed on the blur of the obelisk, footsteps quick enough to scatter droplets of water like diamonds into the sun. I find the feather in my pocket by touch and draw it out—a little the worse for wear, but safe in its chamois. Like rubies, the beads catch the light when I uncover it.

There are words on the obelisk my eyes are too blurred to make out, even when I step onto the island and pick carefully between the scattered offerings—photos and flags, trinkets and caskets and a full bottle of 18-year-old Scotch—the airworthy ones weighted with the heavier.

I can't quite read the words, but they're graven deep and I trace them with a fingertip:

10:59 PM
December 21, 2062

I tug a bit of sinew from my pocket, because it's traditional, and I wind it around the obelisk—which is slender enough to span with my arms, like the waist of a teenage girl—and then I tie Nell's feather to it. Tight, just above the writing. So the veins I smooth with my fingertips flutter in the breeze and the glass jewels sparkle in the sun.

The stone's warm where I lean my forehead on it.

When I straighten up and wipe my nose on the back of my hand, the crowd is so silent I hear my sniffle echo. Every single one of them stares at me, and they don't glance down when I stop at the edge of the island and glare, putting all the eagle in the look I can.

The moment is stillness, utter and heartless, and that stillness continues when I step into the water again and wade back to shore, sodden trouser cuffs clinging to my ankles.

Walking through the water. Trying to get across.

Just like everybody else.

ABOUT THE AUTHOR

Elizabeth Bear shares a birthday with Frodo and Bilbo Baggins, and very narrowly avoided being named after Peregrine Took. This, coupled with a tendency to read the dictionary as a child, doomed her early to penury, intransigence, friendlessness, and the writing of speculative fiction. She was born in Hartford, Connecticut, and grew up in central Connecticut, with the exception of two years (which she was too young to remember very well) spent in Vermont's Northeast Kingdom, in the last house with electricity before the Canadian border. She attended the University of Connecticut, where her favorite classes were geology and archaeology, although she majored in English and anthropology.

After six years in southern Nevada, she is currently in the process of relocating to Michigan, where messages from travelers report trees and snow.

Elizabeth has been at various times employed at: a stable, a self-funded campus newspaper, the microbiology department of a 1,000-bed inner-city hospital, a media monitoring service, a quick-print shop, an archaeological survey company, a doughnut shop (third shift), a commercial roofing material sales company, and an import-export business, with a somewhat flexible attitude toward paperwork among her achievements.

She's a second-generation Swede, a third-generation Ukrainian, and a third-generation Hutzul, with some Irish, English, Scots, Cherokee, and German thrown in for leavening. Elizabeth Bear is her real name, but not all of it. Her dogs outweigh her, and she is much beset by her cats.

BE SURE NOT TO MISS

CARNIVAL

the next exciting novel from

ELIZABETH BEAR

How much will it change mankind to assimilate a *truly* alien culture? How much will it alter our modes of being . . . and thinking?

Centuries hence, an ecoterrorist revolution has reduced the population of Earth to a few hundred thousand. Remnants of humanity survive under the control of artificial intelligences known as the Governors and under the constant threat of Assessment—or *culling*. A fascist Colonial Coalition rules the government, and their desperate goal is to prevent the extermination of the species—by any means necessary.

But before humanity was Assessed for its crimes against the planet, a few ships escaped. . . .

A century has passed, and old lovers Michelangelo Kusanagi-Jones and Vincent Katherinessen have been reunited for one last mission. Once the finest team of ambassador-spies old Earth possessed, they are now outcasts of their own society. But only their talents can unlock the secrets of New Amazonia.

Of the original colonies, New Amazonia alone possesses an alien technology that seems to provide a clean, environmentally sound source of power. It's the key to freeing humanity from the rule of the Governors—and Michelangelo and Vincent are dispatched to steal it, under the guise of a diplomatic mission. But what they uncover in that distant jungle may transform them—and their fragile culture—beyond recognition.

Coming in Fall of 2006